MISSIONARIES

ALSO BY PHIL KLAY

Redeployment

MISSIONARIES

PHIL KLAY

Penguin Press   New York   2020

PENGUIN PRESS
An imprint of Penguin Random House LLC
penguinrandomhouse.com

LIBRARY OF CONGRESS CATALOGING-IN-PUBLICATION DATA

Names: Klay, Phil, author.
Title: Missionaries / Phil Klay.
Description: New York : Penguin Press, 2020.
Identifiers: LCCN 2020016830 (print) | LCCN 2020016831 (ebook) |
ISBN 9781984880659 (hardcover) | ISBN 9781984880666 (ebook)
Subjects: GSAFD: War stories.
Classification: LCC PS3611.L4423 M57 2020 (print) |
LCC PS3611.L4423 (ebook) | DDC 813/.6—dc23
LC record available at https://lccn.loc.gov/2020016830
LC ebook record available at https://lccn.loc.gov/2020016831

ISBN 9780593296455 (export)

Printed in the United States of America
10 9 8 7 6 5 4 3 2 1

BOOK DESIGN BY LUCIA BERNARD

For Jessica, my love,

And for our children,

Adrian Felipe and Marcos Andres

I

report us fairly,
how we slaughter
for the common good

—Seamus Heaney, "Kinship"

1

ABEL 1986–1999

My town sat on top of a small hill by the side of a river whose banks held only sand. At noon you had to walk quickly so as not to burn your feet, but when it rained the river would overflow and turn our central street to mud. All us children would go out, slipping and pushing each other, playing in the mud before the sun baked it hard and the wind carried it away as dust.

To talk about this part of my life is to talk about another person, like a person in a story, a boy with a father and mother and three sisters, one pretty, one smart, and one mean. A grandfather who drank too much and beat everyone at dominos. A teacher who thought that boy had talent. A priest who thought he was wicked. Friends and classmates and enemies and girls he watched with increasing wonder, like Jimena, who had thick curly hair and fair skin and who got pregnant with the baby of one of the local guerrilleros. Most people think that a person is whatever you see before you, walking around in bone and meat and blood, but that is an idiocy. Bone and meat and blood just exists, but to exist is not to live, and bone and meat and blood alone is not a person. A person is what happens when there is a family, and a town, a place where you are known. Where every person who knows you holds a small, invisible mirror, and in each mirror, held by family and friends and enemies, is a different reflection. In one mirror, the sweet fat boy I was to my mother. In another, the little imp I was to my father. In another, the irritating brat I was to Gustavo. A person is what happens when you gather all these reflections around a body. So what happens when one by one the people holding those mirrors are taken from you? It's simple. The person dies. And the bone and meat and blood goes on, walking the earth as if the person still existed, when God and the angels know he doesn't.

So let's not talk about this boy as if he and I are the same person and not two strangers, one who walked in this body before the burning, and one who did after. Let's talk about this boy, whose memories and face I share, as the dead child he is. We can call him Abelito.

Abelito was a fat, well-loved child. Every day he would walk to school in another town, a school run by men from America who taught math and reading but also about the personal Jesus and how a group of priests called Jesuits had stolen the Bible and changed the words to make men follow the devil. The Lord would overcome and save us if we had faith, they said, and faith was a moment when the Heavens shined down and we knew we were saved. The mean sister, Mona, said that she had been saved and that it felt very, very good, but that Abelito hadn't had the feeling because he was going to hell. Two weeks later Mother took him two towns down to the church in Cunaviche to get confessed, and when Abelito told Father Eustacio about Mona's salvation, the old priest had scowled and said it was stupidity, that only a cruel God would condemn and save in such a foolish way, and that God was not cruel, but was, in fact, a terrible and frightening love. And he took that little boy out of the confessional to see the skin-and-bones Holy Christ above the altar, a wooden Holy Christ in agony, with muscles straining and a bloody wound in the side like a mouth come to devour. The statue gave Abelito nightmares, but Father Eustacio said to look on the suffering and know the love of God, to do such a thing to His child. God is love, Father Eustacio said, and He does not hand out salvation to be worn like a crown. And Abelito said, My sister, then, she is not saved? And Father Eustacio said, No, which pleased Abelito very much. And after that day Abelito nodded his head when the missionaries talked about the personal Jesus who would come to them and make them born again, but in his secret heart he remained faithful to the terrifying Holy Christ of Cunaviche.

Some days Abelito's grandfather would take him and his smart sister, Maria, and teach them how to carve boats from chachajo, a good hard wood that also makes the best spinning tops, and they would put them in the river and watch them float downstream. Abelito's grandfather said all water flows to the ocean, and that one day he would go there to die, the place where everything goes in the end.

Maria would carve her boats from balsa, which is easier to work, but Abelito carved from harder wood because he wanted his boats to reach the ocean. Abelito's grandfather had been a lot of places, and told Abelito marvelous things about the lands far, far downriver, out of the mountains and into the coastal regions, where the people were lazy and stupid and spoke Spanish that sounded like they had pebbles in their mouths, where there were snakes that could kill a steer with one bite, and men with skin black as coal, and many other marvelous things.

The first time Abelito met death was with Marta, his beautiful sister, who got sick and neither the priest nor the missionaries could save her, because she'd been hexed with the evil eye. After her death, Abelito's father gave the children bracelets with a tiny wooden cross hidden in the weaving. This will protect you, he said. At the time, Abelito didn't understand why anyone would put the evil eye on anyone else, let alone on someone like Marta, who was so beautiful that everybody was always talking about it, what a beautiful child. Abelito would walk through the town looking carefully into the eyes of the old women to see if they were good or evil, but he never could tell the difference, and could never understand what pleasure anyone would get from killing children.

Abelito's father liked to play games with his children. "Bear" was when he would stand by the river and growl and they would run up and try to tickle him and he would grab them and throw them into the water. "Horse" was when they would climb on his back and he would run down the street shouting "Jijiji!" Abelito would also play cinco huecos with some of the other children from Sona. They would use a stick to draw a big square in the street, and then other, smaller squares inside it. Each child would draw a little letter in each square. An *A* for Abelito. *M* for Maria, who was terrible at the game. *F* for Franklin, who was strong and skillful and who liked to boast and taunt the other players before throwing the ball. Then they'd turn, hold a ball in one hand and a little stick in the other, and throw the little stick over their head. If it landed in their square, they'd try to get the others out by hitting them with the ball. I don't remember who came up with that game, but it was Abelito's favorite. Sometimes men would drive through on motorcycles and ruin the squares with their tires, and none of the children were supposed to say anything or even look mad, because all their parents had told them these men were from the paracos.

More than the games, though, Abelito liked working with his father on their house. Ever since Abelito could remember, they had worked on the house. As a toddler, he'd watched his father hack out a small patch in the jungle. This is where your mother will cook, he'd say, pointing to a square of dirt. This is where you and your sisters will sleep.

Then, brick by brick, he built a wall. Whenever he had money, he would buy a cheap block of cement and the children helped him mix it with water to form bricks, and he would lay them around the perimeter. Boys become men by working with their fathers, and girls become women by tending the fire, but in Abelito's family everyone worked with his father on the house, brother and sisters alike. The work went slow at first, but as soon as Abelito's father finished the big room they moved in, all of them, so they could stop paying rent. And as soon as they stopped paying rent, Abelito's father had more money for cement, and the work went faster.

The missionary school opened up around the time they finished the kitchen, and Abelito's parents sent him and his sisters to get an education. Abelito's first year there was the year many dead bodies floated down the river, and the school closed for a month, and Abelito's father stopped playing Bear with his children. Then the bodies stopped, and the children saw fewer and fewer paracos, and the school reopened.

When Abelito was eight, he saw his first guerrilleros. These were the men that the paracos supposedly fought. He was with his father in the boat and saw a group of ten men and four women on the far side. They wore uniforms and carried long guns Abelito had not seen before. They waved Abelito over and asked him to ferry them across and he did. When they left, Abelito's father told him, "When men with guns ask for something, there are no favors. You only obey."

The leader of the guerrilla was called the Carpenter, after Saint Joseph, and people said the name came from the pity he showed to the children he turned into orphans. He never killed children, they said, even though he ran the risk of them seeking revenge. And sometimes he would make a big show of giving children some of the money he had stolen from their parents. There were worse guerrilleros than the Carpenter, people said, and it could be counted as a blessing that he was the curse God had sent to the jungles around the town.

On the Feast of Saint Joseph he came to town with bottles of aguardiente and guerrilleros holding guitars and drums. Abelito's father brought Abelito to see, and though Abelito's father listened carefully to the Carpenter, he didn't let any aguardiente touch his lips.

The Carpenter was a big man with a rough face, pitted like pumice stone, weathered from a life lived moving from place to place, sleeping in guerrilla camps, lacking a true home. It was a serious face, a face Abelito found impressive, admirable. He wondered what it would be like to live a life that would earn such a face.

The Carpenter said he defended the truth. He said the people deserved respect. Every district should have a clinic, every large town a
hospital. The people should own their own land, and the children
should have an education. Everything should be free and the government should give us work. Then a guerrillera stood up. She was tall and
very fair skinned, with black hair tied tight into a bun and an angry
look on her face. She said after her father died her mother had taken up
with a man who abused her every night. She had taken the abuse until
her younger sister had her first bleeding, and then she had no option.
She'd stabbed that man in the neck and gone off to join the guerrilla,
and the revolution became her mother and father. The revolution, she
said, was a true mother and true father. It had given her thousands of
brothers and sisters. Then she sang a song in a voice many years sweeter
than the look on her face. The people drank and the guerrilleros sang
more songs, and Abelito decided he liked the guerrilla much more than
the paracos who used to ruin his games of cinco huecos. Later, with his
friend Franklin, they would play guerrilla. And Franklin, always brash,
would pretend to be the Carpenter, and deliver judgments that were
cruel and just.

A month later the guerrilla came back to the village and took Alfredo, who was four years older than Abelito, and Matías, who was
three years older, to join in the revolution. This is a paraco town, they
said, and it must pay a new "vaccine," which is what they called the tax
they were imposing on the people. They were much angrier than they'd
been before, and no one was sure why. Some people blamed Marcos
Ardila, the butcher, who they said still had ties to the paramilitaries.
Others blamed Chepe, owner of a bar. Whoever caused it, the price was
paid in the children they took. The guerrilla would have taken Abelito,
too, but they didn't, they said, because he was too much of a faggot.
Here is what happened.

Abelito was playing with his smart sister, Maria, when the guerrilla
came down the road. Tall, thin Alfredo, who was always sick, and short,

ugly Matías, who was kind, were following behind them with big, scared eyes. Maria ran and hid, but Abelito was curious and stayed. The men with guns surrounded him. Do you want to join the revolution? Abelito looked at Alfredo and Matías, who were looking down at their feet, trying not to cry.

One of the guerrilla pulled a grenade from his vest and asked Abelito if he knew what it was. Abelito said yes. The guerrillero handed it to Abelito and told him, "Pull the pin and throw it. Prove you are a man."

Abelito started crying, and the man said, "Look, a little faggot." And they laughed, all the guerrilla laughed except for Alfredo and Matías. All the guerrilla had eyes like flat stones, except for the leader, whose eyes were like sharp little knives. "Throw it, throw it," the guerrillero shouted. But Abelito just stood and held the grenade and cried, and the leader took the grenade back and said, "Go to your mother, little faggot."

Abelito, weak as he was, ran to his mother. He should have pulled the pin and thrown it like in a game of cinco huecos, carelessly, so it landed close enough to kill him and the guerrilla and all the worthless games of the future.

Of course, he did no such thing, and once the guerrilla had complete control of the towns around Abelito, once the paras became a memory, the guerrilla brought in the paisas, and the next game started.

When the paisas arrived in town, they brought briefcases and seeds and promises of a new business, the coca business, in which the townspeople could not lose. Many people became excited—planting, picking crops, working the land, and making money. The paisas paid what they said, and on time. And both the townspeople and the paisas paid the vaccine to the guerrilla.

Mother and Father would argue during this time. Father wanted to make money, Mother thought this was dangerous. An ugly business. Grandfather had told her terrible stories about it. In the end, the family did not join in the business that was helping so many of the people around him buy radios, new clothes, and other things. But still, they were happy.

This went on for two years, and during that time the villages along the river changed. Grandfather complained that all the little towns had become no more than bars with streets running through them, and that all the little girls had grown up to become no more than prostitutes. Mother said that Grandfather should be happy that all the towns were bars—he could get drunk anywhere he chose now, and not just in front of Abelito and his sisters.

There were elections, and then after the elections, gunfire, and half the people of a neighboring town left in fear. The paisas showed up with men with guns, and they were very angry. They said they would only pay so much for coca and no more. They said these towns were all paramilitary towns, and the guerrilla had raised taxes on coca to pay for all the trouble they had caused.

Franklin's brother Santiago, who was four years older than Abelito and was good at numbers, said he had traveled downriver with his father and they paid more for coca in other places. He worked out that, if they paid this much here and this much at Camaguan, they must pay a lot in Cúcuta, and the paisas should be paying everyone much more, more even than they had originally paid. He went into the jungle to complain to the Carpenter, and the Carpenter slapped him and told him that they knew this was a paraco town, and he was from a paraco family, and he should not complain. Then the guerrilla beat him so badly he could not even walk back home, but his father and his brother had to be called out to the guerrilla camp to carry him home. Two days later, the paisas returned and went to his house, took him to the square, and told everyone he was an enemy of the people. The next week his body, all swollen, floated down the river and the town mourned and Father Eustacio came from Cunaviche for the funeral. Franklin told everyone he'd avenge his brother, but no one believed him. His boasting turned sad and purposeless.

A period of great fear began. Without warning, the evangelical school shut down. Maria told Abelito the guerrilla had taken the teachers and made them pay, or were holding them in the jungle until they paid. She said everyone in Colombia must pay a monthly vaccine to the guerrilla, especially the wealthy, and when people don't pay it they must be put in prison until it is paid. But the guerrilla do not have prisons, she said, so they took Abelito's teachers to the thickest parts of the jungle, where there were twenty-foot anacondas that ate men alive, and chained them by the neck to trees. She said they would stay like that, a chain around their necks, until money from America set them free, or they died. But after a time, even this became normal, and the people worked for less money without complaint, and the fear became something in the background, like the heat of summer, something you acknowledge and sometimes even complain about but which you do not expect to change.

When he turned thirteen, Abelito started working coca, which was good, hard work. That same year one of the paisas got Abelito's mean sister, Mona, pregnant. When Abelito's father heard of it, he tried to beat her but found he could not even raise his arms to strike his child, so his mother did it for him with a switch. The family became deeply sad. When they asked the paisa if he would marry Mona, the paisa just laughed, and everyone was too afraid to say anything. Mona said it was better this way. She never said the paisa's name, she just called him "that son of a bitch," and that she'd rather cut his baby out of her own stomach than be married to him.

Abelito prepared for life to change, for his sister to give birth and for him to help his father and mother and sister with the baby, but everything changed, for everyone in the town, much faster than that, when Franklin finally found the courage he'd spent years searching for.

The Carpenter had been sleeping with many of the girls of the town, but especially Jimena. She was fifteen, and had already birthed one of his children. Franklin waited for the Carpenter to come see her. He followed the Carpenter and caught him alone with Jimena, who was very beautiful, and very timid, and had always spoken kindly to Abelito, and who he loved. Franklin stabbed them all over, in the neck, arms, hands, and head. Franklin told me he had wanted to cut out the Carpenter's tongue, the tongue that had told the paisas about his brother's plan, but when he turned the body over and saw his face it had terrified him and he'd run.

Only one man in a hundred will stand up to a true killer, the way Franklin had done. But Franklin only had enough courage in him to do it once. He fled, and his whole family fled with him, while the rest of the town waited like a pig facing the knife.

2

t didn't begin with the bombings. By which I mean, Kabul was no longer Kabul well before then. There used to be thousands of us Westerners, mostly military and contractors, but also aid workers, missionaries, adventurers, diplomats, and journalists like myself, trying to make our mark or our fortune in the "good war," Afghanistan, as opposed to the "dumb war," Iraq. The money we brought kept things kicking in our Kabul, the Westerner's Kabul, the city within the city that was unaffordable or just plain off-limits to ordinary Afghans. People called it the Kabubble, and the Kabubble meant imported steaks at Boccaccio, bootleg Heinekens on Flower Street, and rooftop parties overlooking the lights that crawl up the sides of the mountains around the city at night. It meant a place you could let your hair down, drink alcohol, and tell strangers the lies you told yourself about why you were there, what you were doing, and what a difference you were making.

By 2015, those days were long gone. Troop levels down from a peak of over a hundred thousand to less than ten thousand, and for all the cheerleading for a military exit I've heard from self-righteous European aid workers and twenty-two-year-old journalists seeking to "give voice to the Afghan people," I couldn't help noticing that as the American military left, those folks' numbers thinned out, too. You didn't see as many correspondents, or NGO administrators, or even heavily armed white dudes in cargo pants on Street 15 those days. "The tide has turned," Obama had told us in 2012. Indeed.

Then, early morning, early August, the sound of an explosion. We hear the boom in the office, the window frames rattle, and Aasif, one of my Afghan colleagues, looks at me and says, hopefully, "Maybe the military blowing up a weapons cache?" It's eight thirty, I haven't had my coffee yet, and neither of us is eager to run out to a bomb site and try to count dead and injured.

We both run up the stairs to the roof. Just a few years prior, there would have been a gaggle of photographers and cameramen already there, filming black smoke, placing bets on what got hit. To the extent that people cared at all, they cared then. In 2015, there's a lot less interest in random explosions in Kabul. The offices are depleted, and when we get to the roof it's just Omar, languidly snapping photographs and sucking on the tiniest nub of a cigarette. I'm not sure of Omar's exact age—he was a young boy during 9/11, so he's probably barely in his twenties, but he affects a hard-bitten cynicism. "Big, maybe even big big," he says. "But early for too much people traffic, so I guess"—he surveys the scene with an expert eye—"ten dead." This is how Omar talks when sober. Drunk, I have seen him cry about these things, and speak idealistically about the work he does bringing his country's suffering to the world's attention. It tends to make everyone around him embarrassed.

After calling his relatives and confirming that everyone's all right, Aasif says he'll head down to the site. Since I figure Bob'll want me to write the snap, I go downstairs, call the military press office. They confirm there's been no controlled det, but they can't confirm an explosion, so I write, "Explosion sounds in Afghan capital. Plume of smoke seen rising." I read it over once, twice, press send.

Not a lot of information, but two minutes later, while I'm working on my second paragraph for the urgent, Bob swings by from the back office with a cup of coffee and says, "You beat the AP by two seconds." He places the coffee in front of me, my reward.

I take a sip, finish off the last paragraph, it's clocking in at 125 words, and send it. Four minutes from start to finish. Good enough.

Now the work begins. Aasif's already heading to the scene—he's got a motorcycle, which means he's way better at getting through Kabul traffic than those of us relying on taxis or the agency car. Bob tasks me to write, Denise to work the phones. Denise is twenty-three, and plain looking, but she's so much younger than I am that even when we're together, and even though I know I cut a striking figure when I want to and she ties a head scarf like a homeless bag lady, she turns heads. She's catnip to a certain kind of guy, the kind of guy who's not quite sure his time in Afghanistan has proved his manhood, and besides, is secretly terrified of death and needs to work that anxiety out by fucking the young. "Terror sex," that's what my friend Cynthia calls it, and both of us are a little uneasy that terror sex doesn't hold as much appeal for us as it used to. "I want to be at least as alive as the vulgar," we'll say, quoting Frank O'Hara. But we're not that alive anymore, and not even really sure we want to be. After all, we hold the Denises of the world, and our younger selves, and the men who fuck them, in contempt.

"Can we say this is rare?" Denise asks, a little tentative.

"When was the last one?" Bob's style of instruction is Socratic.

"Three weeks," I say.

"Does that count as rare?" says Bob.

"For a war zone?" says Denise.

"Kabul's not a war zone," I say. "Last bombing killed five people . . ."

"How many dead would it take to make Kabul unsafe?" says Bob.

"Point of comparison. Is Kabul's murder rate worse than New Orleans?" says Denise.

"Is New Orleans safe?"

Aasif calls in, the bomb went off near the Interior Ministry, or possibly beside the Interior Ministry, the police aren't letting him in but he's convinced a storekeeper to let him onto his roof, he's got Omar taking shots of the damage, hopefully he'll get something artful, something beautiful enough to get picked up and extend the reach of the violence, make some dent on the public mind. The great democratic public relies on the intrepid veracity of the free press to cut past the political rhetoric with hard-hitting fact so they can make informed decisions. Which, fourteen years into this war, hasn't happened yet, but hey, maybe could someday.

Denise gets a contact at the local hospital to confirm seven dead, but we don't know who the dead are, and that matters. If they're Afghan forces, ISAF will spin this as a good news story. Afghans stepping up and courageously defending their country, protecting it from greater harm. If the bomb went off somewhere inside the Interior Ministry, though, that will make the Kabul administration seem weak, hopelessly compromised. If it's a civilian target, well, it'll be another data point in the shift the Taliban has taken to kill innocent Afghans. The Afghan government will issue a statement vaguely laying the blame on Pakistan. The U.S. military will say it shows the Taliban's increasing desperation, whatever that means.

Bob turns his computer and shows me a Twitter conversation between @ISAFmedia and the Taliban. "The outcome is inevitable. Question is how much longer will terrorists put innocent Afghans in harm's way?" reads the ISAF tweet. And a self-appointed Taliban spokesman tweeting back: "U hve bn puttng thm n 'harm's way' da pst 10 yrs. Razd whole vilgs. Dnt talk bout 'harm's way.'"

"Worthless," I say.

I look at my watch. I'll want to get to the site before the police have cleaned everything up, in time to get some "color": a newly orphaned child wailing and looking around helplessly for her parents, the green pickup truck used to bring the wounded to the hospital, the shattered glass and ruined fruit stalls, businesses, livelihoods, lives. Omar's photos will help . . . not just the ones we'll use, but Omar's always good at taking a few purely documentary shots so we can run down mundane details that don't do much in a photo but pop in a story, like the elderly Pashtun man in the last bombing, who with blood running down his arms held his coat over the corpse of a woman to protect her modesty. The key is finding a detail that might make someone, some reader looking over the morning paper, drinking coffee, eating a hard-boiled egg, about to rush to work, to make that person stop, and care. It's difficult, in part because these days I find it hard to get those details to even make me care. When I first came here, I was full of rage at the indifference most people back home showed to the deaths of Afghans. All these human beings, suffering, dying, and fighting with unbelievable courage to live in this brutal country, courage that can inspire you for at least a few years. It's a feeling I doubt I'll ever get back. These days the thought will sometimes run through my head as I lie in bed, trying to sleep: I am broken, I am broken, and I do not know how I will ever fix this hole I've carved into my soul.

And then I hear the much larger sound of the second bomb.

3

ABEL 1999

Abelito was in the boat with his father when they came. "Quick!" Father said. He pushed Abelito under the seat and put rags and netting over his body, the stench of stale river water at the bottom of the boat filling Abelito's nose. Parts of his body poked out from underneath the seat. Surely, no one could fail to see him there. But Father made a quick circle of protection with his index and middle finger, sealed it with the sign of the cross, and Abelito became invisible. The guerrilla called out to Father and, as before, as always, he obeyed.

"Everyone must come," they said. "For the justice of the people."

Someone laughed. It was a cruel laugh. Or a nervous laugh. Or both.

Father said nothing, but Abelito felt the boards in the boat shift, and then Father pulled the boat ashore, and he heard the guerrillero saying, "Don't bother to tie it off."

Abelito felt taps on the wood of the boat. His father's knuckles, rapping four times. "I love you," his father's knuckles were saying. Stale air filled Abelito's lungs, the sound of his own heart filled his ears, an enormous sound, as if his heart had grown bigger and stronger to protest his cowardice. The boat shifted again as Father released it, and the current of the river pulled and tugged at the boat until it released the shore. Abelito felt himself moving downstream, toward all the places his grandfather had told him about, but where he no longer wanted to go.

Justice, the guerrillero had said. Abelito knew that meant an execution, but who? No one would have dared speak about Franklin—to speak of evil was to invite more. The guerrilla only knew that those paramilitary sons of bitches in this paramilitary town had murdered the Carpenter, a good and kind man, who always took pity on the orphans whose parents he had killed. Worse, they had killed his pregnant lover, which is not just a crime against man, and not just a betrayal of the revolution, but a sin against God.

I have spent far too much time wondering if there was anything Abelito could have done to save his family. These are stupid thoughts. The most he could have done was die with them, but he didn't have the courage for that.

Instead Abelito, sick with worry, got up and piloted the boat to Cunaviche. The town was filled with scared and angry people. A man in a torn shirt and dried blood spattered around his left eye shouted at a crowd of women with their heads down. Two old indios who Abelito recognized from the town next to his sat in the street, heavy sacks plumped beside them in the dirt, food and pans and tools spilling out from the top. There were people carrying bundles wrapped up in sheets, people with household items thrown this way and that in carts, people with hunted looks, milling about, people who wanted to run but did not know where to go, carrying their lives on their backs or dragging them behind like pack animals. Abelito ran to the church, but outside of the church was only more chaos, more hunted people, more anger.

"Animals!" a woman shouted. He heard the sound of wailing. The sky above was pure blue, mocking the earth below. Abelito pushed his way in through the doors. Inside were more people, more shouting, a crowd bunched in a rough circle near the altar, under the Holy Christ. Abelito pushed forward, knowing nothing else to do, nowhere else to go. As he approached, the eyes of the Holy Christ followed him and only him, ignoring all the crowd, and the wound in the side of the Holy Christ seemed no longer to gape and devour, but to scream along with the people in the street. Abelito pushed to the front of the rough circle of men and women, and at first did not understand what he saw. An old woman, on her hands and knees, scrubbing the floor.

"Father Eustacio was playing a stupid game," a man said. "And he lost."

She was cleaning up some liquid spilled across the floor of the church. It was only Abelito's stupidity, his childishness despite everything, despite every reason to be a man, that did not allow him to see what the liquid was, spattered and oozing across the floor, the awful shape of it slowly disappearing and the old woman moved forward, hands and knees, wiping with rags, dragging the liquid across the floor in an arc, creating a rainbow of one color.

"He had no option," another man said. "If he hadn't worked with the guerrilla . . ."

"They castrated him and let him bleed to death. Why do that to a priest?"

"The paras like to send a message."

"The paras?" Abelito said, the sound of his own voice surprising him. "But . . ."

No one paid him any attention. He looked back at the old woman, making her way through the stain. Blood, thought Abelito. Blood. He felt ashamed. The wound of the Holy Christ screamed. He pushed his way back out of the crowd, out the back door of the church. Heaviness hung over the town. The road down the river was full of people with their bags and carts, leaving. The road up the river was full of people with their bags and carts, coming.

Father Eustacio is dead, he thought. The thought made him calm. The heaviness eased. A voice told him, You must return home. It was the animal instinct that tells birds and beasts at the end of their lives to retreat to their nests, their burrows, to find a fallen branch or rock to die under, so as not to leave death in the open.

Abelito walked against the stream of people coming into Cunaviche, receiving strange looks and, from a Motilon woman, a warning. "The paras," she said. Which didn't make sense to Abelito, it was the guerrilla, the guerrilla. His town had not seen paras in years.

Or had it? Back then, Abelito had no real understanding of the groups operating in and around his town. Paracos and guerrilla and narcos and bandits and police and soldiers and even a few smaller groups, local militias put up by Motilones or other indios. And there were different types of guerrilla, and different types of paracos, and different types of narcos. He knew the guerrilla wanted communism. He knew the paracos wanted to kill the guerrilla. He knew the narcos wanted coca. But he also knew they sometimes worked together. Even the paracos sometimes cooperated with the guerrilla, working out agreements or banding together against local militias that threatened their power. It was all too much. The one thing he understood, the one thing that mattered, was that there was no one in this world a poor town or village could appeal to for protection.

After an hour the road cleared of even the stragglers headed in the other direction, and Abelito found himself alone beneath the clear blue sky. Or almost alone. His mean sister, Mona, and his smart sister, Maria, and his father and mother and grandfather, they still existed in his mind, somewhere near the gunfire he heard off in the distance. Somewhere near the smoke rising in the sky. Hiding in the back corners of his mind was the knowledge of a great evil. He walked to that evil. He belonged there, in the space that used to be a town, with drunk old men, cruel little boys, ugly women, and spiteful little girls. With young wives faithful to their husbands. Young men eager to spend coca money on radios and clothes.

He walked past the house where Jimena had lived before Franklin killed her, and where her family had shut themselves up in their grief.

Empty. The door open on its hinge, somehow knowing there was no longer any point in securing the home. No one would return.

Abelito kept walking, walking to where he should find the friends, families, traditions, stories, games, and songs he had grown up with, where even the dead, like Jimena, remained stitched into the continuing fabric of daily life. But Abelito was not heading to a place of mourning. He was heading to a place of silence, where even memory had died.

He saw Pablo's corpse first. Pablo, older than him, a hard worker, but shy among the other boys, lying facedown. Abelito knew him by his hands, tough, calloused hands. You can see a person's soul in the eyes, they say, but you can also see them in the hands. Pablo's left arm was twisted under his body, the hand just peeking out from underneath his right side, open palm to the sky, while his right arm was straight above his head, the right hand dug into the dirt. Abelito turned him so he faced the sky. Pablo's face was trapped in an expression of terror, with a twisted, open mouth.

Even now, I cannot bear to look at the hands and faces of the dead. Whenever death happened in front of me, I would focus on the arms, chests, necks, legs as the work was done. That way, no one would see me looking away, like a coward. I'd be looking straight at them, but not seeing them, only seeing their parts as the life fled. Abelito was young, and did not know these tricks.

The sky was dark, the road hard to see. Abelito knew his way, even in the dark, but with each step his feet grew heavier, his heart more fearful. He passed Gustavo's house, or what was left of it, one wall caved in and the tin roof crumpled inward. What has happened here? he thought, even though he knew. He had heard about other towns where people were chased off the land, towns become too troublesome so the whole population was turned out, become the displaced, ghosts haunting cities far away.

The instinct to return home had faded, but Abelito had nowhere else to go, no other home. The house he had built with his father and sisters appeared on the road like an empty tomb. He could feel that the circles of protection and prayers, which had kept it safe and made it a place of joy, had dissipated. Abelito reached down for the bracelet his father had given him, with its tiny wooden cross. All the sacred power his father and mother had called on their whole lives, every prayer and blessing, it had been used up to save his life. Abelito walked into his house and felt nothing move his soul. There was less home here than when his father sketched out the shape of the walls in the dirt. He touched his face and felt tears on his fingers. Under his bed he saw the book his teacher at the evangelical school had given him, but it seemed like it didn't belong to him anymore, that it belonged to a different person, to whoever had lived in this house while the blessings still held. He took off the bracelet and cross and threw them in the corner.

He left the house and walked to where he'd seen the smoke. Chepe's. His steps became slower and the dusk deepened into night. When Abelito reached Chepe's he could only see the outline of it in the moonlight, and the outline was wrong, incomplete somehow. There was a terrible smell in the air, the smell of cooked meat, and it stirred Abelito's hunger even as it made him want to vomit the contents of his empty stomach onto the ground. He couldn't move forward.

I do not know how long he stood there. I only know that it was with something like gladness that he saw two men in ratty clothes appear on the road, point their rifles at him, and demand he tell them who he was, where he was going, and what he thought he was doing, so close to a place of battle.

The men were the same age as Abelito, made men and not boys only by their weapons. They had simple, honest faces, though they looked scared and excited. One had a large pimple on the right side of his nose. The other, the barest beginnings of a beard. They made Abelito kneel, and even then, Abelito did not fully understand how the world had shifted, and he thought he had the right to ask questions, to look into the face of another person, to speak words and be heard. He thought this even as they tied his hands behind his back, as he knelt before the smoking tomb of his family, his village, and what was left of himself.

"What happened? Have you seen—"

The first blow came like a shock of electricity, beginning in the right jaw and echoing up into the top of Abelito's skull, jolting through his body, which unbalanced and toppled, dust in the mouth and the world tilted sideways. The muscles of his arms strained once, twice, unaware of the new rules, of the rope cutting into his wrists. The simple, honest faces were shouting. There was no pain, only surprise and the first movements toward Abelito's final death, a slow reordering of the way the world works, in which a boy can be helpless, truly helpless, and a blow cannot be returned with another blow.

Once, Abelito was beaten to the ground at school by Gustavo, a larger and crueler boy than the weakling Abelito had been. Gustavo's beating hurt far worse than the one weak blow from the honest faces, but it had changed nothing in the universe where Abelito lived. Back then, with his own fists, Abelito had fought back. An eye for an eye, a tooth for a tooth, his pitiful fists had tried to shout. He knew he would lose, he knew how it would end—in blood, a chipped tooth, and shame. But while he could, he had thrown himself at Gustavo, and kept a shred of dignity.

The honest faces dragged Abelito up by his hair, hit him again, and more dirt hit his lips, the smoke in the dimming light turned into a column floating leftward, the ground rushing up to the right, and God no longer above. Even then, as they dragged him to his knees a second time, the pain rising with him, Abelito thought if he could only under-stand what they were asking him, or explain who he was, and what he was doing, then it would stop. He still believed in rules. He didn't real-ize he had passed into another world where rules didn't exist. They hit him a third time, then pulled him to his feet, blindfolded him, and made him walk.

Is there any reason to tell of the pathetic things done and said by

Abelito as he walked back to the paras' rally point? Does it help to say that the paras knew they were intruding on guerrilla territory? That they'd come at Chepe's request but offered no help when the guerrilla entered the town, and no help when the gunfire started, or when the guerrilla's rage overflowed, or when the rebellious people were herded into Chepe's bar, or when the fire was set, or when the screams rose, death hidden from the murderers by four walls, smoke, and fire? That they waited until the guerrilla were drunk on death, and then they waited until the guerrilla were drunk on stolen aguardiente? That only then, as the guerrilla were leaving town, disorderly and sated, that the paras opened fire? Does it help to say that the honest faces had reason to be scared, that they were braced for a counterattack? That both the paras and the guerrilla were forcing villagers from their homes, shooting stragglers? That even though they were on opposite sides of the war it was almost as though they were working together to destroy all that people had built here? That the area was full of violence tonight and no one, not even the men with guns, was safe? No. Because those honest faces, faces he could barely catch a glimpse of out of the corner of the blindfold placed inexpertly over his eyes, faces shouting questions about the movements of the guerrilla, their numbers, their leadership, their weaponry, those faces cared nothing for answers.

Abelito's jaw throbbed in tune with his heartbeat. One part of his mind remained fixed on his family, on the fantasy that they were still alive and that he would find them. Another part screamed in terror at what was to happen to him. And another part, a part slowly invading the other corners, obliterating thoughts about himself, about his family, about Chepe and Pablo and Father Eustacio and what it meant that they were gone, was just devoted to pain.

At the rally point were other paras, and the sound of a motorcycle running. The honest faces forced Abelito down on his knees. He heard them talking, and then new voices shouted questions, Abelito answered with the truth, still believing the truth mattered, that the truth could stop what was to come. A balled-up rag was stuffed into his mouth. Another rag was tied over his face, covering his mouth and nose. Abelito was kicked onto his back. The part of his mind devoted to his family and the part of his mind devoted to pain receded. The fear took over. He tried to scream out but the rag stifled him.

Wetness, then. First on his face, lips, spreading through the cloth, soaking the rag, the smell of gasoline and soap. It confused Abelito as the taste hit his tongue. *Why this? What are they doing?* Someone took the blindfold off, and he stared up at the honest faces. Quickly the mixture of gasoline and soap saturated the cloth. Abelito held his breath, unsure of what was to come. Then he breathed. The fumes entered his body. And Abelito's mind, which had been divided between the pain in his jaw, his love for his family and town, and his terror for his own life, that mind disappeared.

I could try to describe what it felt to breathe in the fumes from that mixture of soap and gasoline. I could say, "Fire spread inside Abelito's skull and lungs." I could say, "His nose and throat felt as though they were being burst open from inside," or "His eyes felt as though they were being squeezed out of his skull." But this is not helpful. The pain consumed. Whatever had existed before inside Abelito, memories, desires, dignity, and whatever had existed before outside Abelito, his father and mother, his home, the fields where he worked, the church where he prayed for redemption, these were replaced with nothing more than his sense of his own body, a body subject to pain and a body subject to death.

Abelito held himself still, did not dare to breathe. The honest faces came back into focus, faces that no longer seemed the faces of people like Abelito, like the people he had grown up with, but the faces of something more than human, faces of the masters of his body and of his spirit, masters of what would be Abelito's scream of pain and death, if only he could scream.

The desire to breathe welled up in Abelito's chest, in his throat. The sting of gasoline burned at his eyes. The desire to breathe grew stronger. It became a command. Abelito breathed again.

I do not know how long this went on, how many times Abelito breathed and how many times the pain reduced him to the nerves inside his chest and behind his face, how many times the pain expanded his mind into the universe of his suffering body. When the cloth was removed, there were new questions, and Abelito's mind tried to find scraps of thought to string together into answers. Honest answers—that he was just a villager, a coca worker, that he was searching for his parents—and dishonest answers—that he was a guerrilla, that he was a spy, that he was the Carpenter himself, back from the dead and here to kill all paras—they blended together. They made no difference. The cloth and rag returned, Abelito's mind disappeared into pain, and then there were more questions. If only Abelito could have opened up his body to them, allowed them to shove their hands into his rib cage, grasp his heart, extend their fingers into his brain, along the inside of his throat and jaw, and work his mouth and tongue into the shape of some acceptable answers, he would gladly have done so.

Then a word was spoken, and the honest faces disappeared, and the rag and cloth disappeared, and a new face, an older face, appeared. It was not a kind face, nor an unkind face. It had a thin beard and sorrowful eyes. The owner of the older face cut the ropes holding Abelito, checked his eyes and hands.

"It's good, it's good," said the older face, the face of a man I'd come to know, the face of Osmin.

He held Abelito's body firmly, but not without tenderness. He held him the way the Virgin Mary must have held the corpse of Christ. He said, "What is your name?"

And I said, "My name is Abel."

4

wo bombings in a day is new. New is bad. But for the moment, I have work to distract me. The AP beats me on the urgent. Suicide bombing in Karte-ye Mamurin. As I'm grabbing my bag Aasif calls and I put him on speaker.

"Just civilians," he says from the site of the first bombing. "Broken glass everywhere. Shops and houses. No possible military target." He has Wahidulla, at the Health Ministry, confirming fifteen dead and possibly up to three hundred injured, Police Chief Rahimi confirming they're all civilians.

I'm nervous. Kabul has felt increasingly dangerous the past year and a half, since the attack on La Taverna du Liban, since the Swedish re-porter shot randomly in the street, since the suicide bombing at the Christian day care, since the attack on the Serena Hotel, since the two Finns shot in broad daylight, since the Cure Hospital attack. But I'm smiling as I exit the door.

Moments like these, they're the best part of the job. The part where something awful happens, and I get assigned to *do something* about it. To write the story. To sort through the chaos and find narrative, mean-ing. Sure, it's not giving blood, picking up the bodies, or hunting down the killers. And maybe those lines we recite about journalists writing the first draft of history, maybe those lines will rub the wrong way after you've filed the story. You've sent your work out into the void enough times with only the smallest hope that anybody will care. It even becomes funny when a colleague sends you an email from Washington telling you, "You know I got back from Afghanistan only a month ago and already I catch myself talking about the war as if it's not still happening." And you think, what am I doing here? But before I file, when I'm talking to survivors, when I'm gathering the pieces, and finally when I'm writing, when I'm piecing together the awful parts into some kind of whole that readers can accept and digest, I'm a believer. Doing something means believing in it. It means faith. So when horror happens I don't just have to endure it, the way most people here do. I get to act.

I arrive at the second blast site, where there are still dead in the street, and two shrapnel-riddled cars. Both of them have those back window stickers so popular here. One reads: "Don't Cry Girls, I Will Be Back," and the other, "Don't Drink, It Is Sin," complete with an image of a champagne bottle spilling alcohol onto, oddly, Che Guevara's face. I take photos of the cars, of a can of incense on a chain, still smoking. A woman holding a baby sees me and begins yelling, so I put my phone on record as she shouts. I can't always understand what interviewees are saying, especially when they're upset, but I can always play it for Aasif later.

"I was feeding my baby," she eventually tells me, after she's calmed down a bit. Her baby is covered in bandages. "I saw the roof fall in on me and fell unconscious. Then I heard my husband shouting over and over. He came to me. I was bleeding from my face, my hands, and my shoulders. My brother-in-law lost both of his eyes. My son . . ."

She holds up the baby so I could see the injuries, though he is so swaddled in bandages it's hard to tell. The mother herself looks young, with a pretty face still covered in grime and dried blood.

"My husband, he was saying . . . he was shouting, 'Where are the others? My father, my father? Where are the others?' He was bleeding from the top of his head. He was wild, he did not know where he was. We have lost everything."

Later in the day we'll get the official count for the police bombing—fifty-seven casualties, twenty-eight killed, twenty-nine injured. Add that to this and we haven't had so much death in one day since the Ashura bombing four years ago.

So this is different, this is dangerous, this is news. I should be excited. But midway through the interviews I realize I'm running out of steam. Or maybe I'm running out of fucks. Afghanistan has a way of leaching those out of you, which is why every wannabe war correspondent adopts an attitude of casual cynicism well before they've earned it. It's our version of the military veteran's thousand-yard stare. And I'm looking around nervously, worried about an attack on first responders, worried that I'm putting myself at risk, which is not where my head should be. I push those feelings away, and decide, fuck it, I'll fight the Kabul traffic and head to the first blast site, too. Double the risk, you coward.

When I get there I see this was a much larger blast. The bomb has blown in storefronts, leaving the concrete posts and steel beams and metal railings behind, baring the architectural bones of the market. Walking through a city after a bombing is like coming upon the decayed body of an animal in the woods—enough has been destroyed that you can see the rib cage, a bit of skull and jawbone poking through, the long delicate metatarsals of the feet, enough hints to imagine for yourself the whole skeleton that once structured life.

I walk through the crater, see the edges come up to my waist. Beyond the crater, there's a man sweeping glass and rubble out of a ruined store. I see a young man searching for valuables in the rubble. And then, shadowed in a doorway, a toddler beams at the world, a chunk of rubble in her fat hand, raised high. She brings it down on a battered piece of metal, making a loud clanging noise.

"Ba!" she says, delighted. "Ba ba BAH!"

And she strikes the metal again. And again. And starts laughing. I take out my camera and photograph her joy.

As the sun's going down I head back to the office. Everybody is there—Denise typing away, Omar sifting through photos, Aasif and Bob reading transcripts of interviews with Taliban leaders. I file around 9:40, scroll through my photos from the day. Log in to Facebook, where journalists who've left the country are posting news of the blast with posts like, "I've been there so many times, terrible to see . . ." "More violence in my beautiful Kabul . . ." "Two years ago I did an interview just around the corner from where this bomb . . ." I pull up the photo of the little girl, the happy toddler with the piece of metal in her hand. The girl's face is in focus, well lit, and the background is a nicely unfocused blur, though you can see the devastation clearly enough. I save it to a folder labeled "Memories."

Not much later, around ten, we hear a third explosion.

"You've got to be fucking kidding me," says Bob.

"That was big," Omar says. "Far away, but big."

There's a moment of silence. We're tired. We're all tired.

"Didn't NDS pick up a couple of Daesh recruiters yesterday?" Denise says quietly.

"The Islamic State?" says Bob. "Nah . . . I don't think so. You don't go from base-level recruiting to three linked attacks in a day."

I call the military press office and they're in the dark about the blast as well. "We're not giving out any information at this time," says Staff Sergeant Johnathon Burgett, in a lovely, honey-dipped Tennessee accent. But Aasif gets a source telling us there's been a big blast at the gate of Camp Integrity. Everybody turns to me.

"Integrity is run by Blackwater, right?" asks Bob.

"They call themselves Academi now," I say.

"Whatever," says Bob. "You've fucked half the mercenaries in Kabul, you've got to have a source."

The room goes quiet. Nobody likes that I've dated contractors. Two, to be specific, though one was more serious and the other was more casual fucking. It's none of their business, none of anybody's business, but it got around. Even military folks tend to hold mercenaries in contempt. And then Bob realizes before I do that maybe some ex of mine is dead, killed in the explosion.

"I'm sure all the Blackwater guys are fine," he says.

"They subcontract the outer ring of security to Afghans," I say.

Bob looks disappointed. "Of course they do," he says. "Those fucking cockroaches. With their fucking high-speed gear and their cool-guy shades and their wizard beards. So how much are they getting paid to have Afghans take the risks for them?"

"At least it's not civilians," Denise says.

"You know they finally sentenced the Blackwater guys in the Nisour Square massacre. Life for Slatten. The other guys got, I think, thirty years . . ."

I ignore them, mostly. But it occurs to me that I could dial Diego's phone number. At least, the number I think is still his, if he's still in country, or in Kabul. More likely, he's out doing counternarcotics work in God knows where. Or on one of his R&Rs in the backwoods of Chile, drinking maté and pretending not to be out of his goddamn mind. "I'm not a normal person anymore, Liz," he told me once. "And I don't want to be."

I pull out my phone. We hadn't closed things off in any real way, we just slowly stopped talking. He was always off in a different country anyway, doing work he claimed was "like James Bond, but boring." When I'm reporting on something like this, something that matters, it makes it easier if I can become nothing more than a pane of glass, the medium through which people can look out the windows of their normal lives and see what's happening over here. Diego complicates things, raises up emotional turbulence, changes the weights and measures of what I think is important and worth telling. But if he's in country, he'll know something.

I dial his number. The phone rings and rings, but he doesn't answer, and I'm not sure if I'm disappointed, or happy, or worried. I end up heading to Integrity on the back of Omar's motorcycle, cold wind whipping my head scarf as we head out to the base. Camp Integrity. Sometimes I'm not sure if the U.S. government is just trolling us when they name these things. What else would you name a giant 435,600-square-foot compound run by the most notorious mercenary outfit of the modern wars? Blackwater, Xe, Paravant, Academi. They secured a $750-million contract in 2012 for "information" related to the counter-drug effort in Afghanistan, and they've been running Integrity ever since.

When we were dating, I once asked Diego how the drug effort was going. He pulled out an iPad and showed me a graph tracking opium production against the price of wheat over the past ten years. When the price of wheat was high, opium production went down. When the price of wheat was low, opium production went up. Along the graph were little markers indicating various points at which the U.S. launched multibillion-dollar counternarcotics efforts. They didn't seem to have had the slightest effect on overall production.

"So what's the point of what you do?" I asked him.

He shrugged. "We affect things on the margins. What kind of narcissistic asshole would think he could do more than that? But, hey, there are lives in those margins."

I rolled my eyes.

"You ever known a heroin addict?" he asked. "I mean, you ever seen it?"

"Sure."

"The shit is evil, Liz. Pure evil, no lie."

"And Blackwater pays well," I said.

"It's Academi now," he said, and sighed. "Nobody ever asks a homicide detective if they're going to end murder. The question isn't whether we can win. It's whether it'll be worse if we stop fighting."

Afghan police stop us as we approach the blast site. There are a couple of NDS pickup trucks, two unmarked white vans, an MRAP in overwatch, a lot of people standing around with guns, a few interested onlookers. Inside the ring of police I can make out some damaged blast walls, but can't actually see much else.

"No good shot," Omar says. "But . . . I can work magic."

He gets off the bike and starts walking the perimeter. I head into the crowd and ask people what happened. A couple of people give me the same story—one big boom, then some smaller booms, maybe grenades, and small arms fire. An assault, not just a suicide bombing.

"Dead bodies?" I ask.

Heads nod yes. I'm exhausted, and though this should be exciting, I don't care. Three bombings in one day. Does it mean anything? Yes, no, who knows? I call Diego again. This time he picks up.

"What do you expect me to tell you, Liz?" he answers, sounding frustrated and hostile.

"That you're okay," I say.

"Oh," he says softly. "I'm okay."

Around me, the crowd is thinning. There's little more to see here. Little point, even, to having come. Omar will get decent shots but nothing to beat his work from the earlier bombings. Those are the photos that will run.

"Well then," he says. He sounds tired, or sad. There's something there. "Thanks for thinking of me."

"Diego . . ."

"What, you want a quote?"

I sigh. "I could do it off the record . . ."

"How's this?" I hear him shuffling through papers. "Human lives are brief and trivial. Yesterday a blob of semen; tomorrow embalming fluid, ash."

"Lovely."

"It's Marcus Aurelius. Seriously."

"He doesn't really qualify as news."

Suddenly I'm angry.

"You know what, Diego? Fuck you. Would you feel this way if it wasn't just Afghans who were killed? If it were one of you?"

Omar sees me and approaches. He can see I'm upset. He raises the camera and snaps a photo. I draw my breath in sharply. Later, I'll ask him to delete the photo. I'm here to observe, not to be observed.

"Look . . ." I say.

"We lost one too, Liz. Not Academi. U.S. military."

"Oh."

Omar puts the camera up to take another shot of me and I give him the finger. He smiles and snaps the shot.

"Did you know him?"

"He was Seventh Group."

"Oh." Diego's old unit.

"You know you can't print anything until . . ."

"I know."

"I was with him in Iraq and Afghanistan," he says. "We went way back."

"Oh," I say. "I'm so sorry."

"Yeah," he says. "A good guy. Great soldier. I think he'd have thought it was okay, going out like this. In combat, you know?" He didn't sound sure.

There's more to be done, but Bob texts me, he wants us back at the office. Bob's got better contacts in the military anyway, so I figure, let him work it. On the way back, I look at the windshield stickers of the cars we pass. "Fighter Car. If You Follow Me Will Be Die." "You Are

My Heart Always." One has an insignia of the presidential palace, and former president Hamid Karzai. Another, the face of the mujahideen Ahmad Shah Massoud. And then a Toyota Camry with "I Hate Girls."

The next day, we find out the name of the 7th Group soldier— Master Sergeant Benjamin Kwon, "Benjy" to his friends. We don't get the names of the eight Afghan armed guards who also died, not that there'd be much point in hunting the names down. UNAMA claims zero civilian casualties for that attack, though they put the days' total at 368—52 killed and 316 injured, with 43 of the dead and 312 of the injured civilians. Diego doesn't pick up the phone when I call him to get more detail. The Taliban claims the police academy attack and the Camp Integrity attack, but not the first bomb. Bob takes this to mean it was an accidental early detonation, a bomb headed for somewhere else, aimed to ruin other lives.

The day after, while we're still scrambling, there's a fourth bomb, this one at the entrance to the airport, killing and injuring twenty-one people, though by this point the numbers have blurred to just numbers. As I finish typing up the latest death toll it occurs to me that I'd been pumping out articles on how violent Kabul has become, this city that I've always told my family is safe, that I've told them is the one place in Afghanistan they don't need to worry about me, and that if they're following the news at all they're probably freaking out.

So I call my mom. And my mom is concerned for me, and worried for me, like she always is, but it's pretty obvious she has no idea that Kabul has been exploding. She goes on about how Uncle Carey's mind is a touch battier than it always was, and they're thinking about moving him in with my sister so that Linda can help look after him. And when I tell her about the bombings she just says, "That's why I don't like you over there, Lisette. All those bombs." And when I get angry and tell her this is different, this is new, that hundreds of people have been killed or injured in the past three days alone and that doesn't happen here, she tells me as soothingly as she can, "I know, my love, it's terrible." Because to her, to my mom, a woman who follows the news, who is smart, who is interested in foreign policy, who has a fucking daughter living in Kabul, this is certainly terrible but also just what happens *over there*. It's not a surprise. And I realize that no matter how jaded I've become, I'll never be as jaded as the average American.

"I don't think you know what it feels like to have a child in a war zone," she tells me. "To be a parent is to always have . . ."

". . . a piece of your heart," I say. "I know, Mom."

"A piece of your heart," she says, "traveling around outside your body."

And I'm ashamed, talking to my mother, though I'm not sure why, just that I feel foolish, and that I also have the absurd desire to crawl into my mother's lap, my very petite sixty-seven-year-old mother's lap, though at the same time I'm so angry, or maybe just feeling betrayed, and if I showed up at her house tomorrow I know I'd sit in stony silence while she made me tea and talked about how America is falling apart and it's mostly George Soros's fault. But then she asks me what she always asks me: "When are you coming home?" And I surprise myself with what I realize is an honest answer.

"Soon."

5

ABEL 1999–2001

J ust before he handed me the gun, Osmin spoke of revenge, but that
desire was down at the bottom of a well, under the water, so that all
I could see when I searched for the feeling was my own reflection.
Words like *Mother*, and *Father*, they, too, were under the water, and to
even try to think them made my chest constrict. Easier to forget those
words, which meant nothing. I was a newborn child. Peeing myself at
night, like a child. Blinking in confusion at the light every morning,
like a child. Helpless, like a child. But when I held the gun, I did not
feel like a child. I felt like I had achieved something. I even thought
that, if I died, just holding it meant I already knew what I needed to
know.

"When you are young," Osmin laughed, seeing me changed by the
gun, "you want the strong." I believed him.

Those early days are all broken memories. After Osmin saved me I
had thought he would keep me with him, like a pet. Instead he left me
by the side of the road, vomiting blood. I remember rolling onto my
back, coughing and gurgling, the trees above stabbing the sky. Later, I
remember going to church and hearing the names of the dead, fourteen
names, including the four names I was most afraid to hear. Then my
animal days began. I remember hunger, and stealing food in Cunaviche.

I remember being beaten and fighting back like a wild dog. I remember the twins, Rafael and Norbey, who ruled the wild boys who lived on the street. Then I remember the army soldiers coming to Cunaviche, after which the paras moved back to the other side of the river and we didn't see guerrilla anymore. It was months before I saw Osmin again, walking through the town with a fat young girl on his arm. When he left Cunaviche, I followed him and he let me.

"I remember you," he said.

He told me he could give me the revenge I wanted, and also good pay, but I would have to prove myself. I had spoken to him of neither revenge nor pay, but I nodded as if he had offered me everything I could desire. Then he took me on the back of his moto to a bar by the river. Outside, the honest faces were playing cinco huecos, laughing and smiling with their other friends, rifles slung across their bags. One of the honest faces—Iván, I would later learn—took the ball and threw it at the head of another, who ducked, and the ball went into the river and floated away. They laughed, and Iván took his rifle up to his shoulder. "Think I can hit it?" he said, aiming at the ball.

I didn't want to go closer, but Osmin's face became stern, and the same instinct that brought food to my mouth urged me forward. I knew showing fear would be dangerous. And Osmin laughed and said, "You remember Iván and Nicolás?"

He told them that I wanted to prove I was tough enough to join, and then asked me, "Which one? Iván? Or Nicolás?"

Iván had pimples across his face, and I wondered if I could pop them with my fists. Nicolás's beard was coming in and it made him look tougher. "Iván," I said. When he was in the dust, I looked down and saw blood on my knuckles. There was pain in the air around us. Some of it belonged to me, some of it belonged to him. I reached to Iván, and offered him my hand, and he took it, and stood up, and then Osmin offered me the gun.

"I'll give you what you want," he said. And he did.

We never saw the guerrilla. Once, we shot at trees, and trees shot at us. At the time I wondered about tall, thin Alfredo and short, ugly Matías, and the guerrilleros who took them. Was Alfredo still always sick? Was Matías still kind? Was he still short? Did they take part in the massacre? It didn't matter, I thought. They were nothing to me.

Mostly we worked in the towns along the river, keeping order and delivering justice. We'd set up roadblocks to control who was coming in and out. When people tried to steal from the paisas, we would chase them off their land. Make sure their drug laboratories were safe and their shipments went through. If a town had a problem with delinquents, we would come and help with a cleansing. One time a woman came to us with bandages on her ears. Thieves had torn her earrings right off, skin attached, and when the police caught the thieves they threatened her if she made a formal denunciation. We went to the house of the mother of one of the thieves, waited until her son arrived, and Iván shot him, leaving a big red spot on his chest as he gasped out his life. The police waved to us as we left.

Another time a mayor told us about a butcher in his town who had been beating his wife. He was an older man, gray haired, older than my father, with a big red nose, big thighs, and a skinny chest, ugly like an insect is ugly. We went to his shop and held his arms and Osmin punched him five times in the face. Then we threw him to the floor and kicked him.

Osmin told us, "If a man has to beat his wife, it is because he is so weak that he can't make her fear him."

Osmin wasn't married, but he was twenty-two years old and had almost that number of girlfriends, so I thought he must know something about women. As we were leaving, the man's wife came down to tend to her husband's wounds. She was short and fat and ugly, like her husband, and I felt like she should thank us somehow. I imagined making love to her. But she tended to her husband's wounds without looking at us. We walked away.

I met Jefferson Paúl López Quesada soon after. He arrived with his men, paracos who had trained at Acuarela, who handled weapons with care, moved in formation, and wore crisp uniforms that contrasted sharply with our ratty T-shirts and Osmin's bright-colored shorts. They came in pickup trucks, not on motos, and we all knew in advance to speak respectfully and carefully. Jefferson, Osmin told us, ran all the towns around La Vigia, the big town to the south. He gave orders to all the little gangs like ours, and managed all the money from the vaccine that people paid us to keep them safe.

Even before we saw him in person, I knew who he was. Seeing him in person, surrounded by his stone-faced paracos, was like standing before the burning bush.

Jefferson was short, blocky, and muscular, the body of a pit bull crouched to strike. His face was cold. Even when he yelled, the anger never reached his eyes. He stood in front of us and told us we had allowed something terrible to happen in our area, something that demanded his presence to protect the morality of the people and the justice of our struggle.

Then we all gathered our weapons and gear and followed Jefferson's paracos to a gathering outside a river town. On a small stage, a faggot was dancing in front of an audience of about fifteen or twenty. The dancing faggot's jeans were cut open at the crotch to show his underwear, which was red. We surrounded the men, who looked scared, and Jefferson went on stage, where the faggot in jeans was frozen in terror. "Look, he's got earrings," he said. And then he hit him in the face with the butt of his rifle and stood over him and used pliers to tear the earrings out of his ears. I thought of the woman we'd helped, who'd been attacked by thieves.

The red faggot shrieked, then cried. Jefferson walked to the front of the stage and began a speech about how the faggot life came from America and that for a man to fuck another man is to kneel to imperialism. "We must stay true to our Colombian identity," he told the audience, "unblemished, unmixed, uncorrupted." I had never considered my identity, Colombian or otherwise, but I would learn this was Jefferson's way. Before doing violence, he'd talk nonsense to confuse and to justify.

Jefferson also said that no women were allowed to wear miniskirts, though there were no women there to hear the news. Miniskirts, he said, began in Europe, which he made sound even more disgusting than America. Then we fired into the air and moved in, hitting the faggots with our rifles as they squirmed and crawled away. It feels good, to hit someone with a rifle, especially someone who is like a man, but not.

One of the faggots in the middle of the pack, a skinny man with short hair and a rugby shirt tucked into his jeans, went down on his knees and began to pray to the Virgin Mary. This made it hard to hit him. So in the middle of squirming, shrieking bodies, groans and cries, there was this one little man, on his knees, reciting, "Holy Mary, mother of God, pray for us sinners . . ." with a circle of protection around him. When he reached the end of his prayer, Iván hit him before he could start again, and he fell to the ground with blood coming from a gash above his right eye.

Once the faggots were beaten, Jefferson made a sign and we walked away in two single-file lines, Jefferson's group and ours. But as we left the town Jefferson stopped and had us turn around. We found the men tending each other's wounds, a sight that was disturbing to me, and changed my feelings about what we'd just done. Jefferson took the man in the red underwear and we marched him out of town, and Jefferson and two of his men raped him and then shot him in the head and left the body in the road. Osmin told us that the flame of war burns strong in Jefferson. It is what makes him such a powerful leader.

About a week later, Osmin told me he never wanted to be a warrior, he wanted to be a civil engineer. "Let's be builders, we two." He told me this at night, by the river, when we were alone, and then he laughed, as if he knew it was ridiculous to want such a life and not to accept the only life we had. But here was a chance to change things, because after the killing of the man in red underwear Jefferson had taken Osmin aside and told him he would give him money to build a soccer field, and some one-story houses for the poor, so that it wouldn't just be the ordinary people and the businesspeople who liked us for the way we handled crime and kept order, but everyone.

"Jefferson says you start with fear, but fear is not enough." Osmin sat close to me as he told me this. He was so different from his comandante. Osmin had long limbs and a soft face. Jefferson was shaped like a square. Jefferson's hands were thick, with short stubby fingers. Osmin's palms were calloused, yes, but the veins ran across the small bones on the back of his hands in a delicate way. These were builder's hands, he wanted me to believe.

I liked the idea of building, so construction became my special responsibility. "Because you are smart, and know mathematics," Osmin told me. He even got me an engineering textbook, which we didn't need. We had money to pay men who knew their work, and the textbook didn't have anything to do with building simple houses or community centers or soccer fields. It had a dark purple cover, was titled *Analysis of Structures with Dynamic Loads—Volume II: Systems of Multiple Degrees of Freedom*, and seemed to only involve versions of math that I had never been taught.

"I will learn this by heart," I told Osmin, and I believed it at the time, but then I only got three or four pages in before giving it up. "I need the first volume, then it'll all make sense," I said.

My first project was a soccer field in La Vigia. The contractor I found was a kind man who liked me because I was young. He let me stay by his side, and taught me how to keep books for a project, how to invoice correctly, and how to know when workers were taking advantage. For the next project, the housing, I found ways to save and didn't use all of the money—returning the leftover to Osmin, who gave it to Jefferson, who seemed confused and pleased by what I'd done, and asked for my name and then put his large hand on my shoulder, put his face too close to mine, and smiled. His breath reeked of chinchurría. My knees shook and he noticed. His smile grew. He said, "Good boy."

After that, other projects quickly followed. I loved two things most of all, watching the workmen breaking ground, and then coming back long after the project was done to watch what I'd made in use. It was like the feeling I had the first time I held a gun, but it didn't fade. There was something about seeing children playing on a field I'd leveled, or seeing a family eating dinner in a one-room house I'd built.

One night I walked through the section of poor homes we built on the edge of Cunaviche, simple, ugly houses with misshapen bricks made of sand and cement, and corrugated metal roofs that might blow away in a strong wind. Children ran through the street in front of me, shrieking. Around a corner I saw a small fire where they had tossed their scavenged things—an old tire, broken branches, a wet cardboard box pouring thick curtains of smoke into the sky. I looked through a window that was really just a hole, no glass. The mother inside cooked on a kerosene burner, and a little boy played in the corner, picking up scraps of paper and moving them from one spot to another. I stepped closer to the window, my eyes on the mother's face. She looked Motilon—there were some markings on her nose. Possibly, she was here, cooking in a home for the poor, because of us. Jefferson had made a deal with a group of guerrilla to carve up some Motilon lands in the north, lands that grew opium but which the Motilon had tried to keep from both of us, wanting to stay out of the conflict. Between the two groups, guerrilla and paramilitaries together, the tribe was crushed, and many fled.

I felt warmth toward the woman, and happiness that she had shelter. During my animal days, I had seen women like her, begging with their children by their sides, squatting on colorful rags they brought from wherever they'd come from, and I knew that to the whole world a homeless mother is prey. She turned to look out the window, and I ran. Dealing too closely with the people we helped frightened me.

Jefferson was different. He would make people come and beg him if they wanted to live in the houses he built. Undoubtedly, that woman had come with her children and offered him prayers. Undoubtedly, she kissed his hands, maybe even his feet. She'd made her little boy do the same. Jefferson always made them grovel in front of God and all. "They need to know," he said.

I never needed any kisses or prayers. I had the building itself.

Jefferson liked the way I worked, and he liked that I was quiet, respectful. So he told Osmin I would work with him more often, handling some of the civic work for our bloc, and he had one of his men give me a uniform like his paracos wore. He also told me my wage would go up, from four thousand pesos a day to eight. It was a promotion.

There were only six towns within the area of Osmin's responsibility, but Jefferson had a much wider area, where he didn't just hand out money for charity projects but also money for roads and schools, for neighborhood associations and local candidates. These were cities and towns that our bloc had firmly in control, a control coming from far more than fear or even love, which was the point of Jefferson's little projects. We wanted them to think our money paved their roads, educated their children, healed them when they were sick, gave them everything that the state was supposed to but never had, and everything the guerrillas promised but never provided. That's why when the government money came in we'd meet with the mayors and let them know they could not do anything without us. We would protect the projects as long as we received compensation and as long as the people were told the projects came from us. For the people in those towns, betraying us would thus seem like betraying themselves, removing us from the community like removing one's own backbone.

Most of these projects were handled by civilians, but Jefferson wanted to change things so that a uniformed paraco would always be involved, even if only to be seen. "With you there, in uniform," he said, "they will never be able to pretend the money comes from somewhere else."

This became my responsibility—to remind people of what they owed us. I would stand by Jefferson and take notes as he met with mayors and businesspeople and ranchers. Together we would determine what the town needed—assigning people to houses of collaborators who'd been pushed from their land, making judgments on disagreements over land, or reducing the delinquents and the viciosos. If there was money for building, Jefferson would send me out to handle all the details, to meet with the builders and suppliers, to negotiate prices, and to keep track of the construction. Jefferson was often not around—he traveled back and forth to Venezuela constantly—and even when he was around he didn't care at all about the projects except to make sure he was there when they finished, and that everyone knew he had paid for them, so handling all this quickly became a large undertaking.

I managed well. The men I worked with were decades older than me but they knew I had Jefferson's trust and Jefferson's money. They were honest with me, and spoke to me with respect, especially as time went on and I showed that I was good at the work, and attentive to the details, arriving at a site and complaining about poor foundations, or demanding refunds for a failure to complete projects in the agreed-upon time. I kept careful notes, and I often thought with gratitude about the missionaries who had supplied me with enough knowledge to be able to handle the task.

At one meeting with milk farmers across our area, an older rancher with a white mustache complained about a coming tax. Jefferson's comandante had arranged for New Zealand milk-farm technicians to come share their knowledge, and he was also importing milking machines from Argentina. In return, the milk farmers would have to pay more.

The trade representative, a lazy and stupid man whose election we'd supported, should have handled the issue beforehand, ensuring all understood they had no option. But instead of saying this without saying it, he hissed, "What are you doing? Jefferson will kill you!"

The rancher, a proud man named Rodrigo Serrano, puffed up, mustache twitching. "I don't have any fear of Jefferson," the rancher said, his pride speaking instead of his brain. "I fought the guerrilla twenty years before Jefferson came here, and I didn't—"

"Jefferson does not want you or anyone to fear him," I said, lying. Of course, Jefferson did want fear, but he didn't want that fear to be tested. Threatening rich men is dangerous, and killing them can lead to real resistance. From the milk tax we wanted money, not problems.

The rancher scoffed. "I—"

"You fought the guerrilla twenty years ago?" I leaned forward, trying my best to look eager and curious. "I didn't know anyone here had the guts to fight them before the autodefensas came."

"Yes," the rancher said, surprised and unsure of himself, but also looking pleased. "It was a dangerous time."

"Tell me about it."

"I don't think we have time—" the trade representative began.

"Shut up," I said. "The guerrilla killed everyone in my town except for me. I want to hear how the man defended his community."

The trade representative, who did fear Jefferson, turned white. I had never spoken like that to a man in a position of power. It had never occurred to me, before then, that I could speak to a man in a position of power like that. It changed the atmosphere of the room. Instead of the trade representative and me against the rancher, it became the rancher and me against the trade representative.

"Well," he said, "it started when they kidnapped Nelson Pérez . . ." And then he launched into a story about how his father, who had socialist sympathies in his youth and used to help import weapons from Medellín to sell to the guerrilla, had fallen into a rage after the kidnapping. Using the same contacts he'd used to get weapons for the FARC, he'd gotten weapons for himself and a few other men. They'd waited until the guerrilla came for payment of the vaccine, they ambushed them, and they killed them.

I acted amazed, asked questions, urged him into more and more detail as the trade representative became increasingly frustrated. And then I told him, "Given your history, I think we could come up with something different. Instead of the tax, you could contribute to security. There have been kidnappings on the road north of your lands and Jefferson was intending to post some of our men there. But it is always best to have local people."

The rancher gawked at me.

"How many men do you have?" I asked. "Men who can handle themselves? There will be fighting."

The rancher smiled, looked around for support. "I think those days are behind me," he said.

"Are you sure?" I asked. "You'd avoid the tax."

"No," he said. "No. The tax is fine."

The rich, I thought, are foolish and vain. It was strong knowledge to possess.

Jefferson gave me a raise, from eight thousand pesos a day to twelve, and I began working with all the paramilitary groups under Jefferson's control, from little bands of beggars like the one I had come from to more professionalized groups who spent less time managing cities and towns and more time on the border, working the trade of coca out and gasoline in. It gave me a sense of the world, to see the range of things a man like Jefferson was involved in, and to see how unimportant a little band like Osmin's was to him.

As a child, I thought there were guerrilla, and there were paracos, and they were at war with each other, but with Jefferson I learned that it was so much more complicated. There were cocaleros, like I had been, working the fields and sometimes organizing into little self-defense unions. And there were narcos, who bought and transported coca. And there were police and army. But within each group were different factions. Narcos who worked with us, but not the guerilla. Narcos who worked with the guerrilla, but not us. Narcos who worked with both. Guerrilla who would work with us against other guerrilla. Paracos who would work with narcos against us. Cocaleros who protected the guerrilla. Army officers who asked us to do the work they could not. Police who worked for everyone and no one. Sometimes it seemed like it was all a great game. Sometimes it seemed like hell. And always, it seemed so much bigger than I had imagined. Those days, I would sometimes think with wonder at how little worth I had possessed in the world, and how easily I could have been erased from the earth, and how even a whole town, like the one I had come from, could be destroyed without changing the calculations of the powerful.

But now I mattered to the powerful. I moved into an apartment in La Vigia, far from Osmin and the family he had provided me. I had my own bed. I had a little table and a lamp. I drank beer and soda in peace whenever I wanted. I even got a TV, and started watching *Las Juanas*, which would be my favorite show for years, until I eventually fell in love with Catalina Santana in *Without Tits, There's No Paradise*. I kept the television on while I slept. The noise helped me.

Sometimes Jefferson would make me and a few other paracos sleep in one of his fincas, a beautiful place on the river where the sound of the water both calmed me and stirred memories that risked flooding my emptiness with sorrow. We'd watch movies, especially American action movies like *Marked for Death* or *T2* or *Lethal Weapon*. There were always women around Jefferson, but in the morning he wouldn't let them cook, and he'd make blood sausage and eggs with hogao and feed it to us and demand I tell him how good it was. He'd mete out discipline in the mornings, screaming at those who'd failed him, announcing how he'd dock their pay. Several times he had men beaten. Once he tied a man to a chair and then had his right arm flayed, the skin sliced down the inside of the arm and then peeled down to the wrists to reveal muscle and bone. Each day we would eat our breakfast, unsure of who had displeased him, and what they must suffer. Nervous times, but I was always glad to be there. Jefferson was no great cook, but with him the flavors were sharper, and life felt important.

Sometimes after breakfast he'd take me aside, his strange, uniformed paraco who handled business and politics but not war, and he'd talk to me or have me sit in his house while he conducted business. He was a strange man, wise, filled with advice and knowledge about the outside world. He read newspapers and watched television news and listened to news radio, and was friendly with some journalists, and would answer any time they called, eager to show up, to be photographed, and heard. "You have to be more than a power, you have to be a famous face," he told me. "There is power in fame." I learned to please him by tying each project I was doing to some spectacle, some festival. Journalists will not often show up to the opening of a soccer field, but if you open housing for the poor on Good Friday, it becomes, as one reporter who was in our pay told me, "a story that writes itself." Jefferson began smiling when he saw me, and he started calling me "my boy." And even the other paras, Jefferson's hard, well-trained men, they began to speak to me with respect.

In this way, I found a place in the world. From the animal life of Cunaviche to the family of Osmin's front was the first great step. A life with purpose, and a leader to obey. With Jefferson, though, I became a person on my own. People in the towns came to know me as more than just a paraco. Workmen, ranchers, shopkeepers, and mayors, they greeted me when they saw me. Their smiles were unforced, unafraid. They knew my talents. My eye for details.

One day I went into a small town on the north edge of our area called Rioclaro with a group led by a former soldier named Javier. He had a reputation for cruelty, and as we entered I could see the life of the town dying around us. First, the movements of the adults stilled or turned mechanical, like bad actors on a stage. Next, the children stopped their play and stared at us curiously before catching the mood and freezing in place. All of us gripped our weapons, peered into windows and dark alleys. I wondered what Javier had done here, and whether there was any point in what I did, any way to win the people's love. And then I saw the old rancher with the white mustache sitting at a little table, eyes fixed on a dominoes game. He looked up, a furtive look, and saw me. Recognition. He grinned, stood, and waved. I walked over to him and clasped his hand. In that moment, we were the only two living souls in Rioclaro. Oh, I thought, surprised. I matter.

6

n theory, home was Pennsylvania. And in theory, you're obliged to go home, to pay obeisance to the household gods. To lie to your mother not in word but in deed, because going home is like saying that this place, Fourteen Burnham Street, still has a hold on you, that your roots there haven't withered, that maybe you would go back even if she didn't demand the visits. My mother has a sense of place, a sense of the value of land, of belonging, of community. It's one of the things that helped me develop a feel for Afghans and for American soldiers, who have their own version of tribalism. Being fixed in a community is one way of living, of knowing exactly who you are, why you are, what you are doing. Which is why betraying your family and your hometown by leaving feels like flying.

So any trip home means taking care that you don't get your wings clipped, don't let your mother or your sister or your crazy Uncle Carey love you back down to earth. Which is why the first thing I always do when I'm back home is run. Run until I'm purified. A long, long early morning run through western Pennsylvania. Miles and miles and miles. The cold early morning air, me with nothing but running shorts and a thin shirt against the cold, knowing I'll be freezing for the first half mile or so until the exercise warms my body as fast as the wind steals the heat away. It's my ritual of return, down the hills of Cambria County, down past the businesses and restaurants on Old Scalp Road, down past the camp my mom sent me to in the summers, where I caught my first fish, kissed my first boy, and, more importantly, met Rhonda, the camp counselor who wanted to be a reporter and introduced a thirteen-year-old me to Ernie Pyle and Martha Gellhorn and George Orwell. Rhonda has three kids now and lives a few miles away from my mom and when I'm home I always tell myself I'll swing by and see if she remembers me. Of course I never do. I don't indulge in nostalgia. I run. I run until there are no memories in my head at all, not of Kabul, not of Cambria County, not of Rhonda or my sister or anything penetrating my mind beyond pure sensation, the intake of breath, the burn in my lungs, the ache in my legs, and the elation of mastering that pain with every foot flung forward.

I get in late—flight to Istanbul, to New York, then Pittsburgh, then a rental car pickup and a ninety-minute drive, pulling into Fourteen Burnham Street at 4:30 in the morning—but my mom is awake anyway, waiting in ambush.

"Mom," I try to scold. "You don't sleep enough as it is."

"I'll sleep when I die," she says, and before I can tell her what I always do, that her death will come sooner if she doesn't take care of herself, she wraps me in a hug. She insists on carrying my bags herself, she brings them to my old bedroom, and starts making me a cup of tea.

I'm too tired to handle it, to sit there across from her and watch her love me the way she does. Coming home late at night from Afghanistan, from a job I'm proud of, and there's something about her that makes me feel like I'm seventeen and she caught me sneaking back into the house drunk. She doesn't like that I do this job, and that hurts but I know she doesn't like it because she worries about me, so I sit there and let her baby me. There's a part of me that even enjoys it, even tired as I am, hearing how things are going, how Linda and the kids are doing, and oh just wait until you see little Timmy, he's so much bigger, he's walking now, and oh by the way your Uncle Carey is coming by tomorrow, or I guess today . . . it's so late, he said he'll stop by after the doctor's.

But there's another part of me that feels deeply uncomfortable, because I know why my mother makes such a fuss every time I return. And I think, I want to run. I need to run. The sun needs to rise, or at least start curving some light over the horizon, or bouncing rays off clouds and back to earth, to give me something to work with other than country darkness.

And then she brings up a local family whose son returned from Iraq a few years ago and had some issues, how they weren't sure whether the issues were from Iraq or from him just always being a bit of a scoundrel, from a family that never was the most functional in the first place. I tell her I couldn't answer for sure but I do know that stretch of time in Iraq wasn't so bad and that things had been quiet before the rise of ISIS. My mother stares at me intently and I know what she really wants to know is if reporters get affected like soldiers do. I tell her he's probably fine, that war isn't so bad as people think, that most soldiers wouldn't give up their time abroad and most think it makes them tougher, stronger, better able to deal with the hard breaks you find wherever you live.

"That's true, that's true," she says, "but you know, your uncle, after the war . . ."

But Uncle Carey is the last person I want to hear more about so I shush her, tell her I'm tired, I'm not having more tea, and once I've hustled her to her room I head to mine. There I lay out my things, and sit collecting my thoughts and memories, and once I'm sure she's asleep I change into running gear.

I start out right as the sun is rising, while the night air is departing and leaving bits of fog in the hollows of the unfolding hills. It's in this first stage of the run, before I've really burned myself out, that the nostalgia tries to creep in. Western Pennsylvania is beautiful. Perhaps not as starkly grand as the Pacific Northwest, or as the crueler parts of Afghanistan, where steep cliffs and arid valleys suggest a land belonging more to God than humanity. This land isn't so alien. It's lived in—you pass barns and tilled fields and old homes set off from the road. It's gentle—you head down rolling hills, past quietly meandering streams. Nothing dramatic. It's a warm, simple beauty, one fitting the people I grew up with.

When I get to Old Scalp, though, I start noticing real changes from the last time I was here. A few new stores and restaurants. The local pharmacy has shuttered. Jake Siegel's diner, the Wavetop, is now a Long John Silver's. And as I get to the end of Old Scalp there's the final blow—Hilda's Furrier Fashions and Fur Salon, where I'd worked as a teenager. My second day there I'd gone to open the store only to find that out-of-towners had chucked a cinderblock through the glass and posted the statement: "Until all the cages are empty and all are free our struggle continues. This is not the last you'll see of us Hilda." An animal-rights group based in California had taken credit, confirming everything we ever could have thought about the Left Coast, and Hilda had been undaunted but unsure of how to show it. She was just a regular clothing store. Her furrier had gone out of business a decade earlier and she'd just never bothered to change the sign. So Hilda and I had driven to a shop outside of Pittsburgh to pick up fur underwear, of all things, to put on the shelves. "It was the cheapest fur they had," Hilda had explained when we were stocking it. I'd always figured Hilda would die before closing the place down, and as that thought goes through my head I realize how old Hilda had been even when I worked there, and I turn and keep running, cutting away from Old Scalp and skirting the rest of downtown. I don't like to think this place has a hold on me, but I also don't like to see it change.

My mind's not in the state I want, even though my legs are starting to really feel it, so I cut down Route 20, which was Uncle Carey's favorite road for tricks. A UPS driver by profession, Uncle Carey believed you could, and should, take every curve in the road at twice the posted speed. He thought small hills were launching pads. He thought sober driving was for pussies and funeral processions. His favorite trick was called the bootlegger's turn, where you burn down the road, throw the gearshift to neutral, flick the wheel a touch toward the shoulder with your right hand before yanking it toward the opposite lane while hitting the emergency brake and holding the brake release with your left. This sends the car spinning. Done right, you can pull a 360-degree turn and continue on your way as if nothing had happened. The first time he did it, I was ten, my older sister was thirteen, and he gave us absolutely no warning. I was staring out the window, in the backseat, my sister was irritatingly switching the radio stations every other second, and then my vision blurred, centripetal force smacked my face into the window, and then we were moving forward again. It was so surreal it didn't even occur to me that I should have been terrified until about thirty seconds later, when he slowed down for a stop sign, turned, and gave us his big, goofy, gap-toothed grin.

The other trick he played with us was driving to the railroad crossing, stopping the car on top of the tracks as a train came toward us, and then pretending that the engine wouldn't start. That, I did find terrifying, though in a strange way those times we spent in Uncle Carey's car were useful training for being a war correspondent, insofar as it takes a lot to overload my systems.

I reach the stop sign where Uncle Carey had grinned at us after his bootlegger's turn, the spot where my sister had bawled inconsolably while I stared at Uncle Carey, unsure of what I was feeling, excitement or terror or joy, until I chose joy and smiled back. I raise my arm and slap the metal as I pass, and then slow to cover a long, flat stretch at a medium pace, giving myself a little rest to prepare for the final uphill sprint to get home. I'm running on fumes—if it weren't for being acclimatized to Kabul's elevation this run probably would have knocked me out already—and the last bit's going to be rough. Fourteen Burnham

Street sits near the top of a steep hill looking out over Lower Yoder, and as I reach the crest of the hill there's nothing in my mind except the pain in my chest, which has stopped being an ache and is now a sharp spasm with each intake of breath. And then I see Uncle Carey's Buick in the driveway.

The Buick is a miracle—pretty much every part on it has been replaced, occasionally with parts that would rightfully belong to other cars, it's been wrecked half a dozen times, more than one of those wrecks that should have meant it'd be fully junked, and patched up and repaired so that now it's either a real monstrosity or a piebald beauty, depending on your perspective. Uncle Carey's a "Glory be to dappled things" kind of guy. I have no idea why he's here so early.

I walk through the front door to the spare, clean house my mother keeps. She doesn't believe in the accumulation of "stuff." My mother and Uncle Carey are sitting in the parlor, her with a pinched look on her face, Uncle Carey with a manic grin.

"Lisette!"

He hugs me, my sweat leaving an imprint of my body on his T-shirt. He seems thinner, but he's got his hair, his face is even a little paunchier than last time, and a little redder. It's not as bad as I'd thought, not yet—he looks more like slow dissolution through alcohol than rapid hollowing out through cancer, and I'd be relieved if not for the tension in the air. My mom tells me to sit in the parlor and when I start to tell her I'm going to shower first, she gives me a look that silences me. I find myself sitting in an armchair, leaning forward so that my post-run body touches as little of the chair's fabric as possible, sitting across from my uncle, with my mother hovering in the background, scowling.

"How are you?" I say.

"Tell me a crazy story," Uncle Carey says.

"You know she doesn't like that," my mother says.

"Sure she does," Uncle Carey says, winking at me.

I shrug and start telling him about an arms dealer I'd met, and how he was the last of six brothers, all of them dead to violence, and how he looked as he told me about each of their deaths, and who killed them. I try to tell it almost flat, not so much emotion that my mother will think I'm really bothered by it, not so emotionless she'll think I've gone numb. Midway through, the teakettle goes off, my mom walks into the kitchen, and even though she can still hear I relax and start to get into it, try to get him to really see him.

"No, no," Uncle Carey says. "That's a depressing story. I want a crazy story. Like the one about the guy who got shot in the face."

This was his favorite, about a Marine I knew with a false front tooth that he'd received when he was room clearing and an insurgent shot him point-blank in the face with a small caliber pistol. The bullet blew through his front lip, ricocheted off his teeth, snapped his head back, and knocked him to the ground, but otherwise left him unhurt. So the Marine popped back up and tackled the insurgent who'd shot him. The insurgent was terrified. From his perspective, he'd sent a bullet through the head of his enemy, only to have the man come back at him like the T-1000 from the Terminator movies. There'd been a lot of discussion in the unit afterward that, instead of detaining the guy, they should have set him free to tell stories of the invincible zombie Marines.

"I don't know," I say. "Maybe some other time."

"You could read the stories she writes," my Mom calls out from the kitchen.

"Ehhh . . ." Uncle Carey says, waving his hand. "Why do that when I can get it from the horse's mouth? Besides, you know they don't print the real stories in the paper."

"Lisette prints the real stories," my mother says, bringing in a cup of Lipton's for me.

"You know, you should cover some of the craziness going on in this country!" he says.

"Oh?"

"You should cover the riots. This country is exploding!" He seems excited by the prospect.

"I think we'll be fine," I say.

"You should—"

"Your uncle," my mother says, "is supposed to be at the doctor's."

"Ah," I say.

Uncle Carey waves his hand dismissively, as if this is all no big deal. "I already made my decision. I'm just gonna do symptom management."

"Ah," I say again. My mom had told me Uncle Carey was dragging his feet about chemo. There's a part of me that's glad. When I found out the diagnosis, I checked the five-year survival rates for his stage cancer and the percentages were in the teens. Besides, we both remember how it was for my dad. Sometimes fighting the good fight isn't worth it.

"Did you know," he says, "I've already passed the life expectancy for most folks in this part of the country?"

"Instead, he came here. For breakfast."

"I've been thinking . . ." he says.

"That was never your strong suit," says my mother.

"I've been thinking . . ." he says again.

"Here I thought I had a brother who was a fighter all these years."

"What I've got," Uncle Carey says, "it's not survivable."

Those weren't words meant to be spoken, not in our family, not in that house.

"You know what I've got, right?" he says. "Can you say the word?"

My mother and I look at each other.

"Life," he says, grinning at his joke. "It's a terrible condition. It's got a one-hundred-percent mortality rate."

My mother rolls her eyes.

"You know," Uncle Carey says, and turns to me, "my great-uncle, your great-great-uncle, he died when I was fourteen."

"Yes, the game warden, I know," I say. Great-uncle Alister, shot in some dispute in the woods, no details on who did it, though everybody knew it had to have been somebody from the community. Great-uncle Alister is part of our family lore, and he isn't going to distract me. "With treatment, it's the difference between months and years, right?"

He ignores me and starts telling stories about how he used to dream about Uncle Alister, how they'd go fishing or hunting and how in his dreams he'd ask him to tell him who did it, but he never got an answer. He tells me they weren't sad dreams, they were happy, because Uncle Alister was a happy guy, even if he did get murdered, an event that I know from my mother absolutely destroyed the rest of my grandmother's life, since she could never get over thinking about who did it. I get the point Uncle Carey's trying to drive home, but to underline it, he tells me, "You know, there's a lot of people I'm looking forward to seeing on the other side."

I check my watch. It's nine thirty-five. I don't know why I bothered to check, or what possible difference it could make, now that I know the time.

"You understand, don't you, sweet pea?"

He looks at me with his open, honest face. There's something vulnerable there, and though I do understand, I'm not sure I should say so. We're quiet for a bit and he keeps staring at me, like a child. When I can't take it anymore I quietly say, "Okay, I guess I do," and he smiles and sits back in his chair, and as he moves a flash of pain goes across his face for a moment before he settles whatever it was in his body.

"That makes me very happy." He grins wide. "You and I always understood each other, didn't we?"

"Sure," I say. I avoid looking at my mother's face.

"So where are you on to next?"

"I thought I'd go to New York, see some people, then . . . someplace new."

"Someplace new. Always moving. You get that from me."

"I get that from you?" Except for Vietnam, I doubt he's ever left Cambria County.

He grins. "You know what I mean."

I do know. I sip my tea without tasting it.

Uncle Carey leaves after breakfast and it's pretty quiet between my mother and me until my mother, seeming to have come to some determination, says, "Your uncle never much listened to anybody, but . . ." and I know that what follows is going to be "he might listen to you." Which isn't true. He won't, and I don't want to get into it, or to pretend that I've got the ability to help live someone's life for them, and live it in a way I might not even choose myself.

Over the next few days I try to distract my mother from the Uncle Carey situation. We take a trip to Pittsburgh. We visit Fallingwater and Kentucky Knob. And we visit my older sister Linda and her baby, which always makes my mom happy. Linda is settled. Happily married. She's got one son and is pregnant with twins and she visits my mom all the time and helps out with Uncle Carey and is in general the kind of dutiful daughter nobody would have thought she'd become.

On the way back I try to talk to my mom about why I've chosen the life I have. Perhaps for her sake. Perhaps for mine.

"You remember the freelance piece I did on Karen Wheeler?" I ask her. She takes a moment to place the name, so I add, "Lieutenant Wheeler? With the women's engagement team? Who stepped on a bomb?"

"The one they gave you trouble with, for the photos?" she says.

Wheeler, who would lose a left foot and a good chunk of intestine, had given us permission to take the photos while we waited for the medical evacuation. It had been a painful, protracted affair. The Taliban arrived and shot at the incoming helicopter, so the helicopter asked the soldiers to go to a safer LZ. The soldiers had to pick up their wounded and drag them five hundred meters back to a safer location, by which point Wheeler was screaming curses, only to have the pilots declare that landing zone too hot as well, and they had to drag the wounded another five hundred meters, by which point Wheeler was silent. The images and text together made for a powerful piece, I thought, but the oh-so-chivalrous military PAOs threw a fit over images of wounded women, and ultimately an editor, from the safety of New York, decided it wasn't worth the hassle and that the images were "too real" anyway, because "goriness distracts from the substance here." Which I thought, and still think, was cowardice.

Yes, the photos were gnarly. Yes, you'd never have just run them alone, because that would have been pornography. War photography needs the context the writer provides, because without context it's too easy for photos of life's extremes to become kitsch or propaganda. But writing only shakes the reader if they cooperate, put in the work to go past the headline and the lead and imagine their way into what you're trying to tell them. A good photo stops you in your tracks. Shakes you against your will. So writers need the photos just as much. They need them to put you there.

"Mom, when those photos got canned, I could still . . ." I decide not to tell my mother that I could still smell the shit from Wheeler's open intestines, bled out over her stomach and crotch. "I could still hear her, cursing the pilots. And they were beautiful photos. They weren't just pain and fear. They showed people. They made you look."

"I remember how mad you were."

"At the time I thought, here I am, risking my life to educate Americans about what this war is, and some jerk in an air-conditioned office is saying no. No, thanks."

My mother is starting to look uncomfortable, so I wrap it up.

"But things like that teach you about what you really believe. Because next up I get a chance at another embed, in another rough area, and I'm scared. And I'm like, Here we go. Am I really going to risk my life again to educate Americans about this war after all that, after getting something vital and important thrown aside like it was trash? And then I thought, Yes. Yes I am. Because not every editor is a coward. And because doing that work is who I am. That is what matters to me, more than anything." I say it with conviction, to remind myself I still believe it.

My mother nods. She gets what I'm telling her. That even if I'm not going back to Afghanistan, it doesn't mean I'm staying home. And she keeps her eyes on the road, and she says, "I'm proud of you, don't you know?"

I'm not sure I believe her.

The next couple of days are fine, in part because I promise my mom I'll have a serious talk with Uncle Carey before I leave. It seems to satisfy her, though it weighs on me. I spend much of the time reading with my mother on the glassed-in part of the back porch, looking out over the hills from time to time, sipping tea. My mother has a wonderful way of not asking questions, of practicing patience until things spill out, but this time I don't have so much to report. I don't want to talk about Kabul, or why I'm not going back, because I haven't perfectly worked out the answers to any of those questions, and I don't want to speak out of turn and learn something about myself prematurely. If my father were here, he'd hustle us around, convince us we needed to do something, go fishing or hiking or just out for a walk. "Wild apples are hanging from every tree," he'd say, "and here you are eating Oreos." But of course my father is not here. Even the plants he used to keep out on this porch have died, so there's nothing obstructing our view. Less work, my mother would say, if I were to ask her why she never took care of them. The only conflict comes when my mother gets up to go to church and asks me if I'm coming, even though she knows I'm not, but it's a small spat, an old rerun of fights past, dating back to high school, and it's over quickly enough and then she leaves me there, on the porch, looking out over the hills, sipping tea, alone.

When the time comes to leave for good, I load up the rental car, say my good-byes to my mother, and make my promised trip to Uncle Carey's. He lives about five minutes west of Davidsville, in a perpetually poorly maintained one story with an oversized American flag, a small and tattered Gadsden flag declaring "Don't Tread on Me," an overgrown front yard, and a beautifully ordered, pristine garage. He has a beer cracked open for me before I even walk in the door, and we spend the time reminiscing, laughing about the things he used to do, the scoldings my mother would give him, like he was one of the kids, and the crazy things he did with us in the car that no responsible adult would ever do. Eventually we run that conversation to the ground, and in the silence he leans forward and that vulnerable, childish look comes on his face.

"What do you think," he whispers. "Should I do the chemo, or just have some fun on the way out?"

It's not a question I want to answer. We both know I've been running it through my head since his visit to my mother, that I can't claim not to have an opinion on whether he should die quick or die painfully. It's all that's been on my mind. So I sit there, trying to form what I feel into words. Something about the man he is, about what he means to my mother, and about the crazy things he's done in that old, beat-up car. "I think," I say, knowing the words make me even more a traitor to my mother and to this place than I already am, "I think that old Buick can still do a few flips."

Uncle Carey grins wide, that big, goofy, gap-toothed grin. "Promise me something," he says.

"Yeah."

"Don't come for the funeral. Be somewhere else. Somewhere awesome."

Which is, of course, when I start crying, and Uncle Carey wraps me up in a bear hug, a hug that always used to mean getting lifted up off your feet and shaken around a bit, but not this time. He just holds me as tight as he's able to muster. It's not very tight. I bring myself under control, I kiss him on his cheeks, and then I slip his grasp, free.

7

was still having nightmares when I met Luisa. The dreams were horrible because they were real. Things I knew or had seen happen to other people. I would run through the street without a weapon, Iván chasing behind. Toads for the guerrilla would come to slit my throat. Or Jefferson would come and do to me the things I had seen him do to other people, and I would scream that I loved him, that he should spare me because I loved him and worshipped him more than all the world. And he would tell me that is why he must do this, because a warrior must kill the things he loves.

Because of the nightmares, I would stay out very late, drinking. On the road to Rioclaro there was a gas station where they sold alcohol, and behind the gas station were plastic tables by the river, lights strung across the trees, and a few speakers to play music. I liked it because normal people went there, especially the girls who didn't just want to sleep with paracos because they had money.

I was still a virgin then, though I'd made attempts to cure myself. But taking off my clothes, I'd become terrified, feeling naked even before I *was* naked. In each case the women were whores, confident and unashamed in front of a young, nervous man, and their confidence made it worse. More shameful, each time I failed. More full of fear and dread and a desire to cover myself so deeply in earth no one would ever find me. But at the gas station, with normal people and normal girls, girls who had no interest in a man like me, I felt safe. I watched normal life. Workers sharing stories from the day's labor, girls flirting playfully, the old drinking until they could no longer walk, and boys starting fights that never ended in murder.

Being there reminded me that the world I lived in—of paracos and narcos and guerrillas and criminals—it was just the thinnest sliver of life. Most people are not killers, and even then, as I was still finding my new place in the world, I suspected that a killer is not just a different kind of person, but a different kind of thing. *I* was a different kind of thing, though I had never killed anyone myself. At the river I would see carpenters, bakers, construction workers, shopkeepers, farmers. Mothers, babies sucking on their breasts, calling their drunkard husbands home. Men shouting their fanciful dreams out in loud voices. Girls with cruel laughter and kind faces. Every sort of person was there and yet I, with my pistol tucked in my pants like a gangster in a telenovela, did not belong. I had been torn from the world of those people, and there was no way to stitch myself back in. Even if they respected me, a current of fear kept them distant. I was not alive the way they were. Still, at night, with a beer in my hand, I liked to watch, a pale ghost feeding off the colors of the living.

That's where I saw her. Roberto Carlos's "Amigo" was playing on the radio, there was a table of young people my age, and one of them, a beautiful girl whose name I don't remember, got up and started dancing. In the middle of the conversation, without saying anything or inviting anyone to join her, she got up and began swaying, moving her hips, her eyes closed. She had a perfect body, a shirt that ended an inch above her belly button, long legs and curvy hips. She knew she was beautiful. She must have. Women who are not beautiful don't make scenes like that. She danced and swayed, she sung the lyrics of the song, and the conversation at the table jerked and stuttered. Some of the men stared at her openly, some looked quietly down. Her movements were like a magnet for the eyes—to look away took effort and you could see, in the faces of the boys not looking at her, the effort it took. And when she opened her eyes, she'd point at a boy, sing loudly, smile, close her eyes, and lift her face to the sky while she slid her hands down her stomach as her hips swayed.

And then Luisa got up. I had never seen her before, had not even noticed her sitting at the table with the beautiful girl who drew all eyes even when she wasn't dancing. Luisa was a plain girl, neither fat nor thin but with a stout body, long hair, and large, masculine hands. She was shorter than the beautiful girl, she stood awkwardly to the side, and then started dancing herself. A flicker of awareness appeared in the beautiful girl's eyes as Luisa began to move, and she began to exaggerate her movements. Once more, she ran her hands down from her breasts to her stomach, but this time her hands went lower and lower. I felt a spasm of anger watching her, different from the normal anger a man feels at the beauty of a woman he does not own. Luisa shifted jerkily from side to side, half singing the lyrics, her eyes shifting from the spectacle of her beautiful friend to the boys at her table, none of whom looked at her for even a second. I could see Luisa's eyes, searching, seeking to make contact, to be seen. The song ended, and the beautiful girl collapsed, laughing, into her chair, while Luisa remained standing, waiting for the next song, which turned out to be a slow song, a song you need a partner to dance to, and then she sat down as well.

It was her defeat that gave me confidence. I imagined, perhaps, that she would be grateful when I walked up to her and told her, "I noticed you dancing, and you were very beautiful," but she stared at me, stone-faced, and said, "I know who you are." Then she returned to her friends.

Later that same night, when she had drunk more and so had I, I met her and told her that I did not think of myself as a paraco, but as an administrator of local government. A bridge from the people to the power that ruled them—Jefferson. She looked very afraid of me then, and asked me what I wanted of her, and I told her I wanted to see her here more, and she asked me if she had any choice, and I told her she didn't. Her face went flat. It was no longer a face but an object, a mask. I knew I had made a mistake and I said, "I'm sorry, I don't know what I want to say. Of course you have a choice. But it would hurt me. It would make me very sad not to see you again." The mask shifted, animated back into a face capable of compassion, and she nodded, but after that day she never drank there again.

The next time I saw Luisa, I was with Jefferson. He took me with him to Rioclaro. The little town, it seemed, had become disloyal.

"I blame the mayor," he said.

The mayor, a man named Victor Sánchez, wanted his town to be left alone. Left alone by the guerrilla, left alone by the army, and left alone by us. A place of peace. Jefferson was going to make it clear that was impossible. I was there as the carrot to Jefferson's stick.

"You will offer him money for the town," Jefferson told me. "I will say nothing. He will know I'm offering him death. The trick is to make him think he's taking the money because he cares about his people, and not because he's scared. If he thinks he's doing it out of fear, he'll feel like a coward, and he'll hate us. So there must be a way for him to be the hero, and then he will come to love and defend us, because loving and defending us will be the same as loving and defending himself. So I want you to talk a lot. I want you to be excited about what you can do for his town. The only reason he'll let us in the door will be because he knows if he shuts us out, we'll kill him. Your job is to make him forget he's a coward."

When we entered the town it was hot, and I had dark stains on my uniform under my arms and in the center of my belly where the sweat had soaked all the way through. The town was pretty, with clean, well-kept houses and balconies full of flowers. I thought we'd head to the mayor's office but instead we went to a bar. Jefferson posted his men at the corners of the street and then invited me to sit down with him.

"We're going to visit Sánchez at his home, not at his office," Jefferson said. I understood very well why that would be more frightening.

As we sat and sipped cold beer, I looked out at Jefferson's paracos, posted on the corners, and it astonished me to realize that I was somehow important enough to sit in the shade and drink beer while they sweated.

Jefferson was thinking the same. "You're smart," he told me, "and trustworthy. Usually, the smart ones are not trustworthy. Only the really, really smart ones are smart and trustworthy. They understand obedience."

"Yes," I said, obediently agreeing with him that I was smart, and trustworthy, and that I understood obedience. Two men passed by and Jefferson smiled and waved to them. They scurried away.

Jefferson settled into himself, his face like an outcropping of rock. I didn't know whether I should say anything, so I remained silent. We stayed like that, not talking, ordering new beers as soon as we finished the old ones. The fear we'd provoked in the town, just by being there, began to infect me. Then he broke the silence.

"In ancient times, all wars were holy wars," he said.

I nodded. And he spoke of the book of Joshua, which tells of how the Jews killed for God. How they killed from the rivers to the seas, and from the plains to the seas. They killed to the salt sea, and the way north and south, and the coast that was the land of the old giants, and the people that dwelt in the mountains and in the valleys and in the plains and by the springs, and in the wilderness, and in the south country. They killed the king of Jericho, and the king of Jerusalem, the king of Ai, of Jarmuth, of Lachish, Megiddo, Gezer, Shimronmeron, and many other places. Thirty-one kings. And not just the kings. In each place, they followed the command of God: You shall not leave alive anything that breathes.

"That was real war," he said. "Holy war."

He stared darkly into his beer.

"I fought for the Castaños in Cesar. I fought for them as if I were fighting for God."

I nodded again.

"Osmin told me the guerrilla killed your family," he said. "What do you fight for? Revenge?"

I wasn't sure what to say. When I followed Osmin into this life, it had not occurred to me that I needed a reason to fight. When I saw him in Cunaviche, a door opened, and I did not even think to make a choice, I just walked forward.

"I fight for the people. For freedom from the guerrilla," I said. I had heard him say similar things.

"Only a slave fights for freedom," he said. "Men fight for something more."

I did not know Luisa was Sánchez's daughter until we went to his house and she opened the door. She wore a simple blouse and a sullen face, looking past me as if she did not know me. I knew I should say something to Jefferson. I should tell him I knew her. But then it occurred to me that if I didn't tell him, there was no way he'd know I'd held my tongue. I had a choice. Part of her fate was in my hands. I decided I would say nothing.

She took us to a little sitting room with a few ratty chairs, a table, and squished into the corner, a piano.

"Look at that," Jefferson said. He walked over and pressed a key, smiling like a child when a note struck.

I had never seen a piano before. It had chipped white teeth and unblemished black ones. I pressed a black key, slowly depressing it. Nothing sounded. I hit it harder, and sound rang out in the air. Jefferson clunked down a few more keys. Then he mashed the keys with his hands, sending ugly notes quivering into the air while Luisa scowled.

Jefferson was still hitting notes when Sánchez came in. I greeted him enthusiastically, "Mr. Mayor, such a pleasure, very glad to meet you," while Jefferson clunked upon the keys.

Sánchez looked little like his daughter. He was tall, with a long nose and skin several shades paler than Luisa. A local man had told me he was not from Rioclaro. He had married a local girl who was very dark and who had died in childbirth. "The two types were not a good mix," he said, "and so the mother died, and the girl came out angry."

It was a simple meeting. I told him I knew that his town had been negotiating with the manager of the Telecom office in Cúcuta, who refused to lay phone lines to Rioclaro because the area was too dangerous. This was the sort of problem we could fix. I told him that was all we were here for. We knew about the phones, and wanted to help. Would he accept our help?

"Yes, of course," he said. He even seemed grateful, so relieved the meeting had been about something so simple. Who knows what terrible things he'd imagined we'd come for as we sat and drank beers all afternoon in his town.

I didn't offer him any money, just said that we would talk with the Telecom manager. Money could come later, once he had become accustomed to accepting our help. He thanked us. I would wait until after it was done to tell him that he was asking us to threaten the manager on his behalf. Everything worked beautifully, until Jefferson decided to have the last word.

"You see," Jefferson said as we were leaving, "we have advantages. The state has bureaucracy, limitations, less resources. We don't have bureaucracy, we just solve problems. If you work with us, we get things done."

It was a mistake. Sánchez's face went cold, the way his daughter's had when I threatened her. I looked carefully at Jefferson, with his pitted, square face. It occurred to me that Jefferson only occupied so much space in the world. A cubic volume of flesh and blood. If I ever made my way through that engineering textbook I could calculate how much.

Sánchez let us out politely, and Jefferson clapped me on the back and told me I had done well.

That night I dreamed of what it would be like to sleep with Luisa. In my dream she opened the door for us. Her father sat before the piano and she brought us drinks, lulo juice mixed with vodka, and then she unbuckled my pants. Jefferson and her father sat at the piano and discussed telephone lines. I found myself on the floor, she was naked above me, her unlovely body rubbing against mine. When she took my dream virginity, I cried out, and Jefferson laughed, and her father laughed, but she held me with her eyes and began to devour me. My skin dissolved into hers. She was rooting inside me, fingers in my organs, while I lay paralyzed. Every nerve screamed. My desire for her was like physical pain, like a fever inside the body, and inside my mind and soul. I woke, hard to the point of agony.

I left my bed, got on my moto, and drove the four miles to a bar where I knew I could find relief. There was a girl there, beautiful, and just old enough for her beauty to have lost the innocence of youth, the innocence Osmin was always hunting down and ruining. Her name was Flor. Flor was seventeen, with a daughter, and it was to support the daughter that she worked as a prostitute. I knew these things because I had tried to cure my virginity with Flor, and when I had failed, she had told me of her life, sharing herself out of pity.

"But I like this job sometimes," she had whispered to me, "and I like you. Come back anytime you're feeling better."

There was cruelty in her kindness. The power her beauty held over me was painful. Kindness only twisted the knife. So that night I went to her, wanting to fuck her the way Jefferson fucked—hard, mechanical, discharging a need, masturbating into a pussy. "You shit in the toilet, you come in a woman," he had told me. I wanted her to be nothing, for Luisa to be nothing, and for my desire to disappear.

First, I drank five or six shots, enough to deaden my senses and my awareness of her and other people, enough so that I felt I was swimming inside my own body. This was enough to let the devil inside me, and when I was alone with her I took her and fucked her with hatred, and I released the poison, and then she took my money. I hated myself then, and I wanted to apologize, but for what? She was a whore. This was her job, I told myself, and she had said she liked it sometimes, though even in my haze I could see in her face that she had not liked it. I had hurt her somehow. My soul swam in drunkenness. I tried to give her more money and she said no, and then I said it was for her child, not her, and she took it. I would never speak to Flor again. But my virginity was gone. I had cured myself.

Not long after that Jefferson took me up into the cold mountains, alone. We reached a dirt trail and a little farm at the edge of a mountain pass, and we got off our motos and began to walk.

Flowers were in bloom. I wondered if Jefferson knew I had hid information from him about Luisa. Perhaps, I thought, Jefferson was going to kill me. So I took great care to look not at him but at the trees and flowers. There were trees full of fruit with branches that spread out at the base and then curved upward to the sky. There were trees with deep red and purple flowers with yellow stems that shone so brightly it seemed they had their own inner light leaping up to greet the sun. Jefferson stopped and pointed out two hummingbirds with brilliant blue coloring. One had its beak in an orchid that was strangling its way around a tree branch. The other flittered angrily above. "They're going to fight," Jefferson said. And he was right. As the first bird drank deep from the flower, the other dove down, stabbing its beak into the first bird's neck. Jefferson clapped, delighted as a child. It was strange to see beautiful creatures fight.

We walked for about two hours, and the trees changed as we got higher. Tall, narrow trees shot up, then burst at the top in a star of thin green palms. We walked through a cloud, and mist and haze surrounded the forest. The sunlight, already weak through the vegetation, became further shrouded. Everything appeared through dark layers of suffocated light. As we climbed I felt as though we were moving back through time, to older and older forest, each step taking us further into the past, to the beginning of time, just after God made the trees and flowers but before he made us humans, and before he declared his creation good.

Eventually we emerged into a clearing where we could look out on the valley. The sun returned in all its force. Clouds dotted the mountainside, some level with us, some below us, some high above.

"Stay here," Jefferson told me. And he disappeared into the wood. I turned to look at the view but could feel him behind me, a prickling in my back. If he was about to kill me, what should I do? Should I pray? And to who? To the broken, screaming Christ of my childhood? To Luisa, who had seen me and known me for what I was? To God, who has no mercy?

Jefferson returned with firewood in his hands, and he dumped it on the ground.

"Comandante?" I said.

"Yes?" he said. But I did not know how to respond. He disappeared into the wood, and then again returned with more wood, and he disappeared again, and again, until we had a large pile.

Then Jefferson arranged the wood, stacking it into a little structure, almost like a building or a cage. And he stood before me, staring closely into my eyes. I did my best not to tremble. To this day, I am sure that had I trembled, he would have cut my throat and burned my body there, high in the mountains. Instead, he pointed to the forest behind us. "Go," he said, "and get more."

So I went into the forest, following a little path, and I saw, next to a pile of firewood, the corpse of a naked man chained by the neck to a tree. His head was slumped and his body covered in bruises. I walked to him, knowing this was what Jefferson wanted me to see, and I put my hand under his chin and lifted his face to mine, and Osmin's dead eyes looked back at me. His mouth fell open, as if the dead man were about to speak. I took some water from the canteen on my belt, and I poured it in my hands and washed his face, and then I let his head down and picked up some firewood and carried it back to Jefferson, who said nothing.

I did not ask him why, or what Osmin had done. I simply put the wood on the pyre and Jefferson lit the twigs and I blew the small flame to life. A fire starts slow, and we stood and watched the flames lick upward, and I made a tiny sign of the cross with my finger, and prayed for Osmin's soul.

Jefferson checked the pyre, blew sparks to light the far side, which had not caught yet, grabbed a stick, and pushed a burning nest of twigs further into the heart of the flame. He moved mechanically, without expression, and I wondered whether he was capable of love or horror. Inside my own hollow body, inside the space where my soul had been, echoes of pain and loss rang out, and I knew my nightmares would never cease, and that Jefferson had never slept poorly in his life. The flames slowly rose, and Jefferson took me to the edge of the mountain, the pyre burning behind us.

By this time it was sunset. I looked out on the setting sun and realized that Jefferson had planned all this, down to the timing of dusk. I looked at his craggy face. He seemed satisfied, like a man after a heavy meal. Around me the yellows and purples of the flowers darkened with the fading sun, and the greens darkened into shades of blue and black.

They blended into one another and into shadows, and I realized that this high, in the mountains, I did not know the names of things. We were so far up, among trees and flowers different from the trees and flowers I knew from the river valley. A nature both older and wilder. And I had the idiotic thought that perhaps these things had no name, and like Adam, I could name them.

Jefferson told me a delicate time was coming.

"There are two elections. For Congress, and for president."

He said our man was Álvaro Uribe, who I didn't know much about but whose face I had seen in the papers. Towns that voted for Uribe and his allies were with us. Towns that voted against him were with the guerrilla. It was my job to make sure towns were for us.

Everybody else got to rest. In the months before the elections there were police and soldiers out on roads where there had never been anyone but us before. Our paracos kept the peace and stayed out of trouble. Jefferson even had a man from the International Committee of the Red Cross come to talk to about seventy paracos in a classroom at a school in La Vigia. They sat in children's desks while he told us about "international law," and how it didn't allow torture or "extrajudicial killings" or driving people from their homes. He was describing a lot of their work, and they sat and nodded their heads.

Meanwhile, I scheduled events and meetings with neighborhood associations. I reminded people what they owed us, and who we wanted them to vote for. In most places this was easy. Most people appreciated us, and the delinquents who didn't we had chased out. On the edges of our territory, though, I could sometimes sense awkwardness, expressions of loyalty that seemed forced.

In Rioclaro they didn't even act like they loved us. I reached the village on the night that their neighborhood association was supposed to meet, and when I entered the church basement I saw Luisa. She was standing in the crowd, shouting at the man running the meeting. The man we had selected to run these meetings.

"We are hardworking people," she was saying. "We are good Christian people. We are not the enemies of anyone."

All eyes were on her. Her passion for what she was saying made her face shine. She was so different from the girl I'd seen dancing awkwardly next to her beautiful friend. I felt proud of her, and glad I'd kept my knowledge of her from Jefferson. But what she was saying was dangerous. If a town does not share your enemies, then they *are* your enemy.

I waited until the end of the meeting. Then I approached her and told her the truth, that what she was doing was both stupid and dangerous. There are times in life when you can make decisions, and there are times in life when you should respect the place you are in, and the powers above you. This was one of those times.

"I don't want trouble, and I respect you . . ." she began, and I slapped her.

"No," I said, "you don't."

She stared at me hatefully. She raised her hands, as if about to strike me, then lowered them.

"If Jefferson was here he would break every one of your fingers," I told her. "And then how would you play the piano?"

Election Day we hired buses to bring people out to vote. I coordinated all the schedules, and then after the elections went to La Vigia to find out how the towns voted. To see which towns were for us, and which were our enemies.

The local archivist was a muscular, angry-looking man who walked me over to the town gymnasium, hardly saying a word the whole time.

Inside the gymnasium a group of Jehovah's Witnesses were holding a meeting. They stood in the stands in ill-fitting suits, choked by neckties. We walked underneath the stands, made our way to the stairs, then farther down below, to a room reeking of mildew and bulging with papers, papers in garbage bags and old boxes stamped "Chiquita Banana," papers spilling out onto the floor and papers bound tightly with rubber bands. And in one corner, the newest addition to the chaos, sat a neat stack of binders holding the list of local electoral results.

As I filtered through the filings, it seemed our municipality was in good order. Plenty of votes for candidates who had received Álvaro Uribe's blessing. Few votes for Carlos Gaviria types. As the archivist stared at me sullenly, clenching and unclenching his fists, I took careful notes, mapping out the degree to which the towns in our control voted in accordance with our will. Elections, Jefferson told me, are the most valuable source of information we have. People think they can show their souls in the voting booth and no one will know, but it's not true.

And then I reached Rioclaro, and the numbers changed. A surge in votes for the Social and Political Front. I sucked my teeth and looked up at the archivist.

"What are you going to do with this information?" he said.

I answered him honestly. "I don't know."

It began with small things. Driving into the streets of Rioclaro and firing guns. Leaving flyers telling people to leave their homes. Then, a few days later, delivering invitations to funerals, with the names of living residents of Rioclaro listed as the deceased.

"By the presidential election," Jefferson told me, "this town must not exist."

That gave us several months. First to create a climate of fear. Make the citizens question what was going to happen, make emergency plans, think about what they will take and what they will leave when the time comes. Get them to imagine leaving the only land they've ever known, which had nurtured them and their parents and grandparents, and where they had dreamed of raising their children.

"The goal is to avoid a massacre. Nobody wants a massacre right now," Jefferson said. "If you kill too many people, there are consequences."

My role was to identify the resistance. The only person beyond the mayor I was sure was involved was Luisa, but I didn't want to give her name to Jefferson. So I reached out to people in the town, and found out who mattered, who had influence.

The first was Juan Camilo. Jefferson sent four paras dressed in guerrilla uniforms to find him in his fields, rob him and beat him, and then smash his kneecaps with rocks so that he would never work fields again. A week later, the same four went to the home of Ricardo Gómez Gonzalo and raped his wife and daughter. Jefferson sent out paras to spread the word in Rioclaro that, because of the town's disloyalty, they were no longer going to protect them from guerrillas and bandits. "Rioclaro is no longer safe," they repeated to everyone who would listen. As they left they fired rifles and broke windows. Then they shot Leonel Fernando on his way to sell goods in La Vigia. He fell off his mule and was dragged hundreds of meters before another traveler stopped the animal and found him, bleeding not only from the bullet wound but from cuts and scrapes, bruised by rocks and sticks in the path, almost but not quite dead. I went to the hospital to check on him, and to hear from the doctors that he'd survive. He hardly looked like a man anymore.

"That is the best that could have happened," Jefferson told me. "Not quite death but almost death. It makes less news outside of Rioclaro, but inside Rioclaro he'll be a constant reminder of what it means to stay."

Villagers began leaving. To walk the streets of Rioclaro was to hardly breathe, to be choked by the fear in the air. It only needed one final push.

"That," Jefferson said, "requires death."

When we moved on Rioclaro, Jefferson had his men take the piano out of Sánchez's house and bring it to the center of the town square. Luisa and the mayor followed us, filled with fear and sadness and rage. The edges of the square were slowly filling with scared people as Jefferson's paras beat through the town, driving everyone to witness. We set the piano down at the south end of the square, by the church.

Jefferson pointed to the piano and said, "Who plays?" And the mayor, terrified, pointed his finger at Luisa, now crouched on the ground, face in her hands. And Jefferson stepped over and touched her arm gently. And he said, "Ma'am, I would like to hear you play." And Luisa looked up at her father, the mayor. And the mayor nodded his pale, frightened face, and she let Jefferson lift her up and escort her to the piano as if onto a stage. The fire I had seen in her was gone.

"Play," said Jefferson. And Luisa looked at her father, and her father looked at Jefferson, and Luisa shook her head angrily, some of her fire back, where she'd found it I do not know, and she said, "I'll play the *Appassionata*."

She lifted the seat of the piano bench and pulled out papers with notes on them that she put on the ledge above the keys. Then she sat at the piano, and she gathered stillness around her. The crowd at the edges of the square, whose eyes had all been on Jefferson or on the men with their guns who surrounded them, seemed to fix on her, and the strange thing Jefferson had her doing. She laid her hands gently on the keys. Her hands, which I had first thought too large, and ugly, like a man's hands stitched onto a woman, now looked lovely, and right. And she started to play.

The opening notes were dark and slow. Then she fluttered her fingers, a quick moment of light before it returned to dark. And then more flutters, and more dark, and quick dark stabbing notes struck with fat heavy fingers.

Jefferson grinned and gave the mayor a thumbs-up. He liked a good show, and this was a good show.

To me, it was not a good show. I did not understand why. Perhaps because I was overexcited, or nervous about what was to come. Perhaps because somehow the music dragged emotions out of me. Little emotions I did not know I had, and did not want to have, started flowering. In the hollow core of me, dead feelings moved in the emptiness, stirring into something like life.

Then the music turned, or maybe Luisa was having trouble playing. There was a flurry of notes with a lot of noise but no emotion, and I could breathe.

"Pretty good," Jefferson said. I almost agreed. Her fingers stumbled over each other, the notes clunky, and I could see the awkward girl trying to dance but trapped in her plainness, her powerlessness. And then, a pause, a breath, her fingers lifted off the keys, then back down with force, and the music caught me again. For the rest of the performance, this is how it went. She was not good enough to always play well, but at times she would get it right, and listening would hurt.

She played for a long, long time. When she finished, she looked thinner and frailer than when she sat down. There was a moment of silence. A moment of quiet in the terrified crowd, a moment that had nothing to do with us, with the guns we held, with the man we were about to kill, or even with Luisa, the woman who had played the music.

"Okay, okay," Jefferson said. "Very fun. Now, up."

His voice was strange in the silence her music had created, but he seemed oblivious. Had he heard something different from all of us? He dragged Luisa up off her chair, and our hands tightened around our rifles, we squared our shoulders, and the work began.

We tied Sánchez on top of the piano. A chainsaw appeared, and suddenly everyone who had watched, confused and amazed as Luisa played, knew what was about to happen. A certain degree of calm came to the plaza.

Here is what happens when a man is chainsawed in half in the public square of a small village. First, the noise of the chainsaw makes you realize how quiet everything has been. The kick-kick roar of it goes off. The man about to die cries out but his pleas drown in the violence of its sound. Then the sound shifts slightly. It becomes silkier, gentler, as it bites into the flesh and muscles and guts of the abdomen like butter. It sprays blood and flesh and, when it hits the intestines, shit, which is why we urged Javier to stop sawing them in half at the stomach, but he told us, "That's the reason I do it, to fling the son of a bitch's shit over everything." Then the noise becomes grittier, jerkier, coarser, no silkiness now, as it bites through the spine. There's no sound but the chainsaw by this point. The tip, at the far edge of the stomach, bites into the wood beneath the man and sawdust flies into the air, mixes with the blood, thickening it. The screaming has stopped, Javier is sweating, putting muscle into the work and then, grrrrrr . . . roar, the sound emerges clear, beautiful, unbroken. The spine is severed.

One death, dramatic and public, and Rioclaro became a ghost town. Uribe won the presidential election, and within a year there were talks with the government about the paramilitary groups disbanding. We were all offered a deal. We could leave the paramilitaries, or "demobilize," and there would be benefits for us at a "reintegration agency," and only the paramilitary leaders, like Jefferson, would have to face any jail time, and even that would be light.

Jefferson told me that while he was in jail I should work for him in Venezuela, where there were ways to make amazing amounts of money if you were smart. I told him that I had learned from him not to fight for money, but for God, and he laughed. He let me go. And I stayed in La Vigia, and tried to earn a living like a normal man. I still felt like a ghost, haunting my body rather than living my own life, but over time I decided there was one thing that anchored me to the world. I had saved Luisa.

8

Canadian photojournalist once told me that nobody should ever go straight to New York after spending time in a war zone. It's too weird and the anger will just be too intense. He always made a point to go to New Orleans, which he considers a halfway house back to civilization. Me, I go home and then I go to New York to see my old friend Raul, who's so goddamn New York fancy, and so unapologetic about it, that after enough time with him every ounce of self-righteous anger evaporates, and I move on to a much healthier sadness. But as he chatters, I wonder if something different is going on inside me, if the choice I made to leave Afghanistan and never go back has broken a part of the deal, because I can't assuage myself with the promise to return to the place where life makes sense, and what I'm doing feels important.

"Big step you're taking." Raul grins at me impishly. "Proud of you."

We're sitting in the back garden of a little restaurant off the High Line where all the food is served on special little plates, practically miniature sculptures, teardrop-shaped soup bowls and oval dishes with holes in the center and a cheese platter on a tray where actual grass grows through artfully arranged pebbles and the cheese balances on top. I'm smiling at Raul and telling him everything is great—he's paying—but I feel like a caged ferret. This is also part of the homecoming process—fuck this place, fuck these people, with their wealth and their careers and their comfortable lives—and I've gone through it enough times to know how to let it wash over me and then die off in time to enjoy dessert. Yes, indulging in anger feels cathartic. Who doesn't like to think they're special? That while everyone else is focusing on money and status you're focusing on death and destruction and the terrible course of history, on the war. But Raul has heard me give that speech before, and he doesn't buy it.

"Yeah, I'm done with Afghanistan," I say. And then I add, with regret, "And Iraq." What I don't mention is where I'm going next. That's the real question. I owe Bob a response in two days. He wants me to relocate to New Delhi. Theoretically, I'm supposed to be thinking it over while I'm in New York.

"Too bad," Raul says. "I like getting photos of you with your little helmet and flak jacket. It makes you look like Mrs. Potato Head."

I let out a long breath and a look of concern comes across Raul's face.

"You doing okay, Liz?" he says. "You gonna get the PTSD on me?"

"No, I'm fine."

He stares into my eyes. Raul's my dearest friend because underneath layers of cynicism is a remarkably sweet and loyal man, but I get nervous whenever that Raul comes to the surface.

"I'm tired of covering a failing war," I say, looking away.

"So find another war," he says. "One we're winning. There's probably some nice little war in Africa or someplace."

"Africa?"

"Don't they have pirates in Africa? That'd be cool."

"We don't have a pirates-specific beat."

"That's too bad," he says. "Afghanistan is played out. But everybody always loves hearing about pirates."

"You know," I say, "you haven't asked me, not even once in all the years I've been going overseas, how the war is going."

"Let me guess," he says. "It's going bad." He plucks a piece of cheese off the grass tray. "Did I get it right?"

I sigh. "Yeah. Pretty much."

Raul smiles indulgently. "I read your stuff," he says. "Some of it. You inspire me."

"How?"

"Well . . . I started donating to the International Rescue Committee."

"That's nice."

"I'm not completely worthless. Oh . . ." he says, pulling on the collar of his shirt, "and I've made a real lifestyle change. Can you tell what it is?"

He leans back in his chair with his arms wide, displaying himself to me.

"I changed my wardrobe," he says. "Now I only wear clothing that saves lives." And once more, he tugs at the collar of his shirt.

I lean forward. The shirt is light blue, with shiny white buttons. The last time I went shopping with Raul he bought a shirt that cost more than your average villager in Paktika makes in a year. I'm sure this one is no different.

"Impressive," I say. "How does it do that?"

"Italian-made shirt, the components cut individually, with hand-sewn Australian mother-of-pearl buttons, and"—he grins widely—"a percentage of the profits goes to mosquito nets."

"Mosquito nets."

"Mosquito nets." He smiles. "Did you know that the most efficient way to save a life is to donate money for mosquito nets to help stop malaria? Every thirty-five hundred dollars to send mosquito nets to Africa or wherever saves a life."

"Yeah," I say. "I've heard that."

"Ethical capitalism. Buy our fancy crap, save a life. If every company did this, we could solve all the world's problems."

"There's issues with that," I say.

"Oh, I know," he says, "charity's a Band-Aid, right?"

This is something I've told him. That charity's nice but real problems require political solutions. And political solutions don't happen without a free press bringing real problems to the public's attention.

"And they probably use child labor or something," Raul is saying.

"No," I interrupt, "I know about this. I've read about this."

"About my shirt?"

"About mosquito nets," I say. "Mostly they're great but in the Great Lakes region of Africa, they've been taking those nets and fishing with them. The chemicals on the nets pollute the water, and the holes in the nets are so small they don't just catch fish, they catch fish eggs as well. So the lakes are all getting depopulated of fish. Which means, yeah, you're going to have less people dying of malaria, but it's fucking up their economy and all those people are going to be very hungry very soon."

Raul stares at me.

"I read about it in the *Journal*," I say.

He starts cracking up.

"The fucking fish!" he says. "Oh, that is why I shouldn't even try. Oh man, that is a short history of humans trying to do good in the world."

It takes him a moment to calm himself down, and then he says, "I'm sorry, but you are such a bummer."

The next day I meet with Farah Al-Ani, a former interpreter I'd met years ago when I was covering her army unit in Basra. At the time I hadn't paid her much mind, but then later I interviewed her over Skype so I could write a piece about her at the behest of her old platoon commander. She was trying to get a visa, there were proven threats to her life, and a cousin of hers had been murdered, possibly something to do with her work for the Americans, though nobody really knows. The platoon commander was also, it's worth saying, completely in love with her. She hit every standard of American beauty—she was tall, thin, with curly but not too curly hair, and long eyelashes. Soon after the story went through, her visa application moved forward as well, and I like to tell myself that the piece I did played a role. Proof, I think, that stories matter.

I meet her at an Israeli coffee shop in Murray Hill, and it's a little disturbing to see her in New York, dressed like a New Yorker. Skinny black jeans and combat boots, of all things. She's still pretty, though in a way that seems so much more ordinary than it did in Basra, among the army.

We have coffee and she tells me about her life in New York, why she stays away from Little Iraq in Queens, how she likes the job an army contact had helped her get, and how she's handling the schooling she's trying to do on the side.

"I'm still very grateful to you," she tells me in an almost shy way, and I want to hug her but don't.

On a whim, I ask her if she'd ever let me do a follow-up article. Tell her story of coming to New York, settling in. Maybe react a bit to the rhetoric in the presidential campaign. She physically recoils.

"I'd . . . like to put that behind me."

"Oh. Of course," I say.

"I feel bad, though," she says.

"It's okay."

"Sometimes . . . I do have that desire," she says.

"The desire to tell people?"

"Yes," she says. "But I'm done with that. I have a new life and I want to enjoy it. Some people, they look back too much. It eats them up, and does nobody any good. If God did not make us to enjoy our lives, why did he make us?"

I don't know. This isn't what I'd expected from Farah, and suddenly I feel terribly homesick. I miss Kabul, but more than that, I miss being out of Kabul, embedded with troops. I miss what my friend Kirstin calls the ISAF sound track: the rasp of the Velcro on magazine pouches opening, the crunch of dried mud yielding to the massive tires of heavy armored vehicles, the cough of a diesel engine, the roar of a passing Chinook, the excited shouts from a nearby soccer field, the chirping of birds.

If I take Bob's advice and go to India, I won't have that. A different adventure, I guess, though one disconnected from the type of reporting I've been doing. Working for a wire service is like being the boilerman for a steam-engine train—you never stop shoveling. In Afghanistan, every shovelful was composed of war. I wonder what stories I'd even cover in New Delhi. Last time I checked the news coming out of there, for some reason it was mostly legal stories—"INDIA BLOCKS 857 PORNOGRAPHY WEBSITES, DEFYING SUPREME COURT," "INDIA INQUIRY INTO SCANDAL OVER TESTING SET TO EXPAND."

"You're very American these days," I tell Farah. "Forward thinking. With a touch of pragmatic amnesia."

"Amnesia?"

"Forgetfulness."

She shakes her head. "I don't forget anything. But it's not good to talk too much about the things that happen in war." She laughs. "And I don't want to burden people with my nightmares."

I tell her that if she ever changes her mind, she might be surprised to find out how many people were willing to listen to her nightmares.

"Yes," she says. "That's true, I have met that sort of person before." And then she makes a little dismissive hand wave.

And that ends things, more or less. What is there left to tell her?

The last thing I do in New York is meet up with an old on-again, off-again guy I know from when I was covering New York City politics for the *Daily News*. We have drinks. He rants about Bill de Blasio. I know what he's expecting after the dinner, it's why I called him up, and I wonder abstractly whether I really want to go through with it. He's a perfectly acceptable candidate—decent looking, relatively skillful in bed, unattached, and generally not a creep. It's not like I'm dying with desire, but I wouldn't mind resetting the "last time I got laid" clock so that I can stop hearing it ticking me closer to my grave. Plus, at this point it'd be more awkward than it's worth to bow out. We end up going to his apartment and having what I think of as an "empty-calories fuck," enjoyable but not quite enjoyable enough to be worth it.

I head back to my sublet feeling even further outside myself, and though I know I need to respond to Bob, put my name in the hat for New Delhi or let the opportunity slip, instead of calling him on Skype I decide to email Diego. I'm not sure why, so I leave the subject blank. I type his name, and then I remember Raul telling me to find another war, one we're winning. So I type one sentence, "Are there any wars right now where we're not losing?" And within fifteen minutes he responds with one word.

"Colombia."

II

What good is a revolution
if we're counted among its casualties?

—*Aria Dean*

1

My father was a miner back when that was still a thing, back when you could be a miner and think that someday your son might be one, too. These days he walks with a stoop in his right shoulder, the gift of a rockfall in '83. He's got arthritis, and there's a delicate way he gets up from chairs, navigating himself around the damage he's done to his body. He has raging tempers. Bouts of deep depression. But doing hard work, physical work, he always told me, was the best way of quieting yourself and fastening your mind to God.

When I started out in the teams, I thought it wasn't so different. The work a bridge between my father's life and mine. You could see it in the way a man like Jefe, my team sergeant, prepared his kit. Not with love, not exactly. Not the way a gun enthusiast oils an AR, or a suburban dad fastens bits in his eight-hundred-dollar power drill. No. With a practiced, unconscious care. If you could see that care and then see the way my father prepared, bringing his gear in line—lamp battery, breathing canister, rock hammer—bringing himself in line, each limb, each finger a piece of equipment, then you'd see that connection. Men like us are always aware of the tools our lives hang on, their capabilities and weaknesses, just like we're always aware of our bodies, of our pains and limitations—shot knees, shot backs. Sore muscles strung across rough bones.

Back then I believed my father's work digging coal in the Pennsylvania hills and providing for his family really was a prayer, made not with words but with blood and sweat. And I believed my work was the same. But I was starting to be troubled by the occasional mission that made you question. Like the raid on Ammar al-Zawba'i.

Al-Zawba'i's house was the nicest I ever raided. Not the wealthiest—we raided plenty of pimped-out palaces across Iraq—but it was classy. More books than I've ever seen in any house, American or Iraqi or otherwise. Some were in English. Mostly history books but also a worn old *Huckleberry Finn.* I won't forget seeing that.

While we were flex-cuffing him, his fifteen-year-old son charged down the stairs, coming for us. His jaw hung slack. His eyes were unfocused. He shouted garbled, incoherent words. We could have shot him, I suppose, but we didn't.

"No," al-Zawba'i screamed. "He is ill! He is ill!" His English had what sounded like a British accent, and was far clearer than any of the terps we worked with. He was a former intelligence officer in Saddam's fedayeen, well educated, connected, and knee-deep in the more nationalist and less religious factions of the then-growing insurgency. If I'd known then what I know now, I would have said we should leave him alone and focus on the real crazies, but, you know, hindsight.

The son stopped in the middle of the room, wild-eyed and confused, then stepped toward me. I shifted my weight and slammed my buttstock into his stomach, sending him down hard. The father started shouting in Arabic, very fast and loud, as I zip-tied the son. I guess he was too emotional to reach for his polished English. Our terp, a young Yahzidi kid named Tahseen who within ten years would be murdered by ISIS along with his whole family, exchanged some rapid-fire talk with al-Zawba'i, and then filled us in.

"He was taken by the Angels of Death."

We'd never heard of it. Yet another militia that'd basically named themselves like a heavy metal band.

"They are a Shi'a . . . maybe under Sadr . . . maybe . . . ummm . . . crime . . . they crime . . ."

"Gangsters," al-Zawba'i said, irritated.

"Yes. Gangsters," Tahseen said. "They took him and put electric cables to his head. Now he needs medicines."

"He cannot help being this way," al-Zawba'i said.

In an upstairs bedroom, decorated with stuffed animals and Monet prints, the ex-fedayeen's seven-year-old daughter was cowering behind her bed. We brought her down and tried to calm her. She seemed to have some sort of disability, maybe a genetic disorder. Her left side didn't function right. She was shaking with fear, and my friendly "Salaam aleikum" didn't help. She'd seen a lot already, I suppose, in her short time on earth, and things weren't about to get better. Her eyes were already puffy, she'd already been crying, but she burst out again.

"Where's her mother?"

Our terp shook his head. Not alive, I guess.

"Is there a neighbor?" Jefe asked al-Zawba'i. "Someone we can call to look after your daughter and your son?"

He sat, stone-faced. Any name he gave us, that'd be a lead and he knew it. I shrugged. The house had three desktop computers, two laptops, and seven cell phones for the analysts. We'd have more leads soon anyway.

At one point, al-Zawba'i looked at Ocho and said, "Maybe not all of you, but some of you will die here." He smiled.

Ocho laughed. "If I die here," he said to al-Zawba'i, "I hope I die fucking your mom."

We finished up, and as we prepared to leave, I asked Tahseen what he thought would happen to the little girl.

He looked her over slowly, considering the question, and then said, "She will marry a man who beats her, and have children who cannot read."

I was a junior medic then, an 18 Delta new to Special Forces and a little out of place but getting away with it because medics are allowed to be weird. And I had a baby on the way. Natalia in her third trimester, me a soon-to-be new parent eight time zones away and still wrapping my head around the notion of childbirth, around what was happening to Natalia, and to me, that we were slowly becoming a family, or perhaps had already become a family, while I was over there, driving on endless boring patrols, playing Xbox, and, occasionally, killing people.

"Hey, try not to die, okay?" Natalia told me over the phone a few days after the al-Zawba'i raid. "I'd rather not raise this baby alone."

"Well, in that case . . ." I said.

At the time if you'd asked me why I was over there, despite having a pregnant wife at home, due close enough to my redeployment date that I might miss the birth of my daughter, I would have said I was doing it for my family. That I was experiencing the violence and horror of this place so they didn't have to experience the same things in Fayetteville, North Carolina. That I was behaving honorably. Being a good citizen. A good soldier. A good man. So my child could have a parent to look up to, to see as a role model. So my child could understand that anything good in this world requires sacrifice, real sacrifice, and pain. And I would have said the mission was worth it, that the men we were hunting were truly evil, and we had the videos to prove it. And on later deployments, back to Iraq, still with the CIF, when we were doing the same missions but also training up Iraqi special forces, it was gratifying in a different way. Ninety-day deployments, raid after raid after raid in

Baghdad and in the belt of suburbs around the city, and the Iraqis getting a little better each time. You feel this huge sense of purpose. Like you're really making a difference in the world. And I want my child to see what it's like to have a parent who really puts his heart and soul into what he does, and gets back a sense of identity and value and meaning.

That's what I would have said. The truth, though, is that I loved it. I couldn't have even said why. At the time, I was so young I didn't know what was going on. It was a blur. Before some raids—don't laugh—but I'd have an OCB, which is the official DoD nomenclature for Out of Control Boner, and I'd be thinking, what's with the goddamn chubby in my pants? I'm supposed to be thinking about my sector, about digging my corner, clearing the fatal funnel, but everybody's going to see I'm popping a goddamn chubby! And if you'd asked me the first time I got shot at and survived what it felt like, the best I could have told you was it felt like I'd fucked the prom queen, run the winning touchdown, all that good American shit. And after a raid, Christ, I'd just sit there on my way back, my limp dick against my thigh, not knowing much about what just happened and being able to explain even less. All I knew was that I was in my early twenties, I'd had some ups and downs, but this was the happiest I'd ever felt in my life.

So what happened with al-Zawba'i and his daughter, that was at first easy to forget. And had things turned out differently, or perhaps if Natalia hadn't been pregnant, I can see a very different life that would have unfolded for me. Special Forces, which was supposed to be the unit of warrior-diplomats, of language and culture specialists who could learn the cultural terrain, build up host-nation forces to fight so Americans didn't have to, was already becoming more and more a direct-action unit. Raid after raid after raid. Over the next ten years, the "diplomat" portion of the "warrior-diplomats" would wither, FID missions where you were trying to build up local institutions would be seen as a waste of time, and a dark kind of pure warrior, "see you in

Valhalla" mentality would grip more and more of us. I could have been that kind of soldier, and that kind of leader.

But then, after a long stretch of working with a not particularly competent Iraqi police unit, we got word we were finally heading out on a raid, hitting a target with foreign fighters, no less, the kind of mission where you can expect to get into a gunfight. I was less excited than relieved. Yes, this is what I'm here for. And then, right before we stepped off, Ocho brought up the coming baby. It was almost like he was trying to screw with my head, or knock me off balance just to see how well I recovered.

"Listo para ser padre, maricón?" Ocho asked me in the ready room, smiling, as the air filled with the metallic sound of magazines slamming home. Since I was one of the white guys in 7th Group and didn't grow up bilingual like all the Puerto Rican and Mexican dudes who'd been funneled into SF's Latin America–focused group, Ocho liked to fuck with me in Spanish.

"No, hijo de puta. But it's happening."

"If the kid pops out and you think, shit, that sort of looks like Ocho . . ." he said, putting his hands out as if to say, don't blame me.

I sighed, and picked up an M9. "So," I said, "are you suggesting to a man with a weapon in his hand that you impregnated his wife?"

Ocho chuckled. He was the senior medic. Theoretically, I was supposed to be learning from him, but mostly he just told me stories about having sex with Colombian whores back in the Cali cartel days, teaching me lessons I didn't want to learn. He was in his thirties, looked like he was in his fifties, and talked about sex like he was still a teenager.

"I would never disrespect Natalia like that," he said. "I'm just saying, maybe you spending all this time around a man of my potency did something to your balls. Put the man back into you."

Jefe looked up, caught Ocho's eyes, shook his head, and went back to prepping his kit. The rest of us followed suit. There was a quietness to Jefe, a dignity that could even sweep up Ocho in its wake. His fingers moved methodically, dismantling and then reassembling an M4, moving on to his IFAK, checking the placement of ammo pouches, a choreography identical each and every time, regardless of mission. You wouldn't know from his movements we were preparing for a raid, that there were three Jordanians holed up in an apartment filled with guns and explosives, that people were about to die and that we had no way of knowing if some of those people were in this room. Whether it was a raid or a convoy or a MEDCAP, the movements never changed. And the last thing he did, the very last each time, was to fish a small crucifix out from around his neck, where it hung with his dog tags, kiss it, and tuck it back inside.

Jefe got up the way he always did, slow. It made him look old. He *was* old, and seemed calm. I was young, and thinking about death. I wanted to be more like him and less like myself.

He walked to me, put a hand on my shoulder, and said, "Pretty sure we'll get home in time. You think Iraq is hard, wait until you've got a newborn." And then we stepped out.

It's jarring, the transition out of those deeply private seconds when you're preparing your kit and your body for what's to come. When the work begins, and you're rushing down the backstreets of Hilla or just below the ridge line of a mountain in the Hindu Kush, private thoughts recede. Ideally, *you* disappear and the team's collective will takes over. It's true that sometimes, especially at the beginning of my career, thoughts of death would sneak in. When I was starting out, not enough of us had died yet for it to become normal, and we were still more accustomed to killing than grieving, which requires different muscles, muscles my father knew well, having seen violent death in the mines, deaths where the body was crushed or severed or in some way made inappropriate for display in a coffin.

At first the raid was anticlimactic. Our supporting element, a group of bozo National Guard guys, took it upon themselves to open up on the bad guys with a couple of AT-4s. If you've got serious firepower, I suppose they figured, why not use it? Besides, rockets are cool. The gunfight was over before it began. Then we heard screaming and wailing, and it became clear that the adjoining house was really just a sectioned-off part of the same building, separated not by concrete or brick but by drywall, and those rounds punched straight through into the other apartment, where a family lived.

The first thing I saw inside was a toddler whose stomach had been blown open by shrapnel that hit his little belly crosswise, spilling his guts onto the ground. His mother was crouched over him, mechanically stuffing the intestines back into the dead child's chest cavity. The kid's eyes were open, looking upward, and he had a baseball cap on that read "Pay Me!" It was a fucked-up thing to see. We continued to clear the house, and in the first room to the right there was an old man whose left knee had been shattered so thoroughly the bottom of his leg was just hanging on by skin tissue. He was still alive, if you want to call it that, still conscious anyway, and choking on his own blood. I gave him morphine and he died minutes later. The rest of the family was huddled together, cut up by bits of debris and building material sent flying. I let Jefe and our terp tell the family what had happened to the old man and the little boy, and then watched as Jefe left to speak with the Rangers outside, who were celebrating their first kills as a unit. I wanted to bring them inside to look at the boy, to see what they'd done, but Jefe said it was a bad idea.

"They're normal kids," he said. "It'll fuck them up."

"Good," I said.

"No," he said. "Stuff like that doesn't fuck people up the right way."

I didn't understand what he meant, because I hadn't been to Afghanistan as part of a detachment yet, and hadn't seen the ways people become cold. But I trusted Jefe, like we all did, and backed off.

After that incident, I tried to do the old soldier's routine of lies and half-truths to the family back home. "We got some pretty evil guys the other day," I told Natalia over the phone, speaking about the raid like I was delivering a press release. "Foreign fighters. Guys who came to Iraq because they wanted to kill innocent people."

"What's wrong?" she said. One thing I like about Natalia is that she sees through me. But I knew I probably had the wives' network on my side, voices in her head telling her not to press too hard. Your soldier needs his space.

"Okay, okay," I said, scrambling for what to say, how to deflect. "It's nothing. Just a little strange, you know. Jefe says a soldier's job isn't to kill, but to protect life. It's just that he protects life by killing."

"What happened?" Natalia said, her voice firm.

A part of me wanted to tell her nothing. *She's not a soldier, she couldn't understand.* Or something like that. This part of me spoke in a stern, gruff, manly tone. *She's a pregnant woman, she can't deal with it. Only guys like me can deal with this shit.* Of course, I was really just terrified of what she'd think of me. And beyond that, terrified of what I'd think of myself if I started talking about it.

"We shot a kid," I said. "I did what I could, but . . ."

I'm not sure if that was selfish or brave.

Things were slow after that, op-tempo at a crawl for two weeks and then—one final incident. It began with a photograph.

Jefe showed it to us in the old dining hall of one of Uday's palaces, a place we'd taken over and turned into a briefing room. There was a giant, crystal chandelier, gilded molding around the walls, and a pile of debris from bombing damage. "This is courtesy of Fifth Group," he said, and handed out a photo of an insurgent named Sufyan Arif at, of all things, his baby daughter's first birthday party. In the photo, Arif was tall, dignified, holding on to his daughter with both hands as she perched uncertainly on, I kid you not, the back of a camel. The girl was in a shiny silk dress, Arif was in some fancy sheik getup, and neither was smiling.

"The girl," Jefe deadpanned, "is not a target."

And then he showed us a few more photos, these of flayed feet and severed heads.

"This guy is a real piece of shit," Jefe told us. On the unit laptop he pulled up a grainy video of a masked Arif wielding a knife. In front of him was a weeping young kid, maybe sixteen or seventeen, and Arif put the blade to the kid's neck and started cutting. An amazing amount of blood rushed out, but Arif wasn't getting enough of a sawing action to sever the neck so he withdrew the knife and started hacking. It's the kind of thing we'd all seen before. Most of these guys are pretty un-imaginative when they're filming their torture porn. There's even something weirdly cartoonish about it, like it's a low-budget horror film, not real life. Earlier in the deployment we'd hit a real, no-kidding torture house, and even that was only a bit shocking. On the one hand, we were face-to-face with actual, mutilated corpses. I forced myself to remember that once, these were bodies intertwined with souls and made in the image of God and so on. But after enough of that stuff . . . I forget who said it, that stepping over a single corpse is painful, but walking over a pile of corpses doesn't bother you at all.

So the video didn't bother us. If anything, it was gratifying. Most of us had been in enough murky war zones to lack the near-religious faith in democracy that the war was sold on. If you'd asked our team, "Tell me how this ends," we probably would have answered, "Badly." And though weapons of mass destruction remained a top PIR, and would stay that way through at least 2005, that was rapidly becoming a joke. No one thought we would find those weapons. No one thought that somehow, in some bunker, we'd uncover the reason we were there, the thing that would give purpose and meaning to the chaos swirling around us, to the deaths of the men we were about to lose over the next decade. And yet there we were, the finest soldiers in the finest army in the history of the world, bumbling about, making up our own pur-poses. And the torture houses were one thing we had on our side, a sign, almost like a sign from God Himself, that there was an enemy here who might be worthy of us.

As we shuffled out of the briefing room, I looked at the photo Jefe had passed out. How strange it was to see the child of a man you were about to hunt down. You don't think of the bad guys having children. You think of them having torture houses and hacksaws and stashes of porn, not daughters.

Please God, I prayed, no more kids.

We stepped out, made our way to the target, and ended up facing an unassuming apartment in a middle-class district of west Baghdad. It would have been unimpressive, deflating after all that prep, but part of the beauty of war is how it heightens your sense of the weight and reality of things.

Before you hit a target there's a sharpening to every second, eyes and ears tensed, breath shallow, the vibration of your heart beating, drumming through your chest. Your mind stays calm, detached, registering the fear, the excitement, the small movements of the men you've trained with, each in their positions, as trained and executed time after time so you don't have to see but feel Diego, Ocho, Jason, and the rest, and the fear building in your limbs radiates out to them. Radiating back, there's this sense of control, of power, of yourself as part of a larger organism capable of covering every bloody angle of approach. You pray for something quick. Murderous. And in the long, drawn-out seconds of, well, is it joy? Awe? Something more? In those long, long seconds there are these quick rapid instants, between the blink of an eye, when your instincts, honed predator instincts, they give way to a different kind of alertness. To the alertness of prey. To the knowledge that the men you hunt are meat eaters, too. And that feeling, that sense of yourself and your own mortality and that of the men around you—it lends an aura of the sacred to the profane work to come.

We burst into his house, and the first person we encountered was not Arif himself, but his tiny, young, delicate-looking, and extremely pregnant wife. Who didn't scream in terror. Who didn't weep or shout curses at us in Arabic, like we're accustomed to. Who merely clutched at the wall and started moaning, low, long, and sad. Noises like the ones from birthing videos I'd seen with Natalia before I left, and now here's this tiny woman, tiny but huge with child, stomach heaving, stretched. I froze. I thought she was going into labor.

I helped her to the floor, pushed aside an end table. A vase with yellow flowers fell off and shattered. There were yellow flowers in every room of that house. It's funny what you remember. Her eyes were deep brown, she had a long thin face and dark, dark eyebrows.

Ocho found a very young girl with big scared eyes hiding in a closet, the baby from the photo grown up a few more years, and when we brought her in to be with the mother she calmed a bit. Arif put up no fight, which is more common than you'd think. He was heavier than in the photo, more jowly, with a thicker mustache and thinner hair. He sat sullenly, not looking at us, not looking at his hugely pregnant wife, and I got so angry. Look at her. Apologize. This is all your fault.

We wrapped up quick. Nobody wanted to linger. Toward the end we helped his wife up and he shouted something at her, something beyond the Arabic of anybody in the room. It was the first time he seemed emotional, and as the words struck her she stiffened, went cold, refused to look us in the eye. I've always wondered what he said. It's awkward, fighting a war in people's homes.

Right after, I had all these feelings I couldn't put a name to. Al-Zawba'i's daughter kept popping into my head, and so did the dying toddler. I kept thinking of the noise Arif's wife had made, and I had this fucked-up regret that she hadn't really been going into labor, or, even more fucked up, that Arif hadn't tried to pull a gun on us. It would have been something, to take a guy out and deliver his child on the same night.

I called Natalia on an MWR line, wanting to hear how her thirty-four-week appointment had gone.

"Everything is fine," she said, "fine. Blood pressure's a little high, baby's growing a little less than they want, but she's fine, we're fine, it's fine. Come home soon. You don't want to miss her."

"You should have Inez say a rosary," I told her. A priest had told Natalia's grandmother her prayers had special pull because of her devotion, and she'd never let anyone in the family forget it.

"I'm her favorite grandchild. She's probably praying right now."

I hesitated. There was a lot of turbulence in my head then. I thought of Arif's snuff films, and they calmed me somewhat.

"We got a really evil motherfucker today," I said.

"Oh." I could tell Natalia was confused, to have me switching subjects. But the things were all muddled together in my mind.

"His wife was pregnant, and she freaked out when we hit his house."

"Oh. Okay. That must have been . . . strange."

"It was, it was."

"Do you want to talk about it?"

"Nah."

There was a pause, and then, to close things off, I said, "Today was a good day. It's a better world, with him in prison."

Which was true. Obviously. In training for Special Forces, an instructor had explained the difference between direct-action missions and foreign internal defense missions as the difference between treating the symptoms of an insurgency and treating the disease. A guy like Arif was a symptom. A weak government and a military without the support of its own people was the disease. I understood that. That day was a day for treating the symptoms. Tomorrow, hand-holding an Iraqi unit, would be treating the disease. That all made sense to me. But after those three missions, I couldn't just think about the symptoms and the disease. I was increasingly worried about the patient.

I didn't say this to Natalia, though. I switched back to talking about the baby, and her high blood pressure, and all the reasons neither of us had to worry.

2

here's a gringa hen and a Colombian pig, and one day the hen says to the pig, "We have known each other for so long, and we have always done well together. We should start a business."

And the Colombian pig thinks, Yes, I have known this gringa a long time, though I'm not so sure I've always done well by her. Still, *she's* always done well, so perhaps going into business together will work out for me, too. And the Colombian pig says, "What is the business?"

And the gringa hen says, "We'll sell breakfast sandwiches. I'll provide half the ingredients. You provide the other half."

"That sounds fair," says the Colombian pig. "What is your contribution?"

"The eggs, clearly," says the gringa hen.

"Clearly, yes," says the Colombian pig. "And what about me?"

The gringa hen smiles. She lays a wing on the pig's shoulder. "You? My sweet little Colombian pig. You'll provide the bacon."

My daughter told me that story. My daughter, Valencia. She heard it from her professor of law, who is, like seemingly every professor of law at Nacional, very much a man of the left. She told it to me the way she tells me every little excess or flourish of her professors, with an eye roll. "Not quite a mamerto, but almost," she said, echoing what I have told her often before. But, for perhaps the first time, I detected a question behind her eyes. Perhaps she herself did not know it was hiding there.

"There's some truth to that," I told her. But I didn't say more. We don't talk about my work. It is not appropriate for children to know more about it than the honor it is due, and I still think of her, twenty years old, beautiful, with her mother's eyes and, unfortunately, my weak chin, as a child. But it *is* true. I, more than anyone, would know. After all, for the past twenty years, I have been the bacon.

We left it at that and, in the manner of our family, did not return to the issue. I told myself, as I have told myself many times before, that one day we would have a talk. Or maybe I would write it all down, the true story of my life, without evasions and without the boundaries that distinguish the relationship between father and daughter, in which I must be the authority and the source of wisdom and she the subordinate, incapable of judgment or even of talking back. Maybe I will one day write it down and tell it to her like I would tell a friend, or a priest, or God. If I believed in true friends, or priests, or Gods.

But I think of her professor's little joke tonight, as Valencia does her schoolwork and as my wife, Sofia, chops onions and I tap my fingers on my cigar box, trying to decide whether to pull out the Cohibas or the more expensive La Flor lanceros, given to me by General Campos on the day of my promotion to lieutenant colonel. Tonight, we have Sergeant Major Mason Baumer to dinner. He's what brings Valencia's joke to mind. Because if I am the bacon, then Mason, the U.S. embassy's Special Forces Liaison, is the gringa hen laying my eggs.

"You're sure he likes Italian food?" Sofia says.

"Everyone likes Italian food," I say.

"Didn't you say his wife is a paisa?" Sofia says. "I could have asked my mother how she makes bandeja . . ."

"My arteries cannot handle bandeja," I say. "And Vale doesn't like bandeja. And *you* don't like bandeja. Besides, she's not coming, and it's her family that's from Medellín. She grew up in North Carolina."

"North Carolina, ah," Sofia says. I can tell she's thinking back to the trip we took to Fayetteville. "Probably never had good Italian then."

I give the cigars one more look. Unequal partnership or not, Colombia still needs those eggs, especially as the peace deal looms and the nature of the war shifts. Gringa hens need to be kept happy. I decide upon the lanceros, and let out a long breath, then walk to the dining room to examine the table settings. Everything is ordered. Centerpiece precisely centered, place settings distributed evenly, symmetrically, with one setting on the left for our guest, providing him the view out the window, and one on the right side for our daughter, with Sofia and me at the end, creating an effect that is almost perfectly harmonious. I check the tablecloth, the mats. One is not quite right, I tap it gently on the right side, moving it so its edge runs parallel to the edge of the table, precisely an inch away. I let out another long breath.

"I can hear you," Sofia says from the kitchen. "Stop it. Tonight will be fun. American military are fun."

"Not this one," I say.

"You're a snob," she says.

Perhaps, I think, though it's more than that. The nature of my current job, and my relationship with Mason, revolves around an unpleasant truth, which is the extent to which a third-tier official from the American State Department or Department of Defense can make decisions with huge consequences for my country. Mason is not even a third-tier official, but he *is* one of the principals in the American embassy's MILGROUP, as they call it. And as the man who brings operators in and out of the country, he's the man I work with most regularly, the man most directly involved with our operations at the tactical level. Which means he's a man whose opinion those third-tier officials will care about. I'm an officer, and he's enlisted. He's no suitable partner for me in any sense, and certainly not my social equal. But the Americans view their enlisted as the equivalent of our officers, one of many insults we suffer, and so his opinion matters.

"Mason is a little strange," I say. "Most U.S. operators are"—I make a fist—"more supportive of us."

Sofia doesn't respond. Maybe she will like him. Valencia will definitely like him. Vale wants to be a lawyer, and Mason *should* have been a lawyer. Every operation, every request, from him I get nothing but questions, constant questions, half the time questions with no answers, or no good answers, or answers that are designed for politicians and diplomats to think about, not soldiers. For a while, I've been debating with myself whether or not this means he's weak. Nothing is certain with him, the ground is always shifting, which is terrible in any partnership, but especially in one that involves violence.

"Just," I say, "be careful what you say around him. He's not so easy as the last one."

Mason arrives on time, an irritating habit American military have. Sofia barely has her makeup on, and Vale is still in the bathroom. Mason, leaner than most Special Forces but still a big, thick-necked man, walks into my sitting room and takes a chair, as if it were his apartment, and we're his guests.

"Beautiful," he says, staring out at the room, the paintings on the wall, the battered crucifix my father had recovered from a destroyed church during his war in Medellín, the photos of Valencia.

Sofia offers drinks, and we talk about the weather, about how comfortably Natalia is settling in to Bogotá. Mason's Spanish is flat but clear, easier to listen to than the previous SFLi, a Dominican who chewed on the last syllable of every word he gargled out of his mouth. When Valencia emerges, in a red dress I have never seen before and which her mother would have picked out for her, she greets Mason with a touch of formality. I remember our conversation about the Colombian pig and the gringa chicken and wonder again what she is being told at that school. Perhaps, I think, I should try to avoid talk of politics tonight. It is a delicate time. The peace treaty with the FARC goes up for a vote in October, and though most of my colleagues and family members will be voting no, everyone expects it to pass. The guerrilla will leave the jungle and end the war. Which means both a changing security environment and a changing relationship with the U.S. military. What happens in the next few months will shape the future for men like Mason and myself. This means it will shape Valencia's future, too, and perhaps I should have explained all this to her beforehand but it's too late now—the evening will proceed how it will. And then Sofia claps her hands and calls us to the table.

After both courses there's much praise, and wonder, and a little bragging on Sofia's part. "You can imagine how hard it is to find authentic stracchino in Bogotá," she says, knowing he has no clue what stracchino is. *I* don't know what stracchino is, I only know that I just ate it, and it was delicious. And then, over Sofia's homemade limoncello, Mason ruins the mood.

"Are you worried about the peace?" he asks me.

"Why would I worry about the peace?" I say, though of course I'm worried, and everyone knows it.

"I want to say . . . are you going to vote yes, or no?"

Mason's government is very much in favor of the treaty. So is mine, of course, and I tell him so.

"Then . . . you will vote yes?"

"He won't tell you," Sofia says, smiling slightly and circling a finger over the rim of her glass.

"I'm a soldier," I say.

"The treaty is trash," Sofia says. "I hate that they even call it a vote for peace. 'Vote yes for peace!' Only a monster could be against peace. But I'll tell you a secret . . ."

She smiles seductively and leans forward, her chest on display, a silver pendant gleaming between her breasts. "You're dining with monsters."

She goes over the usual reasons. That it lets the FARC off too easily for their crimes, it lets them keep their drug money, it lets them have representatives in Congress when all they deserve is prison. She points out that even left-wing organizations like Human Rights Watch are attacking the peace for allowing guerrillas who have killed civilians, kidnapped civilians, committed widespread sexual violence, and forced children into military service not to spend a day in prison if they confess.

"There is a saying in America," Mason says. "No justice, no peace."

"I like that," she says. "No justice, no peace."

"What do you think?" Mason says, his eyes casually fixing on mine.

"I'm a soldier," I say, not liking the turn the conversation has taken. What I want from Mason has nothing to do with the guerrillas, and nothing to do with the so-called peace. "Soldiers don't have any business thinking about justice."

"No?" Mason shakes his head. "What do you mean?"

He waits, and I'm not sure what I want to say. That war is like love, that the world is chaos, so two people say to each other, Everything is uncertain. Friends become enemies, health becomes sickness, wealth becomes ruin. But we two, we will create one small space of order in the chaos. I will rest on you, you on me, and we will not break. And in that small space, we will have room for human feelings, maybe cruel, maybe tender, full of arguments or never-ending kindnesses, but more important than the nature of the love is the space we create for it to exist. And that the same goes for the state.

"All my life, and all my father's life," I say, "the government has sent us out into mountains and jungles of Colombia, to the regions where the government has no power. These places have always been the same—before the guerrilla and the narcos and the paramilitaries, there were bandits, there was the Violence, there was chaos. So we carve out order in the chaos. Sometimes I think it is like a man with a machete hacking a path through the jungle. Everybody who follows behind us, it's their job to think about justice, about whether the state is cruel and callous, or good and benevolent. It's my job to carve the path."

"Then," Mason says, "you are yes?"

"To call it a peace is too much, far too much," I say. "I'm a soldier. I've seen guerrillas turn to paramilitaries turn to drug gangs turn to politicians. I've seen massacres over the scraps left behind after our victories. I know the law of unintended consequences. So we need to maintain presence and . . ." I consider whether this is the time to bring up the point of the evening, and decide I might as well. "There's Operation Agamemnon. Already, it's not going well, and this will complicate matters. I don't want to say it, but I'm afraid the job will become too much for the police to handle on their own."

"Ha!" Mason says, seeing the point I'm making. "Switching Agamemnon to the army . . . Well, I think of Agamemnon as law enforcement, not war. Yes?"

"Sadly," I say, "there's not much of a difference here."

Operation Agamemnon is a police-led strike at the Clan Úsuga, alias the Gulf Clan, alias the Urabeños, a criminal group with an estimated two thousand members. It's the largest campaign against a criminal group in Colombia's history, with an order of magnitude more resources than we ever threw against Escobar. Also, given the FARC peace treaty and the peace talks ongoing with our other major group of communist guerrillas, the ELN, it's the most important thing going on in Colombia. But it's police led, which is a problem, and not just because the police lack our skills and are more prone to corruption and infiltration.

Having the Americans on board right now for a shift to making Agamemnon an army operation would put us, *philosophically*, in the same place. The modern Colombian army depends on millions of dollars of U.S. aid for the maintenance of our air power—a necessary capability in a country filled with jungles and mountains—and so despite the international news declaring an end to "the longest insurgency in history," it is critical that all parties involved understand that "war," loosely understood, continues in Colombia. War, and "war," requires continuing support.

Mason turns to my daughter. "What do you think, Val?" Her name sounds dead on his tongue.

"That's my father's business," she says. "I'm in my second year at university, studying law. We talk about the deal, but . . . I don't know enough yet to earn an opinion. I think someone should really know what they're talking about before they open their mouth."

"You'd make a terrible American," Mason says, laughing.

"It sounds strange," Valencia says, "knowing that my father is an operations officer in the special forces, you'd think I would know all kinds of things about what's going on . . ."

"We don't talk about work," I say, "inside these walls. This is a home. Our kind of work has no place in a home."

Mason looks chastened. "I'm sorry."

"No, it's good. Every rule should be broken sometimes, especially for guests. Valencia, do you have any questions?"

She thinks for a moment, and Sofia eyes our daughter with her head cocked. Is she nervous? In truth, the rule is more for Sofia's benefit than Vale's.

Finally, Vale says, "What do you tell your daughters about what you do? Do they know about it?"

"Oh." Mason looks at me warily, and I nod to him, slightly. He leans forward. "At first, nothing."

Valencia nods.

"But kids learn things, I don't know how. When they were old enough we had to have the war talk. The war talk, and the sex talk. Not very fun, those talks."

I have had neither of those talks with Valencia.

"What was it like for you?" he said.

Valencia looks nervously at my wife, then at me. "The only scary time was when I was really young. Five or six, I think." Without wanting to,

I raise an eyebrow, and Valencia quickly adds, "Nothing happened. But . . . there was a time when my mother was very nervous."

There's a moment of silence. My wife looks sad, and then says, "Saravena," the name of an oil town where I'd been tasked with building bridges to a community that hated us.

"That was a difficult place," I say. "It still is."

Valencia doesn't say anything more, because she is a respectful child. I think about making a comment on those days, about being a father and fighting a war, but instead I wave my hand dismissively. Valencia's face is opaque. I had always thought we shielded her perfectly, and the degree of achievement and obedience we see in her is proof that we raised her well and protected her from anything truly damaging, but of course children notice more than you think. Perhaps she knows better than I how Saravena changed me. I was too busy living through it.

"Good," Sofia says, clapping her hands. "No more of that. And much more of the limoncello."

After dinner, Mason and I have cigars in the garden of our apartment complex, leaving the women upstairs. I watch him put one of my lanceros to his lips and take a puff. He holds it awkwardly, and lets too much saliva touch the quickly dampening edges. Odd, for a military man, not to know his way around a cigar.

"Your wife wants the peace deal to deliver justice," he says.

"Yes."

"How about you?"

"I think justice is a lot to ask for."

He laughs at that. "Somebody told me you were on the Raúl Reyes mission."

I nod. Reyes had been the number three man in the FARC. Also, he'd been a clown and a killer, with rodent facial hair and endless crimes from cocaine trafficking to murder. Formally sentenced for eighteen kidnappings, for the murders of thirteen policemen, eighteen soldiers, the thirty-six youths killed in the bombing of Club El Nogal. And he had the obnoxious habit of dressing his murders up in the most trite clichés about the people, and the revolution, and socialism, and justice.

"Did that feel like justice?" Mason asks.

I wonder what he's driving at. The Reyes mission was done in collaboration with the Americans, the type of collaboration we'd like to employ in the Agamemnon mission.

"It was"—I'm not sure how to describe it—"an impressive display."

Basically I'd sat on a base, bored, while the planes flew overhead toward his camp just across the Ecuadorian border, first a group of Cessna A-37 Dragonflys, light attack aircraft carrying 500-pound Mark-82 gravity bombs with a Paveway guidance system strapped on the nose, behind them our Super Tucanos, flying at much lower altitude, carrying conventional gravity bombs, and behind them an AC-47 gunship. The Dragonflys dropped their smart bombs, killing Reyes and those around him. The Super Tucanos dropped their bombs, flattening the surrounding jungle, killing insurgents while simultaneously providing plausible deniability that we were using American technology. Then the AC-47 strafed the area, shot survivors. And it was only then, after all that firepower, that we came in on our U.S.-provided Black Hawks. There weren't many guerrilleros left. We walked through bodies torn by shrapnel. One corpse lay peacefully, as if for a wake, the only sign of damage, pools of blood where eyes should be. And we found a huge amount of intelligence, probably the biggest haul on the FARC ever. And, of course, Raúl Reyes's corpse. Mostly intact.

Hearing that story, you might be tempted to think it was a bomb that killed Reyes. You might focus on the technology, the guidance system given to us by the CIA, or the plane, a light attack aircraft specially designed during the Vietnam War for counterinsurgency. Or perhaps you'd think about the pilot, or the commander who oversaw the operation. But that wasn't what killed him at all. Or, at least, it wasn't the important thing.

"You know what it felt like," I tell him. "It felt like doing the laundry, or taking out the trash. Like something that needed to be done."

Mason takes another awkward pull on his cigar. The only other American soldiers who don't know how to smoke are the Mormons, who have an excuse.

Nonchalantly, not trying to offend him, I turn in profile to show him how to treat a lancero, holding the cigar just to the mouth, drawing in the smoke gently, bringing down the cigar with the smoke held in the mouth, feeling the tobacco hit, savoring the richness, slowly letting it out, then rotating the cigar, exaggerating the movement, and repeating the process. I don't think he notices.

"Take Agamemnon," I say. "Currently it's the police who are leading the fight against the Urabeños. It's logical. They're a drug gang. Let the police handle them. And so they're trying. And when they catch Urabeños, they arrest them and bring them to trial. Would you say that counts as justice?"

"Sure," he says.

"But if the army takes over Agamemnon, well . . ."

"You'll stop putting Urabeños in jail and start putting them in body bags."

"Exactly." I smile. I suspect this is what makes him nervous about the whole thing. Might as well confront it. "Is that justice? Who knows? But last week the Úsaga dragged a sixty-year-old man from his truck, they shot him in the middle of the road, waited for the police to come. Then they killed four police, they killed one army captain . . ." I let out a sigh. "So I don't think now is a time to worry about justice. There are things that need to be done, one way or another."

He says nothing. I know he gets my point, but he won't agree to it, even for politeness's sake. Which is frustrating. What we want is not simply a new front in a war, but access to that thing the Americans, and only the Americans, can provide. The same thing that killed Raúl Reyes, and which the Americans have been using to hunt people in Iraq and Afghanistan and the Philippines and Somalia and Niger and Colombia and Ecuador and who knows where else. And it is something we deserve access to. After all, it started here, in Colombia, thirty years ago.

This was during the war against Pablo Escobar, who had been the herald of a new type of criminal. A drug lord of such scale and wealth that he was able to wage an asymmetric war against the foundations of the state itself, focusing as much on murdering police officers, judges, and politicians as on holding territory. When ISIS started murdering every state worker in Iraq they could find, including garbagemen, as part of their war, they were acting as Escobar's children. Break down all order, all civilization, so the cockroaches can breed in the ruins.

In response, we formed a special unit, the Search Bloc, about whom much has been written. Behind the scenes, men like my father worked with the Americans to create an integrated network of differing agencies designed to tighten the loop of finding targets, fixing them in place, finishing them, exploiting and analyzing the intelligence collected, and then disseminating that intelligence to the agencies and commands able to act on it most rapidly. It created a model in which the operations of special forces, military intelligence, police intelligence, signals and human and image intelligence services were reorganized and integrated to reduce stovepiping, maximize information sharing, and tighten the circle of analysis and execution into a seamless, never-ending cycle.

That system is something often ignored in discussions of military capabilities, because it is not a particular unit, or weapons system, or technology, or style of training, but something more amorphous, a system that ties all of those elements together and multiplies their lethality and speed. This is no exaggeration. The Americans would use the same system in the Balkans, and then would pump steroids into it in Iraq. The outcome: a special operations command that was executing

12 raids a month in 2004 turned into an industrial-scale killing machine that was conducting 250 raids a month only two years later.

An American officer once described it to me this way: "When civilians think about war, they tend to think about the mechanism of death. The heroic Navy SEAL firing a tight cluster of bullets into a bad guy's head. The creepy, mechanical drone delivering a bomb. But those are just the flathead and Phillips-head screwdriver at the end of a targeting system. And it's the system that's the real killer."

The Americans took the system back to Colombia ten years ago, and after a lucky NSA intercept of a phone call with Hugo Chávez, used it to help us kill Raúl Reyes. And Negro Acacio. And Martín Caballero. And many others. Of course, we can run the system, in a limited sense, on our own. In fact, we teach the system to other military allies around Latin America. But access to U.S. assets turns it into a monster.

"I'll be honest with you," Mason finally says. "Most of MILGROUP is on board with the shift. But personally, I think it's a big fucking deal when you switch from targeting a bunch of guerrillas who are explicitly at war with you to targeting drug dealers. Mixing war and policing is dangerous. Plus, high-value targeting is famously useless against criminal gangs."

That's too stupid to take seriously. "And against terrorists, supposedly," I say. "But Al Qaeda, Taliban, ISIS, Boko Haram, al-Shabaab, the Haqqani network . . . it seems a mix of war and policing is all Americans do these days."

He laughs at that, and says, "Why do you think we can't seem to end any of these wars?"

I'm not making any progress, and I should probably leave it there. Enough to learn that the rest of MILGROUP is in support. But I can't help pushing.

"Can I trust you with something?" I say.

"Of course."

"I mentioned to you we've been getting intelligence from a group operating in Norte de Santander with ties to the Venezuelan military."

"Yeah . . . the . . ."

"The Mil Jesúses."

"Yeah," he says.

"What I didn't mention was who they were passing intelligence through."

Now he's looking at me curiously.

"Me," I say. "*I'm* their connection. Or, rather, they reached out to me."

"Huh," he says. "Why? I mean . . . why you?"

The short answer is that it's my daughter's fault. Because she's got a professor who wants to take students to work for a foundation in Norte de Santander. Because I started reaching out to contacts in the area who might know something. And because within a few days a lawyer in Bogotá who, after my father's disgrace, had worked briefly for my family, was calling me on their behalf. Not that I'm going to tell him that.

"Who knows?" I say. "Probably because they wanted a direct line to Colonel Carlosama. And he wasn't going to be in touch with them."

"Huh," he says again. He's not showing much surprise, but I expected that. The Jesúses don't have much discipline around operational security, especially when it comes to avoiding signals intelligence, and so I'm quite sure the Americans already know about me. It's one of the reasons I'm willing to share this little secret with Mason, who probably thinks I'm being recklessly trusting.

"Yes, it's unusual," I say. "And because of that . . . it puts my career in a delicate place."

I let him take that in. He puffs on the cigar awkwardly, and makes a face.

"Friends like that can be a problem," he says, his expression guarded.

"I know. But we wouldn't have had the El Alemán raid without them."

"The one in Norte de Santander?"

That was where we first met, when Mason came to Colombia.

"What am I going to do?"

He doesn't answer. I decide to push him again.

"Are you going to judge me for these . . . friends?" I ask, smiling. "I suppose you only accept human intelligence from angels."

"Not so much."

I smile. "Don't tell anyone about this, by the way. I tell you in confidence."

He nods, warily. Of course I know he'll share what I'm telling him. But he'll feel guilty about it.

"They don't trust the National Police, they will only work with us. Of course, we pass the intelligence on to the Junglas, but you know how easily bureaucratic roadblocks can happen."

Mason shrugs. "Sure."

"And their information about Venezuela is"—I decide to be deliberately vague—"interesting. Anyway, it's just one of many developments that will put us in good standing when we take over Agamemnon."

Mason nods, awkwardly fiddling with the lancero in his hands. I decide I've pushed this line far enough for tonight. Enough to put the worm in his brain. "We can talk more some other day. Enough work for tonight."

Mason holds the cigar up to his face, lets it down, and says, "I'm sorry, I'm trying but . . . I never will understand cigars."

I laugh. "I can see that."

"I am wasting good tobacco here. To me, all cigars taste like lung cancer."

I pluck the cigar from his fingers.

"Next time, you come to our place," Mason says. "You can meet my daughters."

I smile. "I would like that very much."

He claps me on the shoulder. Very American, this Mason. I think he wants to be friends. In the military, in our military, we don't have friends. One year here, two years there, is not enough time to develop friendship, true friendship, that lasts beyond the camaraderie of men who have served together. It is one of the many hardships of the army. The loneliness. The fact that we don't even have the love or respect of our people. Until Uribe, we did not even give the army the tools we needed to accomplish the tasks asked of us, brutal tasks, tasks in jungles and mountains, in towns where the people report your movements to the guerrilla, in the forgotten parts of the country where coca grows everywhere and friends of the state wither and die.

Instead of love or resources or friends, we have duty. It's an iron duty, a duty that doesn't beckon us to glory or to public adulation, a duty whose voice is sometimes so faint, a calling from some other sphere, that we listen to it like the mystics do to the supposed voice of God. A calling only we know, a calling that steels us, that drives us.

But if Mason wants to be friends, we can be friends.

It is late by the time Mason leaves, and I have an early morning tomorrow, but I make myself some tea, pull out a book by an American economist on the use and misuse of land reform in twentieth-century military campaigns, and sit myself down and pretend to read it. The night went well, I suppose, but I also have a sense of something dislodged within the order of my home. A premonition that something has gone wrong. My instincts in this regard have always been very good, so I'm not surprised when Valencia pokes her head into the room.

"Papá," she says, and I incline my head slightly in assent, not taking my eyes off the book. She slips into the room and sits down, dressed in her nightgown. My eyes scan the page I'd randomly opened to and fix on the sentence: "In short, MacArthur had ordered the Japanese to do something that was already in the works." I nod, as if in agreement with a point made by the author, then look up at Vale.

"I had a very nice evening," she says.

"Good," I say.

"You said that the rules about talking of war, that they were lifted for . . . the evening."

"For the dinner," I say.

"Oh," she says.

This is not the right way to handle this.

"For the evening," I say. "It can be for the evening."

Valencia smiles nervously. "You talked about guerrillas, and narcos, and neoparamilitaries, and paramilitaries. And I know that the government used to work with paramilitaries, that paramilitaries were legal, and then illegal . . ."

"Do you want to know if I ever worked with paramilitaries?" I say.

"No . . ." she says, though of course she must want to know.

"So what do you want to know?"

"I read a book by a journalist, Maria Teresa Ronderos . . ."

I know which book she's talking about. Probably the best book about the paramilitaries, which means the most thorough, which means the one that details every last ugly thing about them, and about their links to the army. This is what sending your child to university does. It teaches them to distrust. "That's a very good book," I say, which makes her very happy to hear. That I approve of it means, perhaps, that I agree with its criticisms, which means I must not be guilty. She smiles and nods.

"It's very interesting," she says. I wait a moment, but she's not sure how to proceed.

"I never worked with paramilitaries," I say. There are other questions I could answer—did I ever turn a blind eye to social cleansings, take bribes, kill civilians and claim they were guerrilla, drive peasants from their homes, work hand in hand with murderers and drug dealers. Perhaps she has not articulated these questions to herself yet. I am sure, in her heart, the answer to all of them is no. But education has placed the worm of doubt. "Your grandfather, of course, worked with paramilitaries. He trained them, back when it was legal. It was part of his job."

"Yes," she says.

"And intelligence sources," I say, "are often unpleasant people. An officer needs strong character to deal with them in the correct manner."

"Yes," she says again.

I wonder how to close off this line of questioning more strongly.

"Let me tell you a story," I say. I put down my book on the side table. "I was in one of the very first counternarcotics battalions. We were based out of Tres Esquinas, and we had a couple of Huey helicopters, trash helicopters, but . . . helicopters. One day, a police post radioed in. This was early days, so the operation center was full of paper maps and radios and stale coffee and a lot of people milling about when the policemen came on the radio, panicked. We could hear gunfire crackling. Three hundred guerrilla, they thought. The police post had only fourteen men. And there I am, a new lieutenant in air mobile assault, with some of the best men in the Colombian army, twenty minutes away. Twenty minutes . . . by helicopter. On foot, through jungle and mountain, three days away. So what do you think I did?"

"I don't know," she says.

"What do you mean you don't know?" I say. "There I am, twenty minutes away by helicopter, and these fourteen police officers, fourteen brave men, are calling us over the radio, 'Help us, help us. We need reinforcements. They are surrounding us.' So what did I do?"

She shakes her head. "The question is a trick, somehow," she says.

"After ten hours, the calls became desperate. We have only this much ammunition, we have only this many men left, we have taken this many wounded and this many killed. 'Help us, help us. We need reinforcements.' After fifteen hours, they were rationing bullets, taking so much care with each shot, trying to prevent the enemy from tightening the circle, only firing when it was absolutely essential, because they knew their bullets couldn't last. After twenty hours, they knew they were going to die, they knew that the foot patrol my commanding officer sent out would never reach them in time, but over the radio they kept their honor. They told us, 'When we run out of bullets, we'll throw sticks and stones.'" After twenty-five hours, they stopped that talk. They told us, 'We have only enough ammunition to hold out a few hours more, and then we'll have to surrender. We will try to make it last as long as we can.' After twenty-seven hours, they surrendered. And though usually the guerrillas would have taken them as prisoners, I think the FARC was angered by their bravery. I think the guerrillas were ashamed to have been held off by fourteen men, fourteen against three hundred, for so long. So they lined them up and shot them."

Vale nods, her eyes on mine. "Why didn't you save them?" she says.

"The helicopters were part of United States' Plan Colombia, and the rules then were that we could only use helicopters for counternarcotics missions. FARC columns were moving in to surround Bogotá, peace negotiations were breaking down. We'd plan counternarcotics missions so that we'd end up in a firefight with guerrillas. It wasn't hard to do. The FARC was fighting to gain control of the coca regions around their despeje. If we headed into the same territory and ended up fighting guerrillas because we were moving in on their drug zones, that was fair. The Americans could pretend, and we could pretend. But three hundred guerrilla attacking a police station? A mission like that was clearly military; we couldn't pretend. And if we'd used the helicopters for a mission like that, the U.S. would have taken our helicopters back. So we all sat and listened over the radio as fourteen of the bravest police officers in Colombia slowly lost hope, and then we let them die."

Valencia takes that in, and I sip my tea. Ginger turmeric, good for the digestion.

"These are the kinds of choices you have to make in a war," I say. "In 2001, the U.S. sent us Black Hawks, a much better helicopter. And then, after 9/11, the restrictions were lifted. The narcoguerrillas became narcoterrorists, and as terrorists, the Americans decided they were fair game."

"Are you saying . . ."

"What I'm saying is . . ." I sigh, putting the tea down and putting on my serious face, the face I used to use to deliver punishment when she was a girl. "What I'm saying is that there were other restrictions, too. Uribe was professionalizing the army, starting with special units like mine. No massacres, no drug trafficking, no working with terrorist groups, and the U.S. declared paramilitaries like the AUC to be terrorist groups right around that time. Also, any air mobile unit with documented links to them would have lost their helicopters. That was one of the conditions the Americans gave. So you think I would risk my unit by working with the paramilitaries? We didn't need them, like my father did. Like other units did at the time. We had helicopters."

I cannot read Valencia's face. Perhaps I was too aggressive. She's not a naughty child, she's a young woman. She's going to be a lawyer, she has thoughts and opinions. I can't expect her to simply accept what I say.

"My professor said," she begins, then stops, reconsiders what she was about to say, and then continues, "that the original Plan Colombia, the one we asked for, was for development of the countryside. Roads, schools, and aid to get the farmers to switch from coca to wheat. But the Americans wanted it all to be military."

"The Americans were right," I say, "in that, if not in many other things. You need a functioning army before you can have a functioning state." I feel like I'm lecturing. I don't want to lecture. I want to be honest with my daughter. I want her to know who I am and know the decisions I've made, and I want her to continue to think well of me after my death, after every secret has been uncovered.

"Listen," I say, "you want me to tell you I've never done anything that would cause you shame. Maybe you want me to tell you that about your grandfather, too, but you know he was fired by Uribe, and you know why."

"I know grandfather . . ."

"Lived in a different time, and came up in a different army, and a different Colombia." I stand up, put my book back on the shelf, and turn so that I'm looking down on my daughter. "Men are weak. Don't ask if they're good or bad. We're all sinful. Ask if they're better or worse than the times they lived in. Your grandfather was much better, and deserved much more than he received."

She nods. There's not a hint of judgment in her face, but it must be there. What type of person would she be if it wasn't there? She's lived a safe life, Sofia and I have made sure of that. The decisions she's made have nothing to do with the cold logic that rules my life, or the even colder logic that ruled her grandfather's. Safety teaches a weaker sort of will. Maybe one day, Colombia will be so much better that my daughter will look at me and, surrounded by the thick walls of civilization, staring out through semiopaque glass into the chaos of the past, see a bad, violent man. And beyond me, deeper in the wilderness, she'll see her grandfather, a monster, a general whose unit was implicated in some of the worst abuses the human rights mob likes to hurl at the army. I suppose that would not be the worst thing. If her generation were ever so safe that they could look on mine with disgust, that would only mean that my life's work had been successful.

3

MASON 2005

People told me I'd never understand sex until I'd done it, never understand combat until I'd been in it, never understand life itself until I was a father. But when the day arrived for each of those things, I didn't find myself with any new wisdom. Just a girl I thought I loved. The anxious thrill of being alive. A fragile life I could hold in one hand. And no idea what to do with any of them.

"Think about getting out," Jefe had told me on the flight back. "Maybe not right away. It won't matter so much, right away. But with kids this job is hard."

You don't expect to hear that kind of talk from a warrant officer with over twenty years in. You really, really don't.

"Plenty of the guys have kids," I said. "I mean, *you've* got kids. You've never even been divorced."

"Maria and I are old school. She pretends I've never fucked whores in Colombia. I pretend, too."

I waited, but he didn't say anything more.

"Jefe," I said. He looked at me placidly.

"Yeah," he said.

We stared at each other.

"Look," Jefe said. "The first couple of years don't matter so much.

You can catch up. The kid won't remember. But you stick around much longer, still doing this shit when that little girl is seven, eight, twelve years old?" He paused. "My kids don't know me. And you're not like the rest of us old boys."

I stared down at my feet.

"So you're saying I've got a few years to think this over."

Jefe smiled.

"Maybe," I said, "I'll get out when the war is over."

"Which war?" Jefe said.

"Iraq," I said. "Afghanistan'll never end."

When we finally got to Bragg, Natalia was there waiting for me, a fierce five two in a black dress stretched tight over her bulging stomach, dark eyeshadow framing light brown eyes, and her hair straightened because even though I like her better curly that's what she does for big occasions.

"God," I said. "Look at you, you sexy beast."

"Go on," she said, pointing to her stomach. "Make a fool of yourself."

So I did, touching her stomach, then putting my ear to her stomach, then waiting awkwardly for something to happen until I think I felt the tiniest something and I smiled and stood up and kissed my wife again. Everything, I was sure, would work out beautifully.

Coming back from a deployment, you're strangers. Even if you don't come back to a woman whose whole body has changed, who's spent months of pregnancy alone. Dealt with the stress of you overseas, alone. Dealt with the not knowing, alone. Even as time went by, as Natalia and I got more and more used to the combat commute, me showing up months later, both of us different but still loving each other, forgiving of each other and trying to be kind, it was never a smooth transition. Usually, it takes me a month to fit myself back into her schedule. There's a while where you're dating your wife, and the favorite uncle to your kids. There are plus sides to that, but it takes effort. There's a wear to it.

We're better than most. We talk. Natalia can talk her way through anything, but our talk in the early days of a redeployment is never really talk. It's never aimed at anything other than filling the silence. Maybe because there's too much at stake, because there's no sure path through the confusion, because each deployment is different, and there's so much you want to say but can't express when you're not even sure yourself what you've just been through, and how it's changed you, and how to put that into words.

When I was upset or angry, especially as a teenager, my father would take me and teach me how to change the brakes on a car, or clean a hunting rifle. One time I got in a screaming match with my mother, and after giving me a half-hearted beating—my father's beatings were always half-hearted, mere duty—he took me to Walmart. He didn't say a word while we wandered the aisles, just picked up a five-gallon bucket, some pickling salt, and then six heads of cabbage.

"We're going to make sauerkraut," he said, as if that settled things between us. We took the supplies to the garage, which stank of oil, and there we shredded cabbage, and kneaded in the salt until our hands were raw. I suppose, for all my father's inarticulateness, that this was his one wisdom, the knowledge of how to take my wild teenage moods and convert them to work, while he worked alongside me, ensuring that I grew up always feeling loved.

I thought about that driving home with Natalia, home from my first Iraq deployment, one hand on the wheel and one hand on her stomach, while she kept up a constant stream of chatter and I kept quiet. Happiness traveled up my arm from the life beating under my fingers, and I wondered if I would put the lessons she'd taught me into practice, if I would open up to my own child. She'd been forcing me to talk since college. More precisely, since a month into my time at college, when she let herself into my dorm room, sat on my bed, looked me straight in the eye, and said, "Why are you being so weird?" And then during the next couple of months, proceeded to make me tell her. Or would I be like my father, revealing myself best when working in silence, elbow-deep in cabbage?

"Are you even listening to me?" Natalia asked.

"I . . . driving is just a lot to take in right now."

"Uh-huh."

"In Iraq we'd drive down the center of the road, and cars would get out of our way. Every car that passes, I feel like it's gonna cross the yellow line and crash into us." I stared at that line as I drove, watched cars coming from the other direction, safely on the other side of the line, treating it the amazing way I'd treated it my whole life, as an almost magic barrier, not as something that could be crossed with a slight turn of my wrist, sending me and my wife and child headlong into the oncoming traffic. There we were, in a cost-efficient sedan picked out by my wife, the accountant, the sort of car that most of the pickups on the road could just roll right over without stopping. "Maybe we should buy a tank," I said.

Natalia rolled her eyes. "Haven't you learned by now? I can look into your head." I thought of the toddler with his "Pay Me!" hat and thought, No, you can't. And then I thought of our last conversation about our baby, and wondered if there was anything she wasn't telling me, and whether I could ask, whether it made sense to remind a pregnant woman of a reason to be worried when all we should have been thinking about was how wonderful it was to be reunited, in time for the birth, which would go fine, I was almost certain. Then she grabbed my hand on her belly, moved it lower, and said in a mock-husky voice, "Mason, do you have any idea how horny pregnancy makes you?" I swerved a bit.

Natalia grabbed me, hard.

"Oh, Jesus," I said.

"You know what the chaplain told us?" she said. "Take things slow." She did a stern, preacherly voice. "'Your soldier might not want to rush into anything. Just sitting in a hammock and relaxing might be paradise to him.' Ugh. Is that what you want? To sit in a hammock?"

We got home and had sex. It was quick and I was very nervous. She had me attend to her for a while, and then when I was ready we did it again and it was more relaxed, less mechanical, the two of us enjoying the changes in each other's bodies.

"You're being so gentle," she said, laughing. "Nobody but me knows you're such a gentle, gentle man. Slap my ass or something. You're just back from Iraq."

Natalia and I didn't date during my one year in college before I dropped out to join the army, a year I spent awkward and angry. At the time, I thought the problem was Wake Forest, the popped collars and Beamers and sons of southern aristocracy, like my roommate, Carlton, a two-hundred-pound baseball player I never really got along with. My first night there, lying in the bottom of our bunk bed, wondering what Wake would be like, I saw a stream of vomit, followed by Carlton's big body rushing down, followed by a thud. He was uninjured and unfazed—thanks, alcohol—and I spent the rest of the night cleaning up after him, never getting so much as a thank you. I guess he was just used to other people making his problems disappear. I felt out of my skin. I felt like I was somehow always violating some unwritten code, stepping over invisible lines of etiquette, revealing myself as rough, coarse, unworthy.

Natalia, on the other hand—who grew up in Springfield, North Carolina, whose father had emigrated from Medellín, Colombia, worked in a factory—seemed to feel right at home, the owner of whatever space she entered, including my dorm room. "Did you feel like this in high school?" she asked me once, and when I admitted that in some ways I had, told me, "Well then maybe the problem isn't everybody else, maybe it's you."

The first week I was home after that Iraq deployment, we spent a lot of time talking about our hopes for our daughter. What dreams we had for her. Natalia had us pray every night, not for her health or that the delivery would be painless, but for the strength to be good parents, to teach her right. Even when I'm not sure I believe in God I've always appreciated this about her, that she makes me struggle to find the words to match our hopes. That first week, though, I held back. I didn't mention any of the children I saw on my deployment to Natalia, not because she couldn't handle it, but because speaking such things would make them more real, and I wanted to pretend they didn't happen.

And then at the beginning of the second week, at the Womack hospital, after they took Natalia's blood pressure, took it again, and did an ultrasound, they told us there was something wrong.

"Are you ready to have this baby? Because you're having it today." They told us to go straight to Labor and Delivery. I don't remember who, they were all faceless.

So we told them, yes, we'd go straight to Labor and Delivery. We didn't. We went to the hospital chapel, but the chapel at Womack is small and windowless, with white walls, cheaply made chairs, and an altar that looks like it came from Ikea, a place too ugly to even suggest there might be a God.

"I want stained glass," Natalia said.

She meant JFK Memorial. Five minutes away, given traffic, which we couldn't count on around that time.

"I'm not dying yet," she said.

"This is no joke," I tell her.

"I know," she said. "But luckily I've got an Eighteen Delta with me, in case things get serious."

So we drove to JFK, and we knelt down in the pews, and we bowed our heads. I don't know what Natalia prayed, or who she prayed to, but I prayed to the Good Thief. Natalia's grandmother Inez had told me once it's good to pray to the less popular saints when things are really urgent, because the less popular saints won't be as busy.

Then we headed back, me quiet, in that other place, that focused place, and I had Natalia call Jefe to let him know what was going on, but we didn't call Natalia's parents or mine, maybe so as not to tempt fate. Traffic had picked up, and we got stuck behind a pickup that was overly timid about making a left turn. The pickup had those truck balls hanging from the back, little plastic purple nuts hanging underneath the license plate, and I resisted the urge to shout, or to ram the truck, or to do anything that might raise Natalia's blood pressure, and within about ten minutes we were back in the Womack parking lot.

When we got to Labor and Delivery, they put Natalia on Pitocin to force labor, which was the only way to cure what was wrong with her.

"I don't feel the Pitocin yet," my wife said.

"You will," said the white nurse.

"Maybe it'll be okay," said the Asian nurse. "Latinos have thicker skin, so there's less pain in labor."

The white nurse narrowed her eyes but said nothing, and when they left Natalia turned to me.

"Uh . . ." she said, "that bit about Latinos and pain . . . was that science or racism?"

I wasn't sure. Probably racism, but what good would it do right then to say so? "Science," I said.

At first the only sign of contractions was on the monitor, nothing Natalia could feel. Just anxiety and boredom. For hours. When it started we were watching *Maury*, of all things, and Natalia said, "Ooookay. I think I need you for these."

Soon she was on her hands and knees, making those noises from the birthing class videos.

Natalia held on until she couldn't take it anymore, and she asked for the epidural. They put it in and she immediately passed out. I sat and held her hand, but the nurse told me to sleep, that I'd need my energy soon enough, so I rolled up my coat for a pillow and slept on the floor. I woke around midnight to Natalia screaming, ready to push.

Natalia would push, her face clenched in pain, looking like I'd never seen her before. It was animalistic, and not beautiful, exactly. Awe-inspiring, I suppose. I was watching this titanic thing, this thing I'd been waiting for and preparing for, this thing that clearly was taking every inch of courage and endurance Natalia had, and well . . . I was standing there like an idiot, saying, "You're doing great, babe, you're doing great."

A nurse asked if I wanted to catch the baby and I went in and helped catch her and we brought her up to Natalia's chest and she lay there. She was beautiful, or seemed beautiful to us, our vision distorted by parental love. Now, looking at the pictures, it's clear she looked like a dirty little gremlin. Still. She was making small mewing noises. I wept. With the help of the nurse I cut her umbilical cord, hands shaking. She was on Natalia's chest for forty-five minutes. We sang to her. We recited RinRin Renacuajo, a fairy tale my mother-in-law had told me to memorize. Before they took her away to the NICU, and Natalia went to sleep, they asked us her name, and we told them it was Inez.

Natalia woke me around 2:30 a.m. "I'm in a lot of pain," she said.

The nurse on duty, a super-sweet Texan named Jacklyn, who'd worked in ER beforehand, examined Natalia, pressing here and there on her stomach until Natalia cried out. There was a gush of blood. Jacklyn's hand came up bloody. And then the lights came on and there were people rushing around. I stood by Natalia's head, holding her hand.

"I'm going to scrape your uterus," a female doctor said, "and it's gonna hurt." And she put her hand up my wife's vagina as Natalia repeated, over and over when not screaming, "Please stop, please stop. Please, please, please stop."

When she withdrew her hand, a lot more blood came out. I'm a medic, you'd think I would be able to handle a thing like this. But I didn't know much of anything about labor complications, so I didn't have any base of knowledge that would let me categorize and file away whatever I was seeing, and besides, even if I did, this was my wife. I couldn't just separate out the body in front of me, a physical object in need of mechanical fixes, from the presence of Natalia in pain. She was losing a lot of blood. A lot for a man, and my wife is a small woman.

It didn't just come out in a stream. There were chunks, failed clots. All this, it was later explained, was the fault of the magnesium. I didn't know that. All I knew was that I'd seen major blood loss before, even from men I've loved, but it had never felt like this. Out of the corner of my eye I saw my wife looking at me, maybe in the hope I'd let her know it was all okay, but I couldn't stop staring at the bloody mess between her legs and spilling over the sides of the bed. The pool of it, filled with clumps of clot.

They put in an IV, fumbling a bit. I could have done it better and wanted to offer, wanted to take charge, but instead I stroked her hair, tried to stay out of their way, to not become another issue the doctors would have to deal with. Natalia was looking at me strangely. I smiled at her.

"You're all right, babe," I said.

They gave her a transfusion. The doctor explained in a very authoritative, calm way that it was okay. "Look around, there's not a million people running around doing things right now," she said. It was true. Where did they go?

"That means you'll be okay. This is serious but totally normal. The magnesium is stopping your uterus from contracting so we're going to put you back on Pitocin." Then it was over, and Natalia fell asleep and so did I.

The next morning, I went to see my daughter in the NICU. I sang to her, and I wept. I don't know why. It was still hard to conceptualize this small wrinkled thing as my daughter, or myself as a father. I wouldn't feel like a father for some time, not until I'd spent time fathering—changing diapers, feeding her, reading to her, leaving her for training and then missing her. But even in the strangeness of it all there were physical things that made sense, that felt natural and right. Cuddling her in my arms, holding her on my chest, singing softly to her. It still surprises me how physical an experience it is, having a baby. Babies need contact and you, as the parent, need it, too.

"Can you imagine if we'd had a birth like this a hundred years ago?" Natalia asked me when I came back.

"You'd have died," I said. "You'd have died and then I'd have been sad for the rest of my life."

And that was the birth of my child.

4

JUAN PABLO 2015–2016

The next morning I sit behind General Cabrales in the National Capitol as he briefs the representatives in the Second Commission on the coming change in force posture. "All assuming the nation votes yes," he adds. Of course, it's a foregone conclusion that they will. Every bit of polling says the yes vote is the only outcome. Peace is inevitable. It's an odd thing for a military man to concede.

Afterward, Colonel Carlosama pulls me aside and asks if I know or have had any dealings with Representative Ana Maria de Salva.

"She wants to have lunch with you. You, specifically. By name."

"I don't know her, sir," I say, though I remember seeing her basic information on the handout detailing the members of the Second Commission.

"Liberal Party, but keeps her distance from President Santos. Possibly not a friendly lunch. The general is curious what she wants, so make a note of what she bites down on."

Strange. And troubling. Why me, and not the general, or at least Colonel Carlosama?

He hands me a piece of paper with an address. "La Hacienda. If it's the place I think, it has terrible food. At one."

"One? Sir, I'll miss the—"

"Afternoon session. Yes, lucky you." He looks down the corridors of the Capitol building, at the men and women hustling by, pretending they're deciding the fate of the nation, when it is really decided by men like us. Or if not decided, caused by men like us.

"She's from Norte de Santander," he says. Immediately I think of my conversation with Mason about the Mil Jesúses and Operation Agamemnon, and I worry that I know what this meeting will be about.

"Careful," he adds. "The women from that department . . . they're tough."

I have enough time before lunch to check in with Captain Maloof, the smart young officer who'd given us our briefing on the new members of the Second Commission and, typical of an eager new captain briefing a general, had clearly gone far deeper in his research than necessary.

"De Salva," he says, smiling. "She's interesting." Which is not what I wanted to hear. And he rattles on about·her "low funds" fortune and her "eccentric" voting record, how she runs Chiva buses stocked with liquor to bring people to the polls on election days, how she modernized her gambling operation after Law 643 made the whole thing legal, how she used to drive a bus. Each piece of information is more useless than the last.

"Okay. She's unusual. Is she corrupt?" I say brusquely, annoyed I have to spell it out.

"Oh," he says, surprised. "No, not at all, I don't think."

"Son of a bitch," I say. If she were corrupt, I'd have a better sense of how to handle her.

The restaurant is a cartoon version of a finca, with white stucco walls and framed portraits of Colombian expressions like, "You're going to teach your father to make kids?" "When you're going I'm coming," and "The devil knows more through his age than through being the devil." I'm not sure whether the restaurant is targeted toward nostalgic Colombians or foolish tourists, but whatever the marketing strategy, neither group has shown up. I'm the only customer.

Exactly at one, Ana Maria de Salva walks in. She's a strong-featured woman with straight black hair, eyes of a brown so dark the iris drowns the pupil, high cheekbones, and a haughty manner you wouldn't expect from someone with her peasant background. I stand up to greet her, but she clucks at me in a way that makes me feel I'm being scolded by my mother.

"Good," she says, looking around at the empty restaurant.

She sits and buries herself in the menu, a colorful array of pictures of typical fare—bandeja and church empanadas and lentil soup. I feel I should say something.

"Is anything good here?" I ask.

"This is the worst restaurant within a mile of the Capitol," she says. "Nothing is good."

When the waiter comes, de Salva orders sancocho and I order the steak. It's hard to ruin a steak. "Just warm it," I say. And then for some reason I repeat the instructions I once heard an American soldier give in a restaurant near Tres Esquinas. "I want it to moo."

When the waiter leaves, de Salva looks at me disapprovingly. "I want it to moo? Is that supposed to impress me? I'd think a military man would prove his courage combating guerrilla, not bacteria."

"I've fought my share of both."

"Man discovered fire tens of thousands of years ago, and it has worked out well for him. Maybe you should take advantage of the technology."

"You Bogotános and your modern ways," I say.

"I am not, and will never be, a Bogotáno."

There's not much to say to that, and when our food arrives she stares at me intently, judgmentally, as I pick up knife and fork, cut into my steak, and the juices run.

"Disgusting," she says, as I pop a piece of steak in my mouth and do my best to enjoy it.

She slurps her soup, makes a face, and slurps some more. And then she sits up straight.

"I heard you had a meeting with a lawyer from Cúcuta last week."

I become very still. How does de Salva know about the meeting? It's possible she's connected to the Mil Jesúses, too. I can't be the only person in this rotten city they've reached out to.

She slurps more soup.

"A loathsome man," she says. "With a loathsome list of clients. And when I heard that a senior officer in the special forces was meeting with this man, I thought to myself, why?"

"I've had a variety of meetings while here in the Capitol," I say. "Are you asking in relation to your duties as a member of the Second Commission?"

The lawyer from Cúcuta, loathsome or not, arranged for us to get some rather key pieces of intelligence leading to the El Alemán raid. Which was a success, and a demonstration of how effective the army could be if the Agamemnon mission could be transferred over from the police.

She snorts. "No. I am asking as a representative of Norte de Santander. Which, I'm sure, means nothing to you. Most of us here"—she waves a hand in the general direction of the National Capitol—"don't really *represent*, do we?"

I'm not sure what she means.

"You're from Antioquia, yes?" she says. "That department has seventeen representatives. Seventeen! You probably don't even know who they are."

She cocks her head, eyes me aslant. I think of a bird examining a beetle it's about to snap into its beak.

"I usually figure their party is more important than their department." When I vote, I vote by the party list.

"Yes. Party over department every time. Which means elites in Bogotá decide what is best for people in Tibú. And elites in Bogotá don't care about the people of Tibú, do they?"

I say nothing. According to Maloof, this woman holds enough personal power in her very small department that she can do whatever she wants and still be on the party list. That makes her unpredictable.

"I don't come from the same twenty families as everybody else here. I don't care about them, I don't care about what they want, I only care about the people. I am a representative who *represents*."

Said that way, it sounds like a good thing, but Norte de Santander is complicated, a place where the state often has little presence, provides few services, little order, little ability even to adjudicate basic legal disputes over land and contracts. Where the economy sometimes owes more to smuggling goods from Venezuela and drugs and illegal mining than to anything coming from the central government. What would a true and honest representative of such a place look like?

"That's very good," I say.

She sits back and considers me for a moment, then nods. "I was a bus driver, you know, when I started running the chance."

I nod and fold my hands together, trying to look relaxed, ready to be told a story. She smiles.

"One day, five paras walk onto my bus without paying, they take out guns and wave them at the crowd. Their leader starts walking the aisles while one of his men keeps a pistol resting on my shoulder. He starts telling me I'm pretty, and that pretty girls should do what they're told, and stay calm. Now, listen. Do you think I was scared?"

"No."

"Idiot. Of course I was scared. But I was angry, too. This was my bus, my passengers. The leader walks the aisles, and he's got a piece of paper in his hand, and he reads out two names. 'Albeiro García Camargo. Ciro

Muñez.' I will never forget the names. And Albeiro and Ciro get up. I knew them by sight. They had taken my bus every day for months. Polite. I never had a conversation with either of them. I didn't know their names until that day. And they didn't say anything as they stood up, walked down the aisle, walked past me, and left the bus. The leader of the paras was the last to leave, and he handed me a twenty-thousand note, and smiled a beautiful, horrible smile at me. Two days later the police found Albeiro and Ciro, their bodies wrapped in barbed wire in the trunk of a car. They had difficulty getting them out. It was incredible, people said, how small the space where they fit two grown men."

"I'm sorry," I say.

"Back then, I was angry at the paras. But I'm older now. I think of them, and I think, young boys with guns. Even their leader was no more than a child. You know what makes me angry now? Thinking about the list. Let's talk about the list. Who gave them the list? Who told them who to kill?"

Usually, it would have been power brokers in the town. Businessmen, mayors, or even police and local army units pointing out the subversives, the guerrillas, the union leaders, criminals, leftists, drug addicts, and undesirables. And that's what I tell her.

"Yes." She looks away for a second, seemingly lost in thought, then faces me again with a blank expression on her face. "Over the past decade, we killed sixty-five leaders in the FARC and seven leaders in the ELN. Last year the whole world was informed by *The Washington Post* that we did this with the help of the Americans. They help us make *our* list. But with a treaty coming, I look at our list and I think to myself, if this is breakfast, what will we be served for lunch?"

Ah. I see. Agamemnon is lunch. Deadly strikes like the El Alemán raid, many of them likely to happen in her department. She knows it, and so do I. Does she want to stop the military taking over Agamemnon? That would be bad for the country. Without the Americans providing us aid, the military won't be able to maintain its air assault capabilities.

Without air assault capabilities, we don't have the ability to project power around the country. Without a war, we don't have an excuse for American aid. So now, with the war supposedly ending, we need a new campaign. I unfold my hands and study them. This is delicate.

"The method we used against the FARC," I say, "brought their leadership to the negotiating table. It brought peace."

"Peace. Yes. But the FARC was a military force. What happens when we put the names of Colombian citizens on a list and then"—she waves her hands—"like magic, they cease to be a problem because they cease to exist."

"Colombian citizens?" I say. "Or gangsters? I would prefer we don't become El Salvador, with its gangs."

"And I would prefer we don't become El Salvador, with its death squads," she says, "Or like America, with its fancy death squads."

"I'm sure the various gangs in Norte de Santander would be very happy to hear you say that."

She stares at me silently, as if daring me to take my words back. I keep my expression neutral.

"I know the leader of Los Mil Jesúses," she eventually says. "His real name."

That surprises me.

"Jefferson Paúl López Quesada. Used to be in the paramilitaries. I knew him then. He's a crazy man. Mischievous and evil and charming. Used to be handsome, in an ugly way. I have heard he's gotten fat."

"Heard from who?"

She dips her finger in her water glass. "All my life, we have had little groups." She taps her finger on the wooden table, leaving a little dot of water. "FARC here." She taps it again, next to the first dot, and keeps tapping, creating little dots of water in the space between us. "Paras here. Police here. Narcos here. Peasant union here. And they've learned to live with each other. They have to. Drugs growing in one place, laboratories in another, shipment routes everywhere. There's too much money at stake not to cooperate, so they've learned to operate like little countries, not getting too big, not causing so much violence that the police feel like they need to go in. But of course some countries are good little countries, like Switzerland, or Chile, and they maintain order, punish the bad, build a little infrastructure, even impose taxes. And some are annoying and dysfunctional little countries, like Argentina. And then there are your Urabeños, your Saddam Husseins." She lifts up her water glass, and starts carefully pouring a thin stream of water, forming a pool that spreads and conquers the other dots.

She looks sadly at the table in front of us, holding her water glass over the small puddle surrounded by a few dots of water. It's not a bad demonstration of ink-spot theory, I think, or whatever you might call the criminal gang variant of ink spot.

"Too big. Men always want to be too big. I know I can't stop the army from moving in. But if you're only going to kill the leadership so Los Mil Jesúses can move into the vacuum . . ."

She flips the water glass upside down, dumping the water on the table.

"Shit!" I say, pushing back from the table as the water spills everywhere. There's water on my pants. I breathe slowly to calm myself as de Salva removes the wet napkin from across her mostly dry lap. She's acting a fool, keeping me off balance with these antics, but I know that anyone who has risen up the way she has is a very serious person. I take my napkin and begin mopping up the water, putting things back in order.

"Please," I say, "enough. What do you want?"

"I can make it hard for you," she says. "You know, I have a friend at *Semana* who covered the Soacha murders. Imagine if the press found out that you were linked to neoparamilitary groups. Or perhaps you don't have to imagine. You've seen them go after your family before. Your daughter can have the same experience you did. Reading her father's shame in the press. What's your daughter's name? Valencia?"

My first impulse is to reach across the table and slap her face. I resist. My second impulse is to say something absurd, out of a telenovela— *Say my daughter's name again and I'll cut that filthy tongue from your mouth*—but I'm not stupid. And neither is she.

I sigh, to let her know I have no time for threats. "You're overplaying your hand," I say. "This is unnecessary. This is silly."

She smiles. "I know, when you move in there must be winners and losers. The Urabeños will lose, and that is fine. But I want you to know you're working with a very dangerous, unstable criminal. The kind who creates chaos. If the Urabeños are Saddam Hussein's Iraq, then Jefferson and his Mil Jesúses are ISIS. You understand?"

I keep my face very still. "Of course," I say. "*If* the army takes over Agamemnon, then clearly, I will keep you informed of any developments related to your department. *And* I will be very interested in any information you have that could help shape operations."

She settles back into her chair.

"Good," she says. "I don't just want to know how you will manage the Urabeños. I want to know how you will manage Los Mil Jesúses."

When I emerge into the sunlight, it's only a quarter to two. The meal went fast, and now I have time to think about what to tell General Cabrales, and more importantly, what not to tell him.

I am a representative who represents, de Salva had said. And for all the times I've found myself in godforsaken villages and towns where the heart of the people pumped red, socialist blood, it has never occurred to me before that representing your people and your state might be different things. To do what I do, you must accept that the true will of the people aligns with whatever the central government believes. So if the people side with the despotism promised by the FARC and reject democratic freedom, then they must be forced to be free.

Still, if you consider Colombia a democracy, which I do, then

Representative de Salva represents a problem. The state, it is true, is a Leviathan whose body is structured by institutions and laws and markets and churches, but at the cellular level the Leviathan's body is composed of nothing more than individual people. And no Leviathan is blessed with smooth skin, an unblemished body that glides soundlessly through the waters of the world. No Leviathan truly holds the monopoly on violence, which is the only reason it exists.

So it must be admitted that though most of the people in our Leviathan are cells in healthy organs—pumping blood, processing oxygen—some are cells in cancerous tumors, or in rotted flesh. This makes them no different from the people in any other Leviathan, whatever the pretensions of your Denmarks and your Swedens, from whom we get excellent weaponry. So what does it mean to represent a department riddled with such tumors, such rot, sitting on a fault line between paras and guerrilla and bandits who have provided the only structure the people of your department have ever known, even if that structure is the wildly expanding structure of a cancer? What would a true and honest representative of such a place look like? A representative of the maggots and the worms, of the warm lifeblood, of the clean and the putrid flesh, none of which has any desire to be devoured? I suppose it'd look like Ana Maria de Salva. That's what she wants me to believe. But even if it's true, there's nothing to be proud of in representing such a people.

I'll check out her information, but I will tell General Cabrales nothing. Until I know more, there's no point. I tell myself that despite her threats she can be an asset. I tell myself that despite her threats she has given me valuable information. I tell myself there's no reason for concern. And then, instead of heading back to work, or calling Maloof to demand he dig deeper, or calling our 2 to pass on the information about the Jesúses, I open my phone and call my daughter.

5

N obody likes deploying while their wife is stuck at home with a newborn. You feel like a shitty father, of course. You'll be overseas, getting decent sleep while your wife is holding down the fort. But there was more to it than that. A few years earlier, it was easy to drop out of college, join the army, and break only my parents' hearts. Now I had to nail myself down, become a stable thing for this tiny creature to depend on. Be this kind of man—more husband than lover, more father than killer. Be this kind of soldier—more professional than warrior, more Christian than samurai. And as I started to find those definitions for myself, it made it easier to see the sickness infecting Special Forces, a sickness at odds with the very core of who I was becoming.

The deployment wasn't even a combat deployment, wasn't to Iraq or Afghanistan but to Colombia. A training mission for the Lanceros, this high-speed commando unit which had been stood up specifically for conducting raids on communist guerrilla compounds deep in the Andean jungles. It was, as Ocho would say, a badass unit with a badass mission. But we weren't allowed to take part in any of that. Just there to train, so no combat patrols, no raids, no possibility of any kind of action where we might get shot at and, therefore, have the right and the burden and the thrill of shooting back.

One time Ocho caught me flipping through some baby photos Natalia had sent me, a dopey smile on my face. He said, "Don't get soft on me, maricón."

"Don't you miss your kids?" I said.

"First one is special. I held mine forever. But then I started losing my boners."

"What?"

"It's true, man. You spend too much time holding babies and shit, your testosterone goes down. It's science, bitch. I had to go back to the gym, do lots of legs, get my shit hard."

Ocho was always a wealth of medical information.

"It's just like this fucking deployment," he said. "Drills, training patrols, hand-holding Lanceros who definitely don't need it. By the end of this . . ." He shook his head.

"We're all going to lose our boners?"

Ocho threw up his hands and shot me a look as if to say, Yeah, obviously.

Perhaps we'd have felt better about the mission if it weren't for the fact that our Iraq stories were constantly getting one-upped by the Colombians. One of the Lancero NCOs told me about guarding an oil pipeline close to the Venezuelan border. The ELN would attack all the time. They were never trying to shut it down, which would have destroyed the local economy. They'd attack it a little bit, get some publicity, some credibility to secure bribes from contractors and politicians, and some work for local people who'd be sent out to fix the minor damages they inflicted. The locals would repair the pipe, the guerrillas would let the oil flow for a bit and bring in money, and then they'd do it again.

"You know the oil spill of the *Exxon Valdez*?" he asked me. "When I was there, they spilled ten times that amount. We had six miles of pipe to protect, all of it in heavy jungle. The guerrilla hid in the trees, like monkeys. Quiet jungle, and then gunshots, grenades dropping down. Sometimes they would fill hundred-pound canisters, half with chemicals and half with human shit. My men would get burns from the chemicals, and then the shit would infect the wounds. City people do not know what we went through so they can fill up their cars."

What do you say to that? It felt a bit like hanging out at your home-town's local VFW and getting owned by some Vietnam vet, except these guys were our age or younger. We had nothing to compare with this. And part of the whole satisfaction of joining Special Forces is in ascending to a higher level of badassery. You start out as a civilian, then join the army and earn a little more respect. The next step is going in-fantry or, in my case, the Rangers, which is a step higher than that. And then there's Special Forces, above which is only CAG and DEV-GRU and probably some super-secret squirrel units only the president knows about. And if you're SF, you're supposedly a super-soldier. You go overseas, you work with indigs who are supposed to look up to you, to want to *be* you, while you share with them a camaraderie mixed with a bit of contempt. Indigs are never supposed to be that good—especially not in Afghanistan, where we didn't even respect the non-U.S. NATO troops, where the running joke was that the acronym ISAF might as well stand for I Suck At Fighting.

In Afghanistan, we'd be sneering at ANCOP, screaming, "Get in the fucking dirt! Low crawl or a bullet's gonna blow out your fucking brains! You think we're telling you to do this shit because we like seeing you in the dirt? We're telling you this shit so you don't fucking die!"

In Colombia—not so much. The Colombians are good. They win the Latin American special ops competition every year. They generally didn't have to be berated. It wasn't that they were better than us. We had more schooling, more training, better training, for the most part. As a medic, I had skills they couldn't touch, our weapons sergeants knew far more guns far better than them because they had far more opportunities to train on a wider variety of weapon systems. We had broader capabilities, and way cooler toys. But as soldiers, they weren't beneath us. They'd been through some tough shit. Tougher shit, sometimes.

Toward the end of the training, the Lanceros were heading out to Macarena to do COIN ops, a mission that wasn't dangerous but just dangerous enough that at the last minute we got the word we weren't allowed to go with them, which is when Ocho's shit hit the fan.

"They think we're faggots," he yelled at Jefe in Spanish. "Because we're acting like faggots. How am I supposed to train a son of a bitch when I can't share risk with him?"

Jefe just raised an eyebrow.

"Training up foreign troops to protect their citizens so we don't have to, that's the whole reason Special Forces was created in the first place. De oppresso liber."

It wasn't Jefe at his most inspiring. The definition of foreign internal defense, straight from army manuals, plus the SF motto, was not going to convince a bunch of soldiers that they weren't bored. "Man, Jefe," Ocho said. "You're more into FID than anybody I know."

Jefe stared Ocho down, and Ocho lowered his eyes. Jefe was the first team sergeant I'd ever had. When a team leader is good, they're something of a father figure, and Jefe was very, very good. Humility matched by flawless technical proficiency. The kind of man an aura grows around. I'd never seen anyone try, in any way, to take even a little of the air out of his tires.

"Yeah," Jefe said, "that's what's on the fucking poster."

Ocho looked at me.

"What do you think?" he said.

I looked at Jefe, and at Ocho, not sure exactly what was going on. Technically, Jefe was right. SF wasn't supposed to be just a smash things unit. I'd had that in Ranger Battalion. Ranger Battalion is an eight-hundred-pound gorilla. Ranger Battalion is *supposed* to be an eight-hundred-pound gorilla. It's the reason I left. I was done being part of a crazy collection of angry individuals ready to fuck things up. I wanted to be a bit more than your average eight-hundred-pound gorilla. And SF is an eight-hundred-pound gorilla that can dance ballet.

But I owed Ocho loyalty, too. And I wanted to defuse things.

"I just had a kid," I said. "An easy deployment, it's not so bad."

As we headed out, Ocho turned to me. "Man, when I joined Seventh Group, Colombia was the fucking legend," he said. "All the old heads talking 'bout chasing Pablo Escobar and fucking hot Colombian bitches." He shrugged. "Times change."

Ocho was hardly the only guy who hated being in Colombia. The rest of 7th Group were cycling in and out of Afghanistan, living far from the flagpole, getting into gnarly firefights, dominating their enemy, and then going back to do it again. They'd sit with their Afghan counterpart (if there even was one), sip chai, look at a wall map, and say, "Let's go to Mangritay. There's always good hunting in Mangritay." And then they'd load up the trucks, head out, stumble into a few firefights, come back, rest up, pick another spot on the map, and do the same thing again. Rinse, repeat, count the bodies. Pure war. No one was on the hook for securing a district, or a province, let alone the country. If the gunfight was a success, you were a success. Meanwhile, we were hand-holding indigs an ocean away from the real war.

If Jefe had just bitched along with everyone else, it would have been fine. But he wanted us to *like* the mission. He'd tell Ocho and the rest to shut up when they got on rants about how we were wasting our time, or he'd launch into speeches about Pappy Shelton, who'd trained up the Bolivian Ranger team that killed Che Guevara.

"While everybody else was in Vietnam, getting in badass gunfights and losing the war, Pappy was doing boring training work and winning the war against the most badass commie guerrilla . . ."

"Yeah, yeah," Ocho said. "We all know about Pappy Shelton." He turned to the room. "His brothers are dying fighting Viet Cong, and what does that bitch do? Run to Bolivia."

When a few guys chuckled, Jefe's face went purple. He looked around the room, his eyes eventually resting on me. An ODA team is supposed to be one cohesive unit, one collective mind. It's not supposed to be a place where you have to choose sides between your senior medic and your team chief.

Later that night, Jefe caught me alone, and told me in that quiet way of his, "You know I like getting it as much as anybody. But I've seen too many people blown up or killed in this fucking job to have any patience for that hard-guy bullshit."

I wasn't sure whether he was right, or going soft.

The training itself was otherwise fine, straightforward—room clearing, shooting moving targets, raids, patrolling, specialized breakouts like me and Ocho working with the medics. Which, given that it was Ocho, meant some really specialized training.

One of the Colombian medics had nine kids, and Ocho was like, "That's nine too many."

"You have four kids," I said.

"Yeah," he said. "But I don't care about them that much."

The guy's wife was a conservative Catholic, as in no-birth-control conservative, and since the guy didn't want any more he let Ocho talk him into letting him do an off-the-books, tabletop vasectomy.

"It's a really simple operation," Ocho said when I complained. "It's good training. And it's good for developing trust. If he lets me all up in his balls, that means we've developed a true cross-cultural bond."

Snip-snip. The operation was a success, and it did build a weird kind of camaraderie. Ocho was always better at that team-building stuff than I was.

Meanwhile, our team was decomposing. Things finally blew up into open insubordination when Jefe canceled a patrol we were supposed to take with a Colombian unit. Intel had just raised the threat level in the region, and so Jefe didn't want to risk the chance we'd get into a firefight.

"Fucking coward," Ocho muttered when Jefe broke the news.

The room got still.

"You want to go back and rethink that shit, Ocho?" Jefe said calmly.

"I'm not asking to go on a raid. Just one piddly-dick patrol where there's a least a *chance*, a little fucking chance . . ."

"This is a no-combat mission."

"No shit."

Ocho turned to me.

"When I joined the army," he said, "they taught me how to fire a machine gun. And they said, Ocho, you motherfucker, you don't fire this shit like Rambo, holding on to the trigger until the gun overheats and you burn the barrel like some asshole. You fire in three-to-five-second bursts. So hold the trigger down only as long as it takes to say 'Die, commie, die!' Well you know how many commies I've shot since then? None! I've shot terrorists. I've shot hajjis. But not a single goddamn commie. And guess what, Jefe? There's commies probably a half-hour helicopter ride—"

"Ocho. You sound like a fucking SEAL. Shut up."

"I like these guys. We're friends, Jefe. We're boys. I want to fight with them." It sounded so sad, the way he said it.

"Combat eventually means casualties. This is a no-casualties mission."

"If I die, high on coke, driving two hundred miles per hour, flipping a Maserati, that's a good death. Dying fighting commies? That's a bad-ass death."

"Yeah, well, your death isn't worth anything here."

Ocho threw up his hands.

"Americans die in Colombia, then Congress starts looking at all the money we're spending here and wondering if it's worth it. And we're winning here, you understand?"

"*They're* winning here," Ocho said. "We're not doing shit."

"Exactly, you fucking idiot," Jefe said. "*They're* winning. Which means it's sustainable. Which is the point of our job. You want to die for your country, do it somewhere else. Here, your death is worthless."

Ocho turned to me. "Mason. What do you think?"

A year ago, I'd definitely have agreed with him. A part of my heart agreed, infected by the sickness, this itching desire to leave behind the mission our whole unit was centered around—training indig forces—so we could get into combat and feel like we were really doing something, indulging fantasies of being the warriors we believed ourselves to be, even if in a failing war without anything close to a coherent strategy that could justify the lives we might lose and the lives we might take. But there was another part that was steadily becoming stronger.

"Most of Natalia's relatives live in Medellín," I said. "Ten years ago, we would never have visited them because it was too dangerous to be worth it. I like being able to tell my daughter people like me are why she can visit her aunts and uncles and cousins."

Ocho gave me a look of such disappointment. I knew I'd lowered myself in the opinion of the rest of the team. "Yeah, all right," he said, "fine. But if our next deployment is to Mexico or some shit, I expect to be fucking El Chapo in the ass."

"I'll make a note of that," Jefe said.

The joke of it all is that now, looking back, I can see that the Latin American deployments were the only ones where we were building anything. But how could we know that at the time? It felt like we were just spinning our wheels, while the guys in Afghanistan were doing the real work, a serious mission with a real gunfight every once in a while. Or more than every once in a while.

6

JUAN PABLO 2015–2016

My colleagues thought it was insane that I would send my daughter to university at Nacional. Yes, it was a good university. A great university. But it was riddled with guerrilla cells. A center for knowledge somehow incapable of grasping the most obvious fact in history—that communism is a religion for brutal slaves. Why not send her to Los Andes, or Externado? Not simply her physical safety, but the safety of her soul was at risk. Carlos Pizarro Leongómez, the son of an admiral who went to Nacional and joined the guerrilla, was mentioned more than once. Even if she wasn't fully converted, they told me, the professors there would teach her ways to hate me.

I responded confidently, arrogantly, and worse, idealistically. I told them I was sending her to Nacional *because* of the guerrillas. Nacional, this jewel of the nation's public university system. Harder to get into than the schools my fellow officers were sending their children to, and much cheaper, a factor I couldn't ignore. But still. One of our country's best schools. And I am supposed to cede this territory? Me? A man who has fought and bled for centimeters of worthless jungle, I just give up 1,214,056 square meters of downtown Bogotá to the enemy? No. This is my country. It will be my daughter's university. I will prepare her for the education to come, and make her invincible.

It began with a book. A true jungle fighter takes the enemy's strengths and turns them to his advantage, so when she was applying to university I took her to campus. I came in civilian clothes, since military dress would do nothing more than make her a target. She came wearing a necklace with a cross around her neck. An odd choice, I thought at the time. Perhaps the influence of her mother.

In the center of the university is a large plaza dominated by the giant white wall of the school auditorium, upon which is painted, several stories high, the image of the Argentine communist revolutionary Che Guevara. The plaza's proper name is Plaza Santander, named after the Colombian general, president, and "Man of the Laws," who fought for his country's freedom from Spain. Of course, no one calls it the Plaza Santander. All the students know it as Plaza Che, honoring a man who never fought for Colombia, or for rule of law, or for freedom.

We went straight to the plaza and we stood before the mural. There was Che's face. Che as an icon, his hair like a halo, his eyes sorrowful like the eyes of Christ, looking not at the reality of the world but at his utopia, where none but the free suffered, and all the rest obeyed. And I laughed. I let her see me laugh. I wanted her to know I thought he was a clown, not a devil. Devils have dignity. And then I handed her the book.

"Che Guevara. *Guerrilla Warfare*," she said, reading the cover, which displayed the same iconic Alberto Korda photograph the graffiti artist had used for his mural. It was my old, dog-eared copy from my student days, bound together with a copy of Che's Cuba diaries. She looked up at the sorrowful, proud eyes above us.

"I want you to read this book," I said. "And tell me how to win a revolution."

She nodded gravely.

I left her there to explore the campus and went home delighted with myself. Cuban propaganda, of all things, would keep her safe.

That night, as Valencia was holed up in her room reading, I wondered what she was making of the work, with its yellow pages and its margins filled with notes I'd scribbled as a young man, naively imagining I was preparing myself for life in the army. I'd thought I was readying myself to reverse engineer Che's tactics to crush my nation's enemies. Flipping open the book the night before, I'd seen an old note of mine in the margin of the section on War Industry, next to where Che writes, "There are two fundamental industries, one of which is the manufacture of shoes." There, in pencil, I'd written "Ah ha!" Who knows what I thought I'd learned.

It embarrasses me to admit it, but the book inspired me. The story it tells, through a series of dry tactical lessons, is a heroic one. Start with a small, dedicated group in the countryside. You need only thirty to fifty men—Castro had only had twelve who made it to the Sierra Maestra—but they must be devoted, incorruptible, their moral character vastly outshining the venal brutality of their enemy. They must hide in the wildest, most inaccessible places, forming a nucleus, a vanguard, a focus of revolutionary activity. With no industrial capacity, no ability to produce weapons or ammunition, the guerrilla band must take these from the enemy himself. As they strike blow after blow, slowly a few peasants will join and the movement will gain strength. The guerrilla band will become more audacious, their very audacity will inspire the people, revolutionizing them. As the people revolutionize, the guerrilleros will make more contact with the people of the zone, and the less isolated the guerrilla band will become. Soon, the true war for the state will begin, though the guerrilla's heroism will already have won the struggle for the soul of the nation. What a difference thirty men can make as long as they are men who are pure of heart, saintly in conduct, and fearless in war. Forget the communist ideology, just think of the thirty men changing the world with their virtue. What soldier wouldn't want to believe in such a thing?

I felt only a slight nervousness. Che's notes, if she read them correctly, would provide the first hints of the truth behind the legend. Before his death, Che had many pursuers. The CIA. The Bolivian government. American Special Forces. But *Guerrilla Warfare* reveals the true killer—Che himself. A man so enchained by his own mythology that he not only spouted, but actually practiced, tactics directly at odds with the real story of what happened when Castro's little band of guerrilleros arrived at Las Coloradas Beach in December 1956, ready to ignite the countryside in revolution.

"He's actually quite heroic," Valencia said. "I didn't expect that."

I almost choked.

"Who?" Sofia said.

We were at dinner, Sofia had made one of my favorite dishes, tilapia Veracruz. The sun was setting gently in the west, and through the window to my right I could see long, thin clouds blushing as they feathered over Monserrate. Everything was harmonious and orderly. Except my daughter's mind.

"Che Guevara," Valencia said.

Now it was Sofia's turn to choke.

"Papa gave me his diaries."

Sofia raised one manicured eyebrow. "To prepare you for school?"

"Yes." Of course. She'd skimmed the dry tactics, but lingered on the drama of the diaries.

"How . . ." I said, trying to find my footing. "Why . . . how were they heroic?"

The book I had given her did not describe heroes, but an incompetent, hurried group of eighty men, crouched together in a leaky boat with bad engines, arriving on the island late, two days after the futile Santiago de

Cuba uprising they were supposed to take part in, and arriving in the wrong place, a swampland where the unseasoned and undisciplined revolutionaries lost almost all their equipment as they trudged through saltwater swamps, developing open blisters and fungal infections on their tender feet. They were like nothing out of *Guerrilla Warfare.* They were filthy. They lost medical supplies and backpacks to the swamp. They let their ammunition get wet. And then, like idiots, they grabbed sugarcane from a nearby field as they marched and then tossed the cane peelings and bagasse behind them, leaving a trail a blind man could have followed.

"They make landfall, and they're ambushed at Alegría de Pío—"

"It was *not* an ambush," I said. "In an ambush, the attacking force selects the site ahead of time. They prepare the kill zone, wait for the enemy to pass . . ."

"Yes, sorry, Papá."

". . . and then slaughter them with immediate, heavy, and accurate fire."

"I . . ."

"A well-executed ambush is an act of premeditated murder and terrorism against strangers. In a well-executed ambush, with the right planning and surprise, the victims aren't killed in a fair fight."

"I just meant that it's truly incredible . . ."

"They don't have the chance to fight at all. That was not what happened. Che didn't walk into a trap. He was sitting around, eating a sausage—"

This is true. By daybreak, the men were begging for rest. Their equally lazy commanders permitted them to sleep through the morning hours, after which they looked up to the heavens and saw military aircraft circling above. Even then, they continued peacefully eating sugarcane as the planes circled. Imagine it—you've come to work revolution and, threatened by military aircraft seeking your death, you decide to suck on sugarcane like a child.

As the planes flew lower and slower, Che didn't eat sugarcane. He shoved sausage into his mouth. The first shots rang out. One frightened comrade dropped a box of ammunition. A fat guerrillero tried to hide behind a single stalk of sugarcane. Another kept calling absurdly for silence amid the gunfire. Che himself faced a question—grab a backpack of medicine or a case of ammunition. In his diary, Che described it as an existential choice between his life as a doctor or as a fighter. He grabbed the ammo, and was promptly shot in the chest. When another guerrillero, shot through the lungs, asked the brave Che, his doctor, for help, Che admits he did nothing for the man, telling him, "indifferently," that he'd been shot, too.

Most were killed. The few who managed to crawl away walked until the darkness became too deep to continue, and then they huddled together like dogs and slept, starving and thirsty, a bloody feast for mosquitoes.

"But they started with eighty-two men," my daughter continues, "and right away sixty were killed or captured. And they kept going. Even though Che was shot. Even though he thought he was going to die."

"That impresses you? Trust me, it's not particularly difficult to get shot through the chest if you're a moron in a war zone."

After dinner, I grabbed Jorge Domínguez's history of Cuba from my shelf and dropped it on Valencia's desk with a thud. For added measure, I brought out Che's Bolivian diaries and then, as an afterthought, a first edition of the African diaries, the ones with the introduction from none other than Colombia's native literary genius and political idiot, Gabriel García Márquez. Finally, I handed her a stapled-together report from 1967, one of the CIA's Latin America documents that had been declassified in the '90s and which, in ways that were both revelatory and infuriating, made it clear why the CIA was blindly happy to let Che's diaries loose into the world. In its own way, it was as perfect an example of deliberate ignorance as Che's *Guerrilla Warfare*. As I left the room, I told her what to read, and in what order.

She was still reading Che's way, seeing this idiocy as their baptism, a proof of their hardiness, their ability to regroup and forge a new rebel army out of sheer will. That's why in *Guerrilla Warfare* Che champions self-sufficiency of an extreme sort. The guerrilla band must live off the land, like he did, desperate and isolated but creating revolutionary momentum as a product of his own heroic struggle. But had Castro actually tried this strategy, they all would have died in Cuba.

When I returned, Sofia was sitting, drinking an aromática in our parlor. "Are you going to let me in on your game?" she asked. "Because I'm not sure you're winning."

"Wait," I said.

The books, read properly, would tell a very different story. How after the disaster, Castro reached out to Frank País, leader of the July 26th Movement in Cuba, who sent arms and support to the mountain guerrillas for years. So much for self-sufficiency.

As for the brave guerrilleros inspiring revolutionary fervor, well . . . the country was already rebelling. And not just in the countryside. There was the students' group, Directorio Revolucionario, attacking the Presidential Palace. There was the Cienfuegos naval uprising. The general strike of 1958. An army officer, Colonel Barquín, launched plots against the regime from within the military. The elected and then overthrown president Carlos Prío financed attack after attack against the regime. He even financed Castro, providing the mountain guerrillas yet another urban tit to suckle.

Castro was late to the revolutionary party, but the Batista regime, concerned with more dangerous enemies than a group of incompetents in the mountains, crushed his true rivals for him. José Antonio Echeverría, gunned down after an attack on the headquarters of Radio Reloj, March 1957. Fructuoso Rodríguez, ambushed by the police and shot to death, April 1957. And then Frank País, captured, brought to the Callejón de Muro and shot in the back of the head, July 1957.

Castro didn't come to power as the triumphant head of a unified movement sweeping in from the countryside, electrifying the country with communist fervor. He came to power by process of elimination, picking up the pieces of the movements who'd done more to weaken the regime than his men had. Then, once he had power, Castro crushed his rivals more ruthlessly than Batista ever had, and instituted a new history, a founding myth.

At the Museum of the Revolution in Havana you can learn, I am told, of how a small band of guerrilleros inspired the whole country not just to revolution, but to communism. And because Castro held power, and because the excitement of liberation was still in the air, and because Castro was perfectly willing to jail or murder dissenters, the myth became history. And, through Che, it became tactics.

But the stack of books sat on her desk, neatly piled and unread. The only thing that changed in her room once she began classes was the appearance of a framed print of Albrecht Dürer's *Praying Hands*. Then a tiny two-hundred-peso-coin-size metal icon, imprinted with the image of the Virgin, appeared on the top right corner of her desk.

I didn't know what to make of it. Neither Che nor General Santander, a devotee of the radical atheist utilitarian philosopher Jeremy Bentham, would have approved. Was it evidence of faith? Or placed there the way someone else might place a horseshoe and aloe behind a door?

More troubling was the class she had started. Integral Human Rights. "I'll get it out of the way," she told us. And then, a few weeks later, she told us about her professor, who had been attacked and brutally beaten by a criminal group in Norte de Santander during Uribe's presidency.

"He showed us a photo of him in the hospital," she told us over dinner, a note of unmistakable admiration in her voice. "He had one eye covered with a bandage, his whole face was bruised, but there were papers all over his bed! He was working!"

When we didn't respond to that, she added, "They nearly killed him, and he went on working."

"Yes," I said. "That is not particularly uncommon in my job."

Then she told us about the practical component of the class. Internships with the ARN, the reintegration agency that offered benefits to demobilized fighters. Which was fine. The ARN was not a kindness, but a tool of war, designed to leech FARC manpower.

"And for top students, there's an independent study he's offering next year where the practical component will be done with a foundation in La Vigia, this little town in Norte de Santander, working with victims of the war."

That, I didn't like. Valencia, the daughter of an officer in the special forces, going to a part of the country that was even more infested with the guerrilla than her university's campus.

"I probably won't get it," she said, seeing my expression. "And I don't even know if I'd want to do it. More human rights . . ."

But she was my daughter. She'd be at the top of her class, I was sure. And she was more invested in this professor and these ideas than she let on.

I reached out to the lawyer from the region who'd worked with my father in the past. An unsavory man, but useful back in the time when intermediaries with regional paramilitary leadership could be necessary. I made a simple request, and asked him what he knew about the town, La Vigia, and who controlled it. "Don't go out of your way," I told him. I didn't mention my daughter, or the nature of my interest. Foolish of me to think it would end there.

A few days later he told me it was controlled by an urabeño called El Alemán, and he told me there were patriots in the region who hated the Urabeños, men who were eager to share any information that could help the army in its inquiries. This led to the Mil Jesúses, which led to the El Alemán raid, which led to the mess I am currently in, in which both narco lawyers and members of the House of Representatives in the Second Commission know my name and feel I owe them something. The things we do for our children.

———

It wasn't until she finished her first term at Nacional that the books finally moved. The history of Cuba made its way from her desk back to my library. Then the diaries. The CIA report remained on her desk, next to the icon, and though I wanted to press her on it, instead I waited. People must come to their own conclusions.

The report, easily available online these days, is devastating. No more than eight pages long, with telling little chapter headings like "The Failure of the Guerrilla Tactics," "Ineptitude," "Morale," and "The Guerrillas' Failure with the Peasants," the writer is clearly having fun with Che's disaster. He notes smugly, "The guerrilla tactics that Che compiled in his handbook *Guerrilla Warfare* proved to be empty theoretics." He goes through the well-known mistakes. How Che arrived in Bolivia with a band of elite guerrilla, almost half of them foreigners. How, unlike Castro, Che's band rejected the urban, and less radical, Bolivian Communist Party. The report delights in Che's unwillingness to sully himself with the kind of bargains and power-sharing agreements that were crucial to Castro's success. It delights in Che's adherence to his theory, expecting his magnificent and saintly guerrilleros to inspire the people, who in reality were uninterested or hostile. "The peasant base has not yet been developed," Che wrote in his journal, "though through planned terror we will keep some neutral."

I love that. "Planned terror." From would-be liberator to would-be terrorist of the peasantry. But he even failed at brutalizing them into silence. The peasants turned on him, the Bolivians killed him, and his journal ended up in enemy hands. The CIA document concludes, reasonably:

"When the diary is published, the Guevara legend will only be dulled by this account of the pathetic struggle in Bolivia."

Which is what any sane and rational man would have thought. Did theory ever more conclusively fail in a clash with reality than in the case of the man whose image is painted over the main square of one of Colombia's best universities? Reason demanded that Che would fade into embarrassed ignominy. And so, the Americans let the journal out into the world.

Castro, however, was a true genius, and true men of genius are never entirely sane or rational. They know when to toss the stuffed dummy of reason overboard, grab the wheel, and navigate by feel through the howling pitch and toss that is the chaos of human life. When Castro got ahold of the journal, he used it.

The Cubans published a free edition of Che's Bolivia diaries— 250,000 copies of his supposed suffering and bravery. At the Museum of the Revolution, Che's image dominates—Castro is a hidden figure. The revolution is of the sainted dead, not of the living, making the revolution untouchable, sanctified by blood.

Imagine the CIA's confusion as Che's sainthood began to extend far beyond Cuba's shores. "The most complete human being of his age," said Jean-Paul Sartre. "An inspiration for every human being that loves freedom," said Nelson Mandela. Ernesto Sabato declared that "the struggle of Guevara against the U.S. was the struggle of the Spirit against Matter," which at least had the virtue of being a little true, though not in the way Sabato thought.

This used to make me rage. In Colombia, we have no military celebrities—we only worship enemies of the state. In Medellín you'll still see Pablo Escobar T-shirts. Our television screens are dominated by narco stories, and sympathetically reintegrating guerrillas. Simón Bolívar is neglected. No one cares about the Man of the Laws. Even Uribe is tarred and feathered with the paramilitary brush. There are no official gods.

A simple text, over WhatsApp. "I think I know why you gave me those books." I arranged to meet her at the Che mural. And so, under the eyes of the saint, she told me what she'd learned, dissecting where Che had gone wrong.

"In a way," she said, coming to what she thought was the point of the lesson, "ideology killed him. He fooled himself into believing the myth. There's something a little tragic about it."

Tragic. Right. She pitied him. This man with the soulful eyes and the bohemian hair looking down on us. Good. I didn't want her to look up at the mural in rage, as I might have done at her age. Rage is too close to love. But pity . . . that's a small step away from contempt, which never dies.

"I think it's funny," I said. "He was an inspiration to generations of guerrillas. Carlos Marighella in Brazil. Luis de la Puente and Héctor Béjar in Peru. For Humberto Ortega in Nicaragua. For our own ELN. And they followed his tactics, because they believed in the saint." At least, they did until they realized how bad those tactics were. Which, in some cases, took decades.

"I suppose that is lucky for you."

"Think of them," I said, "decades in the jungle, fighting without a hope of victory because of the unbelievable stupidity of their Che. Think of the men who followed his lessons and died pointlessly, because their hero was a fool who wanted to believe his own legend." I pointed at the mural. "The church should canonize him. The patron saint of capitalism."

"He looks so romantic," she said, her gaze up on the mural, taking in the haunted eyes, the flowing hair, a fake Christ promising fake salvation built upon his martyrdom.

"When you walk by that, I want you to remember that the people who put it up didn't even have enough patriotism to put up a Colombian communist. At least the Universidad de Antioquia has Camilo Torres for their guerrilla icon. And I want you to remember that the people who put it up didn't even have enough brains to put up a true champion of communism. The CIA couldn't have dreamed up a more effective way of sabotaging the guerrilla, corrupting their tactics, and training their armies for failure. But that's the left for you. No substance, no intelligence. Just . . . good hair. Think of that, every time you pass through here. It's the funniest joke in history."

She promised me she would. I left, secure in the knowledge that I had sufficiently prepared my daughter for school. She would take what she needed from this place, but not be changed by it. She would still be mine.

That was months ago. As I head to meet Valencia at a bakery a few blocks from campus, around the corner from the American embassy, I wonder how secure that feeling really is. Whether I really have inoculated her against poisonous ideas so that she can continue moving into the future I have envisioned. And it doesn't help that before I can even begin, just as we've barely sipped our aromáticas, she announces an unexpected plan of her own.

"I was in the Plaza Ch . . . Santander," she says, "looking at the mural. And I was thinking about what you told me. About how ideology kills the mind."

This was not what I had told her. I had told her leftists were stupid. But fine. A worthy lesson.

"You know, for one of my classes my first semeseter, top students were invited—"

"Yes, yes," I say. "The trip to do field work in Norte de Santander." Documenting the violence.

"I didn't say anything at the time, because I didn't think I'd want to go. But . . . I was offered a spot."

She looks at me, her beautiful face still, expressionless.

"Of course you were," I say. "You're a brilliant student."

She goes on to explain the nature of the work, and how we as a society need to acknowledge and respond to the violence suffered by rural populations at the hands of the FARC, yes, but also at the hands of paramilitaries and police and even . . . but she doesn't say the army. She just lets me infer. "It's not dangerous there anymore," she says. "My professor says it's very settled now."

Her professor knows nothing. The Mil Jesúses are in charge now, and Representative de Salva claims the Mil Jesúses are like ISIS. I could tell her that. But she's my daughter. That might make it more appealing. And besides, Representative de Salva is wrong. There have been very few murders around La Vigia since the Mil Jesúses took over, following the El Alemán raid. I've been keeping track. So what to tell her?

My daughter is looking down at her hands, long, elegant hands. Hands unblemished by hard work. Behind the counter, I can see the baker pulling a tray of pan de yuca out of the oven.

"One moment," I tell Vale, and get up and walk to the cash register. I wait while the woman carefully loads the tray of hot pan de yuca onto a shelf.

"Nothing better than a pan de yuca fresh out of the oven," I tell her. She glances at the sign above her, which says the exact same thing.

"Clearly," she says, pulling oven mitts off her coarse, calloused hands.

I hand her a twenty mil note and ask for four pan de yuca. I think about what Valencia is saying as the woman slowly grabs a set of tongs and drops them, one by one, into a paper bag. She hands them to me, counts out my change, and though I still don't know what to say as I head to the table and sit down, when Valencia opens her mouth to say more I raise one finger, halting her. Then I break into the crust of the pan de yuca, letting out the steam.

"This is a good life," I tell her. "If you enjoy the small things."

I tear off a piece, the gooey strands of yuca inside the crust pulling and then breaking, and I put the piece in my mouth. I close my eyes. There *is* nothing better than a pan de yuca fresh from the oven. I chew, then open my eyes.

"You actually want to participate in this clinic?"

She nods her head. "My professor says the spot is still there for me."

I take another bite of my pan de yuca. She starts talking about a revelation she had during Lent.

"I've never done anything like this," she says. "The ARN work is mostly administrative. And we did works for the poor at Santa Clara, but it was always easy. The faces of the people I met quickly faded."

Santa Clara is an Opus Dei school. My wife's idea, but I didn't mind. Opus Dei teaches you to find God in the dignity of daily work, whether it's the work of a poor day laborer or the work of a student, sharpening the tools of the mind. A fine lesson. But like so many young people, and like Che himself, she wants a more heroic role. Never mind that I've warned her, more than once, that a desire for heroism leads to most of the suffering in the world.

"This would be hard," she says. "And it would bring me face to face with victims but also with—"

"Murderers. Kidnappers."

"Yes, exactly," she says. "And child soldiers. Rural poor. Didn't you say, during the paramilitary demobilization, that most of the paracos were confused kids caught up in the violence and we shouldn't judge them by the cruelty their worst leaders spurred them to do?"

I did say that. But the paramilitaries frequently fought on our side, and my concerns have never been about individual justice, but about the progress of the state.

"I know Mom thinks the peace treaty is unjust because it lets them off too easy," she says. "But even if that's true"—she trails off a bit—"even if that's true, if, *ideologically*, Mom is right, there's still another way to think about it."

I feel a bit of trepidation about where she's going, but say nothing.

"As Christians, we're called to mercy." She delivers that pat phrase with an affirmative nod of her head.

"What?"

"Mercy is always an injustice."

"What?"

"If it weren't, then it wouldn't be mercy. It would just be justice."

"Is this," I say, stammering, surprised, "is this a *religious* thing?"

She laughs, a delicate, gentle laugh. My daughter has never laughed at me before.

"Christ spent time among the fallen." She smiles shyly, as if she knows how ridiculous and self-aggrandizing that sounds. "I want to spend time with the defeated and the scorned. And even, in some cases, the unworthy and the cruel."

I sit back in my seat. This is not the turn I expected. I can say no. Obviously, I can say no. She won't go if I don't allow her. Her mother will want to say no as well. But I've led enough soldiers to know that there are times when a young mind must be given strict commands, and there are times a young mind must be held in the hand like a little bird. And if she's spouting religious cant, then this must be handled carefully.

I can say it will be dangerous. That I have learned things about the region her professor can't know. I could tell her about Representative de Salva, about Jefferson Paúl López Quesada, or about my meeting with that loathsome lawyer in the exquisite dining room of a five-star hotel, where we were served wine that cost more than the monthly salary of most Colombians, and the lawyer, fat, his face flushed from a life of decadence, waved his chunky fingers and belched greasy words into the air, making promises I ignored and divulging information I held tight. But that would heighten the appeal for her.

As with Che, it is best to fight with the truth. Deception is always shaky footing. And though she had started by telling me about the dangers of idealism, it is clear she is motivated by something else, something worse, something I have lied to her about my whole life. The first step, then, is to come clean.

"God. Jesus Christ," I say. "We send you to church because that's what a young woman is supposed to do. Are you really telling me you believe in all that shit?"

7

MASON 2007

t started with the fireworm, a five-kilometer-long convoy in Helmand, everything we had in one beastly formation, the only American force in the district, civilization descending into the wilderness, lighting up the first few Taliban brave enough to fire on us, chalking up the first couple of deaths to the deployment tally before hitting the turnoff for Highway 611, turning due east, off-roading into the desert, heading parallel to Sangin and then, exactly at noon, flooding the town, taking it without a fight.

With a base of operations established, the colonel adopted a strategy of sending out small teams, twelve Americans plus some Afghans to draw the Taliban out so we could call in air support on them. Our deadliest weapon, as per usual, was our radio. And all of us were glad to be back in the thick of things, even if sometimes it took its toll.

"Fucking bullshit," Carlos told me as I handed him a few Motrin. "I forgot about the goddamn headaches."

"Everybody only remembers the cool parts of combat," I told him. I'd forgotten them as well—the headaches, the sleeplessness, the frayed nerves that were all part of the game.

We lost people. In May, a Chinook got shot down. Eight died in the crash, and we had to fight a running gun battle to get through to recover the bodies. In June, an IED took out Cliff Weeks, a well-liked team sergeant from another ODA. July, two more dead, one from small arms fire and another from a pressure plate rigged to an artillery shell, an old-school IED method, one of the classics that never goes out of style. And that's not counting the injuries, the gunshots, shrapnel wounds, and lost arms and legs and fingers and eyes. If there's a heaven for limbs, a waiting room in paradise where the severed parts await re-union with their owners, we put in some work filling it up.

We gave better than we got. After one battle in Zerikow, 136 dead. Amazing, at the time, to think battles that big were still happening, that the Taliban was still sending so many people, so many of them so young, into our meat grinder. Hovering above that wonder, the knowl-edge that they were sending so many to their deaths time and time again because they could. Blood, as they say, makes the grass grow. In Afghanistan, it grew tall.

Benjy, our new engineer, said, "All the guys we're killing, you think the Taliban would be collapsing."

All Jefe had in response was, "It takes time."

"We've been at war here for six years," Benjy had said. "By year six, World War Two was over."

Back then, there was a grand total of thirty thousand troops in the country. The army was gearing up to pour bodies and equipment into Iraq because of the "surge," while out in rural Afghanistan it took two months to get mission critical replacement parts because "Iraq." Even if we'd decided to forget about 90 percent of the incredibly rural Afghan-istan and just secure the big cities—Kabul, Jalalabad, Mazar-e-Sharif, and Kandahar—we couldn't have done it. So how do you secure Af-ghanistan, cede zero territory to the Taliban, promote local governance, and develop local forces and courts and economic growth with thirty thousand troops? You don't. So we didn't promise the Afghans money for roads, or schools, or improved health care, or better governance.

Everybody, especially the Afghans, knew that wasn't what we were there for.

The best we could do as far as the traditional ODA mission set was concerned was work with a contingent of ANA, a little group of Afghans living and fighting with us out of a firebase near Sangin. Their senior sergeant, an illiterate Afghan named Azad Khan, had whipped the unit into unusually good shape. According to the outgoing ODA, Azad Khan was not just a great soldier, but something of a legend.

In 2004, he'd been blown up and left for dead by his unit after an ambush where an IED had torn off pieces of his face and mangled his legs. Despite injuries that would have killed most people, Azad Khan found his way back to his unit and back to the fight. And the month before we'd arrived he'd secured the love of his soldiers after an incident in which a young interpreter had been shaken down for money by a group of Afghan National Police at a traffic checkpoint. They'd beaten the terp badly enough to puncture a lung. Azad Khan had told his unit that an attack on the terp for their attached ODA team was an attack on them all, and then he led his soldiers on a raid of the police checkpoint, capturing the ANP who'd shaken down the terp, bringing them back to the firebase, beating them bloody, and then stringing them up by their hands and feet from poles over empty fire pits.

The outgoing ODA's intel sergeant, who was telling us the story, laughed. "We said, 'What the fuck is this, Azad?' And he said, 'We told them we were going to cook them and eat them, like the Americans taught us.' But, you know, they didn't do it. I guess our human rights classes are working."

After all that, I was expecting much more than the squat, ugly, barely five-foot-tall Afghan we met at the firebase, sitting in a loose white shirt, beaming at us "longbeards," as the Afghans call Special Forces, and then urging us to dance with him to celebrate our arrival.

"Za! Za!" he yelled at me, as I started awkwardly moving my limbs around to the music. Ocho pulled out a camera, trying to catch me mid-dance move so he could use the photo to humiliate me for the rest of the deployment. When Azad saw that, he grabbed me by the shoulder, pointed at the camera, and then put up his fist with his index and little finger extended, like he was at a heavy metal concert.

"All right," I said, making the same gesture and mugging for the camera.

"Raaarrrr!" he said.

"Raarr!" I said.

He laughed at me, and patted me on the stomach.

"Longbeards," he said, and gave a thumbs-up.

Later that first night I was checking out one of the guard towers with Ocho, who was shirtless, big muscles and belly fat and scars and tattoos exposed to the cold air, and he pulled out his dick and started pissing out into the desert beyond our firebase.

"This kind of deployment is what I joined the teams for," he said. "Out in the fucking wilderness, alone and unafraid."

"I thought you joined to chase Pablo Escobar and sleep with Colombian whores?"

"Hmmm . . ." he said. "This is better. This is so much better."

It was a deceptively good beginning to the deployment.

"I like it here," I wrote Natalia. "I like the mission. We rarely see the enemy, mostly it's calling in air strikes on piles of rocks. But there's something unbelievably fulfilling about being in a place where you can count on getting into gunfights."

We mostly relied on letters. "I want to hear your voice," Natalia told me before I went out, "but I'm not gonna make it if you're calling me every day and telling me everything." I was relieved to hear her say it. One of the many ways my wife is wiser than me.

We ended up working out a deal where each of us would try to tell the real stuff in letters. That way we wouldn't be putting the other person in the position of having to respond to whatever intense shit we were going through, whether it was our daughter or money or combat, in real time. And it meant I didn't have to switch from war to Bragg in the space of a minute. On the phone, it's so easy to lie, especially about things that have just happened, things you haven't figured out in your own head yet, so you just gloss over them, or tell half-truths, or worse than half-truths, you tell the SITREP version of events, the who did what where and when without the emotions, the list of events recited and dumped on your wife's lap without context or meaning because the whole thing doesn't quite make sense to you yet either, like how funny it was after you crawled through a sewer ditch with the rest of your team and you shot one muj and Carlos shot the other and they fell in just the perfect way, Muj One shot through the pelvis, abdomen, and heart so shit and blood pooled together, and Muj Two spun around by the bullet before face-planting into his friend's blown-away and undoubtedly now dickless crotch, the two of them dead but Muj One with this expression of total shock and pain almost indistinguishable from extreme pleasure, so it really did look like he was receiving a blow job from his friend and it was too funny, really. Not in the moment, because fighting at close range you don't know if you're going to die and it's scary as shit, but afterward, in that next moment when you know you're alive and you know you're going to stay that way and so is the rest of your team, you look over and see Muj One and Muj Two and it's so fucking funny. I mean it almost disturbed me how funny I found it, how the memory made me smile and would come to me unbidden and how that's not really the kind of guy I am but there it is, we all laughed about it, we laughed about so many things. Our job is too serious to take seriously, so we laughed about a lot of things that weren't funny at all, or wouldn't have been so funny if they hadn't also been so terrifying, and here was this pure joke displayed before us, so great that Carlos tried to take a picture before Jefe, ever professional, stopped him.

How to tell that on a phone? Instead, I wrote letters, each word deliberate, though at first I wrote almost nothing of missions. My early letters avoided all that, papered over war, and instead talked about our girl, about what she meant to me, and what it meant being a father and being away from her. Without regular access to the phone, I felt what older generations of warriors must have felt when they wrote home, a sense of separation and of precariousness, of the need to communicate something such that the time here, whatever happens, will be anchored and preserved among those I love. And by writing about my girl and not about war, I was bringing my girl here, letting my wife know, and maybe someday Inez as well, that she was with me, she was essential to me, that even here the most important thing in the world was that I was her father. Which was mostly true.

In return, Natalia sent me more packets of photos like she'd done when I was in Colombia. First came less than a month in. My little lady dressed in a polka dot dress, with lacy frills. With a bow tie. Her fat, happy face smiling up into the camera. Adorable, you understand, a happy sight to see. Something to miss, not just the little girl but also the lost time. Unlike the memory of those dead muj, the photos rarely made me smile.

"The sad thing about what we do," Jefe told me one night as we smoked cigars, dropping the same tired wisdom I'd heard from other team guys but hadn't expected from Jefe, "is that we go home to our wife and kids and know that we can never really explain this to them, what it's like to do this job. That they'll never understand."

I didn't like what he said, but I kept my silence. I knew I was just supposed to nod, as if it were something profound. Was it true? Would my daughter ever understand me? Would Natalia? I'd always thought she knew me better than I knew myself. She sees things so clearly, and has a hardheaded way of cutting through the bullshit team guys like to tell themselves. It would later occur to me that if our wives never came to understand us, it wouldn't be because they couldn't, but because we would never tell them.

The largest operation of the deployment was Operation Adalat, where we threw the Special Forces rule book out the window. The plan was to pin a bunch of Taliban in the Shah Wali Kot valley, head in with a column of Canadian armor (seriously), and kill them.

Shah Wali Kot has only three exits. One team blocked the exit in the north, another team blocked the second exit, and the rest of us moved up with two hundred Canadians in six Leopard tanks, thirteen light armored vehicles, and thirteen support vehicles. The plan was to assault up a mountain against dug-in Taliban positions. "This is some straight-up World War Two shit," Ocho told me excitedly. We weren't all as giddy, but it was pretty fucking cool. After our time as professionals in Colombia—all training, no fun—here was our chance for a mission that was no training, all fun.

By this point we'd also had enough time with the Canadians and ANA to feel comfortable working together. Especially to feel comfortable with Azad Khan, who'd lived up to his reputation and then some. Not long before Adalat we'd set up a traffic checkpoint north of Sangin to try to snag roadside bomb makers. It was the sort of thankless mission where you didn't expect to snag much—the people pretty reliably reported all our movements to the local Taliban, but midway through a beat-up Toyota appeared around the bend, then suddenly stopped, and went screaming into reverse. Since Azad Khan had hidden himself in a security position up ahead in an irrigation ditch, he was able to jump out and fire a burst directly into the car's engine block as it passed him, sending it to a rolling stop. I watched as Azad put his rifle to the ready and approached the car, which had three passengers. Then I heard the driver yelling, cursing Azad Khan, calling him a dog. Our pint-sized Afghan Rambo roared and dove into the car.

"Shit!" Jefe shouted, and we raced over. Two muffled cracks went off, and we stopped and aimed in on the vehicle, waiting for movement. Azad Khan slowly wiggled himself back out of the car's window and turned toward us, his face covered in blood and bits of brain. He was beaming. The driver had tried to pull a gun, his third mistake of the day, and Azad Khan had wrestled it from him, driven it under his chin, and pulled the trigger twice.

The other passengers were very compliant after that, and in the trunk we found an RPK, ball bearings, wiring, mines, and blasting caps. So we went into the Shah Wali Kot feeling very confident about Azad Khan.

The op started with the Canadians calling in artillery strikes in the fields and mountains around the villages to warn local civilians to leave the planned engagement area. So we sat on our asses while we made empty fields explode, and then we waited as a mass of Afghans started trickling past us.

They came not in ones and twos, but as whole families. The first one, a tall, older man, walked with a stoop and held hands with a little boy of eight or nine, who in turn was holding hands with a little girl of seven or eight, and she was holding hands with an even littler girl, and behind the two of them, two women in beautiful, flowing robes that covered them head to toe, even their faces. It was strange to see women, and I was struck with the bizarre desire to walk up and smell them. Azad Khan nudged Jefe and jerked his head toward the women, grinning, then said, "Hubba-hubba." You couldn't see a single, solitary inch of their skin, but I knew exactly what he meant.

More and more people flowed out of the valley. "No young men," Jefe said to me. It was true. There were a few old men, men on crutches. And many, many children, followed by those flowing, mysterious and arousing robes—but almost none of what the army calls "military-age males." All these families, their young men were waiting for us. And as I watched them pass, my excitement about the coming fight curdled into rage. I wanted to grab one of the old men, and shout at them, "We are the best fighters in the best army in the world! We have heavy machine guns and Mark-19s and LAWs and snipers and artillery and close air support and tanks and light armored vehicles and a bunch of surprisingly badass Canadians and a crazy Afghan named Azad Khan and we are going to kill everybody! We are going to slaughter your young men, your boys, your children, and their deaths will mean nothing!" Getting angry can be good preparation for a fight.

Ocho scooped some Copenhagen into his mouth, a clear sign he was feeling jittery, anxious for the damn thing to start. Carlos racked the charging handle on his Browning. Benjy smiled up at me. Diego and Jason bullshitted. Jefe checked and rechecked his kit. I cradled a machine gun, tapped the rifle I had slung over my back, checked my magazines, rockets, water bottles. Touched them all again. Then looked out at the civilians trickling to the district center, and the ANP directing them. Things would kick off in an hour and everybody knew it—no surprises for us, no surprises for the Taliban. Everybody in the valley knew what was about to happen. And then we moved.

Those of us in the gun trucks were supposed to assault uphill, through enemy lines, then turn and assault again, pinning the insurgents while the armored force hammered them from the south with tank and artillery fire, eventually pushing them into the blocking forces. This is, more or less, what happened, with the main assault force of our unit putting up an awesome amount of firepower. Far up ahead, I saw one of the Canadian tanks disappear an enemy position in a mud hut, just totally obliterate it.

Diego raised his arms, delighted. "Are you not entertained!"

"I'm entertained," Benjy said.

"Motherfucking tanks!" Ocho shouted. "Those things are useful."

Early stages went pretty much according to plan. Worst moment for us came a few hours in as we spread out up the valley to clear a few buildings and irrigation ditches behind a berm that hadn't been visible on the three-year-old imagery Jefe had briefed us off of. Behind the berm was a U-shaped building up an incline of about eighty feet. We drove toward it, moving off the main road to avoid IEDs, then dismounting while Carlos fired away on the Ma Deuce. Jefe was calling out Pashtun commands, and Azad Khan started setting up Afghan machine-gun teams. I saw some rusty old Soviet trucks, a water tank, a few small vehicles. We sprinted toward the berm while Jefe gathered the ANA machine gunners and moved them in line with our position. Rounds were exploding all around, tracers burning laser lines through the sky close enough I could have reached a hand up and strummed them the way you would the strings on a guitar. Most of the rounds were coming from the U-shaped building.

Combat is not like people think. It's much slower, more deliberate. I didn't understand that at first, not even after the first couple times in combat, back when I was with Ranger Battalion in Afghanistan. The adrenaline, the confusion, the newness of it all made it seem like a wild chaotic ride. I did not know what was going on, all I knew was my blood pounding through my veins, and the knowledge of death being present, and then, slowly, the knowledge that I was okay with that. I think if there was a time I could have done something really worthy of a medal for valor it would have been then, before Natalia, before I started valuing my life and my future over the experiences of the moment. I would have rushed out stupidly under fire then.

Now I know too much. Not just that I have a wife and child at home, who depend on me and love me, but also, I know the battlefield in a different way. Every movie, every video game, is about the hero rushing forward, killing the enemy, saving the day. The lone, individual hero.

On an actual battlefield, victories generally don't come from one man killing a dramatic number of enemy. Killing doesn't always mean strategic or even tactical success, as anybody who has studied Vietnam or Algeria or the Philippines or any goddamn war in history can tell you. What you want is not corpses but dominance over the battlefield. In that regard, combat is less like Call of Duty and more like chess. Jefe was moving us pieces into position.

Rounds from the U-shaped building were spitting up bits of dust into the air. Diego crept the truck forward, cresting the berm just enough so that Carlos, in the turret on the 50 cal, could fire back, sending heavy rounds exploding through the walls.

I ran toward a group of ANA, grabbed one of their PKMs, crawled uphill, found a spot with just the right angle on the building, and set it in its bipod. Think a bishop, pinning a piece so it can't move without risk. I fired a burst, showing the Afghan behind me where to shoot. "In an arc," I shouted, stupidly in English, and then motioned to him how I needed it.

As we fired, another ODA team set up in the defilade. I looked up at the building. Painted on the side was a message: "This school was donated to the people of Afghanistan by UNICEF."

The assault force stormed forward under the roar of machine-gun fire. Dust rose from the hard-packed ground behind them, and the bullets crackling through the air burrowed through the dust, carving whisps in the air. Something about the sight made everything seem like it was happening at a quarter speed, and it was beautiful.

One Afghan went down, then got up and hopped forward. Spurts of blood came from one leg. Arterial, potentially deadly. An Afghan medic pulled him to a depression and began treating the wound. They were learning.

"Raven thirty, this is Raven thirty-one, where the fuck is our air support," Jefe was screaming over the radio.

Up ahead was an explosion. I saw an Afghan soldier screaming, his legs a mess. At the medics course they say you've got to let the wounded come to you. An SF trained medic is too valuable to risk. But I took an

ANA truck to him and applied a tourniquet. The straps clamped down, viselike, on his arteries, crushing them shut, and he screamed. Up ahead, I saw an Afghan soldier scrambling up the hill, firing from the shoulder, careful, intermittent shots, professional. He threw a hand grenade and crested.

I hauled my Afghan back to the CCP, where Ocho was grinning madly among the wounded, blood spatter all over his sleeves. I got in to help while Carlos up in the gun truck defended our position, firing away as return fire came in from irrigation ditches, grape huts, and compounds up on the hills.

Jefe pointed to a compound where I could see Taliban flitting through the windows. It offered solid lines of fire to split our force. He grabbed me and Diego and some Afghans, leaving Carlos and Benjy to defend Ocho and the wounded. We were the support fire team, we only had machine guns, which aren't exactly ideal for room clearing.

"Hamla!" Jefe shouted to the ANA.

We sprinted forward. The Taliban in the hills opened up.

"Za! Za! Za!" Jefe was shouting. We reached the entrance and Jefe set up two Afghan machine gunners to fire back at the positions in the hills. Azad Khan pulled the pin off a hand grenade, tossed it in, and rolled back away from the entrance. The building vibrated with the boom, and a machine gunner stepped into the entryway and fired his PKM down the hall, shooting from the hip.

Jefe pushed the PKM gunner inside, and while he fired down the hallway we cleared the rooms. From a window I saw an RPG fly toward Carlos in the gun truck. Carlos shifted fire and reduced a grape hut to rubble. We moved to another building, cleared it, then cleared another and another. As we moved forward, the gun truck moved forward, too. Then there was an enormous flash. Jefe looked at me and I looked back at the gun truck.

The bomb had exploded underneath one of the back wheels, setting off the gas tank and the jerrycans of fuel. Flames arced up toward the sky as the truck jumped, equipment flying everywhere, and Carlos, in the turret, launched straight up. His arms spread out, hands clutching empty air, as his body twisted. Then he fell back down, landing on the front of the truck. I was too far away to hear anything, and even if I'd been close, the machine-gun fire would have covered over the sound, but in my memory of it I always hear the thud.

I ran across the field, the machine-gun fire around me not quite registering, reached the truck, and hauled Carlos, heavy with all his gear, to the ground. His uniform was on fire and I burned myself trying to smother the flames. Rounds started cooking off in the burning truck. Inside were more than twenty thousand 7.62 rounds, ten thousand 5.56 rounds, as well as rockets, mortars, recoilless rifle rounds, and grenades, all of which would soon be exploding.

I grabbed Carlos around the underarms and started hauling him to an irrigation ditch about ten meters away from the truck, just by the side of a marijuana field. As I pulled, an explosion in the truck sprayed us with hot frag. I kept pulling. My lungs burned, and my blistered hands screamed at me. Machine-gun fire raked the open spaces around us. We reached the ditch and collapsed in, but it was barely eighteen inches deep.

"FUCK!" I screamed, then rolled over to assess Carlos, who looked up at me calmly, not in shock.

"Benjy," he said.

I looked back to the truck, ablaze. Behind it, just up the hill, a dark figure. The explosion must have blown Benjy through the driver's door and into the hill, saving his life. Out of the corner of my eye I saw Jefe sprinting his way toward Benjy. He moved fast for an old man.

"Leaking from the hip, bro," Carlos told me.

A piece of frag had punched through his hips, shredding his stomach and intestines, spraying splinters of hip bone throughout the abdomen. Clearly the major injury. I scanned the rest of the body. One leg, shredded, bent horribly, bleeding profusely. Due for an amputation at some point, if he survived. I quickly applied a tourniquet, easy. He had burns to his face, hands, unimportant. The patient—not Carlos, but the patient—had sustained a hell of a blow. In an hour or so, systemic inflammatory response would hit. The bowel and abdominal wall would swell, oxygenation would drop, and the patient would need massive fluid resuscitation and possibly inotropic support. He was in the Golden Hour, and I started packing the hip and abdomen, trying to keep the organs sterile and on the inside, trying to give him the best chance of surviving those sixty minutes.

Packing from without is creating a sandwich, I could hear the instructors at Special Forces Medical Training Center telling me, packing from within is filling a cavity. Two layers of pads on either side of the liver, supported by the abdominal wall and the diaphragm. My heartbeat had kicked into fifth gear but my movements were controlled, or something beyond control, past clenched-fist bare-knuckled will and toward a natural set of movements flowing from the training, bypassing language and thought as my chattering brain whined on, reciting injuries and treatment options, but the voice increasingly distant as my hands worked.

"Are you in pain?" I asked.

"Yes," he said. "Hip, stomach. Jesus. Leg. Right leg. Face."

His beard was smoking. So was mine.

"Okay, okay," I said. "I got you."

You have to ask about the pain. Carlos's pain—when talking to him about his pain he was Carlos again, not the patient—it would be the life kind of pain, the kind that from this point would ebb and flow but never quiet. Asking about pain at the site of injury is a way of treating that chronic pain. They're not sure how it works, other than that it does. Perhaps since pain is emotion plus sensation, reflecting care and concern and the promise of help to the patient somehow changes the equation. So we ask about the pain, and so I asked about the pain, and Carlos tried to tough it out.

"Stop the bleeding first," he said. I guess he thought I was going to bust out the drugs.

I grinned at him. "I don't tell you how to do your job."

I moved from the liver to the right gutter. Packed it. I shifted, put my left hand above the spleen, pulled it toward me, packed above the spleen, moved to the left gutter, then the pelvis. Noted accumulation of blood from a mesenteric bleeder. I stopped that with a finger. Then I used a clamp. I didn't like the blood flow. I pulled the stomach down, pushed two fingers past it, slippery, rubbery, until I could feel the aorta. It pulsed under my fingers. This is life, I thought. I looked at Carlos's face, which was pale, serene. I compressed the aorta manually.

Jefe arrived at the ditch with Benjy, who saw how shallow it was.

"Are you fucking kidding me?" There was a stench of vomit. He'd probably puked over himself from breathing in the toxic smoke of the truck.

Taliban were shooting at us directly now, bullets slicing through the marijuana over our heads.

"If I get shot in the ass . . ." Jefe said as he pulled off Benjy's body armor, checking him head to toe.

"Benjy's fine," I said. "Carlos is in the Golden Hour."

"CASEVAC is twenty minutes out," Jefe said.

Huge explosions roared in the hills. The Canadian Leopards opening fire. Azad Khan appeared at my side with a stretcher. I could have kissed the ugly bastard. We got Carlos on the stretcher, started moving. Jefe helped Benjy to his feet and then, when Benjy collapsed, carried him. Behind us, the truck continued to burn. Ahead of us, the CCP, littered with needle cases, discarded bandage wrappers, tubing, shed straps of clothing, and in the midst of the chaos, covered in blood, Ocho.

I pushed fluids into Carlos, as well as antibiotics. Later he would be too weak to fight the incoming infections from all the dirt and grime and evil pushed into his body before they had a chance to really grip him.

"The fucking Dutch," Jefe told me at one point, "can't identify targets, and won't go below their ceiling." Ah, I thought. So that's why we don't have air support.

Carlos seemed certain he was going to die. He'd alternate between joking and telling me things to tell his ex-wife, who'd left him after he cheated on her with a stripper in Fayetteville. I pumped him full of painkillers, kept him talking. Even if he survived the Golden Hour, I knew something he'd soon learn—that you never fully shake the finger of death once you'd been injured like this. Survivors age faster—two to four times as fast, though the doctors don't quite know why. The diseases of old age—coronary artery disease, chronic kidney disease, hypertension, diabetes—strike earlier. It's like the body knows it wasn't meant to live. But there we were, Ocho and I working with his blood drying on our clothes, pushing life as he lay helpless to stop us, the two of us conspiring against his body's right to die.

We put him in the CASEVAC, unsure if he'd survive. It wouldn't be until the fight was over that we'd receive definitive word that he'd made it, or at least made it through the worst. And the fight continued for two more days, with a body count somewhere around four hundred Taliban killed by the end.

After the fighting, the people started filtering back to their towns, and I watched them, wondering what they were wondering. If they were asking themselves who they lost, how many of their brothers, or fathers, or sons were simply never coming home again. Diego pointed to a little boy holding hands with his littler brother. The boy had a mop of black hair, messy, like old pictures of the Beatles.

"In a couple of years," he said, "you think we'll come back and kill him?"

I scowled and Diego laughed.

"You know what's crazy," he said. "Between 2001 and now, life expectancy in Afghanistan has gone up."

I didn't respond.

"I know," he said. "From fifty-five years to fifty-seven. That's how fucked up this country is. This war has actually been good for their health."

"Ah," I said. I wasn't interested in playing Diego's games.

Diego looked back out at the people. "You know what? This isn't war. It's chemotherapy."

I treated my own wounds, small burns and little bits of frag that had ripped little tears across my neck, face, and right arm. All would mostly heal, with minor scars. Nothing like Carlos.

There are two ways to think about severe wounds. One is the very smallness and weakness of the human body, pathetic even compared to other animals, and so easy to break beyond repair, so easy even with the most basic of tools, a rock is enough, and then to think of it in the midst of the sorts of things that happen in war, not just explosions sending earth and brick blossoming but weapons that work by strange inversions of pressure, collapse buildings from the inside, or concentrate force in small spaces that liquify metal and send it shooting out through the air. The penetration of the human body is so easy it almost seems beside the point—such tools should be used for greater creatures than us. We are weak, we are fragile, and so, perhaps, we are nothing. There is wonder in the world—the unbearable blackness of the sky in Afghanistan, its piercing stars, the vibrations of the guns, soundless light on the horizon, flashes like echoes, a moon rising over sharp blades of mountain while tracers carve lines into the night. But man himself is nothing.

But the other way of thinking is the opposite. That the world itself is what is small. Mountains, stars, horizon, so much accumulation of rocks, dust, and an expanse of empty air. Meaningless without someone there to see it. I was once shot in the shoulder. The world around me wobbled and vibrated and collapsed to nothing in the midst of the pain. I applied my mind to the pain, oriented myself, returned the world to its proper place around me. I thought of my brothers, who I was currently failing by no longer being in the fight, by being injured, perhaps badly enough I would need their help leaving this place, under fire, when they had enough to carry without me. I thought of my wife and daughter. And then I looked at my arm, flopped to the side, immobile, mere matter. A thing. Meaningless. And I applied my mind again to the pain, and a finger wiggled, dead flesh suddenly live. There was a miracle there, in the difference between the two.

I didn't write to Natalia about Carlos. I thought about it constantly, but putting it into a letter was too much. Putting things like that into words means facing them head-on, which you shouldn't do mid-deployment. But the more I thought it, and about Natalia, and why I wasn't telling her, the more I started wondering about what Natalia wasn't telling me. Military wives tell each other not to tell their overseas soldier the hard truths, and since soldiers tell each other not to tell their wives the hard truths, intimacy withers on deployments.

I can pinpoint the moment I was certain I loved Natalia. We'd just started dating. I was a year back from my first Afghanistan deployment, with Ranger Battalion. It'd been something of a letdown and I was puzzling over whether I should get out, go back to school, or try out for selection in SF, go to the next tier, where maybe I'd find where I belonged. Natalia, ever certain of where she belonged, was plugging away at her certification as a CPA. The relationship had escalated fast—we were already friends for years, we'd shared some serious things with each other before even getting romantic, so the whole thing felt fast-tracked, maybe even destined if either of us were romantic enough to believe in destiny— and I'd spent the whole weekend with her, Wake Forest being not the most terrible of drives from Fayetteville. We were just hanging out on

Natalia's bed, goofing around. I was playing with her hair. "I'm making you beautiful," I said, as I pulled thick curls over her face, or bunched them up on top of her head. And she was laughing and taking photos of me as I did this, and then taking photos of both of us, her hand stretched out so the camera would maybe get both of us in the shot, though when we developed the film it was just the craziest of angles, my head cut in two or just the top of her hair sticking out everywhere like crazy. And I suddenly had this premonition—the thought of us in middle age, laughing like this. And then later, old age. The two of us like my grandparents, who toward the end had been in a room together at a hospital, where they'd reach out from their separate hospital beds and hold hands briefly each night before they went to sleep, a ritual that kept them alive until, of course, it didn't. And in the midst of that goofing around with Natalia I felt the most profound sense of sadness at the thought of my own death coming toward me, because I knew that would be the end of times with her. When I drove home that night, I drove the speed limit, my life suddenly more valuable to me because of her.

You don't live for your teammates. You prepare yourself to die for them. This is a very different thing. So I screwed up my courage. First by talking to God. And I told God that perhaps it was the ugliness in my life that was worth sharing with my wife, and I wrote her.

You know the little fake Christmas tree you and the rest of the wives sent us, with all the ornaments that had pictures of the guy's kids in them? Ocho and Benjy took all those baby photos out and put in porn, or pictures of Halle Berry or Britney Spears. I didn't tell you that because I was ashamed, and because I didn't say anything when they did. Actually, I was relieved when they did it. It's hard to look at my baby's face constantly, and then go out on missions. I think something about being a father has changed this job for me.

Here's a small story. A simple raid from last week, not very serious—we had night vision, they didn't. They're shooting blind from inside a building, then we hear a boom and whoosh, and then a rumble and crash. Some muj had fired his RPG from inside the building, not thinking about the backblast. It overpressurized the mud hut and blew out the walls, sending the ceiling crashing down.

Jefe radioed our stats back and we got word that the main assault element was done, the targeted personality KIA on objective, prep for exfil, helos twenty minutes out, so we do a quick SSE on the hut. Four bodies. One was old, or Afghan-old, mid-40s. The other three were also military-age males, though younger, teenagers maybe though it was hard to tell, and one with barely any beard at all, a young teenager, still holding the used RPG tube.

Jefe got mad. Fucking Taliban. Using fucking kids. Later that night, I asked Ocho if he thought we'd ever clear the south of Taliban and he just laughed and laughed and laughed, and I asked what were we doing here, if we weren't going to clear Helmand, and he was like, What are we doing here? Knock knock.

Who's there? I said, and he said, 9/11, and I said, 9/11 who? And he put on this angry face, pointed his finger at my chest and shouted, You said you'd never forget!

A pretty good joke, I thought.

Maybe I shouldn't be telling you all this. I don't really have any grand moral or lesson. I was so excited when 9/11 happened, in Ranger Battalion, where we all felt like the lucky ones, the ones blessed to be in just the right spot to do exactly what every American wanted, to get some payback, to do something righteous. And I still feel that. There's some bad, bad people here. But there's also young kids who join in the fighting because they're young kids. It pisses me off and also kind of fucks me up a little bit.

Don't get me wrong. Most days, I love what we're doing. Mission by mission, this is the best deployment I've ever been on. And I saved Carlos's life. Me. I did that. How could I think I should be anywhere else, doing anything else, than this?

After that, the letters got a lot more real, realer in terms of minor things—"Oh, thank God, I have been waiting and waiting to tell you how much I hate Diego's wife . . ."—and major, almost too real things—"when I feel like I'm failing as a mother, which is often, sometimes I comfort myself by telling myself it's not me that's failing, it's you, you failing by not being here, by insisting on being in a stupid war nobody cares about at all. Which means I can relax. If Inez grows up fucked up I won't be the one to blame . . . and then, of course, I feel horribly guilty." And she told me of the balance of joy and stress that is raising a child, and how my absence had tilted that balance to the almost unbearable, functionally a single mother but with the added fear this life brings, the terror of news reports, casualty rolls, the sight of men in uniform driving down residential neighborhoods sending a chill down the spine. Is it strange to say letters like this made us closer?

Before we left, we did have at least one mission that was less pure combat than hearts and minds. It was a VETCAP, a veterinary civic action program, the sort of thing that was far more popular with Afghans than medical engagements, where we went out and cured their illnesses. In the rural region of Afghanistan, human life is cheap. Pain and death, it is understood, are a part of existence, and they follow their own logic. A healthy herd, on the other hand, is pure gold. So Ocho and I were sent out with Diego, Benjy, Jason, and some Canadians to try our veterinary skills on the local herds.

En route, of course, a group of Taliban skirmishers took some shots at us in an untilled field. The fire was unusually intense, and unusually accurate. A bullet nearly grazed my head.

"Diego," Ocho said. "If I die on this dumbass mission, I want my tombstone to read, Here lies Ocho. He gave his life for goats."

They must have prepped the area as a battlefield, establishing fire positions and marking the distances against the trees dotting the fields, using them as aiming stakes.

"You know, we may not have much success training Afghans." Diego smiled at me. "But these Taliban fuckers do seem to be learning. It gives you hope for this country."

Diego called for air support while we maneuvered the Canadians around, playing a game that'd end up taking an hour or two before the Taliban decided they'd had enough and ghosted away. The main casualties were goats. We pushed on to the village and delivered medicine to the villagers' sick herds, curing the same kind of animals we'd just slaughtered and feeling a bit, well, sheepish about it. Perhaps just the exhaustion of something so seemingly pointless led us to slip up on the way back, miss the IED. I don't know.

The explosion that hit Ocho sounded in a pulse, like being inside the heartbeat of an enormous animal, an animal the size of the earth itself, and with a heartbeat loud enough to swallow you whole. It flung Ocho high in the air, thrust me backward, staring at the sky, unfocused, unsure of what I was or where I was or even what I was seeing. Blue patch here, now. Brown patch there. And then, pain. And then, above the pain, a sound. Ocho screaming.

I lifted a hand, bleeding, and held it against the sky. I ordered my fingers to wiggle. All five wiggled back at me. I lifted the other hand. Wiggled. Sat myself up.

There was a crater big enough for a man to stand in and disappear. Against the edges, I could see the outline of other IEDs, undetonated but their positions revealed by the explosion. I heard someone call out a warning. That someone was me.

Ocho was a few feet away from the edge of the crater, the top half of him more or less recognizable, the bottom half smudged. I scanned for other casualties and saw a Canadian guy only six or seven yards away from me, slumped with blood seeping through the body armor, just over his chest. I looked back at Ocho. There was a decision, a decision related to training and not to friendship, love, or camaraderie. Legs or chest?

Ocho was shouting and gradually I understood, he was warning people away from him, warning about movement in general. IEDs all over, any patch of earth. Only one of his arms was moving.

I pulled out my bayonet and pushed it through the dirt in front of me, making my way to the Canadian soldier, away from Ocho, moving at a crawl, digging under the dirt, feeling for the clink of metal, the solidity of a mine.

When I reached the soldier his face was white, his breathing shallow, veins sallow.

"Hey," I told him as I worked from the side to get his body armor off. "I got you. What's your name?"

"Jim," he said.

"Okay, Jim," I said. "It's a small entry and exit wound, not so bad. So you know the deal. You survive the next five minutes, and what happens?"

"I live."

Out of the corner of my eye I saw Ocho applying a tourniquet to his right leg. He roared as he tightened it. I'll never get used to the screams that come with this job. Everything we do to casualties hurts—from dragging wounded bodies across hard ground to the chest seals to the compressions to the IVs—but the vise-like grip of a tourniquet is in a special class. It's so painful it can kill, because the pain makes the nervous system demand oxygen, adding another unfulfillable request to the body's shrunken, weakened veins. But Ocho is a tough motherfucker, I told myself, and if anyone can self-care a pair of tourniquets without passing out, it's him.

"Jim," I said. "Tell me where it hurts."

I took out the chest adhesive seal, which is the size of a dinner plate, and began peeling the adhesive off with shaky, adrenaline-fueled fingers.

Jim told me it hurt to breathe, it hurt in his chest and his foot, which I could see was twisted under him and attached so it didn't matter, not so much, but that's fine.

I applied the seal, which hurt Jim more, but more important than managing pain was stopping the air spilling into the hole in his chest, getting trapped in the chest cavity and squeezing the lung smaller and smaller until suffocation. Blood and oxygen, I thought, and now emotion.

"Do you want fentanyl?" I asked. "For the pain?"

"Fuck. Yeah." Jim was shivering. Ocho was tying on a second tourniquet and roaring again, the tough bastard. Another Canadian guy who'd been bayoneting his way across the ground reached me, and I set him packing a wound in Jim's calf, deep but probably not enough to threaten the leg. Laminated gauze with a homeostatic agent to do the clotting Jim could no longer do for himself, while I put in an IV, fluids plus antibiotics.

"Keep packing until it's full," I said. "Then hold down three minutes."

There were no bullets in the air. No shooting. I started making my way to Ocho, who'd done too good a job warning people away from himself, too good a job telling everyone he's got it, so he was still in self-care, and with every inch I approached it became rapidly apparent I'd made the wrong choice because it wasn't legs versus chest, like I'd thought, it was legs and arm and maybe more versus chest.

His legs were rags, with torn flesh and bone sticking out oddly, calf muscles flopped to the side and covered in sand, looking like breaded chicken cutlets waiting to be thrown on the skillet. The feet no longer attached, muscle and flesh torn off the bone, the signature of blast injuries, whose shrapnel takes the hard bone and whose blast energy takes the soft tissue, the muscles, skin, veins, and arteries pulling up off the remaining bone like the peel off a banana.

Ocho's right hand was split down the middle, as if someone had driven a hatchet between his middle and ring fingers. There were chunks missing out of the meat of the forearm, exposing the large bones there.

I lifted my head, ready to call for Diego and Jeff to clear a path for Ocho to be dragged out, but saw it was already being done. I turned the tourniquet on his right arm and Ocho's bellow was weaker, by far, than the other two I'd heard. I asked about his pain. I squeezed fluids into my friend, resuscitation fluids and analgesia. And Ocho told me, "If you save my life, I'm gonna be so proud of you."

I reached to Ocho's leg and moved aside his dick to place another tourniquet up higher than the one he'd administered himself.

"Now I've got to live," he said. "I'm not gonna die when you're the last person to touch my junk."

When we put Ocho in the stretcher, he screamed in pain, which is normal, more or less, so I didn't realize what had really happened until he shifted, reached over the side of the stretcher, and grabbed his right foot. I'd assumed it had been completely severed, since the foot had been snapped off at the bone, but there was a thick flap of calf muscle still attached, and we were dragging it through the dust, sending pain screaming into his brain. Ocho pulled the foot into the stretcher and clutched it to his stomach, cradling it like a baby with his one good arm, his eyes closed. That's the image I had of him as they put him into the helicopter.

By the end of our deployment to Afghanistan, the 1st Battalion of the 7th Special Forces Group had killed over 3,400 enemy, most of them in a territory that is now, eight years later, still Taliban controlled. Our particular team had sustained no KIA. Which meant, from the perspective of the American public, that it'd been cost-free.

Since we were now just scraps, the team couldn't be kept together, but I'd return to Shah Wali Kot on later deployments. We'd fight another major battle there a few years later. For all I know, we'll fight another major battle there a year from now, or five years from now. Those little kids hustling from the valley, hand in hand with their sisters, escaping the bombardment—they keep getting older.

Azad Khan died in 2010. I was with him at the time, and he said his last words to me. "Sir," he said, bleeding from more wounds than I could ever hope to pack, "I need more hand grenades." When I came back from that deployment, I told Ocho and he laughed and said, "That motherfucker, that lucky motherfucker. Goddamn. He was a fucking motherfucker, wasn't he? A fucking warrior, wasn't he? Goddamn. I wish I could die with some badass shit like that." Ocho still holds out the hope that prosthetics will improve to the point where he can go back to war as some kind of Robocop-style super-soldier with bionic limbs. It doesn't matter if it takes them years to get to that kind of technology, he tells me. Whenever they figure it out, Afghanistan will be waiting, that land he thinks of less as a country than an arena, a stadium for men like him and Azad to do what they were meant to do.

I couldn't have articulated it then but that deployment was the beginning of the dead certainty that I preferred boring Colombia to exciting Afghanistan. I preferred strategy over tactics, progress over bloodshed, winning wars slowly over the thrilling and immediate victories of combat without purpose. When I got back I asked Natalia if she wanted another child, and she said yes.

8

JUAN PABLO 1987–2005

When I was a boy I felt the presence of God. This was, of course, a matter of design. My father sent me to a retreat run by the Jesuits, who are good at that sort of thing. Before my daughter, and before my career in the military, and the hopes for the future they would bring, this would be my first failed love.

They took about twenty of us up to a little place in the mountains. We each had a monastic cell with a tiny window where, for the first few days, we spent our time in almost perfect solitude.

There were prayers and specific passages of Scripture to read. There was a little journal where we reflected on our spiritual progression, such as it was. In the beginning, we were called to bring our sins to the front of our mind, spurring our guilt. Then, we were to calm ourselves by meditation on God's incomprehensible mercy. I remember sitting in my cell, looking up at the small window, at the stone wall with only the most rudimentary of crucifixes, barely more than two twigs strung together. I didn't have any grave sins to call to mind, what boy of twelve does? But still, I prayed, I searched hard for small slights I'd committed, pulled up scraps of memory that could suffice, and held them out for God to look at. Maybe he'd care about them more than I did.

Things got more interesting when we studied the Passion of Christ.

They made it personal, assembling us in groups and urging us to talk about our own sufferings—a task a young man can warm to. The terrible injuries we'd all suffered, or imagined we'd all suffered. Much of what we said was petty, if meaningful to us. And then a boy from a good family, the son of a general, wealthy and handsome, told us that his father regularly beat his mother, and had once thrown him out of a moving car.

"We weren't going very fast," he said, his face pale as the words emerged from his mouth, seemingly unwilled.

The Jesuit scholastic running the retreat, only a decade older than us and clearly with little experience in handling these things, looked terrified. These were the kind of secrets that had consequences when shared. This was dangerous. The son of the general lifted his arm.

"I broke my wrist," he said, fear radiating from him as the words continued to spill out. "I had to get stitches. I still have the scar." He pulled his sleeve back, displaying a faint, jagged line. He stared at it, we stared at it, then he looked up, his eyes attempting to make contact with another set of eyes. But after a person has opened himself, simply to look him in the eye is to assume responsibility for his pain, so the rest of us gazed safely at the floor.

After this, there was silence. I looked around. If no one else were to speak, it would be a betrayal. When you share dark secrets, you must be repaid in kind. I searched my memory, but had nothing. My father, whatever his faults, loved my mother passionately, and loved me the same, and would never have done anything like that.

Finally, one of the other boys spoke, and the group seemed to exhale at once. Thanks to God! He began in a tentative, small voice that slowly expanded into a world of pain and loss. The death of his mother to cancer. A worthy offering. Then another boy spoke, and another, depths suddenly opened, the kidnapping of a sister by the guerrilla here, the loss of a cousin to drugs there, and it seemed as though a secret world had been unlocked, a world in which sin and pain were real, and mattered, and infused us with a terrible sense of the true meaning of the world.

We retreated back to our cells, trembling with the weight of what had happened. There was nothing other than my little window and my little cross to focus my mind, to calm the turbulence in my soul. I knew I was supposed to pray to God. No matter the awfulness of what I'd just heard, such prayers had been made by countless Christians suffering worse crises, suffering martyrdom and torture, pains and troubles far larger than our privileged group of children had been able to produce. But I could not pray. I had no words. And then I heard a sound behind me, and saw a large envelope had been pushed underneath the door to my cell. I lifted it, opened the packet, and withdrew a group of letters tied together with twine.

Each was addressed to me, and when I opened them, one by one, I found they were letters from older boys at my school, and from my parents and relatives. "My sweet, my dearest Juan Pablo," began the one from my father. Each letter was a loving description of me, a catalogue of the ways I had improved the lives of those around me. "When you were born," the letter from my mother began, "my dearest aunt, Blanca Maria, who had raised me more than my own mother, was in hospice care. I took you to see her, you were less than a week old, small enough to hold with one hand, and I put you in her arms. It gave her comfort to know that she was passing out of life as another life was beginning. When she looked at you, the shadow of death passed from her face, and it seemed that all the comfort and promise of the Resurrection settled in her soul. I knew then you would be a joy in the world."

There were letters from other boys as well, boys in the year ahead of me who had undergone this retreat, older boys who we looked up to and who maintained hard exteriors before us but here were telling me, "You are an exceptional, hardworking cadet," or "I can see you doing some great act of heroism," and saying that I was their "brother in Christ." In that place, at that moment, it was overwhelming.

And so the presence struck me. I began to tremble. Tears fell down my face and in my heart I was filled with the most remarkable joy. I walked to the window of my cell, through which I could see the branch of a tree, a bit of sky. A bird flitted into and then out of view, and I had the absurd desire to reach out, cup it in my hand, and kiss it. The stillness in my cell was exquisite. I felt as though the material world had been pierced, and life itself was flooding out from the wound. I was aware of a presence within the room, that I was not alone, though also that the presence was not separate from me. It was larger than my own spirit but somehow suffused with my own, expanding it and extending my senses to an embrace of the cell, the retreat, the whole world. I felt undone, and remade whole. I wanted to call for a priest but also to do nothing more than stand in the stillness. The joy became almost agonizing, having no outlet. And then I spoke the words of the Lord's Prayer.

For a long time after, I was very religious. I spoke about joining the priesthood or a monastic order, cloistering myself away in prayer, removed from the material world, removed even from a sense of normal time, the progression of life and death, my life ruled by the cyclic and unchanging structures of sacred time. I imagined that during my retreat I had opened a wound where the eternal had touched the temporal, and I wanted to live in that wound, expand it, allow it to engulf my universe.

Just before Christmas, the material world intruded. My father was assigned to the 4th Brigade in Medellín. "That's a dangerous post," said one of my school friends, also the son of an officer. It was an odd thing to hear, because Medellín, to me, was my mother's hometown. It was where my grandparents lived, where I had aunts and uncles and cousins spread across the city. So the new posting should have been a return to the land of my own birth, where I'd played with cousins in "Los Altos del Castillo," as my grandmother called their neighborhood, which was really just a part of Las Mercedes. Where I'd gone up into the mountains with my grandmother to visit the town of her birth, where she'd ridden a horse and lived a life that was "poor, but not poverty of the city, because we always had food to eat," and where she'd stayed until the time of troubles after the death of Gaitán and the family fled to the city, only to have unexpected success in the grocery business, allowing them to send their fourth child, my mother, to a school where she would interact with a higher class of people—the class my father belonged to. It should have been a wealth of cousins and grandparents and aunts and uncles, but my father quickly informed us that we wouldn't be coming with him.

"Even if you came," my father told me, "you would stay on base and have to go to school with the soldiers' children. Almost none of the officers are bringing their families, and frankly, the less contact we have with your mother's family, the safer they are."

But my mother insisted we at least visit during the holidays, and so that December I both returned to Medellín and failed to return to Medellín. The streets and buildings remained the same, bits of concrete and steel and glass arranged in the same patterns, but those roads which throughout my childhood had been no more than a means to the loving arms of my grandparents, with their large house, their plants, and their massive oven, an ancient oven that my grandmother still used to run her home business selling cakes, those roads now belonged to a different geography, one shaped not by land and steel but by people. I was a child, barely old enough to stare longingly at a woman but still, somehow I knew that my father was right. This was not the same city where I could buy sweets and coffee with my grandmother at El Astor, walk with my grandfather through San Antonio Plaza, talking to the people he knew, businessmen and shoe shiners and women selling salted mango. Stepping out into the streets now would be as wise as stepping over the edge of a mountain cliff. The city had changed.

Whatever the old web of life and commerce, gossip and backstabbing, old loves and new infatuations, I was no longer a part of it.

"Things have changed," my father said.

After our cold Christmas in officers' quarters, my father asked First Sergeant Santiago Jaramillo, a senior enlisted who had lost a nephew to a cartel bombing, to drive us to the airport. Jaramillo was in plain clothes, driving a plain blue sedan with a warped fender instead of an army vehicle. I thought it odd, but given the narcissism of youth, thought little about it. I sat in the backseat, my mother in the front.

Jaramillo had a shiny, shaved head with a vein bulging just over the right ear. He also swore constantly as he drove.

"Look at this fool!" he'd say as a car swerved in front of him. He'd pull ahead, swerve back in front of the other car, and shout "Faggot!" out the window. Then he'd catch himself, scrunch his thick neck into his shoulders, and apologize to my mother.

"I'm sorry, ma'am, it's these . . . Whore! Son of a whore . . . I'm sorry, ma'am."

He couldn't help it. He knew no other way to drive. In the backseat, I'd giggle at the curses, then stifle my giggles as my mother turned sternly back to me.

But as we rose above the city on long, winding roads up the mountainside, the cursing stopped. We reached a traffic light, Jaramillo slowing at first as the light turned red, then bolting through at the last moment, the car swerving into a hard right, centripetal force pressing me into the side of the car, seat belt cutting against my neck as he skirted in front of oncoming traffic, horns blaring.

It squeezed the breath out of me, but when my breath returned, I waited for the sound. For an "Idiot!" or "Faggot!" or "Son of a whore!" I waited for my mother to say something sharp, but there was nothing. My mother held herself straight, her face in the mirror still, expressionless, her left hand gripped on the edge of the seat and her right on the handle of the car door.

After the second crazy turn I realized we were being followed. Of course, I knew about the kidnappings, but had always felt that only happened to other, lesser people. I was the son of an army officer, I was immune. But no, I realized in the car. That had it backward. I was the son of an army officer. Therefore, I was a target.

When I returned to Bogotá, I had nightmares of being lost in the winding turns of a city I didn't know, a city where every face is like the face of a relative, but then, when I draw near, different. No one knows me, no one can tell me which turns I must take, or even where my final destination must be.

To be honest, I don't know if the two things, the nightmares and the trip to the airport, were related, but they added to the uneasiness of my waking hours, the already uneasy waking hours of a new adolescent, charged with hormones and emotions now heightened by the aftershocks of repetitive, peculiar dreams and the anxiety of a father in a war zone, a war zone that happens to be the city of my family, and a city where I do not belong.

When we returned to Medellín for our next visit, in the midst of Holy Week, I was full of nervous excitement. And it was in that state that I first encountered Juana Peréz.

We came on Holy Thursday and, along with another officer's family, went straight to the 4th Brigade Headquarters under escort. The base was different, packed with people, many of them civilians.

"We've had to convert Fourth Brigade into a refugee camp," my father explained. The general in charge, General Bedoya, was trying to organize something like a witness protection program. The civilians on base were witnesses to the crimes of the Medellín cartel. I think my father wanted me to see them, to know the luck I had in life, to know what drugs were doing to Colombia, and to spend time around people brave enough to stand up to Escobar. I hardly spoke to any of them, spending the time reading instead.

"This will be an education for him," he told my mother. "He'll get to see what this work is and how it doesn't wait, not even for God."

As if to prove his point, on Holy Saturday a canister bomb was launched over the walls of 4th Brigade, right where the officers' quarters were. No one was killed, and my father wasn't displaced, but we did lose water and power for two days, meaning that we had to use the group showers in the building where they were billeting our "refugees." This, too, my father thought would be "an education." And he was right.

I woke very early Easter morning, disturbed by another one of my peculiar nightmares, and left to take a shower. As in my dream, the route I walked was both strangely similar to what I knew and different in ways my sleepy mind wasn't processing. I entered a group bathroom, one I thought I had used before, ignoring the very important sign on the door.

Inside was a corridor with various stalls, each with a little curtain that stopped about a foot short of the floor. One stall was occupied, the water running. I got in the stall across the way, turned on the water, and waited for it to warm. I missed my home in Bogotá, and I missed the Medellín Holy Week of my childhood memories, when everyone in the street put on purple clothes, emptying the factories of purple cloth and creating processions that turned the streets into bright ribbons of color. There at 4th Brigade, you mostly saw army green.

The water warmed, I stepped in, and I heard the other shower turn off, then the other shower curtain being swept aside. Idly curious, I peered through the crack between my curtain and the stall and saw a column of flesh cut across by what looked like black twine, a curious sight. I leaned my head and moved closer to the crack to get a better view. The other person shifted, and there in front of me, no more than a meter from my face, was a naked woman's breast.

My jaw hung slack, my eyes widened. I could have spit and hit the nipple. For a moment I did nothing but look, shocked by the sight. The nipple swayed, moved out of view, and I bolted back to the edge of the shower, my shower sandals splashing water. Idiot! I thought to myself. I was terrified she'd look in around the edge of my curtain. I had the ridiculous desire to sing in a high-pitched voice, or hum, the way I imagined a woman might hum in the shower. I took shallow breaths of air. The antiseptic smell of cleaning solution, carried up by the steam, flooded my nostrils. The nipple swung back into view and I stared, breathless. Blood rushed to my face in shame, but it also, I realized, was rushing to another, much more disobedient organ. I covered myself with my hands. What if she swept aside the curtain? What would I say?

A curved belly appeared before the crack, then shoulders and long, thin arms, here too with the patches of flesh appearing as though they were bound in black twine, poorly wrapped, then all was covered with a white towel. It was too much, and I wanted to weep. Instead I clenched my jaw, controlled my breathing, remained still with my hands trying painfully to bend down that disobedient organ, to tuck it between my legs.

Then the white towel swept upward, and I could see it above the top of my curtain. She was drying her hair, this woman. I leaned again to the right side of the stall, peered through the crack, and saw that the towel was over her face, covering her eyes completely. My body relaxed, slightly. There were a few golden seconds where I was certain she couldn't see me. Without thinking, I inched closer to the edge of the curtain, trying to get a better look than the mere slivers I'd had before.

The woman's whole body, with the exception of her towel-covered head, came into view. She was tall, with skinny legs, long skinny twigs for arms, a beautiful curve to her back, and, as she turned slightly, displaying her marvels to me, the far more exaggerated curve of a pregnant belly. Her skin was fairer than mine, and crisscrossed with what I now realized were stitches, black stitches over still-healing scars. They were all over her shoulders and arms, most of them ten to fifteen centimeters in length, and straight, what I would later come to realize was the work of a weapon. In the moment, they neither added nor detracted from her beauty, such as it was, but only underscored her astounding strangeness. She had a few more scars on the upper parts of her legs, two across her chest, one on the outside of her right breast, but none, thanks to God, across that remarkable belly, smooth and round, her breasts lying on top of it, and from below her stomach, reaching up, her wounded thighs, between which, just visible, a dark patch of hair.

I heard her sigh. Her hands, small with gnawed fingernails, stopped their work atop her head and unwound the towel. I quickly stepped to the back of the shower, again, splashing water as I went, again. Cursing myself an idiot, again. She started singing, "I cannot forget that woman that made me suffer such a long time, I cannot forget that love . . ." And then she stopped and gave a short laugh. I heard rustling. I couldn't see her, I heard only the smallest sounds. I didn't know what she was doing. I didn't have any idea of what a woman does in the morning to prepare herself for the day. And then the door opened and closed, and she was gone.

I reached outside the curtain, grabbed my towel, and wrapped it tightly around my waist, tying my erection flat to my stomach. I hadn't really washed myself, didn't even think about continuing. I wanted to escape. I stepped out into the steamy room, walked the corridor between the empty shower stalls, came to the door, and wondered what could be on the other side. Was the woman waiting, knowing I'd eventually emerge? Was someone new coming in? Perhaps only we two were crazy enough to shower so early, so far before daylight. Perhaps she, too, had nightmares.

I opened the door to an empty corridor and shut it behind me. There was the sign I'd ignored, heading in. "Women," it read.

For weeks afterward, I would wake early from a different type of dream, where I traced my fingers over her rough stitches and her pure stomach, where she looked down on me from her great height and stared into my soul with eyes so powerful they drowned out all vision of her face, where her strong hands reached down, touched my young body on my neck, my shoulders, my hairless chest, reached down and down until I woke up excited and frustrated and ashamed in my bed in Bogotá, hundreds of kilometers and another world away from where she lived and had suffered. I didn't want to have these dreams. I hated them. But they came anyway.

Worse, the memory followed me in the daytime. Of course I had noticed girls before, and wondered about what was beneath their clothes. I had seen images of naked women in magazines older boys had secreted away, showing me glimpses of women with enormous breasts and butts, lips painted to a deep red and faces caked with makeup and buffed to a flawless, inhuman sheen. But the woman in the shower, with her wounds and pregnant belly and chewed fingernails, replaced those fantasy women. The woman in the shower was different. She was real. A woman in the body of a woman, capable of being touched, of being wounded, of giving birth. A woman with a history and a future. The antiseptic smell of cleaning fluid was enough to make me stiffen.

The memory of her worked on me as powerfully, and as incomprehensibly, as my early encounter with what I was then calling God. I don't mean this in the simple and often stupid way in which sexual passion is contrasted with religious ecstasy. The two experiences were not remotely similar—the first a rapture occurring entirely within my head, the second an assault on every nerve in my body. Nor was my reaction to her simply one of desire. If anything, the desire served merely to muddle the other reactions I'd had and add a strong layer of shame to the memory. Unlike the memory of God, which offered a clear path to me, this left me confused. It made me think there was something wrong with me. Sometimes, I blamed that woman. Mostly, I wanted to see her again. I hoped that she had an ugly face, as if an ugly face, or even a normal face, would purge the effect the rest of her body had made on me.

I learned her name, and her story, the following July.

"Would you like to be the altar boy at a baptism?" my father asked me over the phone. "I'm going to be the godfather to a very special child."

This child, I would learn, was graced with the name Harold Peréz, named after the general in whose barracks he had been born. "The mother, Juana Peréz, she is one of our refugees," he said. Juana, my father explained, had been in the Department of Security and Control in Envigado, a city bordering Medellín that at the time was the center for white-collar workers in the drug trade. "Her colleagues had tried to murder her with hatchets," my father said, "so be prepared. She has some impressive scars, and I don't want you staring."

We all had breakfast before the baptism—my father, my mother, an officer from the B2, little baby Harold, and Juana Peréz. I knew her immediately by her hands, even though her fingernails had grown out. And of course I knew her scars.

Despite my hopes, she did have a pretty face. Not beautiful or exceptional, and not with the deep and piercing eyes in my dreams, but the face of a normal young woman of Medellín. Prettier than the average Colombian, but standard for this city. When my father introduced us, she smiled a big smile that shocked me somehow. Perhaps I thought that a woman with such wounds would never smile. Or that she'd only smile looking at her baby, not at the outside world and the people you meet there.

"You have such a handsome son," she said, and I bristled. She turned so that little Harold faced me, his eyes closed and his face peaceful. "Say hello, Harold. One day you'll be big, like Juan."

I didn't eat much at breakfast, even though my mother made arepa de chocolo, which I loved. I was too confused by this ordinary woman who should not be ordinary, who should be weeping in fear or in joy at the gift of life, who should have been visibly overcoming her horrific past through indomitable will, but who mostly just chatted with my father and the officer from the B2 about the food on base getting better, and how she'd started reading the book the officer from the B2 gave her and she thought the author was better even than Mutis.

Then, since it turned out my mother and Juana had grown up in the same neighborhoods, they began talking about the people there—the grocer who let so many people get by on credit that when he retired there was a line of people down the street to pay off debts, my mother's cousins who had worked in a factory making T-shirts, and the bad kids who hung out on the corner when they were both little girls. "I think, maybe," Juana said, "they smoked marijuana," a comment that made both my father and the intelligence officer laugh. Other than that, nothing that she said was especially remarkable.

Years later, in an attempt to exorcise the impression she made on my young mind, I would write a series of terrible poems about her in which she was an idealized figure, an eternal image of Colombia, a scarred goddess displaying her wounds and bringing forth unblemished new life, and so on. The more airy my descriptive language became, the more it jarred against my memories of this breakfast, during which she was too ordinary and lively to be reduced to a goddess of Colombia. I gave up, deciding she was an image of nothing. Or she was the image of a living and breathing woman who had been brutally attacked, survived, and went on to give birth and live her life. Which is enough poetry for anyone to endure.

As the breakfast finished up, though, she caught me staring at her scars, and she asked, "Would you like to hear the story?"

"I'm sorry, I'm sorry," I said, ashamed to be caught.

"No, it's good," she said. "Telling the story is good. I learned that from your father. Though he says you tell these kind of stories with soldiers, and aguardiente."

"I didn't . . ." my father began to say, but then stopped. I don't think I'd ever seen him embarrassed before. My mother shook her head, but said nothing.

"And you tell them over and over," Juana said, "because it is *your* story. Right, Colonel?" My father gave an almost imperceptible nod, and then she gritted her jaw, the lightness of her manner disappearing for a second, before she flung her head back, giving me a better view of the scars on her neck.

"I walk the earth by the grace of the Lord's Prayer and a leather jacket," she said. There was a stiffness to how she spoke, the words sounding rehearsed, a ritual. But as she continued she relaxed into the story.

"Four of my colleagues at the Department of Security and Control . . . Saúl Londoño, Fernando Tenorio, Augosto Posada, as well as Luis Veléz, who is the son of a whore, and I apologize for using that word, but if I used a nicer word I'd be telling a lie. They asked me to come with them in a van. I trusted them, because I worked with them, and because . . ." She cocked her head and looked down at little sleeping Harold. "I trusted them for many reasons," she said.

She explained how silent it was in the van, how Luis wouldn't even look at her, how she refused to accept what was about to happen to her, even though she knew what happened had happened to so many others at the hands of the Department of Security and Control.

"I only accepted it when the van stopped," she said. "Then I knew,

I was about to die. They threw me out of the van, but I fought. I was wearing a black leather jacket, and Luis had a hand on it and it pulled up over my head as I fell to the ground, covering my face so I could not see. And then I felt the first strike of a hatchet."

She slapped her hands on the table. "Boom," she said. And then she tilted her head so her hair fell down to the side, and she parted her long, dark hair—quite beautiful hair, in fact—revealing a hidden scar on the side of her skull.

"I started to pray the Our Father," she said. "I only got to 'blessed be thy name,' and, boom! Another strike of the hatchet. I started again. 'Our Father, who art—' boom. I kept praying, and they kept hitting me, and every time they hit me I started again."

She nodded, as if in agreement with what she was saying.

"Thirty-five times, they hit me," she said, "or they hit my jacket, thanks to God. Thirty-five times I tried to pray the Our Father. That's how many holes they found in my jacket"—she smiled—"and in me. They left me for dead. I wasn't sure I was alive. But I recited the Our Father, and made it further than before. 'Forgive us our trespasses, as we forgive those who trespass against us.' Imagine, praying that! 'And lead us not into temptation . . . ' I prayed, so terrified to reach the end. I was so, so afraid to reach the end. I thought I would finish, and ascend to Heaven or go to hell. And then I reached the end. 'Deliver us from evil. Amen.' I waited. I was still alive. I prayed the Our Father once more. I was in so much pain, I knew I must be alive. I prayed a Hail Mary, just to be sure. And then I got up, my jacket and my body all in tatters, cut up and bleeding, and I walked to a road and stopped a bus full of laborers going to work. I told them to take me right to Search Bloc, but they brought me, instead, to your father, and this is where I've been ever since."

I wasn't sure what to say. I went with, "It's a miracle."

Juana smiled indulgently. "Luis is Harold's father," she said. "Or was. I think if you try to murder your son and his mother, you are no longer a father. Harold is a child of God now. Which is why we are all here today."

At the baptism I wore white robes not so different from Harold's baptismal gown. I was nervous, trying to work myself up to a sense of religious devotion, but mainly struck with horror at what Juana and Harold had survived, and shame at my secret history with her. Harold woke up midway through the sacrament and started screaming. "He's going to sing opera," the officer from B2 whispered. The priest poured water over Harold's head, anointing him. A child of God, I thought, remembering Juana's words. Throughout I kept sneaking glances at Juana's face. I wondered how many children had been baptized in such circumstances, how many children whose mothers barely survived to bring their children into the world. There must be many. Many even at that very moment, women threatened by the drug business, by the political struggle, by angry, jealous, crazy men, desperate men, drunken men, cruel men. Juana Peréz could not have been the first to crawl bloody out of the mountains, or jungles, or ditches, or alleyways, or broken homes. Most women like her die, I knew, but against all odds, some live.

I looked around at the participants. Juana's role was obviously closed to me, and I didn't think much of the father's contribution. Even the priest seemed peripheral, a mere conduit. My father, though, in his uniform, a representative of another ancient order, was not peripheral at all. His ancient order did not just anoint. They had received and protected Juana, entering into her history in a way that seemed profound.

For the remainder of my visit to Medellín I observed my father through an entirely different lens. His days had a monastic rhythm, given not by an eternal structure of prayer but by staff meetings, regular reporting requirements, and the rigid timelines of military operations. His days had a monastic austerity, missing meals and sleep to work and enduring time on patrols full of such physical danger and hardship it bordered on mortification of the flesh. And his days had a monastic hierarchal structure, with conscripts in place of novitiates and General Harold Bedoya in place of an abbot. Everything operated in terms of traditions, moral codes, regulations, and trained responses, just the same as in an order, except that in a monastery all this revolves around the awestruck contemplation of a God existing outside of history, and in the military it revolves around the work of violence, which is what makes history happen.

I did not make the decision then, but as time passed, as the memory of the presence of God faded and as Medellín became habitable again, a place I could walk through without fear, I became more and more drawn to the way in which my father's work impacted the lives of real people, saving lives and creating a space for life to flourish. His wasn't a life centered on money or things, the shallow currencies of the external world, but on people and duty. There seemed something sacred about such work, or if not sacred then something like it, and by the time I was eighteen I knew.

Thus began my second failed love, one that filled me not with the wonder and gratitude toward existence I'd felt in my little monastic cell as a child, but with a painfully sharp sense of duty toward a broken, evil world. I finished university, I went through training, I was commissioned. I spoke the words, completed the rituals, and received not God's saving grace but responsibility over the life and death of thirty-two young Colombians. The responsibility puffed me up with an unearned sense of self-importance, which, especially in the early days of my marriage to Sofia, made me almost unbearable in the company of civilians. Though it was a moral duty I was fulfilling, not a sacred one, in its intensity it seemed to rise to a religious level. Standing in starlit fields with instant coffee packed into our lips like tobacco to keep us awake, hiding in ditches by the side of remote roads, patrolling through ruined towns—the war was more than my job. It was the dark star around which the entirety of my existence orbited, to which family and friends and loved ones and sex and money and God seemed like weak abstractions, insubstantial against the weight of the madness we were fighting.

This is enough to give a young man a sense of purpose. No more is necessary.

And since my father made general the year I became an officer, my career was charmed, one desirable post after another, leading me to seek out new difficulties and challenges. Ways to prove myself. Which is how I ended up in Saravena.

Saravena was a guerrilla town where the people hated us so much they'd walk up to soldiers in the street, look for the youngest, most scared-looking conscript, sniff loudly, and say, "I smell formaldehyde." It was an ugly fight, where the hatred of the people provoked the hatred of our soldiers, who would sometimes take the kind of actions young, scared, hateful, and hated soldiers will do.

Counterinsurgency was in fashion then. My colonel had attended a 2004 Southern Command conference where the American military had pushed population support and development as the critical element of success, something that had amused my father. "The Americans always have a new shiny idea," he said. "I trained with American veterans of Vietnam at the School of the Americas, and all their tactics were based around zones of annihilation and the logic of attrition. Now we're supposed to do counterinsurgency? That's not what they're doing in Iraq. I think they just want to see if we fail before they change strategies."

Our colonel came up with the idea of targeting the hearts and minds not of the adults, who were inflexible in their loathing of us, but of their children. And so he created the "Soldier for a Day" program, in which a soldier would put on clown makeup and a clown wig, to go along with his uniform and rifle, and entertain children at the local schools.

Initial runs were not a success. I assigned the first duty to a young soldier, Edgardo Ramos, with a round face and a cheerful manner and a way of always making his fellows laugh in training. When we entered the school, some of the children's faces turned pale. He did some jokes, pretended to walk into a wall, told them about where he was from and why he was here.

"I was out with my father's cow and the military caught me!" he said. "They said, 'You're going into the military!' and I said, 'What do I do with this cow? It belongs to my father.' And they said, 'You better sell it!' Can you imagine how mad my father was? I send him money every month but every month he asks me, 'What happened to that cow?'"

I thought it was the greatest waste of time I'd ever encountered. After the class, one of the teachers asked to speak to me.

"Privately?" I said.

She looked nervous. "No, no," but then pulled me around a corner from where Edgardo was doing his best to ease the tension in the room.

"This is not good for the children," the teacher said. And then she launched into a story about how the paramilitaries had tried to infiltrate the town a couple months ago, and how they had killed some of the guerilla in a bombing attack, and how after that the guerrilla had tightened their grip on the town, controlling who came in and who came out. "Anyone new," she said, "they killed."

I nodded my head, confused by why she was telling me this, but listening because I imagined she might give me useful intelligence.

"It was right after the first round of killings that the Peruvians came," she said.

They were a group of clowns on a humanitarian mission, Clowns Without Borders, idealists who thought that even children in war zones, especially children in war zones, deserved laughter. They entered town with painted faces and big smiles, and were almost immediately lined up, shot in the head, and left in the street as a warning.

"The only other time these children have seen clowns," the teacher told me, "they were corpses. It was terrifying. Even living clowns frighten me. Even real clowns, not your . . . I don't know what you are doing, or what to call it . . . but it will give them nightmares."

Afterward, I spoke to my colonel about the Soldier for a Day program. Knowing about my father, he normally was solicitous of my opinions, but the dead-clowns story only made him more enthusiastic.

"It's the guerrilla that terrified them, not us!" he said. "Whenever they see clowns, they'll think of the terror of the guerrilla murderers, and the laughter and jokes of our clowns, laughter and jokes which cannot be stopped because our clowns carry guns."

He ordered me to continue the program, and suggested that I put my own name on the roster. "Lead by example," he said. "Practice some funny faces."

There was no way, I told myself, I would play the clown, but we did keep running the program, sometimes even succeeding in making children laugh, or at the very least getting them to marvel at the guns our clowns carried, and to wonder how they, too, could acquire such guns and carry them in the service of the state.

A little later, one of my platoons was ambushed by a large force of guerrilla four kilometers outside of town. It was the most aggressive force-on-force engagement the guerrilla had tried, and it didn't end well for them. Since this was during a brief window in which I had access to air assets, I got in an old Huey to fly out and direct the battle, although everything had ended by the time I arrived. The men, as trained, had driven through the heart of the ambush and routed the guerrilla, miraculously not losing any soldiers and killing a few of the enemy.

As we flew down, I could see the men moving about, conducting the rituals of men after battles—treating their wounded, stacking ammunition, hauling trash, and talking among themselves, telling the story of the combat to each other so that, with the telling and retelling, they could come to some group version of what happened, and what it meant to them. Looking at them from above, from the outside, I felt sharp, almost painful pangs of pride. They had succeeded in the task we had set for them, gone out patrolling in the land of the dead, faced down carnage, and survived.

I left my Huey, saying little but walking among the men, clapping them on their shoulders, showing my appreciation for what they'd been through without trying to intrude. A young lieutenant with haunted eyes delivered his report on the battle, his quavering voice slowly steadying as he slipped into the dry language of the military, taking the jumbled memories of chaos he'd just experienced and squeezing them into the precise categories of official reports. I felt like a priest, taking his confession.

When I returned to Saravena, I was energized. The dead stares of the people, their empty eyes as they looked upon us the way you'd look at the corpses of animals, it meant nothing. We'd had a force-on-force engagement, at a time and place chosen by the enemy, and had won. Within the hour, though, I heard an explosion. Reporting came on through the radio—gas canisters turned to bombs in a road by one of the schools where we brought our Soldier for the Day clowns. Casualties.

A difficult period began. The enemy perfected its methods against us, and we perfected our hatred against the population that shielded them. More bombs in gas canisters, violence against us perpetrated by ghosts. I began taking sleeping pills. First one, then two, then three or four, and still I could not sleep. Beyond the difficulties of our mission, there were troubles for my family, whispers bubbling against my father, sensational reports in the news.

The day my father was fired by Álvaro Uribe, I'd spent the morning on a patrol through a town that had only further hardened its hearts against us, and then I had signed off on a report that listed three eleno dead, though I secretly suspected it was at most one eleno dead, and two civilians suspected of aiding the guerrilla. That afternoon a bomb went off and took the hand of Edgardo Ramos, our first clown, and I'd sat with him, waiting for medical evacuation, holding his one remaining hand while he smiled and laughed his way through the pain and told me, "But I still haven't paid off my father's cow!" I got the news about my father in the evening, and then read through the press reports and the official, emotionless language of the release announcing the firing.

The newspapers told a story of how military recruiters had combed through the Soacha barrio, looking for the mentally disabled and the desperate, told them they had good-paying work for them, flew them to Norte de Santander, shot them, and claimed the bodies were guerrillas to inflate body count and earn promotions.

My father was not directly implicated, but it had happened in units under his command. Someone would have to pay, and not someone too high up. Certainly not the politically powerful minister of defense, who would go on to be president of the country in a few years. No, someone lower down, less connected, but still guilty of negligence if not actively turning a blind eye. Someone like my father.

One of the men implicated, Carlos Viterbo, was now on trial. I'd known Carlos. He was a large, lusty fellow, a lover of women and alcohol, a terrible but enthusiastic dancer, the sort who spouted the usual motivations for joining the officer corps of the Colombian army and who you generally assumed would be a decent officer and, at the very least, a midway decent man. There was no odor of corruption about him. But as I read I knew in my heart that he'd done it, and in my exhaustion and rage at the town of Saravena I almost understood. And as for my father—given the report I'd signed that morning, the deaths I'd chosen not to look too closely at, I understood all too well.

The newspapers suggested this was only the beginning of these revelations, that such things were happening across Colombia as the military exerted intense downward pressure to meet the demands of Plan Patriota. General officers who didn't care to investigate seemingly good news about body counts—corrupt, callous, evil men, the articles implied, men like my loving father—were even now permitting mass murder.

Neither the articles nor the press release admitted to any mitigating factors, to the difficulty of maintaining discipline in an army that was expanding, relying heavily on sometimes poorly motivated conscripts, fighting a brutal war in which growing hatred of civilian populations is inevitable, and where we were operating in new places and under pressures that the army had never successfully navigated in the past. Why bother? Mitigating factors fail to explain when you cross the border to murders of this kind. The only explanation left is the sin all men are born with, a sin that marks us forever as loathsome creatures, fit for death. It is why an army needs iron discipline, to stamp out the kind of freelance killings that reduce our effectiveness as a fighting force and diminish our prestige in the eyes of the public. My father had the bad luck to be in command of one of the units that got caught. But how could I hold him responsible? I loved him, and besides, this is war.

It was all too much to absorb, so as I scanned the articles the words I read were like coins tossed into an empty well. No emotions, but practical concerns flashed in and out of my consciousness. My father's salary. His pension. My mother's hard-won place in a society that looks on newcomers with contempt. My career, the easy path to generalship I'd anticipated. The increased scrutiny I could now expect to fall on me and on my piece of the ugly war in Saravena. And far beneath all these practical worries was a different kind of concern, one about the love I had for my father, about the man he was, and the knowledge that he would never be that proud, unbroken man ever again.

I retired to my quarters with exhaustion written across my face. When I reached my door, I stopped, too tired to open it, too tired to begin again my never-ending struggle with sleep. I thought of the ambush, months before, and the little rituals of the men, the way they cared for each other, and the hope that it brought me, and I realized it was not enough. Such things can sustain a soldier for a time, especially if the troops still have some degree of faith in the fight. But that faith was withering. More and more, we hoped to survive, and to make our enemies suffer. A combat deployment is not like a prayer, sufficient unto itself. The effort and the pain of combat is only worth it if you succeed. Otherwise, it is no more than a net increase in the suffering of the world. What I'd brought men like Edgardo Ramos to hadn't been worth the price of his father's cow.

I turned the knob and opened the door. The first thing I saw, sitting on my bed, was a bright, multicolored wig. Beside it, tubes of face paint, and a note from my colonel. Tomorrow was my turn to be the clown.

When I returned from Saravena, I had difficulties. I'd be in the middle of a meeting, or drafting a report, and a memory from Saravena would strike, some fragmented image, the packed dirt of a jungle trail or the way the exterior of a shop had caught the sunlight. Stupid things like that. And there was an unease, this sense that I was a little thing in a cold universe that was out of my control, and threatening. I don't want to exaggerate these difficulties. I know soldiers who have had terrible problems, years where they could only sleep with alcohol, and spent their waking hours with every muscle tensed, always on guard. My difficulties were minor. Manageable. But nevertheless, it was irritating. It interfered with work, and with my relaxation at home.

Sofia told me I was more impatient than before, more hostile, and I trusted her sense of the matter. She demanded I go to confession. To please her, I went, and the old priest interrupted before I even got halfway through what I wanted to say. "But these aren't sins!" he said. Everything I'd done had been for my country, he pointed out. And even though I agreed, I felt rage coming up my throat.

"Good," I said, "because even if I believed in God, I'd never believe an old fool like you could forgive me."

It was a disproportionate response, further evidence that something was wrong. I wrote down everything that happened on my deployment in a list, and then burned it. I wrote it out again over the course of a week, this time telling the stories of my deployment not as something I experienced, but as something "we" experienced, the strong, unbeatable "we," who cannot be destroyed. My mood turned unbearably black, and Sophia demanded I return to confession.

"I don't care if you believe or not," she said. "You're definitely a sinner, and I'm only going to forgive you if God does."

This time, I didn't go for an old, conservative priest, I found myself a nice young Jesuit. Perhaps I went to him because it was the Jesuits who had introduced me to God in the first place. Perhaps because Jesuits tend to be leftists, and maybe I'd get some fool with a tattoo of Camilo Torres and a heart shaped like a hammer and sickle. The sort who would refuse to forgive me.

That's not what happened. Like Pope Gregory and the emperor, they're not allowed to withhold forgiveness, even if they want to. The Jesuit listened, and then gave me as penance the command to contact the families of every man injured or killed under my command.

"What kind of officer do you think I am?" I said, genuinely offended. "Of course I've contacted the families."

"At the time," he said. "It's been almost a year. How are they doing now?"

He forgave me, and over the next month I went about the awful penance he'd demanded, reaching out to the families and reopening the scars of their loss.

One night during this time, Valencia had a terrible nightmare. She was seven years old, and asked to sleep with us, which I never allowed. "She cannot become weak," I'd tell Sofia, who agreed. This time, however, I said yes.

Our wide-eyed daughter, holding her stuffed rabbit, started crawling up onto the bed. Unwilling to let go of her rabbit, she clutched the sheets with one hand, trying to pull herself up ineffectually until I grabbed her by the armpits, hauled her over my body and into the space between Sofia and me. Briefly, before she turned from me to Sofia, I looked into her eyes, and I could see that she truly was recovering from terror. A yearning as sharp as desire stung me. I wanted to comfort her.

People say a lot of stupidities about fatherhood, as if it were some magical, sacred thing, when in truth it is the least magical, least sacred, and most purely animal thing about us. Holding a baby, changing her, clutching her to your skin. And even before that, watching your wife go through pregnancy, and then labor, this intensely physical act that is entirely out of your control and that, as a man, you can only watch in terror. We have this illusion that we are rational creatures separate from creation, that we can control and shape nature, the way a dike shapes the course of a river. It is a comforting illusion. Then the dike breaks, and you have a bloody screaming child that you bring home, thinking, We are animals, because what you witnessed was not so different from a calving. It gives you a new appreciation for calvings. And then you have a wife whose breasts refuse to give enough milk so during the times you're home, and not in the jungle, you end up feeding your daughter with a bottle. Most of love is communicated without words or thoughts but with touch, the slow synchronization of breathing and heartbeats, things happening below the level of the mind, at the level of your body that feels a part of you and yet, somehow, different. As a military man, I only had this in scraps with Valencia, so the love between us was strong but glued together with abstractions about duty and family that filled in the places when I was in the jungle, physically distant from her and so, in some sense, not fully her father.

For this reason, it didn't surprise me that after I lay Valencia down she wriggled over to her mother. She was so small, our little girl. Sofia kissed her forehead and closed her eyes. But then Valencia reached back, grabbed my hand, and pulled it so that my arm wrapped around her, and she hugged her small arms around my big one like a koala hanging on a tree trunk. It was the first time since I had been back that she had reached for me out of the basic physical needs of a child for love, and not out of a sense of duty, the hugs and kisses a daughter owes a father even if she doesn't know him so well. I felt her calm herself, an easing of the body. My own body echoed hers, and we both feel asleep, the most blissful sleep I'd experienced in months.

Naturally, stupidly, I thought I was cured. *My child's love has restored my trust in the world!* It was a romantic notion, but it was soon made clear to me that the night had only been a strange confluence of psychological states. Still, it had revealed relief was possible, and I learned that I found that relief most readily with her. I came to think of the effect Valencia had on me as being like that sense of God I'd had as a child, of eternity wounding the material world, wounding the boundaries of my own brain and body, and making me part of a larger story, in the one case the cosmic drama of the universe outside of time, a cosmic drama I no longer believed in, and in the other case the narrower drama of a family, moving forward inside of time. It was a love grounded in the world, in one person whose fate, unlike the fate of an unruly city or country, you can guide with a firm hand.

At Valencia's baptism, I had declared my willingness to train her in the Catholic faith. At the baptism of Juana Peréz's son, I had heard an infant scream as the sign of the cross was made on his skull. On both occasions, I had imagined I was witnessing a sacred mystery. My world is so much more circumscribed now, that faith drained. And yet, in my daughter, there is still a movement to the future. All the unresolved failures of my own life can have an answer in her.

III

If I must die, I would like my body to be
mixed in with the clay of the forts like a living mortar,
spread by God between the stones of the new city.

—*Álvaro Ulcué Chocué*

1

N ine months before the dinner party, before they'd smoked cigars and discussed the Mil Jesúses and the intelligence they were giv- ing the Colombian military, Mason had been invited to watch Juan Pablo kill a man. He'd just arrived in country and though the raid seemed unimportant—the Colombians were taking out a midlevel narco who by all rights should have been the police's business and not the army's—Mason decided to go. He wanted to be collegial.

And so, he'd flown to Tolemaida Air Base and there had shaken hands with Juan Pablo for the first time. He'd received a quick over- view on the man they were tracking—El Alemán, a criminal associated both with the Urabeños and with a splinter faction of the ELN—and was then brought into the operations center. There, on the screen, a video feed from a U.S.-supplied ScanEagle drone eight hundred miles away tracked the progress of a medium-size white truck.

"What's in the truck?" Mason had asked.

And with the utmost seriousness, Juan Pablo had replied, "A giant teddy bear."

The bear, he learned, was two meters tall. It was pink. It had a white heart in the center of its chest. It had been tied with a pink bow and placed inside a giant pink box that was then tied with another, larger bow that was, of course, pink.

"We got a tip," Juan Pablo said. Today was El Alemán's girlfriend's birthday. Which meant a party, and a special-ordered present that, once the military had been tipped off, was easy to track. Months later, Mason would realize the tip had undoubtedly come from the Jesúses, and that Juan Pablo had undoubtedly been the conduit. Not knowing that, or the chain of events the raid would set in motion, Mason had merely accepted the information and, with more than a little boredom, watched the slow and painstaking process by which targets are eliminated in modern warfare.

Mason watched the truck navigate mountain roads. He watched the truck arrive at a luxurious finca with a high exterior wall and three separate structures. He watched the debate break out among those in the operations center whether to have a team fly to the X and fast-rope down into the compound, or leave the helicopters on the far side of the mountain and walk to the objective. Hours later, he watched the arrival of El Alemán himself, who came not from the road but from a path in the mountains, riding a mule.

El Alemán had gold chains and emeralds glittering across his chest. They'd later find a 30-million-peso watch on his right wrist and a 40-million-peso watch on his left. He was not nearly as fat as his last known photo, so at first the Colombians were not sure it was him. He'd gotten a gastric balloon, they knew that. They were expecting a skinnier man. But this guy, clip-clopping in, complaining about the pain in his ass to his nearest security guard, was maybe forty kilos lighter. A gastric balloon, yes, and also weeks trudging through the mountains, negotiating with the ELN to secure new coca routes to Venezuela.

Later that evening, El Alemán's girlfriend and other guests arrived. The drones watched their arrival. They watched the dancing and the eating and the drinking. They watched the ceremony of the bear, the untying of one pink ribbon after the next. They watched as the party moved into the early hours of morning, and they watched as El Alemán's girlfriend danced with the bear for El Alemán's amusement, grinding into the fuzzy white heart. They watched as the party wound down, and people went to sleep, and people left the party. One of the drones peeled off to follow a partygoer, an unknown figure who seemed to be, alongside El Alemán, a locus of attention. And then they watched as El Alemán retired with his girlfriend to a room in the northern corner of the finca.

During this, Juan Pablo sat in the back corner of the operations center at Tolemaida, observing but letting his principals run their op, not interfering. The mark of a good officer, Mason thought. The only times Mason had seen him on a radio or phone was when he was talking to higher, running interference on whatever pressures or demands were coming from the full colonels and generals. Juan Pablo trusted his men and trusted their training.

"Wait until the sniper team is ready," a Colombian major said into a headset, his eyes fixed on the screens. "Wait."

Three squads of eight soldiers were deployed, one that would breach the finca, another held in reserve, and the remaining squad split into teams of four, positioned on the northwest and southeast corners of the finca to block and isolate.

"When you're ready."

On the feed, Mason saw small figures racing to a side wall of the compound, the images oddly endearing, a child's action toys brought to life. They were lifting a lightweight ladder to the side of the eastern exterior wall of the finca, and then one sped up the ladder, dropped down inside, and placed an explosive charge on the side door.

A voice came on the net: "Movement."

On "Kill TV," Mason saw two figures moving along the wall, probably guards who'd heard the assault team moving into position.

"Three, two, one."

The explosive charges went off as the sniper team opened fire. One large flash and a cluster of smaller ones. The two figures fell down. The assault squad streamed into the finca.

On screen, it wasn't so different from a U.S. raid, the choreography of men trained over and over to not simply execute a task, but to rapidly adapt to the changes and surprises an enemy compound can throw at you. Speed and violence of execution were key. Mason figured that, with a compound this size, forty-five seconds was a fair estimate of how long a group of U.S. special operators might take, and he began counting to himself.

One-one-hundred. Two-one-hundred. Three-one-hundred.

A machine gun opened up on the roof, a terrified urabeño with limited weapons training firing ineffectual bullets into the night, his burst serving no other purpose than to alert the snipers. They adjusted fire. The machine gun stopped. Three figures squirted out a side door, muzzle flashes lit up from the blocking squad's position, and the three fell scattered across the ground, doll limbs all akimbo.

Eleven-one-hundred. Twelve-one-hundred.

The assault team rolled out of the first structure and into the building where El Alemán had retired with his girlfriend. Flashes of gunfire appeared on the feed, but the eye-in-the-sky couldn't tell who was firing inside the building, and at whom.

Nineteen-one-hundred. Twenty-one-hundred.

The team rolled out into the final building, laying down heavy fire as they crossed quickly out into the open.

Twenty-six-one-hundred. Twenty-seven-one-hundred.

Inside the final building, the squad leader turned into a bedroom, a younger soldier with a light machine gun following behind. There were two figures under sheets in a bed, both sitting up, holding each other.

The squad leader ordered them to put their hands up. Neither did. The squad leader repeated the order, and the man's hands moved down into the folds of the sheet across his lap. The squad leader's finger had been straight and off his trigger, but now it hovered above his trigger, now it barely touched his trigger, now it exerted the slightest pressure as he decided what to do.

Thirty-five-one-hundred. Thirty-six-one-hundred.

The squad leader squeezed the trigger, punching a line of bullet holes in the man's chest like the buttons on a dress shirt, and then the woman threw herself on the man, and the young soldier with the light machine gun opened fire as well, the bullets splitting the woman's head open. They rolled out and into the hallway.

Forty-two-one-hundred. Forty-three-one-hundred.

A voice came on the net stating that the objective had been cleared. Mason stopped his counting and revised his earlier estimate. A U.S. team could have done it in thirty seconds. Juan Pablo, at a far corner of the room, turned from the drone feed to the other officers and warrant officers and enlisted manning the operations center and permitted himself a smile. Then his eyes briefly met Mason's, allowing him to share in the victory before he turned back to the screens.

At the time, Mason had no sense of the significance of the raid, or the events that would result from it. In fact, he consciously tried not to overestimate the meaning of the affair. In ungoverned spaces, killing drug dealers tended to lead not to more law and order but to violent power grabs among the criminals lower down in the food chain. Intellectually, he knew this killing wouldn't change much in Norte de Santander. But still, in that room, it was hard to resist the feeling of a momentous victory. A cleanly executed raid is always deeply satisfying to watch. There is something beautiful about the operation of a perfectly engineered machine.

The first doctor knew who Jefferson was and delivered the news fearfully, uncertainly. The manner of delivery was, at first, more irritating to Jefferson than the news itself, and he took a certain pleasure in letting the doctor know.

"If you're going to tell a man he will die," Jefferson said, "have some balls while you do it." He decided he needed a second opinion.

The second doctor was more professional, and spoke in rapid, clipped words about the necessity of "palliative care."

"What's important now is quality of life," the doctor said.

"I have never given any importance to quality of life," Jefferson told him. "I'm not going to start now."

The doctor paused. "I'm talking about managing what could be, without significant intervention, a significant amount of pain," he said.

Jefferson, who had never shied from pain, found that funny. "I don't give a damn for any man who can't handle pain. The more pain, the better. That's life."

"Yes . . . but . . ." the now somewhat flustered doctor said, before pausing and collecting himself. Then he proceeded to explain how the tumors would grow and expand and begin to press on the organs, how Jefferson would feel it, and how it would begin to inhibit every aspect of his life unless interventions were made to limit their size. And then, delicately, he began to discuss psychological care. Jefferson silenced that talk with a look.

As the man left, Jefferson told him, "If you mention my condition to anyone, I'll cut your dick off and fuck you with it." The doctor nodded gravely, as if this were a normal way of speaking.

Over the next couple of days, Jefferson made no significant changes. The possibility of death was always a part of the business he had spent his entire life engaged in. What did it matter if it was a disease or a bullet, a tumor or a bomb? Natural causes are, of course, crueler. Slower than even the worst tortures he'd inflicted on men over the years. But Jefferson felt no particular fear. He'd never been able to excite himself in that way, with that strange emotion he'd observed so often in other people. It could, he knew, reduce men to paralysis in the face of coming death. Loose their bowels, make them cry out, betray themselves and all they imagined they were. It was a curious thing, and he didn't have it.

What did develop, slowly, was nostalgia. He found himself thinking of the great days in Cesar, where he had risen through the ranks. Of the trust they'd conferred on him when they sent him to Norte de Santander. Of the network he'd built across the border in Venezuela.

He was made for great things, it was clear. And if he had less time left on this earth than expected, that was no problem. It was merely a spur to action.

And it was in the midst of these thoughts that he heard about the death of El Alemán.

When she bought the plane tickets, it had made sense. Bob had told her, just between the two of them, that there'd be an opening in Bogotá soon. It wasn't for five months, but, she told him over Skype, that was perfect. "I want time to write something a bit more long-form."

Just looking at Bob's face, she could tell, even through the grainy, stuttering video feed, that he did not think that was perfect.

"Long-form? Oh, fuck me. Et tu, Liz?"

Lisette shrugged, tried to play it off. "I just want to—"

"I know what you want," he said. "You want eight thousand words in *The New Yorker*. Fuck you. I hope you get a listicle in BuzzFeed."

"What's wrong with—"

"Eighteen Totally Empowering Ways to Brew Coffee, by Lisette Marigny. I can't wait."

Lisette sighed. She'd known he wouldn't approve. And she didn't need his approval. But still.

"BuzzFeed does great reporting. And what the fuck would be so wrong with eight thousand words in *The New Yorker*?"

The video stalled, jerked forward, like cheap animation with too few frames to connect the movement of the characters, making Bob's voice disembodied, and, oddly, more authoritative.

"You don't know anything about Colombia. I let you stretch a bit here because you'd put the work in. What, you think just because you can write a good sentence you deserve an opinion? You haven't earned opinions yet."

Then he went off on a rant she's heard before, one of Bob's old-man, oh-the-kids-these-days rants, about how too many young journalists thought the work they did was just a stepping-stone. How they think just because they're smart they deserve to talk, but a real journalist doesn't need smarts and definitely doesn't need even a college degree but needs only the ability to get people to tell you things. And that's it. The spade work of the wire services, before the color commentary, before the spin and polish. It's the only thing that actually matters.

Lisette, sitting in her sublet in Brooklyn, wanted to believe him. Go out, find what happened, report it as straight and as succinctly as possible—that's the real work. His voice floated in over his frozen face. "All the hot takes in the world shrivel up and die in the presence of one well-reported fact."

"Yeah, I know," she said. "You've said that before."

She considered laughing it off, gently conceding his point but then telling him, "It's my four-month vacation, I can do with it what I'd like. Why not let me fuck around with a vanity project?" Or she could have told him what she'd been telling herself. That she did know Colombia, because she knew Iraq and Afghanistan. That this was an extension of the same war, not the endless war on "terror" but something vaguer, harder to pin down and related to the demands of America's not-quite-empire which was always projecting military power across the globe and just shifting the rationale of why. That Cold War communist guerrillas became War on Drugs narcoguerrillas became War on Terror narcoterrorists. That you keep seeing the same policies or strategies or even people bouncing around the globe. Two U.S. ambassadors to Colombia going on to be ambassador to Afghanistan. Another going on to be ambassador to Pakistan. In 2004, SOCOM had told Colombian troops to focus on counterinsurgency. In 2007, the new counterinsurgency strategy gets rolled out in Iraq. In 2004, a revolution in targeted killing starts in JSOC in Iraq. Mid-2000s, we start applying the same methods to Colombia, the only difference being that we let the Colombians do the actual killing. Then we give them drones. And if the rumors Diego had told her are true, that the targeting apparatus was about to get applied to domestic drug groups, and that the State Department was carefully eyeing the coming success or failure of insurgents in Colombia as they worked to bring the Taliban to the negotiating table in Afghanistan, then she may have had precisely the right kind of knowledge and context to describe the theoretical end of this theoretically successful war.

For all the focus Bob had on a depth of local knowledge, maybe he wasn't seeing the forest for the trees, maybe she had something to say about Colombia that wasn't about knowing the people or the culture but about knowing the systems applying violence across the globe. And maybe, because she "fucked a mercenary" once, and because that mercenary was in Colombia, she was uniquely positioned to get insider access into the next permutation on the massive, industrial-scale U.S. machine for generating, and executing, targets.

But then Bob finished with, "And I know there's not a ton of validation covering a war nobody cares about, but Jesus Christ, Liz, that's why we've got to do it. If you're not going to tell this story, who is? I never thought you'd just give up." Which stung. And she realized that perhaps she couldn't afford to trust Bob with the dreams she's been spinning for herself. Perhaps he'd tear them apart. And also, perhaps, Bob could go fuck himself.

So that's what she said. "Go fuck yourself, Bob." The video feed didn't register his reaction but Bob was a big boy, he'd managed journalists in war zones a long time, she doubted that was enough to draw blood. So she went deeper. She told him he was a fool, because it wasn't 1971, because people don't read newspapers now, because there's no page A26 to flip past, because people don't accidentally get reported facts on the way to the opinion page anymore.

"All the reported facts in the world shrivel up and die in the presence of universal indifference," she said. And then, going further, she added, "People don't even read about Afghanistan, where they at least sort of know there's a war on, and you think doing spade work in Colombia is going to make a difference to anyone? Excuse me for not wanting to shovel words into a hole until I die."

At which point she realized the video feed from Afghanistan had stalled completely, and there was just Bob's frozen face, the mouth slightly open, and a snippet of a word here or there until it failed, so Lisette sent an apology email and went to bed.

The sad thing was, she wanted to believe like Bob did, but he was only right in another world, a world with the kind of media ecosystem that supported his kind of work, and the kind of popular culture where one was expected to have a broad sense of the world, rather than an in-depth, ideologically inflected analysis of the latest Twitter moment. The question was not, Which style of reporting is best in an ideal world? It was, How do you reach people?

In a small town on the border with Venezuela, Jefferson Paúl López Quesada met with a former lieutenant of his, Tomás Henríquez Rúa. Javier had come a long way from the days when he used to chain-saw enemies of the paramilitaries in the middle of town squares. After the demobilization he'd stayed in the region around La Vigia, and when Jefferson ended up in prison in Venezuela had attached his little group to the Urabeños, running extortion as well as handling an increasing percentage of the cocaine trade moving across the border.

"I'm proud of you," Jefferson told him at their meeting.

Javier ignored the praise. He knew the meeting was about the shake-up after the death of El Alemán. Javier told his former boss that he was mostly watching and waiting. "How close are you to the Urabeños?" he asked.

Jefferson told him, and Javier grinned. Javier liked his old boss, and had liked working for him. But more importantly, he knew his old boss had connections with the Cartel of the Suns, a drug trafficking ring run by the Venezuelan military. With the FARC about to sign a peace treaty with the government, the Cartel needed other clients with cocaine to transport. And so Jefferson was moving across the border to expand supply.

"You know," Jefferson said, "in the Castaño days I used to work for El Alemán. That fat pig."

Javier smiled. "I didn't mind working for him," he said. "But I think I will prefer working for you again."

Jefferson would have smiled back but a stabbing pain in his gut seized him. It had been happening more and more. So the best he could work up was a grimace and a firm handshake, which was good enough.

When Diego learned that Lisette Marigny was coming to visit him in Colombia, he permitted himself a fifth beer, then a sixth. He read distractedly for an hour. He did fifty push-ups. Then he stripped naked in front of his bedroom mirror and surveyed what had become of his body. He decided he had become old.

Is that a gray hair? he thought, looking not at his head but at his crotch. He plucked it. And then he laughed. Now it's like I'm twenty again! In the mirror, a thickset, forty-two-year-old man with a hairy belly looked back at him. He'd once had abs. He'd once had that V of muscle moving up from the pelvis and contouring the lower edge of the stomach. Women liked that V, he'd been told.

He was still in good shape. The other day he'd run seven miles with a thirty-pound pack at almost an eight-minute pace. That was impressive. And if Lisette needed someone to run seven miles with a thirty-pound pack at an almost-but-not-quite eight-minute pace, it would come in handy.

Later that evening he texted her on WhatsApp to say that the hotel she booked for herself was popular with sex tourists. The owner brought in prostitutes to spend all day in the hotel's gym, which was where the clients could observe them in their tight spandex. "Maybe there's some journalisty reason you chose it," he typed, hit send, then typed, "But if you want a nicer place, I've got an extra bedroom at my finca." This didn't seem sufficient, so he added, "close to airport, close to Medellín." He stared at the messages, wondering what subtext she'd read into them, then added, "It's got a private entrance so you don't need to see me if you don't want to." That seemed too standoffish, but he'd already sent it, so he started typing, "And I'd love to spend some time with you," but that was too much. He deleted it without sending, scrolled through his photos for a good shot of the view, and sent that. He texted, "Don't waste money if you don't have to."

Traffic jams were good for Abel. The little store he'd constructed on the side of the road leading into La Vigia got decent business—he'd planned the placement well, with little competition beyond the men carrying wares on their back—and since the new construction had blocked off all but one lane and created backlogs of trucks and cars and motorcycles, it seemed like every third car would pull into the parking lot he'd shoveled flat and paved himself. His shop wasn't like any other peasant shop, with dirty shelves and old goods. He'd slowly built it up to look more and more like a real professional store. It had a sign with lights. It had a glass front door. It had a little section under a heat lamp with cooked goods he got from a bakery run by demobilized guerrillas—one of the projects of the Fundación de Justicia y Fe. One day, he thought, he would raise enough money to sell gasoline. That was expensive, and required tanks and machinery and construction he couldn't do himself. But one day, he'd have a proper gas station. He was a business owner. He paid taxes. He paid the Urabeños. He paid the guerrilla. Some days, it seemed all he did was bleed money to parasites. But when there were traffic jams, and the cars poured in, drivers eager to kill some time, stretch their legs, and buy some chicharrónes or cool drinks or aguardiente, those parasites felt like nothing more than tiny little mosquitoes, young baby mosquitoes with skinny legs and long rifles but bellies so small they couldn't ever dream of taking in enough of his blood to even weaken him. Let them feed off me, he'd think. They know no better way to live.

He wasn't like them anymore. He was back in the land of the living. He had friends. Neighbors. It'd been hard, as an old paramilitary. But he'd kept his head down, and lived honestly, and slowly, over time, proved himself. He'd received help here and there, especially from the Fundación de Justicia y Fe, but mostly it'd been a hard, lonely struggle, building his business brick by brick, the way his father had built the home he'd grown up in. There were days when he could even imagine his father looking down from heaven, seeing his store, recognizing his son, and feeling proud.

So he was feeling good the day Jefferson walked back into his life. Construction about a mile south of him had backed up his road, and led to a steady stream of customers seeking a small break from the frustrations of driving. And then, as the sun dipped, a pack of motorcycles weaved through the cars and turned as one into his little lot. One man, short, blocky, with a helmet that obscured his face, got off his moto. The rest stayed put, staking out positions in a military manner Abel knew well. Indeed, everything about the group, down to the walk of their leader as he made his way toward Abel's glass door, seemed familiar. These men were not customers, he knew that. But neither were they strangers.

Abel left his position behind the counter and walked to open the front door. He knew the importance of respect. And then the leader took off his helmet and the face, older and even more worn and pitted than it'd been the last time he'd seen it, was the face of Jefferson.

"Abel," Jefferson said. Then he smiled, looking around. Abel knew how his store must seem to a man like Jefferson, with its pathetic goods and its reek of diligent poverty. "What the fuck is this?"

"Sir," he said. What else was there to say? Jefferson was no mosquito. Jefferson could bleed him dry. He thought of the rumors he'd heard, that Javier had switched allegiances to a Venezuelan narco. He thought of the new faces he'd seen in town, the increased traffic on the road, the increased business in his store, which he'd only thought of as a good thing.

"Come. Close up. You're finished for the day."

There was a customer browsing the shelves but a look was sufficient to make him put the bottle of Postobón back and head out the door. Abel turned off the lights, pulled the cash out of the register, closed the door, and pulled down the metal gate, locking it and then pulling again to make sure it held.

"Is this all you have in the world?" Jefferson said, curiously fingering the gate.

"Not all." Against his will, Abel felt ashamed of his little store, the pride of his life.

Jefferson took him to a very different house than the beautiful old finca by the river where Abel had spent mornings as one of Jefferson's inner circle. This was new construction, modern. Big blank white walls leading toward huge windows opening onto a view of the mountain-side. Pretty, in its own way, but cold. There was a patio out back, and a grill, and servants. An old woman in a French maid outfit standing before a tray of uncooked sausages and steaks. Jefferson's men lounged about the four corners of the patio, rifles slung at their sides. Abel remembered the man whose arm had been flayed. He remembered Osmin's corpse in the mountains.

Jefferson handed him a beer, and Abel drank. And then he started up the grill.

"You've gotten thin," Jefferson said.

So Abel sat and watched Jefferson cook. It felt familiar. Comforting. He had mattered enough to his old boss to be plucked out of the little life he'd built and transported here, to the bigger game. Against his will, that thought gave him pleasure.

"Venezuela, it's a nightmare now," Jefferson said. "I tell you, I could have been a king in Venezuela. But they've fucked that country up. Now, over there, even kings are cockroaches."

Abel nodded, looking around at the house. It was nice. The house of a rich man. But not the house of a king.

"You left me . . ." Jefferson put out a hand, flat, the fingers outstretched, and tilted it this way and that. "Some people would say that you betrayed me. You were like my right hand. What's a man to do without his right hand?"

Jefferson spoke as though the idea that Abel had betrayed him had popped into his head. Abel knew Jefferson to be more deliberate than that.

And then Jefferson laughed. "No!" he said. "You were never my right hand. You think you were that important? You were . . . you were a thumb. The thumb on my left hand. But a hand needs a thumb, yes?"

Abel licked his lips. He wanted to take a swig of the beer. Maybe a swig of aguardiente—there had to be some here. His nerves were no longer deadened, like they had been when he was a younger man. There was even a woman he'd been seeing. Or, if not seeing in any meaningful sense, a woman who was kind to him, perhaps interested. Deysi. A half-Motilon woman with green eyes that could suddenly sparkle when she smiled. She'd lost a husband and a son, Abel didn't know whether to violence or disease or both, but she knew sadness and was kind. She worked as a seamstress, and sold other odds and ends in her shop that he'd go in and buy, things he didn't even need or know how to use. Why was he thinking of her at a time like this?

"It's been ten years since I've been to La Vigia," Jefferson said. "This town . . . it's gone from paras to guerrillas to narcos. I don't know the players like you do. I need a little thumb, to help me hold on tight to the people here."

"I don't get involved," Abel said. "I'm a shopkeeper . . ."

"Not anymore," Jefferson said. "Now you work for me."

Abel felt the vise tightening, and wondered if there was anything he could say. Perhaps if he let Jefferson know that he'd been in touch with military intelligence, that two men from the army had come to his store, told him they knew all about his life and his former associates, and then took him to a small house where they grilled him about Jefferson's old compadres. Odd things, like what type of alcohol does Rafael Ferrara like to drink? How close is El Hurón to his brother? Is Tomás Henríquez Rúa completely insane or is his madness a facade? He'd answered honestly, it was his duty as a citizen. And he was a citizen now, not a para. But to Jefferson, he was the same Abel who'd worked for him, and for that Abel to be talking to the military made Abel a toad, and bad things happened to toads. The military, he knew, would not protect him. So he tried something else.

"I think, when I left, it wasn't because I thought I'd have better luck without you. It was . . . I am weak. I am weaker than you wanted me to be. Loyal. Always loyal to you. But weak. That shop. That shop you saw. That you laughed at. I know. I laugh at it myself sometimes. But I own it. That is what I have built for myself, these past ten years. And I am proud. And I am so proud of that shop. What could I have built for you, if that is all I have built for myself in ten years? I am afraid I would fail you. You need a better thumb."

Jefferson considered that and smiled. Abel tried not to look too relieved.

"Fool," he said gently. "I will teach you to be strong."

Jefferson pulled the meat off the grill, slapping it down on a plate, juices drooling into a pool.

2

t'd been just shy of two years since Diego had seen Liz face-to-face. She was the first woman he'd been with after the collapse of his marriage. In his mind, the second woman he'd ever slept with, period. He didn't count prostitutes, or the occasional late night, drunk bar hookup. As far as he was concerned, that kind of sex wasn't sex, it was fucking.

When she emerged through the gates of the airport, she seemed no older than the last time. Still pretty—beautiful to him, anyway—but tired, and not wearing makeup. Or so he thought. Incorrectly.

"Diego," she said. "What the hell am I doing in Colombia?"

On the trip back, she told him a story she'd got secondhand from a veteran journalist living in Bogotá. He had a source who'd gone to a Colombian narco's birthday party in Las Vegas in the 1990s. The narco had created a fake film company just so he could rent out the Strip and then, under the auspices of a film shoot, run drag races with him and his buddies.

"Did this actually happen?"

"Oh, probably not," she said. "Then they brought a dairy cow up to the penthouse suite at the Sphinx, and hired some crooked veterinarian to sedate the animal and inject alcohol into its udders so they could drink White Russians straight from the cow's boobs."

Diego laughed. "Jesus."

"They sedated the cow," Lisette said. "Last thing it knew, it was partying in the penthouse suite at the Bellagio. Then, once it tapped out of milk, they chain-sawed her and sent the meat down to the hotel steakhouse."

"There's no way this happened."

"Someday I should put together a book of all the stories journalists heard but could never corroborate. It'd be called *Too Good to Fact-Check*."

Was this the kind of story she was looking for here in Colombia? It had been over two decades, the murder rate had been more than cut in half, but people still couldn't get enough of wild drug-lord stories. Colombia, land of violent, extravagant psychopaths. Of Pablo Escobar and his stupid fucking hippos. Lisette had never struck him as that sort of reporter in Afghanistan.

"Would I be in that book?" he said.

She eyed him carefully, the smile slipping a little before coming back.

"Depends. Got any good stories?"

Abel stood outside the office of the Fundación de Justicia y Fe. He breathed in and out, then willed himself toward the door and up the stairs. He paused on the landing. Luisa would not like what he was about to tell her. Could he even tell her? Easier to throw himself head-first down the stairs and hope it broke his neck.

The first time he'd seen her here, his face had gone white. It was only a few years after he'd left the paramilitaries, he'd completed bachillerato, gotten his diploma, and gone to the foundation for help applying to the Agency for Reintegration for a loan to open his store. He'd been nervous then, as well. He didn't like having to admit to people he was an ex-combatant, and he had heard that the workers at the foundation were more sympathetic to former guerrilleros than to former paramilitaries like himself. But he'd never suspected when he opened the door to the office that Luisa would be there behind the counter, head down, a little older and fatter but still the same girl who'd sat and played the piano and then screamed as her father was cut in half.

His first instinct had been to run. But then she had looked up and seen him. At first, her glance was a purely professional acknowledgment of his presence. Then a moment of confusion passed quickly as she tried to place him. Abel held his breath, kept utterly still, as if any movement would give him away. And then her eyes widened slightly. She had placed him. She knew him. She knew what he was guilty of.

They stood like that for a moment, and then another worker at the foundation, perhaps sensing something was off, said, "I can take this one, if you want."

But Luisa had said no, and had sat Abel down, and asked him what he wanted. And when he told her he had graduated from school, she told him he should be proud, and when he told her he did not want to return to fighting, she told him that was honorable, and when he told her he wanted to open a store with a loan from the reintegration agency, she told him she would help.

She had seemed like a saint to him then. And as she got out the forms he started crying, foolishly. And he told her about his family, and about his animal life on the streets of Cunaviche after their deaths, and she had nodded and listened, but said nothing, offered nothing. Only after they had filled out the forms and she had instructed him on the next steps in the process did he have the courage to ask about what had happened to her after the destruction of Rioclaro.

"A priest, Father Iván," she said. "He had known my father, and he helped me find a job here."

He wanted to tell her that she had survived Rioclaro only because of him, but it seemed as though even mentioning it would be profane. And then, after all her kindness, she made one hard demand on him.

"You have some of your own money that you're putting to the store," she said. "Is that money you saved from your time as a combatant?"

He had nodded yes.

"That money is stained with blood," she said. She told him that if he was going to use that money to open the store, then the store wasn't really his. It belonged to the people who'd suffered. And so, every month, he owed it to the poor of La Vigia to give away some of what he made.

"Once you've given away as much money as you made in the paras," she said, "then you'll have earned the store."

Then and there, he'd wanted so badly to tell her that she lived only because of him. But he held his tongue. And when he finally did open the store, her words haunted him. And so, he put aside a little amount each month. As he started earning more money, he'd take his entire stipend from the reintegration agency, a few hundred thousand pesos, and give it to the church. Slowly, he chipped away at the debt Luisa claimed he owed, earning his salvation. And then Jefferson came back into his life.

He'd shut down the shop. No more earning honest money. No more paying off his debt. At night he hunched in his closed store with the television on, his muscles tense, his mind exhausted, and then he'd lay down, unable to sleep. A brave man would tell Jefferson, No. You can kill me, but I am not returning to that life. I am a man now. I am a member of this community, and I will not turn my back on the life I have built here. Abel wanted to do that. But at even the thought of defying Jefferson, fear would rise up. It was a physical presence inside him, the fear. It burned. It tasted like gasoline.

So he agreed to work for Jefferson, though he held out the hope that somehow there might be something he could do to save himself. Perhaps Luisa would know.

The paint on the walls in the staircase outside the foundation was tinged with yellow, and clumped in spots. He touched one of those clumps—a bad, lazy job—and looked up to the placard above the door to the offices, a computer printout of the name of the foundation hung crookedly in a cheap frame. Everything looked even cheaper than it had when he'd first come. Luisa ran the office now, and Luisa had no pride in appearances. Unlike Jefferson, who, though he was just as happy sleeping under a tree with a rock for a pillow as in a palace, always took care to let the world see his magnificence.

Abel put his hand out to the doorknob, then drew back. Maybe she wasn't even in. Maybe she was in Cúcuta, fighting with the administrators of the foundation. He hadn't seen her around town. Hadn't spoken to her in months. Perhaps this could be put off.

But then the door swung fully open and Luisa, in all her glory, stomped out to the landing. She was dressed in work pants and an old, ratty polo shirt that fit her awkwardly. She had the expression of a bull about to charge. And then she caught Abel in her sights, stopped, made eye contact, and gave a short nod.

"Ah," she said. "You know about Jefferson."

Abel, one foot on the landing, one foot a step down, nodded neither yes nor no, but merely swayed indecisively.

"Not now," she said. "Not today. I'm busy. But Sunday? Meet at the bakery?"

His sins would have to wait until then.

Lisette didn't want to raise Diego's hopes, but nevertheless felt an increasing warmth as he took her around, showed off his house, a lovely traditional construction on the side of a mountain. There was something innocent in his artlessness, and it gave her a tender feeling toward him. To think that a grown man, with the kind of life experiences Diego had, could get reduced to an awkward, fumbling boy. It made her feel more innocent herself. Diego, she knew, was someone who still believed in the magic of intimacy. It was what she'd liked about him when they were together, until it'd become claustrophobic and boring.

So when the tour ended at the door to her room, she put a hand on the small of his back, smiling as he stiffened. She leaned in, closer than she had to, and said, "It's really good to see you again." Which was true. He smiled. She took a moment to enjoy both the awkwardness she provoked in him, and the pleasure. And then she stepped past him into her room, smiled, and shut the door.

There, inside, with a door between her and Diego, she took a breath. She walked to the low, roughly queen-size bed, and sat down on the hard mattress.

"Okay," she said to the wall. "What now?"

Bogotá had been a disappointment. A two-hundred-dollar-a day fixer who introduced her to politicians, activists, prosecutors, human rights workers, and judges. And, of course, *las víctimas*. Víctimas of the FARC, or víctimas of the paramilitaries, or víctimas of the narcos, or víctimas of the armed forces. They'd all been activated in the political struggle over whether or not to ratify the coming peace treaty. If you want people to reject the peace, show them victims of the FARC. If you want people to accept it, remind them that there's blood on the state's hands, too. It was the same with Iraq—prior to the war, hawks wanted everyone to know the suffering of the Iraqi people. Not so much after the war started.

There is a naive belief among Americans, swaddled from war as they are, that merely to tell the stories of the oppressed and victimized is a political act. Tell the stories, and the appropriate political answer to the suffering will become apparent. Colombians, who've lived with war for decades, know better. And they especially know how empathy can be weaponized in the run-up to a vote. But that wasn't what Lisette was there for.

It'll come, it'll come, she told herself as she turned in for bed. Diego, perhaps, could help.

The next morning he made her breakfast. Eggs, arepas, and cheese. And instant coffee with an incredibly sweet hazelnut creamer. He didn't even ask how she liked it, he just gave it to her that way.

"This is Colombia," she said, pointing at the cup. "And you're drinking instant?"

"This is the way Colombians drink it." Diego smiled mischievously. "The fancy stuff is for export."

"I hear Blackwater set up a company here to recruit Colombian military to work as mercenaries for the Emirates."

Diego's smile disappeared.

"It's Academi now."

"I hear they're going to send them to Yemen. Which, am I wrong in thinking, is the most fucked-up war we're engaged in right now?"

"Jesus, Liz. Right to business?"

"Well—"

"Hey, how are you? Recruited any Colombians for the UAE recently?"

"I—"

"No, I'm not involved. But really, is that your story? Piddly mercenary shit?"

This was not how she wanted to start things. But before she could respond, he grabbed a *Semana* magazine and started reading. There's an old reporter's interviewing trick—most people can't deal with silence, so if you just refuse to fill the silence with sound, if you just look at your source like you're listening but let the empty moments follow one after another, sometimes sources will start talking just to kill the awkwardness. And when they're doing that, they're less careful, and they tell you things they wouldn't otherwise. Lisette had used the trick many times before. But there, in the silence as he sat and ate, she felt the emptiness she had inflicted on so many sources, and like those sources, almost without willing it, she began to fill it with sound.

"You know John Sack?" she said. "Vietnam reporter? M Company?"

Diego shrugged.

"He said the best journalist to cover Vietnam was Michael Herr, because Herr went crazy. Herr *allowed* himself to go crazy. The only one to actually donate his sanity to the cause of journalism. Vietnam wasn't about putting the pieces together and making sense of it all. Vietnam didn't make sense. So you couldn't just write the facts. You had to write the experience of getting pushed past sanity."

That amused Diego. "Okay. You gonna go nutty on me?"

"I don't know. Herr wrote the Vietnam crazy. What kind of crazy fits this war?"

"Which war?"

"All of them. Here. Afghanistan. Iraq. Yemen. Horn of Africa. Philippines. Everywhere. I mean, what kind of crazy do I need to be to get it right?"

Diego started laughing. "It's not crazy you're looking for."

"No?"

"What, you think we're out there, smoking dope and burning gook villages? That's a whole different era."

"You sound nostalgic."

"I mean, look, what we do is boring at this point. Now it's all . . . long meetings, lessons learned. Here's what we know about the complementary effects of suppression and local development. Here's six different models of how insurgencies respond to the targeting of midlevel leadership. And even when I am out in the field . . . man. The thrill is gone. I'm in my second decade of this shit, Liz."

"And yet, you keep doing it."

"Look, maybe America hasn't been paying attention, but we've gotten pretty good at fighting these bullshitty wars. Just look at the stats. Numbers of police trained. Number of independent indig operations. Violence up, violence down. Things *are* getting better. The numbers don't lie."

Liz laughed. Diego liked occasionally throwing statistics at her when he wanted to confuse her or blunt some criticism she had of the war and his role in it. Statistics take the raw material of war, human beings, and turn them into numbers on a spreadsheet. And for Diego, no matter how fucked up the war, those numbers always seemed to be in the black. "Well, you would say that, wouldn't you?"

He raised an eyebrow. "Why?"

"Because you're out of your fucking mind."

He let out a disapproving sigh. "You're eating breakfast a half hour outside of a town that used to be the murder capital of the world."

"I'm willing to be sold on Colombia."

"Go through the mission set of every unit operating in Afghanistan right now, tell me a single one that doesn't make sense."

But it wasn't the missions. Liz had been doing this long enough to know that. She'd gotten excited about enough units and their local successes to know that deep in her bones. The missions—chase down Taliban leaders here, train ANP there—did make sense. It was the war as a whole that was insane, a rational insanity that dissected the problem in a thousand different ways, attacked it logically with a thousand different mission sets, a million white papers, a billion "lessons learned" reports, and nothing even approaching coherent strategy. Insanity overseeing a thousand tight logical circles. Sure, it wasn't the exhausted, drug-addled insanity of Vietnam. Not pot and heroin and LSD insanity, but the insanity of a generation raised on iPhones and Adderall. A glittering, mechanical insanity that executes each task with machinelike precision, eyes on the mission amid the accumulating human waste.

There was more silence, and then Diego got up and scrapped the remnants of egg on his plate into the trash.

"Crazy would be thinking we can just throw up our hands and do nothing."

Sunday came and Abel made his way to the bakery, where a short former guerrillera at the counter waved and smiled at him. They all knew him there. They all liked him there. He was, supposedly, a success story. An ex-combatant who ran a successful business. No matter that once they'd been enemies, the guerrilla on one side and the paramilitaries on the other. Now they were on the same side—ex-combatants trying to succeed in a world that held people like them in contempt. Luisa wasn't there yet so he ordered two pandebonos and chatted with the girl. Ana Paula, or Ana Sofia, he thought that was her name.

"Look," she said, holding up her hand to reveal fingernails painted not in a single color, but in swirls of red, pink, and blue. "Mirabel did it for me." She nodded to the back, where Mirabel was checking the ovens.

"Beautiful," he said, unsure whether she was flirting with him or not. He felt like he should say something else. After an awkward pause, he went with, "She should do mine," and held up his hand. That got a delighted little laugh, and Abel blushed. He wondered how many little guerrilleras like this had been killed by Jefferson. And how many paras like him had been killed by little guerrilleras. Probably not that many. Both sides had mainly killed civilians.

Luisa walked in and the guerrillera snapped to attention, trying to look businesslike.

"Let's sit outside," Luisa said.

So Abel took his pandebonos, followed Luisa outside, and watched as she wedged herself into one of the low plastic chairs they put out in the street for customers to sit in. She looked bulky and absurd, with the little chair and little plastic table in front, and Abel hunched down awkwardly into a chair himself, feeling like a child.

"Yes, he's returned," Luisa said. "I was waiting for it. I'd heard his group had moved across the border a year and a half ago."

Of course she'd known. Luisa knew what happened in the area better than anyone.

She reached across the little plastic table and grabbed one of the pandebonos.

"It doesn't change anything for us." She bit into the bread.

Abel licked his lips. "It changes things for me."

"I see." Luisa swallowed and looked down the street, scowling. "I drove by your shop two days ago and it was shuttered. Are you hiding?"

"No."

She became still, and then swung her gaze from the street to his face. Which is when he felt it, the shame. He'd felt it many times in front of Luisa, shame was an old friend, no matter that she'd forgiven him. And again he thought that perhaps he should tell her what he'd left out of his confession. Perhaps he should tell her how Jefferson could have had her killed or raped or, more likely, both, and that he'd protected her. He worried, in his soul, that his confession to her was not a true confession because he'd held that back, held it back from the scorn he knew she'd feel if he told her. But that was the one thing precious to him from his time in the paramilitaries, and he didn't want to give it up.

"He wants you to work for him again?"

Abel nodded.

"And?"

He hung his head. Luisa reached across the table and took the other bread roll from him, then sat there scowling, a pandebono absurdly in each hand. With almost comical aggression, she took a bite.

"You know how it is," he said. "Money or bullets. I had no choice."

"Or," she said.

"What?"

"Money *or* bullets. The word *or* means a choice."

Was she being serious? He laughed nervously. "Well . . . it's not a very good choice."

"Yes." She stared at him intently.

"Who told you God gives us easy choices?" she said.

"I . . ."

"For ten years, you have been a good man. Before that, you weren't even a man. You were his . . . *thing.* Die a good man and see Christ, or become his thing. How is this even a choice?"

He couldn't believe it, to hear her talk like that.

"I won't be doing anything illegal for him, just . . ."

"You'll be doing what you did before. Whispering in people's ears. Handing out money. I have more sympathy for his sicarios. That's honest evil."

Her eyes were withering. And for a moment, as the shame tightened its grip, as he forced air in and out of his throat, as he felt his soul wanting to crawl out of his filthy skin, it did seem like a simple choice.

"If you want my blessing," she said, "you can't have it."

But that wasn't it. What he wanted was worse. "What I want," he said, getting control of himself, "is to talk to you about the election for mayor."

She looked surprised, and then disgusted. "Ah. Already working."

Yes. And she was a force in the town. One that needed to be negotiated around. One that needed to be kept only minimally hostile.

"Tell your boss this. We're bringing in some people from the foundation's headquarters in Bogotá to conduct interviews. A lawyer and some students. They're taking statements about crimes that have happened here."

"And you don't want Jefferson to interfere."

"No."

"Then keep his name out of it."

"Obviously."

"And in return?"

"You know what you get in return."

She tossed him his pandebono.

"That's fine," he said. He just needed her to stay neutral. Which she would, because she was smart, and because that was mostly how she'd played it with every other group that had established dominance in the town.

She leaned forward, put her palms flat down on the little plastic table, and pushed herself up and out of her chair. She looked at him sadly, curiously.

"You could have run away. Fled to Cúcuta."

He had thought of that. Losing everything he'd built. Losing the community where he was known. Again. "I have a life here."

"Not anymore."

The shame was ebbing. Relief was coming in. He'd told her, and she'd reacted as he'd expected. But to have it done with lifted the weight somewhat. He stood and nodded at her as he prepared to leave.

"One other thing I want," Luisa said.

"Yes."

"When we're doing the interviews. I want you to come and tell us and the registrar what happened to you as a boy."

He sat down again. She stood over him.

"Why?"

"That's my condition. Tell your master."

And she left, leaving him in the little plastic chair, holding a pandebono she'd taken a bite out of. He bit from the other end, and then thought about the mysteries of saints and the relics they leave behind—hair and fingernails and bones and blood. So he bit into where she'd bit, and chewed the bread that still had a touch of her saliva on it. Perhaps it'd give him courage.

Courage for what, though? Not for death, like Luisa wanted. But perhaps money or bullets weren't the only options. He thought of the two men from army intelligence. And then he thought of the bruja, who sold fabric in a shop in the north part of La Vigia. Perhaps she had a charm, or a spell. There are secret forces in this world. Perhaps he should use them.

In the silence after she had left the finca—to go interview an uribista politician, she'd said—Diego had sat and savored the afterglow of the anger she'd provoked in him. She was fucking up his tranquillity, but that was fine. After a while, tranquillity is just another word for boring.

After a while, everything is boring. War. Peace. Love. Hate. Even Liz, in Afghanistan, had gotten boring. The same old arguments, the same prickly distance whenever he'd drawn close. But there, in Colombia, she was a change.

And she needed his help. She wouldn't ask directly, but she needed him. He liked that. So he called a few other contractors. He called an officer he'd worked with in the Colombian military. And then he'd remembered Mason. Junior medic in the Afghan deployment where Carlos and Ocho got fucked up. An odd guy he never really got along with. Took himself too seriously to deserve being taken seriously. Took the job too seriously to be really good at it. But now the SF Liaison at the embassy.

Diego dropped Mason a line, didn't hear back until early evening. A short email. "Taking the 1628 flight into Medellín this Sunday for a quick trip to Cuarto Brigada. Could meet at the Mall Indiana in Las Palmas, grab a tea or something."

Tea. This fucking guy. And when Liz returned to the finca, her expression guarded, unsure of how they'd left things, he silently handed her a beer, stared out at the darkening view, and told her, "I asked around for you. Got a friend in MILGROUP at the embassy. Might have something interesting." And she smiled, and sipped her beer with him, and they shared a comfortable silence.

Over the next couple of days he kept it safe. Made a show of playing tour guide—bringing out that weird Colombian fruit you eat by breaking a small hole in the shell and sucking out the insides. Pointing out the varieties of hummingbird that would flit down the mountainside. And in the evenings he'd read, and she'd read, and the space between them would fill with the warmth of their past. And then, Sunday evening, he went out to the Mall Indiana.

Since the coffee shops had already closed, he parked himself at an Italian restaurant, ordered a whiskey, and waited until Mason arrived and, true to his word, ordered tea.

At first, they just caught up. Diego talked about life as a contractor and Mason talked about his family, how the two-year accompanied tour was affecting his wife's career, how his two daughters were doing. He even pulled up photos on his phone. Inez, the older one, was, holy shit, almost a teenager already. The younger one, Flor, a little black girl from Georgia they had adopted after the stillbirth, was now a very cute seven-year-old. Diego made the right noises as Mason flipped through the photos, and eventually Mason turned to talk of his career, the choices he'd made, and how his aversion to Middle East deployments had hurt his reputation.

"You know I'm not a coward," Mason said. "I like a good fight as much as the next guy. But, man, I watched Ocho put two fucking tourniquets on his own bloody stumps in a war we both knew we weren't winning. And I thought, what am I doing here? At least in Colombia, I feel like I can make a difference."

Bingo.

"Still?" Diego asked. "There much left to do, after the peace treaty gets signed?"

"If anything," he said, "the peace is only going to make us busier." He stared at his tea. "Actually, I'm starting to worry the Colombians are going to repeat our mistakes."

"What mistakes?"

Mason started talking about a raid he'd watched play out from an operations center in Tolemaida, where Colombian special forces had gone in and killed some drug dealer. Mason's objections seemed to be the usual ones people had against high-value targeting—that it substituted a tactic for a strategy. You'd kill a bad guy and think you were making progress in the war when, as long as the underlying conditions on the ground remained the same, you hadn't changed anything at all. Or maybe even made things worse by further destabilizing the area.

"I think the army wants to muscle in on a police operation against the Urabeños."

"The drug gang?"

"Yeah." This raid Mason had seen was, he now thought, a "proof of concept" to show how effective the army could be. But then, when Diego tried to get details, Mason got quiet and waved him off.

"What about you?" Mason asked. "How are you doing?"

Diego slugged back more of his whiskey, forcing the liquid down. He knew how to play this. "So listen," he said, putting on a very serious, Mason-style face. "I think I may have betrayed the U.S. mission in Colombia."

Mason slowly blinked once, then again.

"Two primary missions, every time we came here. Right? One, to train up Colombian troops. And two? You know what our other, probably even more important mission was."

Mason didn't say anything.

"To fuck as many Colombian women as humanly possible."

Mason let out an exasperated sigh. Same old Diego, he was probably thinking. Underestimating Diego, as usual.

"But me, I'm fucking an American. Actually, it's worse. I'm fucking a journalist."

Mason didn't react.

"Met her in Afghanistan, you know? But you know what? She was useful over there. You remember that leadership beef between Mansoor and Dadullah?"

This had been a struggle between two factions of the Taliban in 2015.

"We first get the rumors, and I'm like, I don't know. Is this for real? What's happening? But you know how it is in Afghanistan, we're always stretched for resources. So I'm hanging with my girlfriend and I think, Hey. She's smart. She's learning the language. Why not get her to figure it out? So I tell her, Look, deep background only, but maybe you want to get your ass to Zabul. I hear there's a civil war in the

Taliban. She packs her bags and gets there right as the whole thing blows up for real, and pretty soon she's putting shit out on the wire—"

"News stories? Open source?"

"Yeah. And we got nothing in Zabul except a little SigInt, but she IDs a Haqqani guy nobody even knew about who was trying to broker a truce, three days later we nail this guy by his cell phone . . . I forget whether it was a drone strike or . . . shit, no. A fucking SEAL team took him out. SEALs for sure. Fuckers killed civilians, too."

"SEALs." Mason grunted. Everybody hated SEALs. The joke when the DEVGRU guys killed bin Laden was, *Oh wow, after ten years of shooting every unarmed civilian in the room, the SEALs finally got the right guy.*

"Yep," Diego agreed. "Fuckin' SEALs." Bitching about the SEALs was good. He could see Mason nodding in agreement. Mason was the kind of guy who thought he knew better than everybody else how things should be done. He was too fastidious, too disciplined, too much a believer in the nobility of the mission for what was too often an ugly war. It shouldn't be a reach to get him from *thinking* he knew better than the rest of the military to him *doing* something about it.

"Your girlfriend know you were using her?" Mason said.

"She knows every source got an angle. Shit, I told you she was smart."

"Sure."

"It gets better though," Diego said, leaning in, breathing whiskey breath over Mason. "Now she knows the town, so when she hears about what happened, she heads back to cover the funeral. And there were some very interesting people at that funeral."

"You sent your girlfriend into the middle of a Taliban civil war just to generate targets."

"Oh, fuck you," Diego said. "I let her know there might be a story there. Her choice." Then, in a mock-heroic voice: "She is her own sovereign individual." He gestured grandly with his whiskey. "We are all our own, sovereign individuals."

Mason smiled. "Yeah . . . I'm a soldier. And a dad. And a husband. I haven't been my own sovereign individual in decades."

"There's got to be someplace everybody's ignoring. Something going on where we're not involved but maybe should know more about."

And then Mason was quiet for a moment, and Diego let him be quiet. The wall behind them showed a cartoon artist's version of Italy, with goofy-looking Roman statues and cathedrals and leaning towers and men in striped pants offering pizzas. Should he say anything more? No . . . Mason had to work it through on his own. There *was* something on his mind. Diego could see that. Of course there would be.

"Send her to Norte de Santander," Mason said.

And then he told him why.

3

The night before she left Lisette realized, rather pleasantly, that she wanted to sleep with Diego. There was nothing else for her to do. She'd packed. She'd prepped to the extent that prepping was possible. And the next morning, early, she was getting on a plane and leaving any complications behind. But Diego was, in some ways, a delicate man. Prone to sudden spikes of pride. And he'd given her what she asked for, a decent lead. A possible story. Not so he could sleep with her. If he thought that's what it was, if he thought *she* thought that's what it was, the tenuous thread between them would snap. So fucking Diego was probably not on the table.

Unless, of course, she could offer him something less ephemeral than a good-bye fuck. She had come to like Medellín as she had not Bogotá, that city in the flat bottom of a bowl beneath the mountains, filled with buildings sticking out of the earth like used cigarette butts. Medellín was a wilder, more organic thing, with its neighborhoods in the draws of steep mountainside. During the day, the buildings crawled upward into the lush green slopes, and at night the city lights poured down from the ridgelines like glowing rivers. The people were more hospitable, more blunt, and more honest. Even the politicians seemed to lie more honestly. It was a good place to be, and a place she'd like to return to once she was done in Norte de Santander. Could she promise

Diego that? That she'd return? Yes, she thought she could. So maybe, just maybe, fucking Diego was on the table after all.

For dinner, he did what he called an "asado," which as far as she could tell was just throwing steaks on an all-wood fire. He worked the grill while she relaxed, took in the view, drank beer, chatted lazily, and eyed him in a way she could tell made him uncomfortable. He kept looking back at her, the furtive look you give a suspicious stranger trailing behind you in a bad neighborhood.

He was a large man with a handsome face. Thick hair just starting to gray. Brown eyes and stupid tattoos. Skulls and daggers and U.S. flags. There was nothing chiseled or sculpted about his body, she knew that. His torso was thick and had all the definition of a sandbag. And he was hairy. But he was strong and solid and, at times, startlingly tender. She watched the ripple of muscles in his forearm as he flipped the steaks. He flashed another furtive glance back and she grinned at him, this object suddenly come into her possession and which she was, for now, pleased with. He turned back to his *very manly* grilling of the steaks, and she let her laughter break out again, the laugh only slightly nervous.

"This is so nice," she said. And she could see him visibly relax. He nodded yes, so pleased that she was pleased.

She wasn't sure where the strength of her desire came from. Maybe from the pleasure of having a new direction, possibly even a purpose. Maybe from the length of her last dry spell. Maybe, even, from a book. A professor at the University of Antioquia in Medellín had suggested she read what he assured her was one of the finest poets to come out of Norte de Santander, Gaitán Durán, and so she'd picked him up only to find that he hadn't written much of anything useful about the department she was heading to, but had written a ton about sex and death, about the implacable march through history toward our deaths that can only be demolished by eroticism and poetry, because all is death or love, because love is the fiesta in which we most remember death, and so on. It was good stuff, somewhat out of step with her more mundane and less self-important take on the act, but it'd probably had an effect. So maybe that was it. Or maybe it was just one of those things. A desire that struck rarely but powerfully, she didn't know where from, mixing with loneliness and swelling, intensifying, doubling, quintupling. Maybe it didn't mean anything, this kind of desire, and maybe it should be distrusted, but as the light darkened and the flames from the grill provided an ever greater proportion of the light on their faces, the surrounding night covering and enveloping them, she became sure. She wanted him.

He took the steaks from the grill and wrapped them in tinfoil.

"We should let the meat rest a bit," he said.

"Come here." In her nervousness, she barked the words out like a command. He turned, surprised.

"You gonna ask me nicely?"

Now she overcompensated, attempting a girlish playfulness. "No," she said. "I'm not nice." And when he just stared at her, confused, she repeated, "Come here."

He walked over, his face wary. When did she get so bad at this?

There were lights far down the slope of the mountain, maybe from boats on the waters of the Embalsa de Fe, the lights below brighter than the stars above. And then he was standing over her as she sat low in an absurdly flimsy plastic chair, but he just stood there, waiting. She felt a surge of anger, at herself, at him for being so passive, so stupidly inert. And what did he want from her anyway? For a moment, she considered turning away, telling him, Forget it. Forget I said anything. But that would be a failure of some kind. Perhaps a failure of nerve. Her hands were slightly shaky but she affected a pose of confidence and started unbuttoning her skirt as he stood there, doing nothing, nothing, not even a change of expression. And she watched him watching her, her nervousness turning to mortification with him looming there, mute, a silent silhouette above her, and she reached and grabbed his hand, and then she was guiding his hand down and he was letting her, and she let out a breath, and he stooped, then knelt before her, the skin of his hand chilled from the air but then warm and damp against her and he knew what to do, kneeling, as he guided his fingers inside her underwear and then inside her, entering her with his index and then middle finger as well, stroking upward and then, after a slight nod from her, pulling her underwear down, kneeling down deeper, bringing his face to her and then his tongue.

She looked at the fire and at the lights below, and she breathed deeply, and made little sounds not so much of pleasure but of deep relief, tension flowing outward, into the darkness, and she felt very relaxed, very much in the right country, at the right time, in the right place, doing the right thing.

After she was done, he kept rubbing her, playful, sending shocks of pleasure that became almost painful and then, finally, were painful, and she pushed his hands away, and they were both breathing heavily. She considered reciprocating but then thought, No, let him wait. And she said, simply, "Let's eat."

They unwrapped the steaks and sat down and, at first, ate in silence. It was only after a few minutes that Diego asked her, "Honestly, Liz, what are you doing here?" He spread his hands out and gestured to the valley below.

"I burned out." It felt shameful to say it out loud.

Diego smiled. "Yeah," he said. "But here you are, back in the saddle again."

Lisette laughed. "Why'd you leave the army? And don't say 'money.'"

He leaned back and eyed her carefully. "I don't know," he said. "Maybe it was the wrong call. I was done with army bullshit."

"It's strange to see you someplace that's not Afghanistan," she said. "Doesn't feel real."

He nodded.

"But it's nice."

They chatted a little more of this and that. Nothing important. They finished their steaks, which were bloody. She didn't normally eat her steaks that way but it tasted good. And with that taste on her lips, she let him lead her inside to his bed.

Two days later, Lisette was sitting in a beat-up pale blue van with no air-conditioning, no shocks, and hardly any stuffing left in the seat cushions, heading up Ruta Nacional 70. It was hot. Thirty degrees Celsius and climbing. She was sitting shotgun. In the middle section of the van, scrunching next to the boxes of gear she'd brought with her, was Juan Agudelo, a middle-aged professor of law at Nacional with a crooked nose and a mostly bald head. Crammed in the back were the two students Agudelo had brought along with him, a pair of eager young things who were there to cart gear, type off transcripts, and generally handle bitch work. And next to Lisette, driving, was the foundation's regional director, Luisa Porras Sánchez. She was a tough, heavy, square-shaped woman with dark hair, a strong jaw, and utter contempt for journalists.

"It was not my decision to bring you here," Luisa had told her flatly when she arrived. "Bogotá insisted." Local players in the peace movement sometimes had a bit of resentment against the Bogotá-based national players, the people with university degrees, European funding, and plenty of abstract notions about conflict resolution and transitional justice. "And, of course, we're responsible for feeding you," Luisa had continued. "Are you going to write something worth the cost of what you eat?"

As shtick we nt, it was pretty good.

They emerged from the city into flat plains of sparse grass and grubby trees with half the leaves missing from their branches. Ahead of them were brown, ugly mountains.

It had been easier finding an NGO operating in the region than

Lisette thought it would be. A friend of Bob's had tipped her off to a New York hedge fund manager who, inspired by a complex mix of conservative politics and liberal sympathies with the human rights movement, was funding the documentation of human rights abuses within FARC territory and surrounding areas. She'd reached out to New York first and received an enthusiastic response—"Try to get your article out before the peace vote"—which had then made connecting with the local actors easy. They knew the money they were getting from abroad came with implicit demands.

"How does Norte de Santander . . ." Lisette wasn't exactly sure how to say what she wanted to ask, or if Luisa might find it offensive. "Are there more problems here, in Norte de Santander . . ."

"Poverty here has, for my whole life, been consistently above the national average," Agudelo's matter-of-fact voice came from behind. "The government has a metric—the BNU—Basic Needs Unsatisfied. In Santander, it's about twenty percent of the population. Here, in Norte de Santander, about thirty."

They approached a river, and the colors of the landscape became richer, more lovely.

"Because . . . the violence?"

"Our manufacturing is weak. Only about half of children are enrolled in school. But, yes, the violence makes it worse. Criminals raise the costs of legitimate business, push people into the illegal economy, which makes them dependent on the gangs."

"Or the guerrilla."

"The guerrilla have lower taxes," Luisa chimed in, "so they are bad, but not as bad as the gangs."

"We're going to a town . . . the control is by Los Mil Jesúses, yes?"

This, Luisa didn't like. She eyed Agudelo, who shrugged.

"How do you know them?" Luisa asked.

"They're interesting."

"No. These groups are not interesting."

Luisa fixed her eyes on the road. A new tension hung in the already suffocating air of the van.

"Lina said you were writing an article about the foundation," Luisa said. "Is that true?"

"I am interested in your group."

"My group." Luisa shook her head, then pulled over to the side of the road and slowed the van to a stop. She turned to fix her glare on Lisette. "Listen to me. You are here because national wants you here. Because publicity for us can drive money, and we are always starved. Starved. Not because *interesting* groups like Los Mil Jesúses need more attention. If you're not going to write about us, get out."

The students in the backseat had their mouths open. Lisette sighed and glanced at Agudelo, who merely raised his eyebrows, as if to say, It's a good point, why don't you respond?

"Okay," she said. "I already told you. I am interested in your group."

Luisa stared at Lisette, then shifted the van into gear and pulled back onto the road. They drove for a long time in silence. One of the students fell asleep. Lisette stared out the window. A brown river slouched beside the road—thick green vegetation to their right, brown and desiccated trees to their left.

There was little talk for much of the rest of the trip. Lisette closed her eyes and tried to sleep, waking only as they approached La Vigia, the town that Diego had assured her the U.S. military was unusually interested in, and which had experienced a power shuffle after the Colombians, using U.S. tech and tactics, had killed some high-ranking muckety-muck in one of the bigger Colombian drug gangs. If Diego was right and it was indeed a place where the second- and third-order consequences of the use of force were playing out in ways that made people in Bogotá nervous, then it was as good a place as any.

The outskirts of La Vigia were simple houses, earthen construction haphazardly placed that slowly yielded to a more orderly grid pattern of roads lined by white cement houses with metal bars on every door and window. There was road construction ahead, limiting the road to one lane, and Luisa slowed to a stop behind a line of cars and trucks. As far as characters went, Luisa wasn't a bad one, and maybe there would be a role for her in whatever story Lisette ended up telling. Surely worth profiling, if she could get on her good side. Which she was certain she could. The ones who were the most theatrical about how tough they were usually cracked easy.

Luisa, noticing Lisette's eyes on her, gave one loud sniff. "Violent people are boring people." She said it as if responding to something Lisette had said. "Broken children who can only do one thing. Crap-asses who could never work a real job. Set them on good land, already tilled and planted, they'd sit around, stroke their guns, and cry as they starved."

The line of cars moved forward and then stopped in front of a shuttered store on the side of the road. Without the breeze from the windows, the van quickly became unbearable.

"We have a bakery here," Luisa said. "A bakery is a good place to train them to be human beings. You have to get up early. Work with your hands, but also talk with real people. Customers. Some townspeople don't go to our bakery. There's a lot of stigma against ex-combatants. But what are we going to do? The paramilitaries killed my father, now I give them jobs baking bread."

That was interesting. Lisette made a note to run that down. A woman who worked to rehabilitate the kinds of combatants who had killed her father held a natural appeal. Add that to her "I'm such a tough cookie" swagger . . . She'd come off well on the page.

"Do you rehabilitate guerrilla also?"

"More, now. It is harder. This was a paramilitary town. One ex-guerrillero who went through our program, oh, five years ago? He was killed. Of course, we don't know why, but there is more hatred against the guerrilla here and now we have more of them and it makes it difficult."

"How many get other jobs outside of the bakery?"

"Real jobs?" Luisa said. "Hard to say. We don't let them stay at the bakery too long. They have to go out, find other employment. And it's hard, because the economy here is not very good, there is a lot of poverty. And there's always more ex-combatants than we have positions. We try. Some businesses help, some don't. The success rate is not that good. But we have to grow a human being out of a pile of shit, so what do you expect?"

Lisette laughed at that, and heard Agudelo let out a sigh from the backseat. The construction workers started waving more cars through and Luisa started the car again, air moving into the vehicle.

"You know," Lisette said, "you should sell me your work. Not tell me it doesn't always work."

Luisa smiled. A real smile. She knew she was being complimented.

"In Bogotá, they can afford lies. Here, we cannot."

Despite Luisa's bluster, La Vigia seemed like a nice town. The streets were tidy, and full of industrious-seeming people. There was a small central park with a carved book inscribed with the Ten Commandments. It was safe to walk around at night. And there were more jobs than elsewhere in the region. Palm oil processing. Leather goods. La Vigia had three bars, one modestly pretty church, and a disproportionate number of old men playing dominoes. More than one local expressed surprise and confusion to see an American journalist there.

Lisette tried not to put too much pressure on herself in the first couple of days in La Vigia. She told herself she was engaged in a more open-ended form of reporting than she was used to, and she should give herself time, learn the rhythms of the town. So she hung out with the foundation workers, chatted up the old men playing dominoes, tried to befriend the local Defensor del Pueblo, and avoided getting frustrated by how difficult it was to get an honest answer from anyone about what had happened in the town since the death of El Alemán.

Mention the name Jefferson, the supposed big scary narco boss, and townsperson after townsperson described him to Lisette as a businessman. The construction at the north end of town—an expansion of a processing center for palm oil, which farmers harvested in the surrounding areas—that was him. And the talks with the cell-phone company to build a tower and connect La Vigia to the rest of Colombia, that was Jefferson, too. He was changing things, they said, for the better.

And if she asked if Jefferson was associated with the Jesúses, she got a mixture of silence, half-hearted nods, or explanations that the Jesúses were merely a local neighborhood watch, the product of townspeople getting together and throwing out the criminal elements so that legitimate businesses could thrive. Diego had promised her an unstable region where the drug trade mixed with communist guerrillas and refugees poured in over the border. Instead, she had a thriving community where life was improving.

"Business is very good," one bar owner told Lisette. "There's fewer bad types on the street, and a lot of the Venezuelans have money."

"The *Venezuelans* have money?" Lisette asked.

"The town keeps the bad Venezuelans away," he said.

"The refugees," Lisette said.

"Yes," he said. "The refugees bring many problems. I have sympathy! Don't look at me like that! But we are a little town, and it is hard enough to deal with our problems. The poor Venezuelans, they're the ones who voted for Chávez! They wrecked their country, now they want to come here."

"How does the town keep the bad Venezuelans away?"

The bar owner just smiled and laughed and wagged a finger in front of her face.

She also sat in on some of the sad stories being recorded by the foundation, visited local businesses, and listened to the debates for and against the peace vote. It was a "yes" town. More or less.

Something of a break came when the Defensor del Pueblo offered to set her up with a dairy farmer. "He knows the history and is part of a new program you might want to cover," he had said, handing her a brochure that read "Strengthening Communities with Milk."

The farmer came in a rusty pickup truck, a battered old thing with a newish but still weathered front door of an entirely different color from the rest of the vehicle. Uncle Carey would have approved, and the truck made her like him even before he stepped out. He was a large old man with big bony hands that looked like they'd been carved from driftwood. He told her, "Ah. You're a pretty gringa."

"Yes," she said. "I am."

He drove fast, taking them quickly out of town and onto rural roads, one big hand spinning the wheel as they skidded across stones and dirt.

"I called Luisa, because they said you were with the foundation, but Luisa said different." He hit a curve fast enough that Lisette involuntary clutched at the door handle for stability. "She said it probably wasn't a good idea to talk to you but I could make my own mind up."

"Tell her I say thanks for . . . the good word," she said, trying to nonchalantly put on her seat belt without drawing too much attention. If Luisa was warning people away from her, that was a real problem.

He looked at her and chuckled. "The buckle doesn't work."

"Ah," she said.

"I told Luisa, I can talk. Why can't I talk? It shouldn't be a death sentence to talk."

"Are you nervous? To talk?" she said. "Many people said to me the Jesúses are good for La Vigia."

He nodded. "In many ways, yes. In other ways, no different than the others."

The road crested over a ridgeline and then they were descending into a valley. "Where we're heading, I've got two hundred head of cattle. So I pay the vaccine. Fifty mil a head. Same as a year ago."

La vacuna. The vaccine. What people called extortion payments.

"Twenty years ago, I pay the vaccine to the FARC. Fifteen years ago, I pay to the paras. Ten years ago, I pay to the Elenos. Five years ago, I pay to the Peludos. And then it was the Urabeños, and the Peludos, and then the Urabeños." He shook his head. "This place was a football and they'd kick it back and forth."

"You think that the town will obtain more stability with the Jesúses?"

"I pray for that, yes, but"—he held up one long finger—"that is not the most important thing. I always paid the vaccine. Always. But that only protected me around La Vigia." He pointed due east. "I ship milk down to Cunaviche, along the way, I hit a roadblock, I've got to pay the vaccine to the Elenos. I go north . . . Peludos. South . . . it changed—one day this group, another day—but you understand. And if you wanted to buy equipment, or anything, really, that had to be brought from outside, it was so expensive. Do you know how much it used to cost here to buy a can of Coca-Cola? Thirty mil."

That was about ten dollars.

"I like Coca-Cola," the farmer said. "But I never bought it."

"And now?"

"From here to Cunaviche . . . one vaccine."

"How? Are the Jesúses working with the Peludos? The Elenos? Did they fight them? What happened?"

The farmer shrugged. "I started drinking Coca-Cola again."

"What about your"—how did you say *ranch hands*?—"workers? Do they drink Coca-Cola now?"

"Don't tell them you're here to learn about the guerrilla. Some of my men are from the north, and they have a different attitude."

When they got to the farm, he was primarily interested in showing off his cattle—a group of big, healthy-looking animals grazing in a mountain valley. It reminded her a bit of home, coming down the curve of a hill to see cattle grazing in a field edged with trees, though here the fields were rougher, the greenery was richer, the view stretched out farther down mountains so much steeper and wilder than the Pennsylvania hills. Bordering the field was an open-air structure with a tin roof and a few support beams. The farmer pointed to this. "Where we process our milk, and the milk of smaller farmers who want to sell with us," he said. This was the part of the project the Defensor del Pueblo had wanted her to see, since much of the equipment had come through government programs.

The farmer took her into the field, stepping through mud and around cow shit, right up to one of the larger beasts, whose dull eyes were just a few inches below Lisette's.

"These cows are half American," he said proudly. "Half gringa. Here, touch her."

She put her hand out and stroked the nuzzle of the animal. The cow's eyes flattened backward, then relaxed, and she continued chewing.

"We got straws of semen from America," he said. "Holstein and Swiss brown. Santos signed a treaty that let Europe sell milk here and the prices . . ." The farmer made a low whistling noise and pointed his finger down to the ground. "The government had to help us and they sent us semen. It is very good, the semen. The cows we breed give much more milk. So for me, it's not so bad that the price of milk went down. But for the little farmers who come to us to process their milk it is very bad. They have the same old cows. Five, six liters a day. Not very good. The semen only went to the bigger farms. If you're a poor campesino, with one or two cows, what are you going to do with a straw of semen from America?"

In the processing hut, where the musty smell of the farm took on a sharper tinge, he took her to a delicate-looking man with shoulder-length black hair and a thin mustache who was pouring milk from a large metal jug into a square trough covered in what looked like cheese-cloth. The man's brothers and parents were cocaleros, the farmer explained, and he was willing to talk to an American.

"I did not know you were a woman," he said.

And since he seemed uncomfortable, Lisette simply asked if she could follow him around, see what his work was like, and he agreed. Lisette started by asking simple questions—how long he had worked at the dairy farm, how he liked the work, what were his duties. She shared information about herself, that she had been in Iraq and Afghanistan.

She didn't want to push him too hard, but he could be an important source. The cocaleros, or coca growers, were an interesting group. They were mostly very poor people who, of all the different players who profited off narco trafficking, received the least amount of money. And since they were tied to the land they farmed and were thus the easiest to target and control, they suffered at the hands of the police and the army and the narcos and the guerrilla and the American-supplied planes that sprayed poisonous chemicals over their fields. But in Norte de Santander they'd formed unions and self-defense groups. A couple of years ago they had even shut down all the roads in the department and forced a response from the president of the country himself. If she could get him to trust her, he might serve as a bridge to a group with a very different sense of what was going on than any of the townspeople she'd interviewed.

An opening came when the farmworker mentioned that times were currently difficult because his father had become sick and couldn't work like he'd used to. Lisette shared that she had an uncle who was dying of cancer. "Uncle Carey," she said. Sometimes, with a potential source, if you opened up about your own history, especially a history of pain, it would make them feel as though they had to pay you back in kind. Lisette, who rarely talked about such things even to good friends, would often talk about them with sources. In her mind, the fact that it was a part of her work justified it. What she didn't admit to herself was how cathartic it could be, pouring out your heart to a stranger and trying to find links between their pain and yours.

"I'm very sorry," he said.

"He lives in a part of America that is very poor," she said. "He tells me they are the forgotten Americans, because people in the cities do not think about people like him." And she spoke of how pretty it was where her uncle lived, and how coming to the farm had reminded her of it, because there were farms where he lived, too. And also a lot of drugs.

He listened, and told her he was glad to work in milk and not in coca, like the rest of his family. He said some people he knew had wanted to switch from coca to farming palm oil, but that it was dangerous to switch crops. The narcos didn't like losing supply. He said that near the border with Venezuela a cocalero had switched to palm trees, thinking it'd be easier, and the Jesúses nailed him to one of his trees like Christ on the cross. He said the palm oil had oozed from the man's hands and feet.

Later, she asked the dairy farmer about this story and he laughed and told her that young palm trees don't produce oil, and don't have a trunk you could crucify a peasant on. "Even a very small campesino," he laughed, "and campesinos are often very small." These were just rumors that floated around, he said, probably from the Jesúses themselves, since having people believe in murders was easier than murdering, and these groups were full of lazies. "This is the problem in this country. People believe in easy money." He kicked at a pile of dirt, as if to say, What I do here is not easy.

On the way back, thinking of Diego and his statistics, she asked him if life was better with the Jesúses, and he said, Yes. More money, more businesses, less fear. Then she asked if people out in the countryside felt the same, and he said people in the countryside always complained, but they had reason, because their lives were hard and the troubles always fell on them first.

As they made their way through the main streets of La Vigia, he passed by the central square and Lisette saw two naked women with brooms in their hands, sweeping from one corner to the other. The farmer tensed and drove past, stopping outside the foundation as if he hadn't seen anything.

Around the square, some people gawked, some people studiously avoided looking toward the square, and one imperious-looking man sat on a horse, surveying the scene. "Who's that?" she asked, and the farmer sighed.

"Javier Ocasio," he said. "He has done this before." He gestured to the naked women. "This is how he likes to punish women who don't follow the rules."

"What rules?"

"The Jesúses have a lot of rules," he said. "Don't look at him. Just go into the offices and stay inside."

Lisette was used to men trying to "protect" her by not letting her do her job. She left the car and walked over to the square while the farmer watched. The air was warm and dry, she felt a lightness as she made her way to the figure on the horse, a lean, severe-looking man with scars on the left side of his face.

Javier Ocasio tugged the reins of the horse slightly and the animal reared, its front two hooves going up, striking the earth and then resettling, the animal slowly shifting sideways so that now he was facing her, his eyes trained on her, and she felt even lighter as she walked forward, unafraid and self-conscious of her lack of fear, pleased with it and, as she approached, even a little self-congratulatory about where it was bringing her. Finally, she thought, a man who knows what's actually going on.

━━━━━

The farmer watched the gringa journalist make her way to Javier and then, remarkably, he saw Javier smile. The naked women in the square, guilty of who knows what infraction against morality, against the duties of women and mothers toward their families and toward God and toward Colombia, kept sweeping, heads down, seemingly immune to humiliation. The gringa reached up, her hand extending to Javier, passing him something. A card of some kind.

God. Jesus. He set the truck in gear and rolled forward. What a fool he'd been. Luisa had told him not to trust the gringa. He'd thought she was being surly. Being Luisa. So he'd spoken openly of the Jesúses to her. He'd taken her to his farm. And worse. Unforgivable. He'd introduced her to his men. Mother of God. Son of a whore. It had been too long since there were murders in La Vigia, and he had gotten too rich. His instincts for avoiding trouble had dulled.

He sped through the city streets and then out of La Vigia. The muddy river at the side of the town curved away from him, and ordered fields flew past, followed by plots of palm trees, and then he made a turn sharp enough that he had to lean into it, his body weight balancing against the force pulling him leftward, and then he was up into the mountains, passing a tall, yellow guayacan tree, barreling forward and only breathing easier as the trees became sparse and the road dipped and he saw his farm before him.

Admitting his stupidity to everyone was not possible, so when he got there he simply asked the worker who'd talked about the Jesúses to help him load milk jugs into the back of the truck, and then asked him to join him on the trip.

"I need an extra pair of hands today," he said.

As they left the farm, though, he turned right, not left.

"We're going north," the worker said.

And that is when the farmer told Aníbal that he should spend a few days with his family. That he should let them know, and the rest of their family in the ACCV, the coca growers' union, that there was a gringa journalist who claimed to be working with Luisa's foundation but wasn't.

The worker looked at him strangely, and the farmer suddenly felt foolish. Paranoid.

"Who is she working for?"

The farmer had no idea. All he knew was that Luisa didn't trust her, and that she had walked right up to Javier Ocasio as if she knew him.

"The Jesúses," he said.

It was a tentative conclusion, but it was one that would soon become gospel truth in the north, where coca prices were low, discontent was high, and resistance had already been growing for months.

4

efore coming to La Vigia, the only women Valencia regularly saw
who looked like Luisa were homeless indio women, begging on
the streets or selling trinkets, women Valencia had sometimes
given food to when she was on charity missions with the nuns at her
school. "Victims of the guerrilla," her father, Juan Pablo, would say.
Now she was hundreds of miles away from home, and a woman with
the sort of flat, dark, peasant face she unconsciously associated with
poverty and helplessness was ordering her around. And sometimes be-
rating her for her stupidity.

There was much to berate her for. Valencia's responsibilities included
setting up equipment, recording audio during the interviews the foundation was conducting, typing up transcripts, sorting them according
to various metrics and which types of atrocities each fell into, loading
the information into the foundation's database, and running any other
duties Luisa and her staff could throw at her and at Sara, the other
student from Nacional. She barely had time to eat, barely time to think.
"The goal is peak efficiency," Professor Agudelo had explained to them
at the outset. This meant, in practice, that Valencia listened to atrocities during the day, typed them up during the night, and ate and slept
who knows when. She was tired, and, despite the training on the equipment she'd received back in Bogotá, prone to making mistakes.

On her third day there she had plugged the microphone into the wrong channel, the input set wrong on her control track such that she thought she was recording audio but, in fact, had nothing. In the common room afterward, in front of Sara and in front of Professor Agudelo, Luisa had lost her temper and shouted at her, "When we are interviewing victims, we have to be perfect! You think it's easy to tell a story like that?"

She didn't know what to make of Luisa. She knew the stories about Luisa's past, about her father's murder and how she'd come to La Vigia a refugee and risen up to be the foundation's indispensable woman in this region. One of the other workers had told Valencia that Luisa had even helped in the reintegration of ex-paramilitaries directly involved in her father's death. A few spoke of her as if she were a living saint. Valencia wanted to feel that. Awe. Proximity to a holy person who had dedicated their life to forgiveness and redemption. But when the squat, fat, unattractive woman barked an order at Valencia, some deep, patrician instinct rose up and she found herself quivering with indignant rage. She wasn't proud of the reaction. She tried to tamp it down with calls to Christian humility. But whenever Luisa barked at her, it stirred. A coiled, angry emotion she didn't want, but was nevertheless hers.

One day a sleepy-eyed older gentleman arrived to tell the story of his kidnapped daughter, and he seemed so frail, and initially spoke so softly that Valencia had set the levels on the lavalier microphone much higher than usual. It was fine starting out, as the man talked about his business and his family, subjects that would tug a faint smile onto his thin, dry lips, his voice coming out in a whisper. But as he moved on to the changes wrought by the encroaching guerrilla his voice took on a harder, and louder, edge.

"I knew they'd come for me," he was saying, and over the headphones his voice was distorted, as if there were a bee buzzing in the equipment.

Valencia looked back to Luisa, and behind her to Ricardo, the short, skinny, and unimpressively mustachioed registrar officer who rarely looked up from his papers and who, throughout the process, always did his best to blend in with the cracked, off-white wall behind him. He even wore shirts and pants of a similar color to the wall, and he sat motionless, like an iguana on a rock.

"I got letters, invitations to a funeral with my name as the deceased. Even a Mass card." The rancher laughed, the noise coming through with that same buzzing noise. "I thought that was nice."

The only way to fix the levels was to stop the interview and change them on the battery pack for the wireless microphone that she'd attached to the old man's belt. Which would disrupt the process. And there was an art to the process. Valencia had come to respect that.

Luisa would walk in, hefting her weight around in a kind of powerful, bulldog way that exuded authority, plump herself down, and begin. There were no tears, no hugs, and no expressions of surprise. She'd heard it all before, *all* of it. If she showed compassion, it wasn't through a gross parading of emotion, but through careful and attentive listening. She asked probing questions, accepted the gaps and distortions that come with painful memories, but also pushed into those gaps, finding context, making the victim gather up the broken shards of experience into something that could be strung together into a story. As they talked, the registrar would constantly make notes on a lengthy form, only at the very end asking a few targeted questions.

People understand their lives as stories. Or they try to. In the worst cases, cases Professor Agudelo had warned them they'd encounter, people cannot understand. They struggle to turn what happened to them into a coherent whole. And Ricardo's form, which would be submitted through the Victims' Unit to the government, was a long series of open and closed questions designed to break apart individual stories into different metrics of victimization relevant to the different categories and benefits they are due. Questions designed to assess eligibility, need, vulnerability, harms suffered. Questions about the perpetrator, questions about criminal versus politically motivated violence. Questions that, by necessity, implied a hierarchy of suffering, and a hierarchy of victims. Questions that produced results that could, in the end, be fed into a computer and compiled into graphs, columns, and pie charts.

To simply follow the questions, going one by one through the form with a victim, would be to subject them to a kind of mental torture. "For the victims," Professor Agudelo had told them, "it can feel like we're putting their life through a sausage grinder. We don't want them to feel that way but we do need the sausage." Luisa's job was to get the necessary details without going through them in a manner that denied the specificity of what the victims had suffered.

It was especially when going back through the transcripts that Valencia had learned to spot the sensitivity and care with which Luisa pulled out details from the participants, helping them build a narrative while clarifying everything Ricardo needed. It was a delicate, almost beautiful process. And Luisa had delicately, beautifully, brought the old man to the heart of what was clearly going to be a very painful story.

"One moment," Valencia said.

Everything stopped. Luisa's head swiveled slowly. Valencia walked over, reset the levels, and returned to her spot at the laptop. Luisa said nothing, merely continued the interview.

Afterward, Valencia braced herself for shouting and screaming, but in a way what happened was worse. Luisa sat her down and said quietly, "We have to show these people respect. If you are not capable of that, you need to think very hard about what you are doing here, and what type of person you are."

Those words weighed on her. She'd come out here to be a different type of person than she was in Bogotá. To experience something different from the comfortable life her parents had provided her, going from one safe space to another. Apartment to car to school. School to car to mall. Mall to car to apartment. Apartment to university to law degree to professional career. That path ahead seemed so very rational and orderly. But she liked to think there was also within her a series of wilder desires. Did she want to secure a place in the world or to change it? Did she believe in miracles? Did she believe in God? Was there something inside her, call it a soul, that could be connected to the brutal life of her country in a way that could not be scoffed at, pushed aside, dismissed as unreal? And what would she have to do to earn such a soul? So far she'd transcribed interview after interview until the tales of suffering lost their uniqueness and blended into the numerically designated categories of the government form. If these stories were a challenge, then she was failing to meet it. And Luisa knew.

That night as she prepared for bed she told Sara what had happened. Sara put a hand on her shoulder and said, "I know Professor Agudelo thinks Luisa is amazing but I think maybe there's something he doesn't know." And when Valencia asked her what that was Sara smiled and said, "Maybe she's a complete bitch."

Valencia laughed uncomfortably. Valencia's father had told her once that a true leader must sometimes show a little cruelty. Your men won't respect you if you don't, he claimed. Softness and sentimentality and kindness are no virtues, and men, in their hearts, know they are often deserving of a little cruelty.

"I screwed up. Again. I deserved it."

"You're working for free in la quinta porra. And you're studying law, not electronics. You think Luisa would do better? Without you, *she'd* be screwing up with the microphones. She should be thanking us every day."

Sara had a hard kind of prettiness. Angular cheekbones, a tough little nose, dark brown eyes perpetually narrowed, and a small mouth in a perpetual frown. Perhaps she, too, was a true leader.

"I think I get nervous around them," Valencia said. "The victims."

"You should," Sara said. "One of them grabbed my ass the other day."

"Have you ever heard stories like this?" Valencia asked.

"My father is a journalist," Sara said. "I've heard stories like this all my life."

How to respond to that? Valencia wished she were back in Bogotá, back in her nice, safe, boring life. At school, sitting in Professor Agudelo's lecture hall and listening to him preach, she had imagined a heroic role for herself, documenting abuses in one of the poorest and most violent stretches of the country. There was an element of almost Christian witness in it. And sacrifice. When, years ago, he had been attacked by the Black Eagles, they'd fractured his eye socket, broken several ribs, and slashed his arms, chest, and legs. Luisa's father had been murdered. Even Sara was familiar with this world. What did Valencia have?

⸻

Abel had people keeping track of each and every soul entering the foundation's office. He knew about the two students and the professor from Bogotá. He knew about the American journalist. And as the days stretched forward and townspeople and peasants and drunkards and drug addicts and fools made their way across the town square, he began mapping out a network of the people in and around La Vigia who believed in the promise Luisa held out for them. That their sufferings would not go ignored. That justice might be slow, but was coming. That things in this town could get better.

Most of them were harmless people with no power: displaced indios who begged or sold trinkets on the roads outside of town. Subsistence farmers who lived on bits of reclaimed jungle. Madwomen and drunks who dirtied the face of La Vigia at all hours and who would soon, he figured, fall victim to the kinds of "cleansings" he'd once practiced for Jefferson. But there were surprises as well. Fermín, who ran the gas station near Abel's store. Sebastián, a hunchback who sold rice.

He had pity for them. Come tell your story, the workers at the foundation had said. Come. We'll have a registrar officer from the Victims'

Unit there. We'll handle the paperwork for you. The state of Colombia has declared that you are owed reparation. And though the government is the government and so the money does not always come, still. You play the lottery, don't you? This is no worse.

Fools. And he'd soon be one of them. But not at the foundation's offices. He'd told Luisa he couldn't be seen going in. He couldn't become one of the names on his list. "That's fine," she'd said. The national office wanted video at the site of a massacre, and so he could go with her team out to where his family was murdered. He'd wear a microphone, and stand in front of their cameras and tell them what had happened. It was ridiculous. And it was the price she demanded.

Abel stood up from the desk he had in the back room of his store, a back room that held his bed, a little portable gas burner to heat up food, and several boxes of goods for the store, which he feared might never open again. He doubted that he would unshutter it while Jefferson ran La Vigia. And who could displace Jefferson? Jefferson had all the connections to the Venezuelans—it was how he kept the ELN and the Peludos and even the Urabeños playing nice. It made him untouchable. Immortal, perhaps.

Abel walked out of the back room into the silent, shuttered store, bags of crackers and chicharrónes sitting on shelves, never to be sold. He grabbed a bag of chicharrónes, opened it, and began munching. He walked behind the counter. On a low shelf underneath the register, he knew, was a small cloth pouch. He'd got it the day after meeting with Luisa. Inside was a boiled and dried toad, its forelegs tied together with colorful strings. "Bury it in a place of death," the bruja had told him, "and say the name of the man you want to ruin."

He'd been holding on to it ever since, unsure of what to do. What would be the right thing? It wasn't all bad, his work. When Jefferson lived in a town, he wanted that town to run well. For the people to have housing. The roads to be paved. The schools running. Petty criminals kept in line. "You can have all the money, and all the sicarios you want,"

Jefferson had told him once, "but if you don't have the people's love, you will never be secure." Jefferson was a dangerous man, it was true. But most of the work Abel did made things better for the people in La Vigia. Perhaps that's what really matters.

He was no hero, he knew that. Heroism was what Luisa did. Heroism got towns destroyed, women raped, men tortured and murdered. Perhaps he should burn the list of people going into the foundation. Perhaps he should tell Jefferson to go fuck himself, be tortured to death, and go up to Heaven as a saint. Or perhaps he should take the toad with him to whatever was left of Chepe's bar, bury it where his life had ended, and whisper Jefferson's name. That was not just any place of death. It would be powerful. The most powerful place he could complete the spell.

He knelt down, grabbed that cloth pouch from where it was hidden, and held it tightly, feeling the toad's bound legs with his fingers. Would ruin for Jefferson mean ruin for La Vigia?

———

With some victims, Luisa would ban all men from the room except for Ricardo, who was so small and self-effacing that it was less like having a man in the room than some kind of man-shaped plant, a fern with a sparse black mustache. This generally signified the victim of sexual crimes, usually rapes, though in one case a former guerrillera described her forced abortion at the hands of a FARC doctor. Guerrilleras are supposed to sleep with their comrades, but they're not supposed to get pregnant, so the FARC doctor induced early labor at six months, took the still-living baby away, and then left it to die slowly in a basket, an event the guerrillera told us was no abortion but "the execution of the son of two revolutionaries." It was during one of these cases that Valencia first saw Luisa slip.

The victim's name was Alma, a woman who said she was in her

thirties but had a round, childish face, with fat cheeks and a shy, pretty smile. And Alma began telling a story about how when she was young she had a paramilitary boyfriend named Osmin. Osmin was very handsome, she said, and she knew that he had other girlfriends, which made her jealous, but she was only thirteen, and he bought her things, and suggested to her that another life was possible. One day he invited her to a party at one of his boss's homes, on the river, near Cunaviche.

"Jefferson?" Luisa said, her tone flat, seemingly disinterested. This was her slip. Alma spooked, drawing back and tensing, her whole body defensive and closed off.

"I think this was a mistake," Alma said.

"No." Luisa turned to Valencia. "Strike that from the record. Leave it off the transcript."

She turned back to Alma.

"I know about him. I am from Rioclaro. Do you understand?"

Alma nodded, and started again.

She told her story coldly, robotically. In some ways, she was startlingly ineloquent. Repeating flat phrases. Cursing again and again without emotion, describing the story in a way that made it seem less something that happened to a person than to a thing. The sequences of actions were laid out like a shopping list. Alma goes to the party. Alma sees drugs and people having sex. Alma runs, frightened, to a back room. Alma is found by Jefferson. Jefferson brings in Osmin and a few others. Jefferson gives her some aguardiente. Alma starts crying because she doesn't want to drink. Jefferson slaps her. Jefferson tells her it is his house and she is very rude. Jefferson laughs while she drinks. Jefferson says, "Look at this fucking whore." Jefferson says, "Osmin told me you want to become a woman."

"I was an idiot," Alma said, her voice suddenly full of life, full of bitterness and hate. "A stupid girl."

Carefully, but with a series of insistent, methodical questions, Luisa pushed Alma forward in the narrative. Alma told how the rape began, and how Jefferson didn't take part, but would call in other paras from the party, the youngest ones there, each time calling out, "Hey Jhon, you want to eat?" "Hey Abel, you want to eat?" And then he'd tell them that Alma wanted to make them men. Some seemed to take pleasure in causing her pain, slapping her or roughly shoving fingers into her. One put his hands over her eyes so she couldn't look at him. Alma described one boy, maybe her age, who moved over her, his penis completely flaccid, and he mushed it repeatedly against the bloody mess between her legs, calling out, "Yes, whore, yes," pretending to rape her for Jefferson's approval.

She said everything flatly, without emotion, but as she described the rape she began punctuating the story with the phrase, "It was horrible," said in the same flat tone. "Another boy came. It was horrible. I was in so much pain. It was horrible. It was so horrible. I called Osmin but he looked away. It was horrible. It was horrible. It was horrible."

At the end, Jefferson made Alma thank each one of her rapists for "pleasing her." This seemed to bother Alma more than any other aspect of the rape. The flat tone shifted to the hateful one. "I looked each one in the eye. Thank you, you pleased me very much. Thank you, that was so good." She took a breath. "If I looked away, he made me say it again."

Valencia found this unbearable to listen to. She stared at her hands, ashamed even to be in the same room with this woman. Her lunch, greasy fried pasteles, turned in her stomach. She wanted to vomit.

"What did he say to you?" Luisa asked. "I mean, what did he tell you to say? The words."

"I told you. He made me . . . I thanked them."

Luisa asked again, Alma hedged again, Luisa asked her to remember. Valencia nervously stared at her computer screen where the audio wave appeared in mountains and valleys of indifferent data. She thought of Luisa's demand that during the interviews she give the victims her complete attention, and to not show any pity or shame. She forced herself to stare into Alma's face, which was blank, unaffected, as if the words were coming from some other person. It was not how she imagined a person would sound, telling such a story. Was there a right way for the story to be told? And was there a right way for the story to be listened to? What should you feel as you hear it? Should you cry? That would be the wrong thing. A disgusting, self-indulgent thing. So what? What do you do with stories like this? Later, she would transcribe it and hope the Colombian state threw Alma some money, though it was not clear the rape constituted a political crime. The other day Sara told her about a woman whose husband had refused to pay the "revolutionary tax" to the FARC, and so he'd been tied to a pole while four FARC raped her in front of him. That was a political rape. Rape as a tool of war. Would Alma's rape count?

Eventually, Alma settled on a specific phrasing. Jefferson, who did not participate in the rape so much as orchestrate it, stood above her and said: "Tell them they pleased you. Or we can give you more."

Luisa nodded. "You were smart to do what you did," she said. "They would have killed you."

Alma nodded in response to Luisa's nod, but her face showed she neither understood nor agreed.

"What you did, very hard, after that torture. You're a berraca."

Alma, unconvinced, nodded again.

"Believe me," Luisa said, with that authority she wielded. "I know."

Then Alma told how she stayed with Osmin after the rape, even though he held it against her, and even beat her, and blamed her for having been with so many men. Osmin told her that girls who did what she did ended up working for Jefferson in a brothel in Cunaviche, but he had protected her, even though she was dirty. Then Osmin got her pregnant, but she miscarried, and he said it was a sign. He left her, and disappeared soon after.

"People said the guerrilla had caught him and tortured him to death," Alma said. "I heard that and felt nothing. I was like a corpse, then. I was a corpse when he beat me. I was a corpse when he slept with me. And I was a corpse when I became pregnant. Of course the baby died. A corpse can only give birth to dead things."

Alma told them that she fled to the guerrilla not long after that. There was no life for her in her town, where she was a tainted woman. And she told them how, in the FARC, she began to feel freer, and how there were more opportunities for women, even though the new recruits were also supposed to sleep with their campañeros, which she found difficult at first. As she told of her life in the FARC, her flat tone became inflected with other notes.

"My first combat, I went with the machine-gun detachment," she said, smiling. "There is no discrimination in the FARC, the women fight in the front. But I only had a pistol. Still, even if I had to go with nothing but my own two hands, I would have gone. I'm not afraid to fight. The smell of it excites me. It's like nothing else. I've never been scared. For me, it's like going to a party. I would sing and jump and skip because it makes me happy fighting."

It was, by that point, only mildly surprising to Valencia to hear that Alma was an ex-guerrillera. One of the people she had come here, in a spirit of Christian compassion, to forgive.

Luisa asked Alma why she left the FARC.

"To have children," she said. "I have two children now," she said. "My husband and I are very happy. But the corpse, the corpse of the girl I was, many days the corpse reaches up and grabs me, and it is terrible. I would like it to stop."

Luisa walked back to Ricardo, who pointed at a place on the form, and Luisa nodded, walked back to her seat, asked Alma a few family history questions in a light tone of voice, about her mother, father, and their backgrounds, and then the interview was done.

In the common room, Valencia lingered by the smelly fridge rather than joining Sara and Professor Agudelo at the table. It felt as though something should be said, though more than that it felt as though nothing should be said.

"To work!" Luisa shouted when she popped her head out of her office and saw her like that, useless. As she shook herself free of lethargy, Luisa added, "Tomorrow is easier. We will take a trip to a destroyed village. With a man who was in the paramilitaries. A man who still works for Jefferson."

Luisa laughed, but no one else said anything. Sara raised her eyebrows slightly.

Professor Agudelo rolled his eyes. "Oh, don't let her bait you. It's just the same kind of work. You'll see."

And the next morning, they got in a van and drove to a shuttered shop on the road into town, where a man in his late twenties was waiting by the side of the road. He shook their hands, and he told them that he was a victim, and an ex-combatant, and that his name was Abel.

The journalist was a woman. Muscular, thin, pale. A face that could have been pretty when she was younger but seemed to have been out too long in the sun. Afghanistan and Iraq, she'd said. Abel figured there was a lot of sun there. And of all the people in the van—the professor, the students—she was the only one who really spoke to him, or gave him a kind glance. He felt an old feeling, shame. It reminded him of when he'd just left the paras. Then, it had spurred him to change his life, to move forward. Maybe it was a good thing.

The first relic they passed was the old missionary school. Simple. Concrete. Also shrunken in the way that all childhood grandeur shrinks under adult eyes.

"This was the school I told you about," he said.

The journalist seemed to notice something in his voice, some betrayal of feeling, and she turned to the professor and said, "We stop?"

He grimaced and slowed the van down, made a U-turn, and drove back to the abandoned building. The professor nodded to one of the students. "Sara, you'll want to get this." And as they all left the van Sara hefted her camera to her shoulder, then walked over to Abel, reached without asking to the battery pack for the microphone the other student had threaded up through his shirt and pinned to his collar, and turned it on. She didn't ask, she just did it.

"What do you want me to say?"

Sara shrugged.

"What happened here?" the journalist asked.

"People said the guerrilla kidnapped the teachers but it wasn't true."

He walked in front of the padlocked doors. The camerawoman moved slowly in, closer and closer to his face. He looked past her, to the professor.

"They left. They'd been threatened by both sides. Guerrilla. Paramilitaries. So they escaped in the middle of the night. Safer that way, but I think we told ourselves they were chained in the jungle so it wouldn't seem like they'd abandoned us."

"Were they good teachers?"

"Yes."

The journalist made a motion with her head toward the doors, with their rusty lock, and then at the three shattered windows on the side of the building.

"Empty rooms," Abel said.

The journalist snapped a few photos, then they got back in the van.

The next set of ruins was a house with no roof, with trees growing inside and thrusting their branches out of the windows. The professor slowed the van but Abel shook his head.

"No, not here," he said. "This was abandoned." He tried to remember the name of the family. Cabrales? Rovira? "Not from the guerrilla."

"Did you know Luisa when you lived here?" the professor asked.

Abel shook his head. He didn't think Luisa wanted anyone to know too much about their past.

"Okay," the professor said. "Take us to where it happened."

So Abel took them to where it happened. A cluster of abandoned buildings, all overgrown, some with walls knocked down, and the faint outline of what had been Chepe's bar before the FARC had hustled his family and friends inside and burned them to death. He walked down what had been the main street. Sara filmed him and the journalist photographed him as he knelt down and touched the dirt. He cupped some, and then poured it through his hands. It seemed he had split in two, and there was one Abel who was walking the grounds of his old village, doing the things he was supposed to do, and another Abel watching, wondering what they were thinking that he was thinking, what they were feeling as they watched him and imagined that some great feeling was going on when in fact there was nothing. Nothing inside at all. He walked to the overgrown footprint of Chepe's bar and pulled shoots of grass from the earth, and let them fall to the ground. There was nothing inside him.

Click click click. He could hear the journalist taking photos. He could feel the weight of the microphone's battery pack on his belt. Click click click. The only thing that cared less than that reporter about what had happened here, about his parents and sisters, was that camera. Mechanical. Indifferent. Click.

"You told the foundation," the reporter said, "that . . . was it Gustavo?"

"Gustavo was tortured."

Sara began taking slow, careful steps toward him, like a cat stalking a bird.

"But you weren't here. How do you know?"

That was a good question. He couldn't even remember where he'd first heard what they'd done. He just knew he believed it.

"Torture is very important," he said. "It was the same in the paracos. Your new fighters are children, but you have to make them men. So when the FARC catch a defector, or a paraco, or someone who stands up to them, they gather the youngest children, and they take the prisoner out and they cut off the fingers and the ears and the nose, and then cut open the belly and pull out the guts while they're still alive."

The journalist nodded. She swung her camera around and caught him in its eye. He froze. Click.

Abel looked down, away from the eye. He shrugged. "There are more painful ways to kill a man. It's not for punishment. It's for the children. To educate them."

"Did you do this?"

"My group had different methods," Abel said.

The journalist stared at him. Her eyes were gentle, soft, but fixed on him, as if she were waiting for him to say more. When the silence began to feel uncomfortable, he added, "When I demobilized, I confessed all my crimes."

He stepped onto the ground where Chepe's bar had been. Where his parents and sisters had died. This was their grave, if they had one.

"Yes. But I hear the man you committed crimes for is back in La Vigia."

"Yes."

He knelt and scooped out some earth, making a small hole. He put one hand to his pocket, where he had the pouch with the toad.

"You see over there," he said, pointing across the road. "That is where they came from." The students and the journalist turned and looked, and he slipped the toad into the earth unseen.

"Did Jefferson help you . . . with justice for what happened here?"

Abel smiled. Osmin had thought he'd wanted revenge, too. He pushed the earth on top of the toad, covering the hole. Now he only had to say the name.

"Jefferson," he whispered. He looked up at the gringa journalist. "No. Jefferson did not help me get justice."

———

The checkpoint wasn't manned by the Jesúses, but by men in uniforms that, as they drew closer, appeared to be those of the FARC. They were maybe four hundred meters in front of them, the road heading in a straight line up to a slight elevation, with a stream on one side and heavy vegetation on the other, where there was no real room for cars to maneuver.

"This is strange?" Lisette said to Agudelo, who was slowing the van and looking back at Abel, who seemed tense, his jaw clenched.

"Turn around," he said in a level voice. "Turn around."

As Agudelo brought the van to a crawl, Sara, who'd been filming Abel's tour of his ruined hometown, took the camera she'd been using, a Canon 5D, and put it in her lap, facing upward at the windows of the van. Lisette watched her press the button to record, and Lisette smiled. Good.

Two men cradling rifles emerged from the side of the road, about a hundred yards away, and waved at the van to keep going. The checkpoint was past those two by about four hundred yards. There were three vehicles waiting to be inspected. The first, a gray sedan, moved forward, past the checkpoint; the next one, a truck loaded with scrap metal, came forward.

"Just a shakedown?" Agudelo said, looking back at Abel.

Lisette looked up at the men closest to them, one of whom had placed the buttstock of his rifle to his shoulder. It was still pointed down, but Lisette figured he could be up and firing accurately in under a second. If that was an AK, the max effective range was four hundred meters. Even if it was poorly maintained, even if the men up ahead didn't know what they were doing, it'd be capable of shooting through the engine block of the van at two hundred meters.

"Go," Lisette said, motioning up to the checkpoint. "They are . . . close."

"They are not FARC," Abel said. "They are not . . ."

Agudelo shifted gears and the van stuttered forward.

"Turn around," Abel said.

Lisette pointed to the men with rifles, who were now less than a hundred meters away.

"It's not safe," Abel said.

"Who are they?" Agudelo asked.

And then they were passing the men with rifles, who smiled and waved and it calmed Lisette a little. A bribe, that would be all. She removed the memory card, slipped it into her pocket, and shoved her camera into her bag. No need to give them reason to loot anything.

Agudelo checked his rearview mirror, the van still moving forward, closing the distance to the checkpoint, which was now about two hundred meters away. Lisette looked back at the students. They'd been unusually cold to Abel, to the point of rudeness, but now they were all looking at him as if he might have some kind of answer. Clearly there was something about this guy that everybody knew except her.

"They're looking for someone," Agudelo said.

"Do you still work for Jefferson?" Lisette asked.

They came to the line of cars just as the fighters were waving the truck with scrap metal forward, and the final vehicle, a motorcycle, moved in between the fighters as Agudelo brought the van to a stop. Lisette heard laughter. The motorcyclist was making some kind of joke. She turned and smiled at Abel, as if to assure him it would be all right, then turned back and saw one of the fighters slap the motorcyclist on the back. It was an oddly comforting sight. Normal. Friendly.

"No bribe," Agudelo said, puzzled. And he, too, looked at Abel. "They're not asking for money."

Perhaps they were looking for someone. And then the motorcyclist was speeding away, and the fighters were motioning to Agudelo, and the van was moving forward, and there were rifles pointing at the car, and the passenger side door was opening, and hands were reaching in, and Lisette was gripping the seat, and someone was shouting, and it was Agudelo who was shouting, and the rifles pointed at the car, and the hands tore at Lisette's seat belt, and Agudelo gripped Lisette's hand, and Lisette gripped back, and she felt a blow in her side, and the blow registered dully in the sudden charge of fear and adrenaline, and Agudelo was pleading, and Abel was shouting, and more blows came, and Lisette's fingers slipped, and she felt the sun in her eyes, and she squirmed in their grasp, and she planted one foot against the side of the van, and she kicked with all her strength, and the man holding her fell backward, and she fell backward, and the world spun and then stopped, and dirt and trees made a wall before her, and the man moved beneath her, and she twisted, and she kicked, and she moved herself a foot toward the trees, and a hand grabbed her leg, and a boot exploded against her breast, and a boot exploded against her ribs, and a boot stomped on her calf, and she fell to the earth, and a fist struck her face, and a boot struck her face, and the muscles of her neck twisted with the force, and she fell to the earth, and something struck her side, and her legs, and her legs, and she fell to the earth, and then her side, and then her legs, and then her side, and then . . .

Quick Spanish. Lisette only caught a word here and there. A fog. Pain. A sneaker lying two feet from her face. *That's mine.* Agudelo's voice. And another voice. A man's voice, a pleasant voice, a jazz singer's voice, deep and rough. Breathing hurt. She breathed. Sound faded. She slowed her breathing. Took it gentle. Shallow. So shallow she hardly got any air at all. Agudelo's voice saying . . . something. The deep voice responding. "She works for the Sia." Lisette wanted to laugh, it was funny, wasn't it? Sia was a singer. And waves filled her head and pushed the sounds away, converted the sounds into incomprehensible bits of accent and intonation hovering somewhere beyond understanding. She breathed out, and in. She heard "the Sia" once again, and again she wanted to laugh. Sia wasn't a singer. Sia was how Colombians said "CIA." And it was funny, wasn't it? And then sounds were directed at her, the sounds were liquid, a stream of Spanish punctuated by three syllables, "Liz-EH-tee." Her name. She focused, but the words had ended, there was only the sound of the engine of the van, and the van slowly turning, going into reverse, then forward, turning slowly until it was heading back the way they came, back to La Vigia, and up above Lisette in the window of the van were the faces of the students, terrified, longing, and then blue sky and the sound of the van leaving her behind.

5

The previous winter Mason's father took his eldest, Inez, and taught her how to fell a tree. He didn't ask if he could, just left with Inez and an ax, a chain saw, and a peavey. When she came back, Inez showed Mason her hands, where the slow repetition of wooden handle rubbing against skin had raised blisters, and then ripped those blisters off. And as Mason treated her, Inez spoke excitedly of how to recognize the dangerous snags high in branches. How to tell whether a log should be cut from the bottom or top, how to handle a tree that hangs up on the way down, how to work your way around a large piece of wood by attacking the outer parts before sinking your blade into the core. How to pile a face cord four feet high and eight feet long with each end perpendicular to the ground so you don't need end posts.

"You need to take care of yourself, Pops," he'd told his father, who didn't even bother to reply, to say he wasn't dead yet, or some other cliché. He knew he should feel disapproval—his aging father had risked his health doing hard manual labor, risked his daughter's safety doing a dangerous and unnecessary chore. But as his daughter babbled excitedly, he mostly felt jealous.

It snowed the next week, barely enough to dust the ground, but still enough to qualify as a state of emergency in Florida's Panhandle. All the schools were closed, and there were forty-three road accidents in their county alone by 11:00 a.m. Natalia and Mason's father took the kids mud-and-slush sledding, and instead of resting while they were gone, Mason put on work gloves and earmuffs and went out to the tree-line at the back edge of his property, where Inez's face cord was sitting under a green tarp, waiting for the spring and summer to dry it out and make it ideal firewood, the kind of thing that saves you a damn bit of money getting through winters in Pennsylvania but is two hairs shy of useless in northern Florida.

Above him was a midsize black locust. He circled the tree, eyed the branches. There's a way of seeing when you're felling a tree that's different than just sitting out in nature admiring the view. You judge the lean of the bole, the tangles in the upper branches, the side most weighted with limbs. The looking feels not so different from the doing, when you set the choke, yank the starter rope, tap the throttle trigger, hear the scream of the saw, and as you sink it into the meat of the tree, turn the screaming saw to a satisfied purr. Yellow heartwood spat out from the whirring teeth. Mason circled the bole, cut above the gap to make a hinge. The tree, severed from the earth, began to sway. He shut down the saw, rushed from the sounds now snapping through the air, felt the displacement of air, and then, with a crash, the tree hitting earth.

The cruel thing about the path Mason had chosen was that he no longer got to do the real work of his job, the work of the hands and the body. He sat in meetings. He wrote white papers. He discussed the economics of the drug trade, the adaptations of guerrilla units to high value targeting, the differing interpretations of human and signals intelligence. He watched the slow, amorphous cultural changes within military units, police forces, civilian populations long exhausted by violence. He used graphs and figures and papers by political scientists filled with statistics and mathematical squiggles, giving the veneer of hard knowledge, though he knew in his heart that everything he did was at best an art, if not educated guesswork. It made you wish for the simplicity of the teams in Afghanistan, even though Afghanistan was not exactly an advertisement for the simple, physical approach. So he understood why it was important to his father to take Inez, who Natalia insists in no uncertain terms will be going to college, and teach her how to fell a tree.

Nine months later, sitting in the EAC meeting on the kidnapped journalist at the U.S. embassy in Bogotá, listening to David Matíz, the predictably squirrelly CIA chief of station, giving the ambassador predictably squirrelly answers about the Mil Jesúses and whether or not the U.S. has had visibility on them, he pictured that tree, lying on the earth, bare branches veining the sky. He thought about the satisfactions of a job well done, and the calm such a job brings.

All day, all around him, chaos. There were more military and intelligence guys running around embassies these days than diplomats, and when something like this happened, an AmCit held captive, ripe for potential to turn into the kind of news story that brings political pressure to bear, they went crazy. Just walking into the building he could feel the hum of mad energy, like walking inside a kicked beehive. And that mad energy delighted him.

A hostage story is a simple story. Beginning, middle, end. Beginning: AmCit gets kidnapped, the military and intelligence services spring into action. Middle: AmCit suffers brutal treatment, the military doggedly pursues intel on the captors. And then, one of two endings. End one: AmCit dies. End two: Everybody is a fucking hero.

At the EAC, most of the people at the table had nothing. Defense attaché gave a generic rundown on the situation in Norte de Santander. The Legat had a little bit on the Mil Jesúses, or "the MJs," as everybody was calling them, which conjured images of a group of Michael Jackson clones moonwalking cocaine across the border. The Legat cast the group as some lightweight narcos capitalizing on the peace and on Agamemnon, the police operation against the Urabeños. The RSO and the head of MILGROUP had little more. And then there was David Matíz, who harped on the MJs' connections to the Venezuelan military.

"Think of them as an independent contractor," he said, explaining that the parts of the Venezuelan military that ran drug trafficking were as rife with corruption and nepotism and mismanagement as the rest of the country, and so essential functions were often subcontracted out to entrepreneurs like Jefferson—ruthless and competent former paramilitaries with experience on both sides of the border.

"The MJs play it cautious, though," Matíz said. "They haven't turned up a lot of bodies. They somehow took over urabeño territory without starting a turf war. They're low profile, so a kidnapping like this, of an American, is out of character. That means something significant has changed or perhaps it wasn't them."

And then it was Mason's turn to speak, and he went over the assets they had in country ready to assist in the search. He didn't mention Diego, or his suspicion that the AmCit was the "girlfriend" Diego had told him about. He hadn't been able to reach Diego at all that morning, he couldn't be sure this Lisette Marigny was in Norte de Santander because of him, so what good would it do bringing it up? He hadn't shared any classified intelligence. Merely suggested a geographic region, and a particular group, to look into. Plus, there was something weird going on with the Colombians and the Jesúses that was more consequential, more worthy of the ambassador's time.

"One other thing," Mason said. "A few months after the El Alemán raid I had an odd discussion with Lieutenant Colonel Pulido. He told me he had a source in the MJs."

"And you didn't mention this to me?" Matíz said.

"I did, actually," Mason said. Matíz had told him, at the time, that he didn't care about penny-ante narco groups in Bumfucksville. "You weren't interested."

The ambassador raised a hand, made a "cut it out" gesture. Mason shrugged. It was the truth. And besides, it was pretty rich of the CIA to be bitching about *him* not sharing critical intel.

"The MJs have been pretty low on the priorities list, that's true," Matíz said. "I'll see what the Colombians come up with."

CIA guys were odd. In some ways, they were very similar to army guys. Same drive, mission-orientation, susceptibility to tunnel vision. But they had absolutely no sense of teamwork. You make your bones as a young case officer flipping people, getting foreign nationals to betray their home country in exchange for money or ideological satisfaction or a million other things that case officers learn to exploit. Perhaps that ruins the belief in team spirit.

As Mason left the meeting, he collected his phone from security and stepped into the Idaho room, which was covered with maps of the Gem State. He pressed the power button, the little screen turned on, connected to the network. He waited. He scrolled through and opened WhatsApp and refreshed. And, sure enough, up popped a message from Diego. It read, "We have to talk."

"Oh," he thought. "Great."

At lunch with the lawyer, his increasingly troublesome contact with the Mil Jesúses, Juan Pablo debated telling the man that his daughter was in Jesúses territory. It was a quick, lopsided internal debate, in which a small voice suggested he threaten the lawyer and demand the Jesúses guarantee her safety, while a much louder voice screamed that you cannot give these kinds of men any leverage at all. And so, before the meeting, he texted his daughter, "I love you, be safe," hoping she'd have time to stop at an internet café to get the message, but he did nothing else. Until he knew more, there was nothing to be done, and for her sake it was important to stay disciplined.

It was at moments like these that he wished he could pray the way his father had, with the firm conviction that there was a saint out there listening, offering help. But prayer was a hole to bury hopes in, there was no reason to think that his daughter was in any more danger than anyone else, and there were decisions to be made.

The restaurant was one of the most expensive in Bogotá, and everything from the view to the china to the paintings on the wall was beautiful. Everything except for his dining companion, a round, mutton-chopped man whose weathered face and red-veined nose were so ugly it seemed like a provocation, as if he were deliberately insulting the world with his ugliness.

The lawyer ordered for both of them, choosing a tasting menu in which each item was followed by a description of where in Colombia the dish came from—four varieties of fish from the coast, lemongrass-scented rainforest ants from the Amazon, delicate wild rodent meat from the semitropical forest, and so on.

"I can't believe rich people eat this garbage," Juan Pablo said. Circumstances, he thought, merited the rudeness. He wanted to signal where things stood.

"That man you asked me to look into," the lawyer said, smiling. "What was his name?"

"Jefferson Paúl López Quesada. The head of—"

"He's a businessman now," the lawyer said. "Confessed in the demobilization, served time for his crimes. But—and you may find this interesting—he's old friends with General Baute, from his days back in Cesar. And the rodent meat? It's delicious."

Baute. Of course. Cesar. Of course. There was a little town in Cesar that had been held captive by the paramilitaries for a full four days. They raped women in the streets. Dragged a mother through the dirt, tied her, naked and bleeding, in a pigsty. They executed fourteen townsmen they accused of being guerrilla supporters—shooting some, taking a chainsaw to others, and in one case forcing a man to drink acid that tore through his mouth, esophagus, and stomach, killing him from the inside. It was one of the cases the left like to yowl about, since some para boss had later said the army was involved. Baute, specifically.

"I read Jefferson's file from the demobilization," Juan Pablo said. "General Baute should get better friends."

"Would you like me to pass that on to him?"

"If the general wants to share useful information about his friend, he doesn't need to pass the message through you."

The lawyer laughed, and a runner appeared with the first of their dishes. The ants. Even though he knew they were on the menu, it surprised Juan Pablo to see them, sitting there. They weren't dressed up or mixed with vegetables or anything. They were just ants. On a plate. The lawyer reached over and waved his hand, wafting the odor into Juan Pablo's nostrils. Lemongrass.

"It smells good, yes? In Bucaramanga, they say eating queen ants puts steel in your dick."

The lawyer grabbed one of them and popped it into his mouth, cracking into the shell with his teeth and then slurping up the protruding legs, finishing the performance off with a smile and a sip of wine.

"Listen to me," he said. "The Jesúses have no need, no reason to kidnap a reporter. This is the truth."

"So who did?"

"Who knows. There are so many problems out there. Especially outside the main towns."

"What kind of problems?"

"Elenos. Crazy cocaleros. They have these little unions up there now, filled with ex-guerrillas. Remember when they shut down all the roads? The coca price has gone down, so the countryside is very angry."

"Who, specifically, do you suspect?"

"I only know who didn't do it." The lawyer plucked another ant from his plate, flourished it in the air, and dropped it in his mouth. "Has Representative de Salva contacted you?"

Juan Pablo laughed. Of course her name would come up. Honestly, he should have thought of her before. "It's none of your business who I've spoken with."

"Don't trust her."

"I don't trust anyone," Juan Pablo said. He decided that de Salva would be the first person he called as soon as he left this dinner. Then he picked up an ant with his fingers, inspected its crisped, lemongrass-scented head, fought down his disgust, and popped it in his mouth. As he bit down, the flavor flooded in, not just of lemongrass but of other, subtler textures, a slight acidity tinged with sour notes but also some creaminess from the insides of the abdomen. It was revolting, yes, but that was mainly because of the idea of it.

"This is much better than I thought it would be," he admitted.

"Rich people don't eat garbage," the lawyer said a bit testily. "Rich people know how to live." He picked up another ant and held it up for inspection. "If life isn't about hunting down every strange pleasure and tasting it, then what is it about?"

As it happened, Juan Pablo didn't have to call Representative de Salva. There was a request waiting for him. This time, the meeting happened in her office, and was straight to the point.

"Have you heard?" de Salva asked. "The Americans want the Jesúses to be moved up to a Class A."

Juan Pablo sat back in his chair. He hadn't heard that. Categorizing the Jesúses as a Class A Organized Armed Group meant the military could target them with everything from raids to aerial bombardments.

"That's fast."

"No," de Salva said. "I don't think it's fast at all. I think it needs to happen, and as a member of the Second Commission I can assure you that there would be support."

"I see," Juan Pablo said. "We don't even know if they're involved."

"The classification doesn't mean you have to target them. It simply removes bureaucratic obstacles if you need to act quickly. That's all it means."

"True," Juan Pablo said. But it was also false. The classification merely changed the rules of engagement, yes. But his unit was a machine designed to gather actionable intelligence, match it to the current rules of engagement, and produce dead bodies. In practice, de Salva was asking for a death sentence.

"With an American missing," de Salva continued, "and the support of the special forces, there will be no problem issuing the classification."

"And we do this because . . ."

"It is the right thing to do. And will earn you a friend. And as word gets out that the Jesúses are being taken seriously, I suspect you'll find new sources of information willing to talk."

All this was true, and even reasonable. But after agreeing to de Salva's request, and passing that information up to Colonel Carlosama, Juan Pablo found himself wondering why the haste. He understood, from the U.S. embassy point of view, why they'd want administrative hurdles to targeting the Jesúses removed in the event that a violent solution became necessary. But why would de Salva have been so keen? He could think of one possible answer. And that was this—the Jesúses didn't have the journalist, but de Salva wanted them administratively placed·on the chopping block before the army found out.

———

The thing about Colombia was that it was always easy to get a job. Contractors outnumbered soldiers five to one, last time Diego had checked. It allowed the U.S. government to claim a low footprint in Colombia, when, in fact, its fingers were everywhere, doing police and military training, crop eradication, logistics and maintenance. And Diego's specialty, electronic surveillance.

The trick wasn't getting a job. It was getting *the* job. Diego wanted to be there, in Norte de Santander. On the ground or, at least, in a plane, finding Liz. And that meant calling in favors not just within the contractor community but within the military as well.

"You owe me," he told Mason at a bar in the Zona T. "You're the reason she's there. Does the embassy know that?"

Mason wasn't ruffled. "They know that I met with you and told you the situation in Norte de Santander was interesting and underreported. I didn't suggest she head out to coca country, wouldn't have suggested it, and if she'd checked in with the embassy like reporters are supposed to we would have told her not to do it."

But Mason helped. He helped quite a bit, which meant that perhaps he was lying about what he'd told the embassy. And within a few days Diego was seated behind a Colombian pilot in a single-engine AT-802U Air Tractor stuffed with radios, forward-looking infrared cameras, and other surveillance equipment. Air Tractors were agricultural planes usually used for coca eradication, so the thinking was that this particular plane would cause less suspicion than a King Air.

"The only problem is the guerrilla like to shoot at these," the pilot told him as they taxied down the runway on Tolemaida, "so maybe we try to avoid coca fields."

They touched down in Tibú, where soldiers from Counter-Guerrilla Battalion 46 helped them refuel on a makeshift dirt runway, and then, with ten hours' worth of flight time filling their tanks, headed for La Vigia.

They flew at treetop level, deep green below them and clouds above, the shifts and turns of the plane felt immediately in the stomach. Headwinds, crosswinds. Diego didn't like being helpless, didn't like being just a passenger, so he focused on his equipment, the video feed from the thermal cam showing the occasional person, family, or even a microwave. Microwaves meant narcos.

The clouds ahead of them clustered and darkened, a storm front moving across the Catatumbo. They skirted it, the weight of the plane rolling, the nose dipping, the big, fuel-filled nose of the Air Tractor obstructing Diego's view, making the cockpit feel a bit smaller, more cramped. The motors roared, they climbed over a ridge and then dipped down below and the motors quieted, or maybe that was just Diego's imagination, and the flight felt calmer as holes poked through the cloud deck, light piercing down.

Then they were above La Vigia, doing long, slow loops, listening, taking photographs, looking for anything useful. From the air, a city or town is a simple thing. The heart of La Vigia was a small, neat grid of streets and buildings, with one central park that was roughly half the size of a football field. With the supposedly God's-eye view of the airplane, it might seem there was nothing much to this town, and certainly nothing mysterious. But down below, on the streets and in the buildings over the past six months, something strange had happened. A reordering of the connections between people. How they moved. Who they talked to. Who they feared. In a normal operation, Diego's job would be to help map that dynamic. To learn the rhythms of the town. To understand what would happen if a thread in the social fabric were tugged here, or a hole punched there. But this was not a normal operation. The lives of the people below him only mattered if they could help him find Liz.

Police captain Victor Hernández Nieto wasn't expecting the call. Yes, since the kidnapping of the American, his carabineros had been working overtime, reaching out to every contact they had. Yes, Army assumed it was Mil Jesúses, but he knew better and he'd let the Operations and Intelligence Group know. And yes, he had some ideas about what might be going on, but still, he didn't expect anyone to call him.

It had become obvious very early that the military had muscled its way into the lead for the journalist's recovery. This was undoubtedly what the Americans wanted. So when a call came through and the voice on the other end of the line announced that he was a lieutenant colonel in the special forces and he wished to get Nieto's honest assessment of the situation—not just the kidnapping situation but the security situation in La Vigia and the possible repercussions any military actions might have—he didn't quite believe it.

"I know you police sometimes have issues with our style of doing things," the lieutenant colonel, Juan Pablo Pulido, said.

"I don't have a problem with your style," Nieto said, choosing his words carefully. He knew nothing at all about this lieutenant colonel. "I think there is a time and a place for a more . . . for your approach. I simply wish there was more coordination."

"And here I am," Juan Pablo said, "coordinating."

Nieto considered complaining about the raid on El Alemán, which had happened on his turf and which he had only been informed of as it was happening. As far as he could see, that raid hadn't led to any decrease in narcotrafficking. If anything, the opposite. And most of the individual players hadn't changed. Javier Ocasio, a former army officer turned paramilitary turned narco, had been a lieutenant for the Urabeños in La Vigia before the takeover and was now the second in command after the takeover. Meanwhile, sources had dried up, and Los Mil Jesúses had solidified control of the town. They'd put up a candidate for mayor to challenge the insufficiently corrupt incumbent. They'd put pressure on the head of the local police outpost, a talented noncommissioned officer named Diego Murillo, who had recently claimed to be sleeping with a loaded pistol under his pillow. And the Fundación de Justicia y Fe, which he'd tangled with in the past but which did good work in the town, claimed to have had their movement and operations increasingly curtailed in the name of "public order." In short, the space for civic-minded leaders to operate was withering.

"I should mention," Juan Pablo said, "that we have requested that Los Mil Jesúses be listed as a Class A Organized Group."

"Ah." That changed things. "You want to know what kind of havoc might occur if there's a decapitation strike."

"Well, yes. Yes, of course."

There was something the lieutenant colonel wasn't telling him. It bothered Nieto. But he went on and started to explain the challenges such a strike would present. That Jefferson had somehow brokered a peace with the Urabeños but that if the army took him out the truce probably wouldn't outlast his death. That the second in command, Javier Ocasio, was generally considered unstable. That Nieto didn't have the resources to control the chaos that would follow a decapitation strike. And then the lieutenant colonel interrupted.

"There's a couple of university students in the town," Juan Pablo said. "With the foundation."

"Ah."

"It would look bad if a few children from Nacional got caught up in something like this."

Nieto started to chuckle. Of course! God forbid the violence in La Vigia affects someone from the capital! And students at a university, no less! Valuable lives. Lives of the sort that got him a direct conversation with a senior officer in the special forces.

"Is there any way," Juan Pablo went on, "of escorting them out of the town?"

Unbelievable.

"Oh, I really wish there was a way," Nieto said with great pleasure. "But you know what us poor rural police forces are like. Underfunded. Underequipped. We just don't have the resources for that kind of thing."

The conversation was short after that. Toward the end, the lieutenant colonel did ask one more fairly significant question.

"There is another theory I have heard," he said. "That this kidnapping was not the Mil Jesúses. That it was a cocalero association in conflict with the Jesúses."

"Ah," Nieto said. That was unlikely, but not out of the question.

"The FARC started as peasant self-defense forces," the lieutenant colonel continued. "If the cocaleros aren't just organizing, which is bad enough, but turning to violence, that is something we need to know. So is it possible?"

What he thought wasn't as important as what consequences it would have in terms of where army resources were deployed. The army's approach was the kinetic intelligence approach, knowing the territory so as to prepare the battlefield. Pushing hard. Rustling feathers. Kicking up dirt to see what settles. An approach well geared to units that helicopter in, shoot things up, and then leave others to deal with the consequences. The approach he had been trying to bring to his region, with limited success, was the approach he had been taught at the General Santander Police Academy back in 2004, a form of intelligence gathering that was less about generating targets than expanding a network of sources and community relationships, knowing every block on a street, every rural road, and every peasants association. Then you know who lives there. What they do. Who matters. Then you can do prevention. Then you can expand the "culture of legality." Or hope to.

The raid on El Alemán had blown things up in La Vigia, opening the door to Jefferson and the Mil Jesúses. But he still had good networks in the rural areas. If the journalist was out there, he'd get firm intelligence eventually, and then he could let the army know. Until then, maybe it wouldn't be terrible if they started kicking up dirt in La Vigia. He'd lost control there anyway.

"Your source," Nieto said, "and the valuable intelligence they provided. Was it for the El Alemán raid? What I want to say is . . . is the source connected to the Mil Jesúses? Because the Mil Jesúses are the only group that matters in La Vigia right now, and no one does anything without Jefferson's approval."

That was, like all the best lies, more or less true.

6

As they raced back to La Vigia, as Agudelo spit questions at Abel, as Abel furiously punched numbers into a satellite phone he'd produced from seemingly out of nowhere, Valencia felt a shiver go through her. Not from fear. She felt her heart beating faster. She felt the sharpness of things. The trees speeding by, the poverty of the shanties ahead of them. There were people walking in the street, people who seemed more alive than they had an hour before. Like many young people, who value their lives little because they have such little understanding of what effort it took to wrestle them into existence and tend them into adulthood, Valencia had wanted to be close to the spirit of destruction that her father had taught her from an early age to think of as the true essence of her country. Now she was part of it.

"I don't know who they were. No, not Elenos, no. Amateurs." Abel had the large, boxy phone to his ear, panic on his face. Valencia assumed he was speaking to Jefferson. "They lost control. They could have beat her to death. No one took charge, no one gave orders. Amateurs."

Valencia reached over and grabbed Sara's hand and smiled. Sara startled.

"This will be a story when we get back to Bogotá," Valencia said. It was a bizarre thing to say, and later she wouldn't understand why the words had left her mouth, but Sara smiled and seemed to calm a little, so perhaps they were the right words for the time. Valencia found herself wanting to giggle. It was a reaction she'd later feel very guilty about.

When they reached Abel's shop, Agudelo skidded the van to the side of the road, turned to Abel, and said, "Out!"

"That was not us," Abel said.

"Out!"

Only once he was gone and they were back on the road did Valencia open her mouth.

"I should ask my father what is going on," she said, half to herself.

Sara looked at her strangely, so, by way of explanation, Valencia said, "He is a lieutenant colonel in the special forces."

"What?"

Valencia said it again. Quiet followed.

Eventually, Agudelo said, "You should have told me that a month ago, girl."

Sara was looking at Valencia with a wide-eyed expression. It occurred to Valencia that perhaps she had just put herself in danger. These people might not be her friends.

The town whipped by. As they approached the central square of La Vigia, Agudelo began speaking in quick, clipped sentences.

"News of this will get out very quickly. When we get to the offices, you will email your father. You will tell him you are fine. You will tell him that we have dealt with kidnappings before. You will tell him that the organization will ensure everyone's safety. You will tell him that leaving La Vigia immediately might worry groups in the region. This is nothing new for us. I will notify the university and we will discuss what to do next. This is nothing we have not dealt with before."

There was silence in the van.

"With an American?" Valencia said.

"What?"

"You have dealt with a kidnapped American before?"

Agudelo scowled. "That's not important."

Sara turned and eyed Valencia. Of course it was important. They both knew it. It changed everything. Actions would be taken here that would never be taken if it was just some poor cocalero, or townsperson, or lawyer, or human rights worker, or student. They should be prepared. They should call her father. And her professor, the one supposedly in charge, didn't seem to understand why.

Agudelo parked the car, swung open the door, and marched them up the steps to the foundation's offices. They barged through the door, and there, sitting in the main room across from Luisa and a few frightened-looking members of the foundation staff, was a tired-looking middle-aged man with a mustache and a jowly face.

"Agudelo," Luisa said in an even voice, "I'm glad you're here. I don't think you've met Jefferson López before."

L isette was in pain, but that didn't matter. Pain she could deal with. She was a runner. She'd long ago learned to abstract herself, to treat the body as an object, dispense orders, and float free. When they forced her to move and the pain spiked and nearly obliterated her consciousness, it was almost a relief. When the pain wasn't overpowering her, what she felt in its place, suffusing every part of her body and resting like a weight about her chest, was shame.

She had been abducted. She had been abducted and hadn't taken any of the normal precautions because, hey, it was Colombia, not Afghanistan. It was the guerrilla, not ISIS. Through her own stupidity and arrogance, she'd gotten herself kidnapped, and now her family would suffer and her friends would suffer. She hadn't told anyone where she was going. There wasn't anyone waiting for a phone call at the end of the day. She hadn't noted the lack of traffic coming in the other direction from the checkpoint. She hadn't called ahead to find out what conditions were like. She hadn't called the ELN's representative to the

European Union to let them know she'd be in their turf. She hadn't registered with the embassy (no one registered with the embassy, but still). She imagined Bob's disapproval. "You're acting like a twenty-year-old freelancer for *Vice*." And she imagined her mother and her sister, terrified for her, anxiously awaiting news of her death while preparing for Uncle Carey's.

After her beating, they'd loaded her on a truck and driven down what felt like exceptionally bumpy dirt roads. Her kidnappers hadn't bothered to blindfold her, and at first she took this to mean that they were heading to her execution. As time passed and they drove past fields filled with the soft round leaves and red berries of coca plants, she noticed the nervousness of her captors. Sometimes they'd mention "el plan de Jorge." She heard the names of towns. And she thought, these guys are really bad at this. It was not an entirely hopeful realization.

Eventually, the truck stopped at a shack by the side of a coca field, sheltered under larger trees to provide some degree of protection from the gaze of herbicide-spraying planes. And out of the shack, a simple, rough concrete construction, emerged two men. The first was a sweet-faced young man in his midtwenties wearing a loud T-shirt with pinks and blues and red zigzags splashed across his chest, along with yellow, graffiti-style words like "ZAM!" and "FOXY!" and "SEX!" The other, older and thicker and shorter, had a tight braid necklace and an extremely faded shirt with the cracked remnants of Che Guevara's image still visible. On a second look, Lisette could make out bits of lettering floating at the top of Che's head, and she realized it was a shirt for the '90s rock band Rage Against the Machine.

Diego had once told her a story about the weirdness of looking through a scope and seeing a Taliban fighter in a Van Halen T-shirt. "All this old U.S. culture shit, the excess T-shirts that never got sold, they make their way to these countries like ten years too late," he'd said. "And then you're looking through the scope getting all nostalgic, like, 'Yeah, man, I danced to that song with Zhanna Aronov at my prom.'

And then you shoot the fucker." She had exactly two seconds to wonder if the shirt was some kind of political statement or just another bit of evidence of the reach of U.S. capitalism. And then they dragged her off the truck and the pain spiked again.

She was standing before them. Or, rather, standing above them. They were short. Really short. And her body was aching, she was trying to stand straight, as though there was some kind of pride to be found there, but she looked at the ground and it seemed like a much better place to be.

The shortest one, the one in the Rage Against the Machine shirt, seemed to be in charge. He inspected her silently, then turned to her captors.

"Why is she bleeding?"

Her captors looked at the ground.

"Did you take her phone?"

They said nothing, and he stepped forward and grabbed her sides, feeling for her pockets, and his touch against her caused pain to bloom, an onset so fierce her vision disappeared and she found herself holding him, arms on his shoulders and her legs weak underneath her, clutching him for support, and he threw her off, thinking she was attacking him, and she fell to the ground and one of the others kicked her, but it barely registered. So strange, that his hands were so painful, not meaning to be, but work boots colliding into her bruised side, the sound of it a dull thump against bruised meat, painless, as if it were no more than the distant sound of a woman pounding a piece of veal in another room. She couldn't feel it. Above her, somewhere, was a scuffle, and a shouted word whose meaning she didn't catch. Then Rage Against the Machine knelt by her and said, "I am sorry." She felt his hands on her pants, her phone sliding out of her pocket, and then, in a resigned voice, Rage Against the Machine saying, "Now the Sia knows where we are."

And she wanted to laugh, she did. But also, she was pretty sure they were going to kill her.

Jefferson was fat. That's all Valencia could think, seeing him in the flesh. Not obese, and not fat in the way Luisa was fat, where her bulk contributed to a kind of presence. He was just fat. He looked like what he said he was—a rich rancher who lived well, ate well, and liked to spread his money around. He had a small black mustache, a checkered shirt, tan work pants that were too big for him, and a pistol tucked into his belt. He was unimpressive. Somebody's rich uncle.

"Jefferson," Professor Agudelo said, acknowledging his presence flatly. The other workers and students stood around the room, waiting for something to happen. Luisa looked at him with visible disgust.

"I heard you were attacked," he said. "I am so sorry."

So this was a paramilitary commander. This was the man who'd cornered Alma, called out, *Hey Jhon, you wanna eat? Hey Hector, you want to eat?* and then watched as they raped her. There was a rumor that Jefferson had killed Luisa's father. There was a rumor that when he came to town, he'd tortured every Urabeño who wouldn't swear allegiance. He should look more substantive. He should have a scar on his face, a long crooked scar. A square jaw. Jefferson's face was pocked, as though he'd had acne as a child, and it was fleshy. His eyes didn't fix on any one person, but seemed to float lazily around the room as he asked questions about what happened and what the journalist had been doing outside of La Vigia. As the first shock of fear subsided, Valencia began to feel oddly disappointed. Look at him. Just another lump of flesh and blood, like the rest of us.

"The foundation will put out a statement to the media," Jefferson said, "saying that the journalist was taken by the guerrilla."

"We don't know who she was taken by," Luisa said.

"I am telling you what you will say."

"Bogotá will not put out a statement that is not verified," Professor Agudelo said.

"Then verify it."

Jefferson stood up and a flash of pain came across his face. He looked weak and almost pathetic for a second, but then he got control of himself and looked proudly around the room. He walked to Valencia.

"Where are you from, pretty?" he said.

"Bogotá."

"You're studying law?"

"Yes."

He shook his head. "You should be a beauty queen first. Then go study law."

Valencia said nothing, felt nothing. Jefferson turned to Sara, who stared at him hatefully.

"You," Jefferson said. "You go study law."

He turned back to Luisa.

"I want it known that it was country people who took the journalist."

"And if we do this for you," Luisa said, "what do you do for us?"

It seemed to surprise Jefferson, who paused, gave Luisa a measured look, and then laughed.

"It will be very bad here if that journalist is not found quickly. Am I wrong?"

"Perhaps," Luisa said.

"When death comes," he said, "he doesn't come to take just one."

Luisa smiled, her lips tight.

Jefferson stood up. "The police sergeant should be here soon. Let him know what happened. Country people!"

⸻

Luisa knew it wasn't Jefferson. She knew he was smart. She knew he was methodical. She knew he wouldn't jeopardize his position with some foolhardy, dramatic act. She also knew he was popular. She knew he was trying to build an empire. She knew that, in her little corner of Colombia, he wasn't even the worst option.

So what to do? In the main room, Agudelo was briefing the students on the foundation's protocols for things like this. Luisa sat behind her desk and thought. For some reason, the kidnapping of this journalist was a threat to Jefferson. That pleased her, but she tried to ignore that pleasure. What was good or bad for Jefferson wasn't important. The only thing that mattered was what made life better for everyone else.

Agudelo, finished with the students, came into Luisa's office.

"We need to get the students out as soon as it is safe to move them."

Luisa hunched down in her chair, leaned forward, and stared at her hands. They were large, and strong. Pianist's hands, her father had believed, though in her heart she knew that she never played as well as he pretended she did. It had been a long, long time since she'd played the piano.

"There is less violence in La Vigia now that Jefferson is in charge," Luisa said. "He's a monster, but he's rational. Did you know he's been telling townspeople to vote yes to the peace?"

"He wants the FARC gone. One fewer rival."

"Sometimes what's good for Jefferson is good for us. Sometimes it's not." Luisa drummed her fingers on the table. "You have friends. Journalist friends. In Cúcuta."

"I do."

"Well," Luisa said. "You and I need to think very hard about what we're going to tell them."

After giving her statement to the police sergeant, Valencia went to La Vigia's sole internet café. She could have called from the foundation's phone, but she needed to get out of the office, and Agudelo reluctantly agreed. As soon as she connected her phone to wi-fi, text messages from her mother and father popped up. "I love you, be safe," from her mother. And "I love you, take care," from her father. It was suspicious. She went into WhatsApp and called her father's cell phone.

He picked up on the first ring. "Let's not talk about work."

That left her silent.

"Let's not talk about work," he said again. "We always talk about work, and I don't want to talk about work. I want to talk about you and how you are doing, my dear."

It took her a second to get it, and then, once she did, she felt like a fool.

"Oh," she said. "That's fine." Maybe someone was listening in. Maybe her father was being paranoid. Whatever it was, it meant that her father already knew what had happened. Of course he knew.

"When are you leaving?" he asked.

"Nothing has changed."

"No sooner?"

"I don't think so."

What else did he know? Who had done it? Why? She wanted to tell him about it. That she had been *there*. That she knew what it looked like when someone was beaten bloody in front of you, and that she knew what it felt like when you did nothing, *nothing*, to stop it. The excitement she'd felt at the time was fading and in its place was guilt. Shame. A sense of remembered helplessness echoing through into the present, where she was still helpless. And as he talked, as he assured her that all was good back home, as he seemed to subtly suggest that she need not worry, that there were some issues that her father was going to *take care of,* she felt that helplessness coming to the fore. Here was her father, insinuating that he was going to take care of her, even here, in the place she'd come to be her own person.

"I have information," she said carefully. How could she tell him about Jefferson, and what he was demanding the foundation tell the media?

"No, it's good, it's good," came the quick reply. And he started talking about her upcoming semester, and she tried again to let him know that things weren't as they seemed, but he cut her off again and said, "It rained today, very hard. The news said it wouldn't so I went out without an umbrella and got wet. But you can't always trust what you hear on the news."

"Oh," she said, "okay." And then he told her he loved her, and that everything was fine, and that she should do exactly what her professor told her to do, and he hung up.

She went back to the offices, where Ricardo was sitting alone next to the chair Jefferson had occupied a few hours earlier.

"How are you?" he said. "That must have been very frightening."

Valencia nodded, pulled out the chair Jefferson had used, and sat in it. Her skin prickled.

"I want to do something," she said.

"Have you finished your transcripts?"

That wasn't what she meant.

"I know," Ricardo said. "It's boring. But really important work tends to be. Trust me. And Luisa. And your professor."

"Of course."

But she didn't trust Luisa. And Professor Agudelo was a fool. And what was Ricardo but a factotum? And what had any of them done when that criminal had sat in their offices and laid out his terms? Her father had ways of dealing with men like that. It troubled Valencia to feel that way, but she did.

As a girl, Valencia had taken to praying for murderers, for rapists, for criminals and narcos and terrorists. That they'd give up their evil and reconcile with Christ and be redeemed. She'd prayed for Osama bin Laden and she'd prayed for Tirofijo and she'd never, ever told her parents about it, not even her mother, who would have understood but who also would have suggested that perhaps she should be praying for her father and his men instead of those who tried to kill them. It had seemed to her that the extent of the evil committed by the objects of her prayer must, in some way, be proportional to the virtues displayed in praying for them. But looking at the chair in which Jefferson had sat only an hour ago, and at the door to the room where Alma had testified her orchestrated torture at Jefferson's hands, the very idea of praying for his salvation seemed grotesque. Perhaps this was what her father wanted her to know when he dismissed her reasons for coming here as childish nonsense. Perhaps losing one's sense of mercy was part of growing up.

She got up and left the offices and went to her room. When she opened the door, she saw Sara was sitting on the bottom bunk, reading a book by Moreno-Durán.

"I looked into cases from the demobilization under Uribe," Sara said. "You know that Jefferson can't be touched by the law? He served time under arrest. Two years. He served in a special prison with other bosses in the paramilitaries. They had their own rooms and special meals cooked for them."

"Two years?"

"He confessed to all kinds of things, extrajudicial killings, forced displacements, gender-based violence." She said the clinical words with loathing. "That's what he got."

Two years. That was 730 days. Surely, he'd ruined more lives than the number of days he'd spent in a comfortable prison. How many hours had he spent in jail per life he'd ruined? Per farmer thrown out of his lands, per trade unionist murdered in cold blood. She thought of Alma and the corpse of the girl she'd been, reaching up and clutching at her still, all these years later. What had Alma's suffering added to his jail sentence? An hour or two? Less time, perhaps, than Alma had been trapped at that party.

Sara pulled out a little flip phone from her pocket. "The camera on this isn't very good, but I got a photo of him before he left."

On the screen was a slightly blurry image of Jefferson.

"What are you going to do with that?"

"I don't know."

"Why'd you take it?"

Sara shrugged, her eyes on the blurry image. "Instinct."

They both looked at the photograph. Jefferson was standing by a window, a scowl on his ugly, puffy face. Valencia could imagine this photo on the evening news, as she'd seen so many other photos of FARC leaders or drug lords or criminals over the years, their faces posted after one of them was captured or killed and the army or police released one of the surveillance photos they'd used to track them down.

"We could give it to my father," Valencia said.

That hung in the air, but then Sara shook her head. "And what's he going to do? Jefferson is an old paramilitary. He's probably got more friends in the army than your dad does."

Valencia didn't want to get into an argument, so she ignored that.

Sara stared at the photo. "Why is that son of a bitch so interested in what happened to the gringa?"

"Because she's an American," Valencia said. And she told Sara about her conversation with her father, and her suspicions about what might, even now, already be in motion. "The army will try to find her. And when the army comes into a place . . ."

"Ah." Sara nodded. That was why Jefferson wanted the foundation to tell the media it wasn't him. He didn't want to be a target when they came looking for the gringa. "This is a real problem for him."

Valencia nodded, slowly. "Yes, but . . ."

"Luisa's going to help him."

"So he'll be fine."

It was a little revolting to say the words out loud.

"That bitch." Sara tossed her book onto the windowsill. "I'd like to do something to hurt him. Even a little."

And Valencia agreed. Yes. That would be good. And then they were quiet, each with their own thoughts, until Sara held up her phone, displaying the image of Jefferson, and asked, "Do you use Twitter?"

t had been some time since Agudelo had seen violence up close. During his six years with the Sofia Peréz Lawyers' Collective, from 2003 to 2009, it'd been more common. The Uribe years were hard for the profession. State authorities would accuse lawyers like him of being guerrilla sympathizers, and the paramilitaries would take action. Six judges, 12 prosecutors, and 334 lawyers killed. He'd known one well. Alejandra Cortéz. Raped and murdered. He'd seen a coworker approached and held by two men who spat in his face and told him they'd kill his daughter. And then, his own assault.

At the time, everyone kept telling him what amazing strength he had, what resilience. He had a photo of himself from then. It showed a brutalized man in a hospital bed, his face distorted by the damage, one eye half shut, dark swelling flesh pressing against it, stitches along the jaw and the top of the head, an overlarge bandage comically perched upon the nose. But the man wasn't lying back, resting and recovering. He was sitting up, eyes down on the papers strewn about his hospital bed, working. He kept the photo in his office; a reminder of what a brave person he had seemed at the time. But only seemed.

The men who assaulted him had clubbed him in the head, knocking him unconscious with the first blow. He never even saw them. Never experienced the horror of being physically helpless, at the mercy of the merciless. He woke up in a fog, with a kind, panicked stranger shouting in his face that an ambulance was coming. As the blood returned to his brain, then to his tongue, his first concern was not for himself but for the stranger. She seemed so worried, he wanted to put her at ease. "I'm okay. That's not necessary," he'd told her. It wasn't until he got to the hospital and they told him what had happened that he realized he'd been attacked, and not hit by a car or some other thing. By that time he was on painkillers, and so the knowledge didn't land with much force.

That was why he was able to appear so unperturbed by what had happened. His experience of violence was not like other people's.

So it shouldn't have surprised him that the kidnapping would leave him shaken. After hashing out a statement for the press with Luisa, he went to the bathroom and threw up. It felt good. A physical expulsion of the stress and fear that he had not permitted himself to show. As the men had beaten Lisette, sound had faded and time had slowed. His vision had tunneled. Normal physiological reactions, he knew, but the drive back seemed to stretch into eternity, his hands seemed to obey his mind only after a half-second delay, and he had to carefully breathe in and out as white spots exploded at the far corners of his vision, trying keep his heart steady, his blood pumping, his van on the road, and his mind alert.

Soothed by the vomiting, Agudelo cleaned himself, splashed water on his face, and considered his situation objectively. Perhaps some residual mental trauma had been triggered. Perhaps his older, weaker body was less equipped to handle such things. Which meant he needed to care for his body so that he could be useful. Sharp. He needed a walk.

He left the bathroom and headed through the offices, trailing his hand along the uneven wall. Terrible construction. Ugly, yellow-tinged paint. He walked out and down the steps to the bakery. Two old men sat at a table. In the back, two thin, young ex-combatants, young enough that if you'd added their ages together you'd still have fewer years on earth than he did, pulled bread out of the oven.

Luisa had built a good thing here, but good things were fragile. La Vigia was underdeveloped and bordered Venezuela. It was surrounded by difficult terrain that couldn't be effectively policed. It would never generate enough legitimate business to be worth the government's time, but it would always produce enough illegal profit to make it key territory for narcos. What did protecting human rights look like in a place like that? It looked like ugly bargains. Which was what Luisa, who hadn't so much as blinked when she learned that the man responsible for the death of her father had returned to La Vigia, was good at.

Ricardo walked past the door of the bakery, saw Agudelo inside, and poked his head in.

"I'm heading to the Defensor del Pueblo," Ricardo said. "To go over a few things."

Yes, he thought. The work continues. And though he wanted to join him, he instead walked out to the central square and looked at birds and thought about the last hour of his friend Alejandra's life, and whether there was a God and a devil, whether Alejandra would live again in paradise, or whether that was it, the end of her story a mind full of pain and terror, no redemption, nothing saved.

Rather than continue their work in their rooms, Valencia and Sara snuck out to the internet café and wrote down a list of crimes. They edited it three times, combing through for compromising details that might help identify victims. They didn't want anyone targeted. But they also wanted to add substance to the accusations, so that any journalists they tagged would have his backstory laid out.

"But they already know," Valencia said. "It's public record."

Sara said, "Yes. But there's knowing, like, Oh yeah, I'm pretty sure I know that. And then there's *knowing*, like, Yes, absolutely, I have seen the evidence. And then there's people talking with each other about knowing. And that's the most important thing. People don't have the guts to believe what they believe unless other people are talking about it."

"Who told you that?"

"My dad."

"The journalist."

"Yeah."

Valencia wondered what her father would say. When she started at Nacional, he'd explained to her the difference between information and intelligence. Information, he said, was just that. Data. Ones and zeros. Intelligence was relevant, actionable, secret information you could use. Think of the difference between holding a booklet with the rules of a card game versus that moment when you're playing the game and suddenly things click. Ah, this is how you play. Intelligence was what you used to play the game. At universities, they claim to be offering knowledge. But knowledge was only information until you learned to weaponize it.

"Why does it have to be on Twitter?" Valencia asked. "Why not just set up a fake email account and email a reporter?"

"Then it's just an anonymous accusation," Sara said.

"This is an anonymous accusation, too."

"If we put it on Twitter, along with a recent photo, that's news. Reporters don't need to verify the accusations. They can report on the *existence* of the accusations, which is just as good. Two months before the peace vote, this is a good story. A former paramilitary kidnapping a reporter."

"Within hours the foundation is going to say it was the guerrilla."

"Perfect. It'll be a mess, with lots of different theories for people to argue over. Don't you see it's better this way? If we give them something to argue over, it keeps the story alive. It keeps Jefferson's name in the news."

Ah, Valencia thought. Intelligence.

"And," Sara said, "if we want to be extra clever, we create another account, and a few hours after the first thread have that account respond, adding more charges, along with at least one thing they can verify."

And so that is what they did.

———

Jefferson woke up in pain, as he did every morning. Exhausted, as if he hadn't slept at all. The doctor warned him about this. It would only get worse. He got up, walked to the bathroom, and popped some pills for the pain before even urinating. He hated this. Not the pain so much as what it made him. Weak. The drugs interfered with his mind, his clarity. But recently the pain had begun interfering with his mind even worse than the drugs. It was a battle he felt himself losing. He'd rather kill himself than lose, and though he didn't fear death, he did have unfinished work that required his attention. That required his mind, and his energy, and most cruelly, his time.

Does Javier know? It seemed impossible that Javier didn't know. But he kept Javier busy. Busy, rich, and at a distance, a strategy designed to maximize his safety and Javier's loyalty. Javier would happily retire him if he sensed weakness.

There was a cosmic unfairness to his situation. He'd spent years developing contacts in the Venezuelan military, years establishing a base across the border, years preparing the ground for his expansion inside Colombia itself. And the conditions were perfect, like a sign from God, this majestic reordering of the power within Norte de Santander, the receding of the old ideological forces and the targeting by the police and then army of what would have been his most powerful rival, the Urabeños. This was a wilderness ready for exploitation. This was one of the key drug routes, and with the right series of moves it could be his within a few years. A few years. He laughed. In a few years, I could be Carlos Castaño. I could be Pablo Escobar. I could be Che Guevera, Osama bin Laden, Barack Obama.

His phone rang, and he saw from the number that it was Luisa, the fat bitch from the foundation.

"Who did it?" he said.

"The foundation put out a release, you can see it on their website. It says they were dressed as guerrilla."

"Who did it?"

There was a pause, and she said, "Father Iván wants to talk to you."

Father Iván. Who worked it out with the cocaleros and the indios and ex-guerrilleros and a couple of other groups that had been causing trouble.

"Fine."

He took down the details and considered the matter. He was mostly in the dark, but he knew a few things. They'd reached out through Father Iván, a priest who had worked with ex-guerrilleros. They'd asked to meet in territory that used to belong to the FARC. The cocaleros there, who used to sell to the FARC, had been more troublesome than in the regions closer to La Vigia. They'd complained about the prices he paid, the taxes he'd charged. He'd even had to kill one man who'd tried negotiating a better price from the Peludos, who controlled the territory to the north. Undoubtedly, there was anger over that. And any number of guerrilleros had returned home in recent years, so there was presumably a reserve of ex-combatants with military experience. Perhaps one of them was rallying resistance. A failed revolutionary, returned home but missing the sense of purpose war gives to young men. If so, Jefferson could handle him.

His maid cooked him a simple breakfast—eggs and arepa—and he forced himself to eat. His body needed fuel to fight the disease and to power his day, it was that simple. He was even starting to feel a bit better about the situation when he turned on the news and there, on Caracol, was the image of the reporter. And he turned the sound up, and he continued to eat, and then he heard his name, and he looked up and saw his own picture. A recent picture. Wearing the same shirt he'd worn the day before.

He closed his eyes as a wave of nausea came across him. This had to be the foundation's doing. They were making a play. They thought he was weak. And they knew that right now he couldn't afford to slaughter them. But Luisa should know he could be subtle when he had to be.

"I'm famous now," he called out to his maid. She hadn't seen the television, and clearly had no idea what he was saying, but nodded anyway, pretending to understand.

This wasn't the worst thing. Fame was dangerous, but it had its own kind of power. He'd learned that from his old comandante, Tomás Henríquez Rúa, when they were incarcerated together after the demobilization.

Rúa was famous for being crazy. That was one of his aliases. The Crazy Man. He was famous for fucking young virgins. That was another one of his aliases. The Drill. And in prison, that fame followed him around like a tiger on a leash. Everyone respected him, held him in awe. Rúa had more power than the warden, than the prison guards, than anyone. And since Jefferson was in his circle, the blessings fell on him, too. He had eaten better, and fucked prettier whores, than he ever had outside prison. In some ways, it had been the happiest time in his life.

In their second year there Rúa had thrown a party in the common area of the jail. Everyone thought of Rúa as a madman, but he had a genius for connecting with the people. Jefferson had studied this and learned from him. That party was his masterwork. Rúa brought in three tiers of prostitutes. Red, black, and yellow. The highest tier came dressed in red, escorted by armed guards, dripping with perfume, clothing bulging with fake asses and tits, reserved exclusively for Rúa's inner circle. The middle rank came in black. They were all pretty enough, or if not pretty they were young enough to feel fresh, and they only fucked men who'd been in the autodefensas. The cheap whores, for common use, old and strung out, dressed in yellow. It had been especially inspired, he thought, to insist on the uniform colors of clothing. As the prisoners danced and fucked, as the whores went down on their knees and sucked prisoner after prisoner off in the far corners and corridors, behind columns or right in the middle of the dance floor, you could see how people ranked. The whores were human jewelry marking concentric circles of envy, with Rúa at the center. It was like he was a God. It was being a God.

In the middle of the party Rúa had brought out his weapons, his arsenal, to show off to the whores. Somewhere, Jefferson had a photo of himself in prison, holding a Jatimatic SMG just like Sylvester Stallone on the poster for *Cobra*, but with two whores in red crouched at his thighs and making sexy faces.

And then some idiot drunk on aguardiente pulled the pin on a grenade. He'd laughed and tossed it to a whore and she'd screamed. The grenade fell on the floor and only then did it dawn on the idiot what he'd done. Jefferson remembered the man's face as the realization hit, and Jefferson had grabbed Rúa and dove to the floor as the grenade rolled into the pulsing crowd, and then there was a flash and a bang and blood and screams.

Of course, the prison guards immediately came to find out what happened. Jefferson had his men bar them from the common area while Rúa directed others to clean up the body parts, take the corpses to the basement of the prison, and dissolve them in acid. Nothing, they told the guards, nothing at all has happened. Some fool set off a firework.

Meanwhile, Rúa demanded everyone else stay on the dance floor. Everything was okay, everything was normal. And Rúa ordered them to keep dancing.

There was blood on the floor. There was blood on the ceiling. Some of the whores had bits of skin blown into their hair. Some were bleeding. One man screamed that he needed a doctor and Jefferson had his men slit the man's throat. They turned up the music. Reggaeton played. They danced.

That was power. Pure power, built of fear and envy and desire. It was the most beautiful thing Jefferson had ever seen.

He opened his eyes. The news had moved on to a piece about the health effects of only eating the same kinds of foods that were eaten by cavemen.

7

Father Iván followed behind Misael Castillo as he walked the northern side of his land, touching one spoiled palm branch after another. He'd come to the farm to ask Misael not about his crops but about his nephew, Edilson, who was apparently behind this idiotic kidnapping. Misael, on the other hand, wanted to talk crops.

"Idiots," Misael said, and Father Iván nodded in agreement. This was a field of African palm, perfectly legal, and now a full two thirds of the man's trees were dying. The planes the government sent out to spray coca had accidentally hit here, destroying his livelihood. And worse, because they both knew what those chemicals did. Father Iván figured that Misael's children would be shitting all night for the next couple of days, and nothing good would ever grow on this land again.

"There's no coca around here," Misael said. "We were sick of government planes ruining our fields. That's why I switched to palm."

"I thought you switched because the price of coca went down."

"That, too." Of late, Misael had been a booster of palm oil. He'd tell anyone who'd listen that it put more money in his pocket than he'd ever had growing coca. And he was a leader in a local collective of farmers who were getting free seeds and fertilizer from Oleoflores, which promised to send trucks to pick up the product, just like the narcos did with coca. He was building his family a brick house. And the work was cooler—under the shade instead of in the sun. But there were more important things at hand.

"I need to know what your nephew wants before I talk to Jefferson," Father Iván said.

"You know how it is up there." Misael tugged on a withered palm frond and held it up for inspection before discarding it in disgust.

Father Iván had some idea. The arrival of Jefferson into the area had coincided with a drop in the price of coca, so there'd already been a lot of anger up in the north, where Edilson had been trying to organize a local union. It got worse when the Jesúses had murdered a cocalero who'd tried selling to the Peludos, and then, days later, this American had arrived, setting off all kinds of conspiracy talk.

"I have no idea what he thinks he's doing," Father Iván said. "And I'm starting to suspect he doesn't either."

Misael walked to the edge of the trees and stared out into the jungle.

"Palm is good work," Misael said. "A harvest every eight days, regular income. But if I plant new trees, it will be a year and a half before they produce oil. If I plant coca . . . the money will come faster."

"What will you do?"

Misael stepped into the tree line and Father Iván followed him. Nettles caught against his skin and he had to push through the underbrush. He should have worn work boots, like Misael.

"I'll have to cut out more forest," Misael said. "Cut and burn. Awful work. And then I'll ask around. Maybe my nephew can negotiate a better price with Jefferson for coca. Maybe the price of palm oil will go up. Or down."

"This country is growing more coca than it ever has," Father Iván said. "The price of coca isn't going up."

"People always think they can tell," Misael said. "But no one knows. I will wait and see."

That was fair. Anyone who tried too hard to anticipate the market always ended up a fool. With the price of coca, the price of palm oil, there were just too many factors to consider. The opening and closing of drug routes. The law requiring diesel retailers to mix in 10 percent biofuels. The cocalero unions bargaining for better prices. The new palm oil companies sending trucks out to remote places. The six thousand soldiers patrolling Norte de Santander. The seven dead farmers whose funerals Father Iván had officiated, all of them shot when the counternarcotics police descended on a coca field and opened fire. The aerial spraying of crops. The fungus moving across the coast, poisoning coca plants at the root. The temperature and the rain. The lack of good roads. The decisions of farmers and narcos and policemen and drug addicts and presidents and mayors and weather systems and God himself, all factoring in to determine the forever varying price of a kilo of coca leaves and a kilo of palm oil, so that men like Misael could make decisions about what kind of life they were going to live, legal or illegal.

In one sense, it was magical, the way the market worked. But in another sense, the sense Father Iván had come to after years of documenting the wreckage—the murdered trade unionists, campesinos, human rights workers, and others—there had come to seem something sinister about it. Perhaps everything you buy ought to include a surcharge of a drop of blood. Or, depending on the product, an ounce.

"Hey, father." Misael was looking upward, and Father Iván followed his gaze. High up in the branches was a metal box. Snaking upward from the box was a long antennae, hidden among the branches. Father Iván had never seen anything like it before. Military? Police? Military.

"Okay," he said slowly. "Misael, you must tell your nephew he needs to figure out what he wants right now. Because if he's going to negotiate with Jefferson, it has to happen immediately."

—

A crowd of children greeted Jefferson when he arrived at the hut, a rectangular bohío with crooked wooden planks and a thatched roof. The youngest were naked, the older ones in dirty pants, fading blouses. One girl of about eleven had a brightly colored beaded neck-lace, and eyes so dark they seemed to glow. She stared at him as if he were the strange and pitiful one, emerging from his Land Rover, pistol prominently tucked in his jeans, two men with assault rifles at his side, and a caravan of Jesúses in trucks pulling watch at every possible route of egress from the village.

Jefferson did not like children. They were what would last after his death. So he moved through the crowd and strode inside the hut, look-ing for the priest. Inside was dark and quiet. A shape floated before him. The shape moaned. His eyes adjusted, and the shape materialized into a naked woman, pregnant, massively pregnant, and floating in midair. Her feet hung a few inches off the ground, rope and some kind of leather harness around her upper torso and strung up to the crossbeam of the hut. It was a woman in labor, hung suspended so that gravity could help the baby out. Jefferson was familiar with the practice, but had never seen it before. Other women huddled around, nuns in dark habits. One of them lifted a hand and said, "Out! Out of here!" And she moved for-ward, as if ready to throw him outside herself.

The pregnant woman moaned. Jefferson felt his nausea returning. He stumbled backward, out to the crowd of children. He breathed once, twice. His guards followed awkwardly behind. A breeze carried the scent of animal shit. His men fingered their trigger guards.

He breathed again. He had been scolded like a child. It had hap-pened in front of his men. He considered heading back in, but to do what? Beat her? That wouldn't regain him any respect. Nuns have a power. And women giving birth, they also have a power. He'd never understood it. Even Javier, who took more pleasure in torture than in sex and food, had an odd thing for new mothers. Jefferson found it stupid, disquieting. But it was there.

So instead, he turned to his guards and said, "Indios are animals," and they laughed. Fine.

Up the road, he saw a black cassock. Father Iván, presumably.

Waving excitedly. A large cross hung from his neck, like a priest in an old movie.

"No, no," Father Iván called out. "Not in there."

Father Iván was tall and thin and covered in sweat. There were dark stains under his arms and across his stomach. His face shone with it. A droplet of sweat sat on the edge of his nose. Another moan came from inside the hut.

"Idiot! You told me . . ." Jefferson began, but then stopped as nausea rose up again.

"Yes, yes, sorry. But one of the women in the village," Father Iván gestured to the bohío, "well, you saw."

They both stared for a moment at the hut where the indio woman was hanging, giving birth.

"Maybe it's a good omen," the priest said. "A very powerful thing, what's happening. Us men aren't so impressive on a day like today, are we? We can't start a life."

"I've come in enough women to have started a few lives."

The priest laughed. He motioned down toward the stream on the far side of the road. There was a man sitting there on a log next to a dirty white cooler.

"That's Edilson," he said.

"He's the fool behind this?"

The priest sighed. "Please," he said, "try to understand. These are very poor, very desperate people. Times have been very hard for them, and you have been very hard on them, too. They thought capturing a CIA agent would give them leverage."

"A CIA agent?"

The priest began explaining a rather convoluted theory about Jefferson's links to the foundation and the American journalist, who had suspiciously come here from Afghanistan.

"She's just a stupid gringa," Jefferson said. "Not CIA." He was pretty sure.

"Oh." The priest shook his head. "Well, they didn't understand all the problems this would cause."

What difference did it make, whether they understood or not? Jefferson started down toward the stream. "You coming?" he said.

"I . . . cannot."

Of course. The priest wanted to keep his hands clean. Jefferson called out over his shoulder, "You know what my father told me when I was a child? He told me, 'I'd rather slit my throat than have my son become a Conservative or a priest.'"

"My father told me the same thing," Father Iván called back. That made Jefferson smile.

Edilson stood up as Jefferson approached. He was an unimpressive little man. Not very tall. Not much of a mustache. Who was this fool? Did he understand what he'd unleashed?

"The military is coming for you," Jefferson said before Edilson could open his mouth. "They have spy planes up in the air. Have you noticed? Planes that fly low but don't spray crops?"

Edilson looked up toward the road, then back at Jefferson. "We have demands," he said.

"They're coming to kill you," Jefferson said. "I told them who you are."

It was quiet. Edilson nodded, clearly unsure what to say. He turned to the cooler.

"Would you like a beer? We have Aguila Light."

Edilson lifted the top of the cooler and pulled out a beer. His hand was shaking. Jefferson saw Edilson follow his eyes to that shaking hand. He put the beer down.

"Nervous?" Jefferson asked.

"We have demands," Edilson said again. "All you have to agree to is a fair price—"

"Are you talking about coca?" Jefferson said. "Is this all over coca?"

Edilson seemed taken aback. That was good. Jefferson wanted him off balance. He had a very different sort of negotiation in mind than the one Edilson had probably come prepared for.

"Idiot." Jefferson scowled. "Your men who took the gringa. That was well done. Are they ex-guerrilleros? How many men do you have?"

"Many."

Jefferson sighed. "I'm going to need to know how many men you have. And how many of them know how to use a weapon. Ex-guerrilleros are good. They're trained."

"I—"

"The people out here, do they trust you? The cocaleros?"

Edilson raised his head, a confident look in his eyes for the first time. "They do."

"I think that's true. You couldn't have hidden from me if they weren't protecting you." Jefferson pointed his finger at Edilson's chest. "That's worth something. That's worth a lot. I don't like this anger between me and my growers."

"The price you pay for coca—"

"I told you. Coca is nothing." He waved his hand. "It's worth nothing these days. This country is stuffed with it."

Edilson shook his head, still not understanding.

"You little farmers sit on land that is worth far more than anything you will ever grow on it."

That interested him. Jefferson could see that.

"This area is difficult for the police to patrol," Jefferson said. "And it's right on the border with Venezuela. Do you understand?"

Edilson nodded.

"Coca leaves will never make you rich. But this territory, right on the border . . . It is very important to a lot of people. Jesúses. Peludos. Urabeños."

"We—"

"Listen to me. If the army comes here, no one gets rich. If the army comes here, we are all fucked. So first, you are going to give me the journalist. And I am going to give you fifteen thousand mil."

"I'm not here for the money. I'm here for my people."

"That is why you're going to give me the journalist. Because if you don't, I'm going to hunt you all down and kill you and have my men rape your wives and your daughters and your mothers. And that is not good. But if you work for me—"

"If I *work* for you?"

"Yes, if you work for me. I can't have these problems over a couple of angry cocaleros. You will work for me, and your men will control this territory for me, and I will pay you a salary, and that will be better for everyone."

Edilson stared back, bewildered. He wasn't much to look at, Jefferson thought, but he'd built up a crew of fighters, and he'd shown some balls. Perhaps he could be useful. Perhaps this whole thing wasn't a complete disaster.

"But first," Jefferson said. "You have to give me the journalist. Or we are all fucked."

Very soon, Jefferson had worked out a rough agreement, Edilson had called out to his men on a handheld radio, and a small boat began making its way downstream. Inside was nothing dangerous. Just the American, hands tied and blindfolded.

———

Intelligence officers are conspiracy theorists by vocation. You *want* them to see enemies everywhere. Peace treaties are smoke screens, violence an inoperable cancer, and civilians the sea our enemies swim in. At a presentation at the Escuela de Inteligencia that Juan Pablo had attended in 2009, a professor there had proclaimed, "This is Colombia. This is the country of the conquistadores—the bandits, the criminals, the terrorists of Spain. And they are our grandparents, our ancestors, our forefathers. We have their evil and their mischief in our blood. This is why we must always be vigilant. This is why we will never have peace."

No matter. Sift through the paranoia, find the actionable intelligence. That was Juan Pablo's approach. It was a bit more concerning, though, when the malice was directed at him.

The sergeant from the CIME clicked on a slide, up popped a photo of Luisa Porras Sánchez, and the eyes in the briefing room began crawling over him. Sánchez led the so-called human rights foundation his daughter was tangled in, and the connection between the foundation and the kidnapping was looking stronger by the hour, especially since that peculiar photograph of Jefferson had surfaced on Twitter, of all places.

"Head of the local office of the Fundación de Justicia y Fe," the sergeant said, his eyes not on Colonel Carlosama, who he was officially briefing, but on Juan Pablo. Everyone's eyes were on Juan Pablo.

In the past day, Juan Pablo had spoken up for the Jesúses. They'd been getting conflicting reports. Human intelligence sources telling them the journalist had been taken by guerrilla, police intelligence fingering the Jesúses, the foundation itself putting out a statement that it'd been guerrilla, American signals intelligence picking up suspicious traffic suggesting the Jesúses.

It was an unusually sensitive question. Given ongoing negotiations with the ELN and the peace treaty with the FARC, a high-profile kidnapping by the guerrilla would have been a political problem for the president and his supporters. Given the military's push to take over Agamemnon and other operations against BACRIM, adding the Jesúses to the list of Class A groups would be a welcome step in the next phase of military targeting against nonpolitical actors. These considerations meant that the evidence pointing to the Jesúses was highlighted, and counterevidence ignored. But to Juan Pablo, who tried to resist that kind of political pressure, the whole thing didn't make sense, and he'd said as much. Why would the Jesúses kidnap a journalist?

He'd held his own in the argument for a few hours, and then the news reports came out, showing the photo of Jefferson in what a human intelligence source confirmed was the offices of the Fundación de Justicia y Fe. Suddenly, the foundation's statement fingering the guerrilla was not evidence for Juan Pablo's cause, but proof that the foundation itself was compromised. And proof Juan Pablo was a fool.

"Porras's father was mayor of a rural town near La Vigia," the sergeant said. "A guerrilla sympathizer. He supplied the ELN with weapons. He was executed by the paramilitaries in 2002. She's in La Vigia now, they say to interview victims of the FARC, but their office has seen a parade of former guerrilleros coming in and out. And we have a source that claims her relationship with Jefferson goes back fifteen years."

"Back to when he was in the paras?" Juan Pablo broke in. "Really?" The sergeant was spinning bullshit theories as real intelligence, trying to fit a narrative on top of a set of facts that didn't yet make any sense. Was he the only one who noticed?

"It's not impossible," Colonel Carlosama said. "The paramilitaries and guerrilla could work together sometimes, especially the factions more interested in narcotrafficking than in politics."

The colonel raised an eyebrow, awaiting a response. Juan Pablo could feel the eyes of everyone in the room. Everyone in the room expected him to defend Jefferson. They expected it not because they thought he had good arguments that he was convinced by, but because he had a daughter with the foundation and it made him emotionally compromised. He knew he should hold his tongue, but he couldn't stand stupidity.

"If Porras's father was executed by paramilitaries back when Jefferson was running the paramilitaries in that region, chances are that it was Jefferson himself who ordered the killing. And now you're saying they've been friends for fifteen years?"

Colonel Carlosama, no fool, nodded his head in agreement. Juan Pablo felt the pressure ease, fewer skeptical eyes on him and more on the briefing intelligence sergeant as the room of military men instantly adjusted their mood to the mood of their commander.

"At some point in the previous decade he underwent an ideological shift," the sergeant said. "Perhaps he felt betrayed by the jail time he had to serve after the demobilization. After prison he went to Venezuela, and there he became radicalized and developed deep links to the Venezuelan military. We think that La Vigia is his beachhead for exporting the Bolivarian Revolution to Colombia, and Luisa Porras Sánchez is helping prepare the ground for his expansion throughout the department."

Colonel Carlosama put a finger to his lips and sat back in his chair, eyes on the picture of Porras Sánchez. He leaned back in his chair, stretched slowly, and then sat forward. "These days," he began, "the main thing the Venezuelan military is exporting is not revolution but black market petroleum."

"Yes, sir," the sergeant said. "But Venezuela is also importing cocaine. Now with the help"—the sergeant clicked to another slide, this showing the thread on Twitter and the photo of Jefferson—"of local organizations like this foundation."

The pitying glances returned. As the sergeant went on about the foundation where his daughter worked, and how tracking the foundation had generated leads, Juan Pablo realized that he was not simply present at a wrongheaded intelligence briefing. This was an attack on his own credibility, on the reputation of his family, and perhaps on his career.

Afterward, Colonel Carlosama invited Juan Pablo to share a cigar outside the operations center. Carlosama came from a wealthy family and usually stocked the best brands, but the cigar he handed Juan Pablo after rummaging through his desk was nothing special. An Occidental Reserve Robusto. A good enough brand. But cheap.

The colonel lit his own cigar, a Quai d'Orsay, by putting it right into the flame like an amateur. Then he handed over the matchbook.

"It's a different country now," Carlosama said. "Less than thirteen thousand murders across Colombia last year. When I was commissioned, the number was closer to thirty thousand. So it's a different war, too."

What was he driving at? Juan Pablo struck the match, held his cheap cigar above the flame, and spun until he got an even burn.

"The other day General Cabrales and I had drinks with the commander of second division. He told us, 'The army of speaking English, of protocols, and human rights is over.' He thinks if we're going to keep the peace, we'll need a freer hand."

"And General Cabrales?"

"He had concerns. If the peace goes through, we're going to be responsible for controlling parts of the country we have never really had under control. Places where sometimes"—Carlosama waved his expensive cigar—"the army has made mistakes."

He was talking about civilian massacres, extrajudicial killings, and the rest of the litany of accusations people like Juan Pablo's daughter's professor liked to hurl at the army.

"It happens," Carlosama said, "when you're fighting that kind of war. But now . . ."

"Those kind of mistakes will cause more problems than they solve."

"In the long term, yes. The army as a whole needs to be more disciplined. But I think most officers would not agree. They want more freedom." He smiled. "If your daughter goes into human rights work, she can help keep the pressure on us to stay disciplined."

"She comes home in two days. After that, she won't be doing any more of that work."

"Hmmm . . ." Carlosama puffed on his cigar. "You're up for promotion to colonel again. Of course, they'd be fools not to promote you, but have you thought about what you might do if they don't?"

Juan Pablo raised an eyebrow. This thing with the foundation *had* compromised him.

"A man with your skills," Carlosama said, "would do very well even out of the military."

"A contractor job?" Juan Pablo said. He'd always sneered at those. Officers trained by the Colombian state only to turn around and offer their skills to the highest bidder. A former boss of his was currently luring officers away with promises of high wages in the United Arab Emirates. But he didn't want to think about that. He wanted to think about operations. Especially with his daughter being where she was. "Any luck with the beacon?"

Carlosama smiled. "Our infiltrado—"

"The storeowner? Abel?"

"Yes. He says Jefferson doesn't read books, so they're going to put it in a DVD box set of American action movies."

Ah. That made sense. On CENTRIXS, the secure data system connecting U.S. and American intelligence, Juan Pablo had seen discussion flying back and forth as to which American movies were most likely to be appreciated by a bloodthirsty former paramilitary possible communist narco. One faction had been championing the works of Sylvester Stallone, another those of Steven Seagal. Last time he'd checked, Seagal was winning.

"Have the Jesúses been classified yet?"

"It will happen. There seem to be political considerations." Carlosama put his cigar to his lips and puffed, but most of the embers had died and he barely pulled in any smoke. "I won't mind them being Class A."

"More business for us?"

Carlosama scowled and waved his hand dismissively. "We'll have more business than we can stand with the Urabeños soon. No. But I don't like the Jesúses. One, I don't like how a tiny group in Norte de Santander has reached all the way to Bogotá. Two, I don't like their Venezuela connections. And three, I really don't like the feeling that they've been playing us. I'd rather have my narcos stupid and violent than smart and quiet."

Carlosama pulled again on his cigar, this time getting nothing.

"We won't be doing anything prematurely, though," he said. "You handle this like it was any other drug dealer. I'm sure you can do that . . . despite . . ."

"My daughter being at risk."

"Oh, I don't think she's at risk," Colonel Carlosama said. "She just got in with some bad people."

Carlosama lit another match, once again putting his cigar end right into the flame. Juan Pablo looked down at the dead embers on his own cigar.

"Hold it above the flame, not in it," Juan Pablo said, not quite caring if he was giving offense. "You want to taste tobacco. Not ash."

———

Lisette sat in the back of the Land Rover with Jefferson, unsure of whether or not she was still kidnapped. The guard in the passenger seat had what looked like an M60 sitting awkwardly between his knees, muzzle sticking up in the air. It was a huge gun, way too long to handle easily in the car.

Just a few days ago, being in a car like this, looking at the handle of Jefferson's gun resting against his ample belly, would have been terrifying. Now, she was just so very, very tired. And so very much in need of an aspirin. But to show them, and to show herself, that she still had some pluck, she decided to talk.

"You should buy M4s," she said. "I understand that a gun, a big gun . . . it seems scary. An M4 seems a toy. But to leave the car rapidly, M4 is better."

Jefferson smiled. "You like guns?" he said. He grabbed the gun in his pants by the barrel, pulled it out, and turned it over, as if offering it to her.

He waited a second, then laughed again, and put it back in his pants, an awkward process that involved him pulling at his waistband while pushing against his belly fat and inserting the barrel in the space created. Why not just use a holster? This guy could afford a nice holster.

"Yes. I like guns," Liz said. "I used them when I was a girl."

"Good."

He leaned back and scowled, as if in pain, and that was it for conversation. As they left the village behind and crested a ridgeline, Jefferson took out an Iridium satellite phone, punched in some numbers, and began what was apparently an upsetting conversation.

"But how?" he said. "How? I have her."

What followed was rapid-fire Spanish that Liz quickly lost interest in trying to track. Her body was sore. She wondered idly if she'd end up with PTSD after all this. She'd once read that only 4 percent of the survivors of the Hanoi Hilton had PTSD, as compared to something like 85 percent of American POWs in Japanese camps during World War II. She tried to remember why. The Hanoi Hilton guys had all gotten lifetime passes to Major League Baseball games. That probably didn't factor in.

She tried to think of the techniques of other captured journalists. Exercise, establishing a routine. Someone had said that was important. Writing letters to family in your head. Prayer, if you've got religion. The first time he was captured, by Qaddafi loyalists in Libya, James Foley claimed that prayer had helped him. That path wasn't open to Lisette, but perhaps it was basically the same as meditating, or the mindfulness training that was supposedly popular with CEOs. She imagined a slightly paunchy corporate so-and-so in the sauna at the Harvard Club on Forty-fourth Street in New York, a towel draped across his neck, his legs crossed yogi-style, finger and thumb delicately touching as he gathered his energy, focused on his breathing, and prepared himself for a day of attentiveness to the moment, to his stock options, and to positive thoughts.

Jefferson ended his call, his face red, and looked her in the eye.

"You stupid whore," he said.

Lisette decided she was probably still kidnapped.

———

It amazed Abel how quickly the curse had taken effect. He didn't understand at first. When they were taking the journalist, he simply panicked, too much in terror to think about what it meant. It was only later that he realized, when a delivery truck pulled up to his store. A delivery truck with nothing to deliver, but inside the truck were the same two men from military intelligence who had asked him, a year ago, everything he knew about El Alemán and his links to both the Urabeños and the guerrilla.

"The store is closed," he told them. "We don't get deliveries anymore."

"Okay," one of the men said. "Then you'll help us change a tire."

They took a tire off a back wheel. One of the men followed Abel into the store, and while the other worked he asked Abel about the kidnapping. Was it really the guerrilla, as the Jesúses were telling them? Maybe some splinter faction of the Elenos.

"It wasn't the Elenos," he said.

The man said, "Then it was Jefferson." And that's when Abel realized the curse was working.

Abel shrugged. Just that, a shrug. If his boss knew he was talking to the military, he would be dead. If it wasn't for the curse he'd planted, the curse only he knew about, Abel would have been terrified. But knowing about the curse and feeling, for the first time since he was a boy, the circle of protection his parents had always dressed him with, he had just enough courage to tell the man that he'd keep an ear out for information, and that he'd be willing to do whatever it took. The man handed Abel an envelope with a little money inside. Not enough to risk his life for, but still something to set aside for when he reopened the store. It was funny to think that way. As if reopening the store was a possibility now.

They told him if he wanted to stay out of jail, he needed to continue to be cooperative.

"I'm not doing anything illegal," he said.

The man laughed. It was such an odd thing to say, especially in a place like La Vigia. What did the law even mean here? Perhaps in big cities, in places like Cúcuta, or Medellín, or Bogotá, people walked around with a sense that somewhere, outside of them, was this thing called "law." In La Vigia, there was none. There was a way of doing things. Talking about your boss to military intelligence was not the way of doing things in La Vigia.

"I'll work with you because I want to," he said. It made him feel like a brave man.

They left him with a phone. "This uses the Integrated Communication Network," the man said. "It's secure, so we can speak freely." And it was over this phone that Abel had agreed to give Jefferson a gift, a gift the military would prepare for him and deliver to his store.

A few days later, Abel went to meet Jefferson to discuss the mobilization for the peace vote, carrying the gift under his arms. A DVD box set of Steven Seagal movies, tied with a red bow. Abel had examined the package carefully. It didn't seem suspicious. There was no obvious place where the electronic beacon was hiding. And, they'd told him, it was on a timer, so it wouldn't give off a signal for the next few hours, just in case Jefferson had it examined.

Abel held the box out awkwardly to his boss. He regretted not removing the bow. A bow was unlike him.

"When you used to show us movies, at that ranch you had near Cunaviche, these were my favorite," Abel said. "I wanted to get you a small present, to thank you for bringing me back where I belong."

Jefferson laughed and took the gift. "Thank you, thank you." He examined the box, reading off titles. "*The Patriot. Marked for Death.* That was a good one. Did you know he's making a movie with Mike Tyson?"

Abel did not know that.

"That will be very good."

And then they discussed the peace vote. Jefferson had surprised Abel when, a few months ago, he had told him he wanted the vote to succeed. This was an old paramilitary town, and the peace was unpopular here, but if they could turn people in favor of the peace it'd give them a sense of how much influence they had before the more important elections, like the one for mayor.

"Oh," Jefferson said. "That journalist. We found her. We'll figure out what she knows and then turn her loose. Things will return to normal."

As he was leaving, Jefferson stopped him and said, "Come by tonight. I'll send someone to pick you up. We can watch a movie, like we used to." And he'd hefted the box of DVDs.

So. Jefferson wanted to spend time with him. Him alone. Abel nodded. The invitation sparked fear but also, somehow, pride. Jefferson had always treated him differently.

After the meeting he went right back to his store and took out the special phone the military had given him. If he called them and told them that Jefferson had the gringa, there would be consequences. Serious consequences, though he wasn't sure what they would be. The forces operating at a higher level in his country had always been mysterious to him. He called. He delivered his message. And when he hung up, his heart was racing. He was afraid, and anxious. He wanted to go find Luisa, and tell her what he'd done. He knew it was important. But he couldn't tell anyone, and so instead he decided he'd go see Deysi, ask her if she'd like to go dancing Saturday, and keep the knowledge of what he'd done to himself, a jewel he could take out and polish if he felt the need.

He would never be a saint, that was clear. But he had done three dangerous things in his life. First, protecting Luisa back in Rioclaro. Second, using the curse. Third, giving Jefferson the beacon. He doubted most men in his place would have had the courage to do any of those things, let alone all three. He didn't know what would happen, but even if what he'd done didn't free him from Jefferson, he'd tried. He wasn't an especially good man, he knew that. But he was better than most.

———

Jefferson sat across from the journalist, feeling old and tired. He knew what he should do. Move back across the border to Venezuela, put out the word he'd been killed, allow Javier to rename the Jesúses. Then he could return with a new name but the same connections. A temporary setback. Hide out a few months, come back. But a few months meant more to him now than it used to.

"I should kill you," he said.

Her face was impassive. Perhaps defiant. It was also a mass of purple and black and green. Those idiots in the countryside had fucked her up. She was taking shallow breaths. Probably a few cracked ribs. He'd had his men stash her in a back room with a bed, a television, and a window looking down on a maybe forty-foot drop to a river. There were no other houses anywhere in sight. If she was in better shape, this wouldn't be a secure place to keep her. But in her condition, she wasn't going anywhere.

"I should do like ISIS," he said. "I should get a big black flag, and I should put you on camera, and I should make you pray to Allah, and then I should cut your head off."

He hadn't planned on saying that, but he liked the sound of it. He could see it, the grainy execution video. Why was it always a grainy video? Where do you even get cameras so bad these days?

"How sad I'm not Muslim," he said.

The journalist nodded slowly. There was no visible sign of relief. She swallowed. She was afraid, he could see. He smiled at her, to show her that he meant well.

"I thought you were going to free me," she said.

He nodded. That had been his plan. But it was too late. The lawyer in Bogotá had told him the Jesúses had already been put on the military's hit list. What difference did it make now if he killed her or let her go?

"People will look for me," she said.

"Family? You have a husband? Children?"

"No."

"Ah." He shook his head. "That means nobody cares."

He could tell she was trying to decide what was the right way to respond. He wasn't sure himself. He didn't think he'd kill her. It still made more sense to let the whole thing defuse. Maybe even try to position himself as a hero, as a local businessman who negotiated with the cocaleros to rescue this stupid gringa. Maybe if she made him famous, it would protect him.

"The American government cares," she said. "And they don't pay for kidnapped people."

"What do they do?"

"They send Navy SEALs—to kill."

Jefferson laughed. She was trying to intimidate him.

"If they send a Navy SEAL, I'll fuck him in the ass."

"Okay," she said.

"I'm going to think about you," he said. And he left her there.

Later, as he ate an early dinner, he saw he had a message from Javier, asking to meet. Undoubtedly, Javier wanted to know why the journalist hadn't been released. That was what he should do. But he allowed himself to wait, allowed a fantasy to flower in his mind.

In the fantasy, the Americans sent Navy SEALs in to get the journalist. They came to a house where they thought she was being held, but which was, in fact, a trap. A trap for killing gringos. In the fantasy, his men slaughter the SEALs. All except one. It's the Navy SEAL who killed Osama bin Laden. Not the clown he'd seen taking credit on television, but the real one, the one the U.S. government doesn't want you to know about. He's a big man, very strong. He looks like Dwayne Johnson, the Rock, but white. And maybe that's his name. Rock. Steve Rock. The true killer of Osama bin Laden. And Steve Rock has biceps the size of soccer balls. Steve Rock has a dick as thick as a Coke can. On his chest, Steve Rock has a tattoo of an American flag and on his back Steve Rock has a tattoo of Steve Rock killing Osama bin Laden. Steve Rock is large. Steve Rock is glistening. Steve Rock is like Ivan Drago in *Rocky IV* and Arnold Schwarzenegger in *Commando* and Jean-Claude Van Damme in *Black Eagle*. Steve Rock's hair is long and his eyes are blue and Steve Rock is crying. He is surrounded by the bodies of his fellow SEALs, all of them piled on the floor, their bodies riddled with bullets. And Steve Rock fires his machine gun into the air until he is out of bullets, and then Jefferson steps out of the shadows, and Steve Rock throws down his weapon and the two men square off, the younger, stronger man against the older, sicker one. But Jefferson is wise, and Jefferson is vicious, and Jefferson knocks Steve Rock down with one punch, Jefferson flings the blood of the fallen SEALs in Steve Rock's eyes and kicks him through a window, Jefferson lures Steve Rock into a tight space where his size and strength are a disadvantage, and Jefferson conquers Steve Rock. He takes him to Venezuela and parades through the streets with Steve Rock in a cage behind him, and the people throw flowers at the feet of Jefferson and rancid meat into the face of Steve Rock. And Jefferson is declared the new Uribe, the new Chavez, the new Castro, the new Che Guevara.

Of course, Jefferson would still have to die. The gringos could never let him live. That's how it would have to go. And it would be best. A man like himself didn't deserve to die from a disease, stumbling downward on the path of life. He deserved to die while climbing to the heavens. He deserved to die while still fully alive. He deserved to be on T-shirts.

———

When the notification came through, Mason was at his terminal, going through emails. They were mostly dull, administrative tasks. Logistical hassles with a training op in Larandia, details on an ODA team's forthcoming redeployment, a reminder about the planning committee for the embassy's Halloween party. That last one he flagged as important. He was taking the girls and didn't want it to be a shitshow like it'd been the year before. And then a new email came in with an innocuous subject line. "FWD: ISR shift Tibú to La Vigia."

It was from the colonel who ran MILGROUP, who had just typed "FYI" above an exchange he'd had with one of the embassy's DEA agents. Mason scanned it quickly. A few ISR assets were being transferred from the police mission in Norte de Santander to support a hostage rescue mission near La Vigia.

So there it is, he thought. The colonel had already approved it. There was nothing for him to do.

He got up from his terminal and stretched. He felt vaguely dissatisfied, though it was a good thing that the mission was a go. While they had a lock on the journalist's location, it made sense to move fast. Kidnappers could easily disappear with their captives for years within Colombia's mountains and jungles.

He walked down to the colonel's office and popped in his head. The colonel, a bald, muscular southerner, was a bit of a Sphinx. He had a southern drawl and liked to play dumb, but could surprise you sometimes with the depth of his knowledge or his ability to see around corners. Last Halloween, he'd put on a white T-shirt, grabbed a mop, and made a highly popular appearance at the embassy party as Mr. Clean.

"Sir," Mason said, "this thing in La Vigia is going tonight?"

"Looks like," the colonel said. "Fingers crossed."

Fingers crossed. Right.

"You need me to stay late?"

"Nah."

Right.

"I miss being in the field," Mason said. "Wish I could be out there."

"Don't we all."

Mason thought about saying more, perhaps voicing some of his concerns about the shift that seemed to be happening, in which the Colombian military was taking over more and more of what should have been police functions. But the colonel already knew all that. Better to just wish the guys on the ground well, and to pray the hostage didn't get killed.

He went back to his terminal and finished up for the day, clearing out his in-box and shooting an email over to the Colombian police unit that had just had their ISR assets stripped. Then he left the embassy.

Tonight, a team of highly trained Colombian soldiers would be moving in and performing the most complex type of operation commandos are tasked with—hostage rescue. Even now, they would be preparing, going through the plan, analyzing a model of the target structure, gaming out all the possible curveballs the operation might throw at them. Soon, they'd be preparing their kit, gearing up, perhaps saying a few prayers, or listening to pump-up music, or whatever little rituals were specific to that team. They had a clear, unmistakably good mission, with an innocent captive and an evil captor. What a luxury. They didn't have to worry about the things he did at his level. The allocation of resources, the politics behind which unit or branch of service got which mission, and whether or not helping the military shift its focus from killing guerrillas in the jungle to killing drug dealers in coca territory would turn out to be a mistake. Instead, they would have the simple, immediate experience of the battlefield.

It was lucky that the embassy didn't need him. He'd just spend the night full of envy. Besides, he'd told his oldest daughter that either this week or the next he'd help her with her Halloween costume. They'd gotten a picture frame, and a poster of the *Mona Lisa*, and they were going to cut out the face so Inez could stick her head through and walk around as the iconic painting. So far, he'd been too overworked to be able to come home early and help her put it together. Today was as good a day as any to start.

Over the next couple of hours, Jefferson's fantasy dissipated and the real world came intruding, sticking its ugly face in the door and whining about practicalities. The journalist's capture had attracted national attention. The army was now hunting her, along with the police. Until they found her, nothing that he had built here was safe.

Still, it irked him to just let her go. How could someone be so valuable to so many people, and nothing but useless to him? And if he just let her go, would the unwanted attention cease? His name and face were known now. He couldn't fade back into obscurity. But maybe he could use that to his advantage. He had, after all, rescued her.

So he went back to the journalist's room, had his men open the door, and he told her how things would go.

"Journalists have a code," he said, and she agreed, yes, of course they did. And he asked if that code included protecting sources, and she said yes, of course, that is the most basic part of the code, and then he asked if she'd like him to become a source.

"Yes," she said. He could see the relief across her bruised face. The knowledge that she might survive.

"I think it's important that you tell people how I rescued you," Jefferson said.

"I need a doctor," she said.

"I know what you may have heard about me, that I'm a narco. That I was in the autodefensas. Did they tell you that?"

"Yes."

"Who? Who told you that?"

"I knew about you before I got here."

That made him happy.

"I was in the autodefensas," he said. "Proudly. Everything I have ever done, I have done for the poor people, the forgotten people."

The gringa nodded.

"In La Vigia," Jefferson said, "we have been victims of the guerrilla first, and then the narcos second, and the government third." He laughed. "I prefer the narcos. They kill for money. The guerrilla kill for insanity."

"And you?" the journalist said. "What do the Mil Jesúses kill for?"

So many things. "The Mil Jesúses is a prayer. Do you know it?"

"I saw it on the internet. Before I came here."

"Give up Satan!" He pointed his finger to the sky, then realized that was not where Satan was generally said to hang out, and redirected his finger to point it at the gringa. "You cannot count on me because on the Day of the Holy Cross I said a thousand times . . . Jesus, Jesus, Jesus, Jesus, Jesus, Jesus, Jesus, Jesus, Jesus, Jesus."

He closed his eyes as he said the name of God, as if in the grip of powerful emotion. When he opened his eyes, he saw her staring at him blankly.

"If the demon tempts me on the hour of my death, I will tell him he has no part of me, because on the Day of the Holy Cross I said a thousand times . . ."

He paused, and locked eyes with her. A few seconds passed.

"Jesus?" she said.

He nodded. Yes, go on.

"Jesus," she said. "Jesus . . . Jesus, Jesus, Jesus Jesus Jesus Jesus-jesusjesus."

He clenched his teeth and sucked in some air. She did not seem to believe him, but that was fine. She just had to tell people what he wanted her to. "Okay," he said. "Good. It is a good prayer."

"Yes," she agreed.

He shifted in his chair, straightening his posture. "I would tell you that the people of La Vigia have been forgotten by their government, but that would not be true. The government has never cared about us. Bogotá cannot forget a people it never knew. To them, we are nothing. The province of a province. The land of no one."

"And this land? What is it to you?"

"The birthplace of a new Colombia."

Then he ordered his men to drive the journalist to a clinic an hour south, where she could get her injuries attended to.

"If you want to talk more," she said, "I don't need the doctor. I can wait."

Cracked ribs could lead to pneumonia, he told her. Get it looked at, we'll talk later. Meanwhile, he would have someone call a reporter to meet her at the clinic. And the first thing she needed to tell them was that Jefferson Paúl López Quesada was the one who rescued her.

"On the way back," he told his men, "pick up Abel, and bring him here."

After she left, the nausea and pain returned. He popped a few pills, and then popped a few more, and sat in his house, and turned on the TV, and was bored by the news, and ultimately decided not to wait for Abel before watching one of the DVDs he had given him as a gift. So strange, that so few of his men thought to give him gifts. It was something to keep note of.

"Abel."

Deysi was seated in her shop, sewing. She was short and plump, with a youthful face that must not be so different from the one she'd had as a girl, before the violence had come and taken her family from her. Her fingers, though, were worn and calloused, with cracked skin and blotches, and they moved rapidly and assuredly when she was doing the sort of intricate work that required a needle and thread, and not a machine. It was remarkable to see her make patterns blossom on fabric, like watching the flurry of a musician's fingers somehow drawing music from simple, nylon strings. Abel liked to watch her work. He liked the serious expression that came to her face. He liked even more when she looked up and said his name and gave him a smile. She was smiling now.

"I'd like"—Abel looked around the shop. He hadn't come with an excuse to be there, so he looked around and randomly grabbed at a roll of purple fabric—"two meters of this."

"For what?"

Good question. What on earth could he do with two meters of purple fabric? "It's a secret," he said.

She smiled again, amused, and he felt full, overflowing. He wanted to tell her that he was going to see his boss tonight. That they would watch a movie and he would leave and maybe that would be the last time he saw Jefferson. There were forces at work in the world changing things for the better.

"Very mysterious, Abel."

There it was, his name again. When she said his name, he felt like less of a stranger, looking in on real life. He felt like he belonged.

"You know," he said, "you were always kind to me, and I never understood why."

She stopped her needlework and looked at him curiously.

"The first year after"—he didn't want to say it—"after I left the paracos was very hard."

She nodded her head.

"I was very lucky. Mr. Bejar gave me a job. Not everyone liked that. One day, after he'd paid me for the week, a couple of men followed me home and hit me with a brick." He laughed gently. "I woke up with no money and a big headache."

For a long time, he'd lived in fear. He lost weight. He moved. He grew a mustache and combed his hair a different way. He thought about changing his name. A stupid thought, in a town this small.

Those were paranoid days, when he'd refused to sit near windows, and something as simple as an overheard argument from his neighbors would set off fantasies of the guerrilla coming to torture him. Another paramilitary he knew disappeared and Abel was certain he'd been taken by the guerrilla, a gasoline-soaked rag stuffed in his mouth, and left like that until the fumes burned through his insides. But Deysi had always smiled at him.

"That's terrible," she said.

Now what? Ask her to go dancing on Saturday? This wasn't how the conversation was meant to go.

"That was a long time ago. It wasn't so bad, and maybe . . ."

"What?"

"Maybe I deserved to have a hard time, coming back." He ran his fingers over the purple fabric. "I've tried to pay for what I've done."

"No," she said. "You are a good man. I've always seen that."

He nodded. He didn't think anyone had ever told him that before, and now he had nothing to say. He felt silly, and happy to have come, and he paid for his two meters of cloth and left, full of life. Deysi was a very good person, he thought. And that, plus the knowledge of the curse working its terrible power, led to a change in Abel.

When he walked out everything seemed very different than before he'd walked in. There were birds singing and of course he'd heard them before but it seemed like a sudden shock that birds sang like this, all the time, and he never noticed it. As he walked down the street to the central square near the offices of the Fundación de Justicia y Fe, he saw the trees in bloom and a young boy climbing up one of them while two men hustled off somewhere very important and an old woman stared at the sky and smiled as if there were nothing more important or glorious to do than enjoy the sunshine. Everything was the same as it had been before, but sweeter.

You are a good man, she'd told him. He went to the church and stood before the statue of the Virgin and said a prayer of gratitude. Then he walked to the outskirts of town and returned to his shuttered store. Even this, too, was transformed. No longer a gloomy ruin, it looked the way it used to in the mornings when it was still in operation . . . a shop that had been closed down to rest for the night and was waiting for him to start the day fresh.

He went behind the counter and pulled out a ledger, now covered in dust after these months with the Jesúses. It was where he'd kept track of the money he'd given away, following Luisa's instructions, where he'd calculated how much left he'd still have to pay before he had atoned for his time in the paras. What an odd thing he held in his hands. This many dollars left, I am a sinner. This many dollars paid, I am forgiven. Jefferson returns, I am damned. I give his location to the army, I am saved.

He spent the next few hours going through the store and taking notes on the orders he'd have to make to stock his shelves and reopen it again. It was half a fantasy, half a real plan. And it was in the midst of this fantasy that some Jesúses knocked on his door and told him they'd take him to Jefferson.

"Do you know Steven Seagal?" he'd asked them in the car, but no. That was before their time. They were young, like he had been, with pimples on their faces. They liked superhero movies. They didn't care about the names of the actors, they liked Ironman and Batman and Thor.

As they drove, he wondered when the army would come for Jefferson, and if this was the last time he would see him. Perhaps the curse would strike tomorrow, and he really would go on to open the store. Perhaps he really would ask Deysi out dancing. Perhaps she'd say yes.

Perhaps they'd marry and have children and name them after the loved ones they'd both lost. Perhaps there really was a life ahead of him. Perhaps he'd die an old man. And perhaps, at the Last Judgment, as he stood between the hope of paradise and the threat of hell, Christ would look at his whole life, not just at his small spurts of courage, when he saved Luisa or when he cursed Jefferson, but at the long slow act of courage it took to open a store, return to civilian life, master his fear, greet his neighbors without shame, and slowly, over time, see himself reflected in their eyes as a good, upstanding man.

When they arrived at Jefferson's house some of the fear returned, and the vision fled, but he got out and asked the guard at the gate for a cigarette. It would calm him, he thought, before he had to go see Jefferson and pretend everything was normal.

This is when the shooting started. And because Abel was at the gate, next to an armed guard, the first shots were at him, penetrating his torso and his skull, leaving him with no time to cry out in pain or fear, no time to tell the army commandos rushing forward that he was their informant, no time even to whisper a prayer before he died, aged twenty-nine, at what he had desperately hoped was only the midpoint of his life.

Diego's palms were sweaty. He felt useless, and fat, wedged into his back seat in the cockpit, the straps digging into his flesh, immobilizing him while down below younger men in better shape flowed through buildings, searching for his girl.

His girl. That was funny. Was she? Wasn't she? It didn't matter. He wanted her alive. He wanted to be the one to save her and if he couldn't be on the ground at least he was here, hovering above, a guardian angel, whispering directions as the men below stormed the compound.

Still, he hated it. Removed from the action, sweating ugly blotches into his shirt, sitting in a glorified crop duster overloaded with electronics, hoping she didn't die in the gunfight. And how stupid that would be, after everything she'd done, making friends with Taliban, covering Haqqani arms smugglers, driving out into Indian country with Marines and soldiers and getting into firefights, to die in some bumblefuck backwoods of Colombia with some penny-ante drug dealers? Life makes no sense, and there are so many ways something like this can go wrong. If the bad guys inside act like fools, if the soldiers storming the compound pull the trigger when they should have held fire. Even the Delta guys sometimes end up killing the people they wanted to save. And God, he so wanted her to be alive. That was all that mattered.

When the raid began, and a squad of Colombia's finest commandos began shooting their way through the Jesúses stationed in and around the house, Jefferson had just reached the butcher shop fight scene in *Out for Justice*. Steven Seagal grabbed a cleaver from a thug and drove it through the thug's hand, into the wall behind him, leaving him stuck, arm raised absurdly, blood pouring down. It was a good scene. Steven Seagal always had clever things like that. Like where he kills the bad guy with a corkscrew. Or where he drives his thumb through Tommy Lee Jones's eyeball until the goop runs out. Jefferson had once driven his thumb through a man's eye like that, and it hadn't been quite as cool as in the movie because the goop had squirted more than oozed, and some had gotten into his mouth.

At first, Jefferson didn't notice the sound of the shooting. Maybe three or four crucial seconds as his mind, dulled by pain and painkillers and exhaustion, registered the sound he knew so well. Perhaps it was the Urabeños. Perhaps it was the police. Perhaps it was Javier. It could even be the Navy SEALs.

He got up, unsure of where he'd put his pistol, which was still tucked

in his pants. He wasn't afraid. He grabbed it and pulled and accidentally jerked the trigger as it came from his pants and an explosion registered as the bullet grazed a testicle, penetrated his thigh, and lodged
in his femur. He stumbled and fell against the side of the couch. Everything moved slowly. But he brought the pistol up. There was a blur of
movement and then two explosions in his chest and he slumped to the
floor. Colombian soldiers in tactical gear flowed into the room, checking corners, securing the area. Jefferson stared at the ceiling. He felt
another explosion in his chest as one of the soldiers dead-checked him.
Adrenaline coursed through his body, quickening his mind in a way he
hadn't felt in years, while blood poured from the holes left by high-
velocity rounds. This was good. This was a death in combat. This was
a good death.

On the television, Steven Seagal disarmed a gun-wielding butcher as
Richie and his goons got away.

8

lma was not surprised when some of Javier's men grabbed her off the street and told her they knew she was a toad. It was foolish of her to have gone to the foundation, and to have told her story in the first place. Even if Luisa hadn't said Jefferson's name, everyone there would have known who she was talking about.

"But we'll make you a deal," one had said. He was the tallest one, and seemed the oldest, but he was still young. Baby fat on his cheeks. A loud voice meant to project authority but, in fact, showing only his fear. The other two huddled beside him, one scrawny and the other very young, with skinny arms and a round belly and a nervous, boyish smile that Alma would have found sweet in other circumstances. They reminded her of the guerrilleros she'd fought alongside.

"Javier told us to make it look like you got hit by a car."

Alma nodded her head, understanding how the game was going to be played, and the oldest one explained the bargain. You're going to stand here, on the side of the road. And we're going to get in our truck, put the pedal to the floor, and accelerate toward you. If you stay there, if you don't run, you'll die a quick death. We'll go as fast as we can. If you run, we drive to your home and kill your children.

And so Alma stood in the road. It was the end of the day. She had a bag of yuca she'd paid for with a bag of coca leaves. Food for her children. She asked them if they'd bring the yuca to her family after they killed her and the oldest one laughed. But then the skinny one said, "Why not?" And so she gave him the bag and stepped out into the road.

"Here?" she said. And they told her, yes, there, and put their truck in reverse, stopping only a hundred meters away, then shifting to drive. The road was muddy. She wondered how fast their truck could accelerate in the mud. Would the strike kill her? Or would she still be alive? Would she bleed out in the road or would they go in reverse, run her over to finish the job? She knew she was stupid for speaking out against Jefferson, but she had no regrets. She did not allow herself regrets. Her youngest would be too young to remember her mother. Her oldest would have to tell stories of her. The truck spat mud as they hit the pedal, wheels spinning, and then it was advancing toward her, too fast for further thoughts, and she faced it the way she'd faced battle, for this was just another form of combat, wasn't it? And the front of the car impacted with her chest so powerfully her whole rib cage shattered inward, her heart exploded, and her mind disappeared before she struck the ground. And the boys looked upon her body sadly, because she'd shown courage and none of them were sure if they could have done the same. And then, because they weren't without pity, they drove by where she lived and flung the bag of yucca out of the car, the heavy bag flying only a few feet before crashing to the ground, the seam of the bag splitting and yucca spilling out into the dirt for her children to later find, and wash, and eat.

People were afraid of Javier. He knew that, and it was a problem. All the best commanders he'd worked for knew how to inspire both fear and love. And though he knew he could inspire an intense loyalty among his men, especially among those he worked with closely, and most especially among those he had killed with, among townspeople he inspired only fear. This made him an excellent hammer. Javier handed out justice, a justice so severe that when Jefferson stepped in and stayed his hand, it seemed like the mercy of God raining down from heaven. People didn't just fear him and love Jefferson. They feared him so that they could love Jefferson.

As a younger man, Javier thought power was the ability to make a man beg for his life. That was the most pure, most direct form of satisfaction in this world. But as he grew older, he had come to see how limited it was. More like the pleasure a child feels eating a candy bar than the pleasure a grown man feels having a well-cooked meal.

Now that Jefferson was dead, what pleasures awaited him? He thought this as he was still in hiding, lying low, waiting for the storm to pass. When the news had come of a military raid, Jefferson dead, along with six others, Javier thought it was the beginning of the end. But nothing else happened. No more raids. No attacks on laboratories or warehouses.

Already, he knew it was safe. Already, he knew the surveillance teams were leaving the jungle. The aircraft absent from the skies. This little corner of Norte de Santander was too poor, too remote, too far from Bogotá for the military to devote resources to. It was why Jefferson picked it. Javier only needed to keep Americans out, and keep the countryside pacified, and then he could focus on what Jefferson had excelled at—inspiring devotion.

Two weeks before, he had ordered a shirt from a store in Cúcuta. It was Armani Exchange. A "Regular Fit Short-Sleeve Geo Camo Yoke Shirt." The torso was a shimmering gray. The sleeves had a camouflage pattern. It fit him tightly, and he buttoned it to the neck. The sleeves cut off midbicep, showing the swell of muscle. How many forty-seven-year-old men looked like this? How many men sculpted themselves this well at any age? Protein powder, creatine, energy powders, regular weight training, and the discipline from the military combined into a body everyone should admire. He had the right mixture of maturity and vigor. He had spent maybe twenty minutes admiring himself in the mirror, smoothing out the creases of the fabric so it was one pure, straight shimmer of beauty from his neck to his waist. Jefferson, who the people loved, had been fat. Jefferson had never had a particularly impressive body, but toward the end he was just fat. And haggard. Javier was superior. A gentleman.

He went to La Serpiente de Tierra Caliente, the one place in town Jefferson had permitted women to disobey the rules of the old manual for the autodefensas about skirts and lewd behavior. "You have to give people at least one outlet," he always said. Javier took several of his men and went to that one outlet, dressed beautifully, with a body sculpted beyond anything anyone else in the town could achieve, and waited to be admired.

Of course, they didn't admire. They never did. They looked away. Afraid. Even the whores. And he didn't want whores. Disgusting, diseased. He walked through the room, standing straight, not wanting to crease his shirt, and if a woman ever caught his eye it was by accident, and she quickly looked away. Or sometimes she would hold his eye, but that was always whores who did that. They're mostly whores, women.

There was one, short and pretty and a little fat, and she danced and danced and danced and didn't look at him once. Not even as he stood beside her and stared. She was dancing by herself, not even with someone else. An hour or so later, the short and pretty and fat one got into a fight with a tall and dark indio-looking woman, and he had his men break up the fight. He was furious. And it was worse when he found one of them was a mother. That's what she told him. Please, sir, my children are at home. He should have killed her, if there were justice in this world. But of course, Javier was a man, he could control himself. Instead he gave them his usual punishment. Cleaning the town square. Naked. To show their whorishness to the world, and to teach them shame.

Women used to throw themselves at Jefferson. They threw themselves at him and he never wanted them. Jefferson had only fucked whores, which Javier found disgusting. Though, as time passed, Jefferson fucked no one at all. Perhaps he'd been ill, toward the end. He wasn't as sharp as before. And then there was the absurdity with the gringa journalist. Such a stupid thing to let spin out of control. Such a stupid thing to allow that woman, Luisa, to bring into town anyway.

Perhaps Jefferson would still be alive if he had let Javier deal with the problem. Perhaps he'd still be alive if he'd followed Javier's advice and shut down the foundation. Now the news was full of talk about the raid on Jefferson, bringing up accusations of old crimes from the paramilitary days, rapes and murders and other things.

Javier's first action was to reach out to Jefferson's contacts across the border and to assure them they still had a stable partner. His second action was to reach out to the Urabeños and let them know that their access to local routes into Venezuela still depended on their willingness to work with the Jesúses. But his third action was to send a warning shot to the foundation.

Javier was sure it was the foundation who had sent out that photo of Jefferson at their offices, accusing him of crimes on that website "Twitter." Until now Javier had never heard of Twitter, or had any idea it could be capable of causing him problems, this website where anyone can go and make baseless accusations against brave men who fight for their communities.

He had summoned Abel and together they went down the list of people who'd visited the foundation. When they found the name of a former guerrillera, Alma, the sort of person whose death would bother no one but Luisa, he had ordered some of his men to kill her. And then, as they were on their way, he remembered some of the lessons he'd learned from Jefferson and radioed them to tell them to make it look like an accident.

Now that Jefferson was dead, the people at the foundation were probably feeling good about themselves. Perhaps they hadn't heard yet about the guerrillera. So he went to them, just to let them know he was still in charge. Luisa was in, as well as the students and the foundation worker from Bogotá.

"I heard terrible news about someone who visited the foundation," he said, a smile across his face. "I want to assure you, we had nothing to do with it." He said this in a way to let them know that he had everything to do with it, and left feeling very pleased with himself. Dogs were being brought to heel.

Jefferson had his skills, but his permissiveness had led to his death. When Javier was in charge, he wasn't going to run things so loose. He'd close La Serpiente de Tierra Caliente, he'd leave that bitch Luisa's body in a ditch, he'd bring order to the town. It was necessary. It was right. But could he also do what Jefferson had done? Could he make people love him for it?

———

Even though Javier had not said the name of the person they'd killed, Valencia knew, somehow, that it must be Alma. Of all the stories she'd transcribed, Alma's had been the one that struck her the most powerfully. She wasn't sure why. Perhaps because of the way she looked, or the way she told the story, or simply because she'd been one of the hated guerrilla and yet Valencia had sympathized with her and even celebrated her story in her mind, the fact that a little chubby woman like that used to go into battle cheerfully inspired her, even though she had gone into battle to kill men like her own father. It had to be Alma.

Luisa told them they would first go to the clinic on their way out of town. "I want you to see," she said. They were both still denying they had anything to do with the Twitter account and the photo of Jefferson.

Nevertheless, they packed their bags into the van, feeling like the condemned heading to an execution, and made their way to the clinic. And in the clinic Luisa bulldogged her way past the doctor and into a room with a corpse under a sheet. It was a small corpse, Valencia could see that. And then the doctor nodded to Agudelo, and Agudelo gathered the students around the corpse, and the doctor removed the sheet, and Alma's dead face and crushed body stared up at them.

"It was a road accident," the doctor said.

Luisa said nothing, but she crossed herself and then reached down and held Alma's hand. She remained like that, still and silent, while Agudelo shuffled Valencia and Sara back into the van.

Afterward, Agudelo drove back to Cúcuta through the stifling heat. And he ignored Sara when Sara said it was her, it was her fault, it was her idea, not Valencia's. And Valencia stared at Sara as she accepted the blood guilt, and envied her, envied her courage in speaking those words, the liberation of being able to admit your sins. Yet she stayed silent.

Sara punched the back of the seat in front of her, then punched it again and again until Agudelo told her to stop. Valencia stared at her hands. She wanted to speak but shame suffocated her. She found it difficult to breathe, and then she couldn't breathe, her breath shallow and quick, the edges of her vision collapsing in, the stifling air too thick to force down her throat, and then Sara was talking to her, calming words, and she fought to control her breathing, but there was this heaviness, this crushing, unmaking pain. Her soul, if she had one, screaming at her in protest of her stupidity, her narcissism, her desire.

There was silence for a long time, but as they crossed over the Tibú River, Agudelo started speaking. He said it was good that they knew they had blood on their hands. That to live in a country like this was to have blood on your hands, that the lives they lived in Bogotá were paid for in blood, and if they wanted to continue in this work it was the most important thing to know. Most people will never get to stare at the corpses of the men and women who die because the elites of this country don't see it in their interest to fashion a just society, and it is a sight they should always remember, no matter what work they end up in, but especially if they continue working in human rights.

"This is no kind of work for messiahs," Agudelo said. "This is no kind of work for saviors. We only want the guilty here."

And then Agudelo waited, as if he thought they'd respond, but what was there to say? And so he added, "You think I haven't made mistakes? I've made mistakes. I've never made mistakes this stupid, but that's your generation. Inventing new ways to be fools."

Valencia heard nothing, saw nothing but the body, the broken, distorted body lying in the clinic. And God, if there was a God, reached into Valencia's body, and squeezed her lungs with His large hands, and ran His fingers down her nerves, and breathed hot breath over her eyes, and He tapped her heart once, then twice, as the blood rushed and drained and rushed and drained through her, and then He drew back, leaving a hole behind where air rushed in. If she could have wept tears of blood she would have wept tears of blood, and Agudelo kept speaking, making elliptical statements about this kind of work, and the mistakes he'd made, and what they must learn from it.

Two days later, when she reunited with her father, that feeling had not left. She had not slept, had not done much of anything but trace her guilt. She may not have driven the car that ran Alma down, but she'd taken a shot at a drug lord, in the drug lord's territory. Of course someone would die as a result. And the fact that it was Alma who died felt like something beyond simple chance. It felt like a judgment of God. She only admitted all this to Agudelo on the plane ride back to Bogotá, and Agudelo had responded with nothing more than a grave nod.

After that, she remained silent about what happened. Valencia had cried when she reunited with her mother and father, but she didn't tell them why. Discussion of the kidnapping, and what happened afterward, was limited. Even in these circumstances, her family's rule about what they did and did not talk about remained in effect. Valencia went back to school. She studied, she excelled, life returned to normal. Her mother had her talk to a psychiatrist and a priest. She told both about watching the journalist torn from the car, but with neither did she confess her sin. The psychiatrist sniffed around for evidence of trauma like a pig rooting for truffles. Finding nothing, she'd declared her a perfectly healthy, normal, resilient young woman. The priest took her through her paces, going down the usual catalogue of sins and pronouncing her forgiven.

Of course, she didn't tell him her real sin. He would have forgiven her, and it would have felt like blasphemy against the seriousness of what she'd done to believe forgiveness could come so easily. *I have done evil, and the evil cannot be erased by a priest with some magic words.* Later, when her faith returned more fully to her, she would describe this feeling as the sin of pride.

She and Sara got coffee, and Sara seemed strangely fine. She spoke of the coming peace vote, of her new boyfriend, who'd thrown a Molotov cocktail at a police vehicle during a student protest a couple of years ago, of how Human Rights Watch was allying with the conservatives to trash the peace.

"Left and right long ago collapsed into each other. This is what capital does," she said, as if that explained things.

Valencia tried to get her to talk about La Vigia and was cut off. "It was a waste of time," Sara said. "I'm done with human rights."

"You're dropping the class?"

"I'll finish the class for the credits, but then I'm done," she said. "You know, half the people here would think Agudelo is a hero, but he's just as stuck in the past as the FARC." Then she launched into what seemed like a rehearsed rant about how fixating on whether guerrillas or politicians or soldiers or narcos are playing nice obscured how "technocapital," whatever that was, jumped forward, outsourcing and automating, sending T-shirt jobs to Vietnam and the rest of manufacturing to robots.

"Have you thought about what we did?" Valencia asked.

Sara stopped. "I never met Alma," she said, as if the name were a strange new dish she was tasting for the first time. "I only saw her coming in and out of the offices. I never heard her testimony."

"Would you like to?"

Sara's hard features softened into an expression of surprise. Perhaps fear.

"I have the audio," Valencia added. "I could send it to you."

"No."

It was only after she'd been home for a few weeks, and after her father had noted for the fourth time that she still didn't seem to be herself, that he decided they needed a night out. He took her to the restaurant on top of Monserrate, and they ate, and he spoke to her of the journalist and how terrifying it must have been and so on. He told her about the possible end of his military career, and his plans to continue using the skills he had acquired for the good of the world, but that his next step might mean even more time away from home than usual.

"I got someone killed," she said. And she told him about Sara, and the photo of Jefferson, and what they'd done with it, and how it had gotten Alma killed. And she saw how her father was stunned into silence. The sun was setting over Bogotá, her breath was coming short, and she focused in on herself, determined not to cry or in some other way shame herself further.

"Mother of God," he said. "Mother of God. That was you? Mother of God!"

Miserably, she nodded.

"Mother of God," he said again. He controlled himself, reached forward and held her by the chin, bringing her face up, staring intently in her eyes, as if searching for something there. "Of course," he said.

He let his hand down, but continued staring at her. "Of course," he said again. And then he smiled. "I'm proud of you."

"What?"

"I'm proud of you."

And he explained how they'd been getting conflicting reports about who had taken the gringa, and why, and her little stunt had focused attention and, critically, *resources* on Jefferson. All of which had led to his death.

"You killed that son of a whore," he said. Her father. Who didn't curse. "Like you wanted to. Clever girl."

"But . . ."

"This woman. Alma?"

She nodded. She could not say her name.

"You were in a war, my dear."

She nodded yes.

"People die in battle. Yes?"

She shrugged her shoulders.

"I know," he said. "I know. I know well. I know what it's like to lose men. You'll have to find her family. Send . . . money. Something. It will make you feel better. And it's good to do. But listen to me well. I know what it is to lose men."

He reached down and covered her hand with his.

"Some officers can't risk their men in battle. They don't have the guts for it. They lose a taste for boldness. They just want to protect their men, and themselves. They're cowards. In the long run, they get more people killed. But you, my daughter. My daughter." He was grinning widely now. "You're in some little town in the countryside, surrounded by narcos and guerrillas, and what do you do? You take action. You take *bold* action."

She shook her head.

"I know," he said again, and he put his palm over his heart. "The deaths, they weigh on you. Daughter, I know. I know very well. And you remember her well. I know you will. Alma. Your first casualty. But don't lose heart. This is the person I raised you to be. Just . . . in the future, pick your targets more carefully. You caused a lot of problems."

He leaned back in his chair and looked out over the city.

"Look," he said. "The sun is setting."

So it was. And as it set he spoke of the beauty of their country, pointing to the shifting colors over the mountains, over the white modern high-rise apartments, the old colonial buildings of the Candelaria. "Bogotá is a beautiful city," he said.

"Bogotá is a graveyard," she said, parroting a phrase she'd read in a Juan Gabriel Vásquez novel.

"That's every city," he said. "Every city, every town. Every village worthy of the name."

While he spoke, she stared silently out at the same city and mountains he did, but saw a different place. As a girl, she had wanted a simple faith. A sense that she was a sister to all mankind, connected to all creation, that the natural beauty and wonder of the world was a caress of God. Looking out on her city, that was gone, replaced with emptiness, churning, her soul exposed, every nerve raw. This is not my home, and this is not my father. As he spoke on and on and on, she felt herself unraveling. She was nothing but an unforgiven girl in an ugly world. A shuddering sob broke through her. The beginning of her period of mourning. And her father held her hand, and his love for her felt painful and cruel, and she wondered, if there was a God, if that was what His love actually felt like.

———

Luisa went to see Javier first. It was a task that frightened her, and so she tried to remind herself as she walked over that he wasn't really human. Perhaps he had a tumor in his brain. Perhaps he was possessed. If there was indeed a human soul inside his body it was dying of thirst in cracked, dry soil. He wasn't anything to be afraid of. He would be pitiable, if only there were enough of a person there to be worth pitying.

But the problem for her was that he wore the same face as the thing that had severed her father in half. Whenever she saw him in La Vigia, mounted on horseback, patrolling the town as if he were its chief of police, it provoked one of those irritating reactions in her. Terror.

Sunlight on frightened faces. The smell of shit and rot in the hot sun. But fearing him was as foolish as fearing the chain saw that had torn through her father's spine. They were both no more than tools. Mechanisms in a broader system. Though, of course, the sight of chainsaws made her shudder, too.

When the young fools hanging outside Javier's office told her he'd be around shortly, that he was handling business, she smiled. Business! Officially he worked in the export of leather goods.

"I'll wait inside," she told them, almost adding, Until he oozes back this way.

On the wall of the small waiting area were photographs of Javier. Javier on a horse. Javier in his old paramilitary uniform. Javier behind Jefferson at a construction site. She made herself look at them. She'd be facing his real face soon. Might as well face the memories now.

In the days when Father Iván was helping her and a few other refugees who had stayed in the area, rather than flee all the way to Tibú or Cúcuta, she'd seen visions of him before her constantly. She'd felt isolated from all mankind then, but she wasn't alone. She always had Javier Ocasio with her.

She had gone daily to the chapel in Cunaviche, knelt before the bloody Christ on the eastern wall of the church, and prayed the 88th Psalm. The only psalm in the Bible without hope. She asked God if He showed His wonders only to the dead, if His love was declared only in the grave, His faithfulness only in destruction. And she had received no answer, but was comforted nonetheless.

Staring at Javier's face, the last words of the psalm echoed in her memory. *Your wrath has swept over me, your terrors have destroyed me. You have taken from me friend and neighbor—darkness is my closest friend.* She had come so far since then. She was not that girl. She knew so much better how to handle the Javiers of the world now.

When Javier finally arrived, she got straight to the point.

"I respect you," she lied. "Like few people in this town do."

And he growled. *Growled.* These men were children.

Carefully, without suggesting he had anything to do with her death, she brought up Alma. It was her opening gambit. To suggest he pay her family a condolence payment.

"With Jefferson gone," she said, "everyone knows blood is in the water. This is a delicate time. And her death has angered people."

"No one cares about a dead guerrillera."

"I have ways of knowing what the people of this town care about," she said. "Things they won't tell you. It is useful knowledge."

That surprised him. He had obviously never considered that she could be anything more than an irritant. Before he could reject the possibility, she added, "Do you want to rule over a town of people who support you, or a town of toads, croaking your every movement to the government and to the Peludos and to the Urabeños and to the police?"

She could see him considering the question seriously.

"How much would you suggest?"

She named a ridiculous figure, a year of income for a woman like Alma but an easy payment for Javier. Then she explained that it had to be exorbitant. A miserly payment would be worse than nothing. If he wanted to be a king, he had to show a king's generosity. Now, at the beginning of his reign more than ever. He said he would consider it.

As she left, she decided to use the payment as a benchmark. If he made it, it'd show his intentions. If he didn't, she'd evacuate the office, wait for him to get himself killed, and only move back in once a new order had established itself. She'd seen cycles like this before.

Everyone expected her to catch the next flight to America, to head home and lick her wounds. Concerned, faintly patronizing emails came from around the globe. Friends, family, colleagues. The only one she really appreciated was from Bob.

"Here's my take," the email began, followed by a bullet-pointed list of threat assessments for the area, best practices for journalists, and how the actions she'd taken racked up. It was lengthy, a display of Bob's precise attention to detail and fine-grained nuance. And pedantry. It concluded, "Yes, you could have done better. But we both know that most of the journalists we admire take far bigger risks. What happened was not your fault, except insofar as you were doing good reporting and pissing people off."

It wasn't true, of course. She didn't have anything to report, not even enough of a handle on the area to know who had kidnapped her, and why. When the Colombian military had showed up at the clinic where she was being treated for cracked ribs and the early stages of pneumonia, they'd been up front about their annoyance at her presence in the region, her inability to answer even their most basic questions about who'd been holding her, and what their relationship was to Jefferson.

Nevertheless, Bob had suggested she put together a pitch for a story about her kidnapping and what the situation in Norte de Santander said about the coming peace deal. "Remember the old *New York Sun* style guide," he said. "A reporter can't begin a story with the word 'I' unless they've been shot in the groin. And since you haven't been shot in the groin, the piece has to be about the peace deal, not you." She didn't know what her story said about the peace deal, but she bullshitted a few hundred words, sent them to Bob, who revised them and sent them to an editor at *The New York Times Magazine*. Who emailed her directly to say she was interested. It was the best break she'd ever received in her career, and it depressed her.

"Take what you can get," Diego told her at a Japanese restaurant in Bogotá, where he'd flown out to see her. "You deserve it."

"It's quite a way to earn a story," she said. Though she hadn't earned it, not yet. Her pitch was bullshit, but her story couldn't be. She had more reporting to do.

"You know," Diego said, "I'm the guy who found out they were holding you. If only you'd had the good sense to stay kidnapped for a day or two, the Colombians would have rescued you—"

"Or got me killed trying to rescue me."

"—and I would have been the knight in shining armor responsible."

"Sorry to disappoint."

"Of course you had to go rescue yourself," he said. "That's very on brand, Liz."

"I didn't rescue myself," she said. "I wasn't worth keeping."

"I think I still deserve thank-you sex." It was only partly a joke.

"They broke my ribs," she said. It was only partly a rejection, leaving the future more open than she'd intended. But perhaps that wasn't such a bad thing. And she did accept his offer to convalesce at his place outside of Medellín, which is where she finally broke the news to her mother that, no, she was staying in Colombia. She wasn't going home.

She did it over Skype. First, she carefully applied makeup to conceal the remaining traces of bruised skin. Then she angled the camera on her laptop so the mountainside would be behind her, a calm, beautiful scene that might help explain an attachment to the country. And at the time they'd agreed on via email, when her sister would be free and when Uncle Carey was generally most lucid, she dialed up her mother.

On the screen were her mother, her sister, and in the bed behind them, Uncle Carey. He'd lost maybe seventy pounds. After the initial Hellos and Oh, my god, Liz, it's so good to see yous, as well as the initial tears from her mother and the initial detailing from her sister of How Worried Everyone Was and How Awful It Was, her sister trained the camera on her iPad on Uncle Carey so they could show her to him. His eyes seemed to light, and he made an incomprehensible grunt that both her sister and mother would later make much of. In the past weeks, there'd been less and less of Uncle Carey every time Lisette did this, which was one of the reasons she rarely Skyped anymore. They told her excitedly that these days his eyes only lit for her and for her sister's babies. What might he do when he saw her in person, not over a video screen? And how soon could that be?

Lisette didn't know how to tell them. When his eyes lit, it moved her, yes. It really did seem as though the man he had been was calling her through the cage of his dying body and failing mind. But that idea frightened her too much to dwell on, and she told herself that whatever was left of Uncle Carey was gone. His mind had totally deteriorated to a few randomly firing neurons. That wasn't the real Uncle Carey. The real Uncle Carey lived only in her memories. And the Uncle Carey of her memories had told her to be somewhere else when he died. Somewhere awesome. He would have thought of her kidnapping and escape as an adventure. He would have thought Colombia sounded awesome.

"I'm not coming home." She just blurted it out. Bad news is easier done with quickly.

"Jesus, Liz," said her sister, managing to sound both unsurprised and deeply disappointed.

Her mother, on the other hand, simply looked down at her hands.

"You come home after something like this," her sister said. "You come home and let your family take care of you for a bit. Just for a little bit." Liz didn't know what to say to that, and the silence dragged on, and her sister added, this time with a pleading, almost pitiful note, "For a few days."

Her mother said nothing. And so Liz tried to explain. That it was like getting in a car accident. If you didn't start driving again right away, if you didn't get back on the road immediately, before the shock died away and the fear set, it'd screw you up for life. It'd mean the fear would be there every time you got behind the wheel. And she couldn't do her job with that fear. She had to get out there again.

"Why can't you just . . . come home? Rest a bit. You said they want you to write about what happened to you. You don't need to be in Colombia to do that."

"I don't know what happened to me."

And that was the crux of it. She didn't know who had kidnapped her. She didn't know why. She didn't know what their connection to Jefferson was. She didn't know what his real interest in her was. She didn't know why he'd released her. She didn't know what that meant for La Vigia. She didn't know what La Vigia meant for the military. She didn't know what the Jesúses meant for the region. She didn't know what it meant for the cocaine trade, for Venezuela, for the U.S. military, for civil society, for the politicians who had been involved in paving the way for the raid or the diplomats and soldiers involved in giving it the okay and carrying it out and being deeply disappointed when she wasn't there. She didn't know what it meant for American interests in this country that had been the largest recipient of American military aid in the Western Hemisphere for decades. She didn't know what it meant, period. So what did she have that she could write about? Some shitty things that had happened to her. But shitty things happened to people all the time. It doesn't make a story.

She couldn't go home. She had to be working here, someplace awesome, someplace still unknown, and not there, where people thought they knew her, and wanted to tie her to the worn old image of her they carried in their minds. Home was a trap.

———

Mason was ashamed of himself. Throughout the kidnapping, the rescue mission turned straightforward raid, the aftermath and after-action reports, he'd kept silent about his role in the journalist ending up in La Vigia.

"Who, exactly, would it help if you tell them?" his wife had asked, fixing him with that cold accountant's stare of hers.

"It could, maybe—"

"Maybe?"

"You never know what could be import—"

"So it'd help nobody."

"I don't know that."

"You have two daughters who need a father with stable employment."

"They're not going to kick me out of the army for—"

"If they want to screw you"—she pointed her finger directly at his chest—"they'll find a way."

And so he'd kept quiet, working with more than usual diligence on marshaling support for the Colombian mission to recover the journalist. And all had turned out well. The journalist was safe. A narco boss with Venezuelan ties was dead. His wife, assessing the profit and loss, assured him there was nothing to worry about.

But there were things that bothered him. Like how the Jesúses had gone so quickly from a potential Colombian asset a few months ago, when Lieutenant Colonel Juan Pablo Pulido had first mentioned them, to the top of a kill list. Whatever. It was above his pay grade. And in Colombia, it was possible for a career soldier like himself to believe that the folks high above his pay grade could be trusted with the mission he was carrying out. The yearly death toll in Colombia was half what it was when he'd first shown up here a decade ago, as a young medic. The peace treaty with the FARC was going up for a vote to the Colombian people soon, heralding the end of the longest insurgency in history. The evidence on the ground was that the folks high above him knew what they were doing. Or they were lucky, which was just as good.

And then the day of the peace vote arrived, and the great democratic body of the Colombian people collectively shrugged. Only 37 percent turned out to vote. Of those voters, a bare majority said no. No to the peace. And the day after the peace vote, Diego texted him to ask if he'd like to get drinks with him and Lisette Marigny, this woman who'd caused so much trouble.

They met at a bar in the Zona T. She was a tall, sinewy woman with light eyes and a firm, masculine handshake. She gave off no sign of having endured any particular horror.

"You know your boyfriend moved mountains trying to find you," he told her over drinks, thinking he was doing Diego a favor. Not that Diego deserved it.

She raised an eyebrow at the word "boyfriend." Diego seemed to visibly shrink into the rolls of fat that'd been building up ever since he'd left the army.

"I . . . inflated our relationship a bit," Diego told her, "when I was trying to get in on the search for you."

"You motherfucker." Mason shook his head and turned to Marigny. "This asshole. You know he was shit in the teams."

He almost walked out then and there, but Marigny stepped in, thanked him for what he'd done, and then the conversation stuttered and jerked but eventually restarted. He and Marigny talked western Pennsylvania, they talked Afghanistan, they talked the weird and disappointing peace vote, and he decided that, aside from her taste in men, there was a lot to like in Lisette Marigny.

"What do you think will happen?" she said.

"You mean, What does the embassy think will happen?"

"I'm not angling for anything, honestly. Still finding my feet in this country."

"The vote doesn't matter," Mason said. "The president has enough power in Congress to push it through anyway. They'll make a few changes, claim they fixed it, and force it through regardless of what the people want."

"Is that a good thing?"

Mason shrugged. Realistically, it meant there'd be no political will to *implement* the peace, which meant less efforts in the poorest, most violent parts of the country, which meant fertile ground for BACRIM and narcotrafficking, which meant guys like Diego would be able to find employment in Colombia for a long, long time. "What do you think?"

"I don't really understand this country well enough to have opinions about it one way or the other."

Diego laughed at that. "That's the luxury journalists have. For guys like us, shit here moves too fast for us to wait to have opinions until we understand things."

"When I came here," she said, "Diego promised me a good war."

"Consider the competition," Mason said. He knew *he'd* rather be here than in Afghanistan, or the Horn of Africa, or the Philippines. "I think he delivered."

On the way home, Mason decided that was true. This was a messy war, but that was the nature of war. And as wars went, it was a good war. Which meant, regardless of the particulars of this or that operation, his efforts were spent for a good cause. His country was a force for good here. His was a good country. His service to it was a way of being a good man. That was the faith, anyway.

IV

To remain a great nation or to become one,
you must colonize.

—*Léon Gambetta*

J uan Pablo waited to see who would come for the bodies. On the video feed before him was the aftermath of the latest air strike near Hodeidah. A wedding tent. Broken instruments. Bits of colorful clothing. If the camera resolution were better, he'd be able to see flesh, teeth. Children's slippers and severed fingers. Targeting here was not like targeting in Colombia. It was less squeamish.

He'd arrived in the region a few months before. A Colombian company that had a deliberately obscure connection to an American military contracting firm had, upon seeing his résumé, practically rushed him onto the plane to the Emirates, where, supposedly, he was going to help with training and internal security. Most of the Colombian troops here were ground forces. Cattle, more or less. They'd already flown to Yemen and were there, fighting a primitive war with sophisticated weapons. But given his experience and his fluent English, he was placed in a targeting cell staffed mostly with Americans and Israelis, working with a team of analysts constantly flooding the operations center with data from ISR aircraft and drone feeds and sitreps and forensic reports, sifting through and finding people to kill. He was also making more money than ever before in his life.

His wife was talking about moving to an apartment in El Nogal. He was considering sending his daughter to Externado, which wasn't necessarily a better school but was where she'd be less exposed to bad influences. It was all possible now. Money made everything easier.

"Look." Jeffie Sung, a thin, jittery American drone pilot, motioned to the video feed from the drone, where a bongo truck with a crudely painted red crescent on it made its way to the site. Jeffie, who'd flown Predators for the U.S. military, now flew the Chinese drones the Emiratis used. And since his shift overlapped with Juan Pablo's, and since he occasionally needed to speak to Latin American ground troops but didn't speak Spanish, they'd built up a good working relationship.

"The Red Crescent hasn't been operating here," Juan Pablo said. "Let's see who this is."

The truck stopped and a group of young men emerged and began collecting the bodies in a workmanlike way.

"This is the strange part of the job," Jeffie said. "Watching the cleanup."

Juan Pablo nodded. "Does it bother you?" he asked.

"No."

"Good."

"And you?" There was something peculiar in Jeffie's tone.

"I'm not without heart."

Jeffie laughed, even though it was true. Juan Pablo took no pleasure in watching these scenes. But in war, only sociopaths are guided by pleasure. He told himself he was guided by duty. During his time in the Emirates, he'd been trying to determine what that was, exactly.

"Oh, and I've finally got my damn liquor license." Jeffie pulled from his wallet one of the little Alcoholic Drinks Licenses that permitted non-Muslims to buy booze in the country. "Want to swing by after our shift, have a little whiskey?"

"Well . . . yes," he said, his eyes on the screen. Two of the men loaded a child-size figure onto a stretcher. He kept his eyes on the figure as it made its slow way to the truck, was unloaded, and then the men went back for more, the next time picking a corpse the size of an adult.

He pointed to the screen. "Regrettable," he said.

Jeffie shrugged. "Emirati pilots suck," he said.

It *was* strange. Juan Pablo knew he was looking at the aftermath of a wedding party. He knew this war killed civilians by the thousands. He knew disease would soon claim worse. He knew cholera was spreading from Sana'a to Aden. He knew children were dying of malnutrition and he knew that Hodeidah was the central port for the vast majority of humanitarian aid coming into Yemen. So he knew that as they closed in and choked it off, more children would die. Regrettable, very regrettable. But necessary.

The Houthis, of course, had killed thousands even before the Emirates and the Saudis had intervened. They fought a dirty guerrilla war, laying minefields indiscriminately, getting six-year-old children to drop grenades in the turrets of tanks, establishing a totalitarian police state in the areas they'd taken over. They were primitive tribesmen, he told himself, their brightest idea the restoration of a seventh-century theocracy run exclusively by blood descendants of Mohammed, the sort of medieval idea Juan Pablo would have found hilarious if it wasn't backed by Russian and Iranian technology. He shook his head. A bunch of tribesmen who would probably struggle to construct a working electric lightbulb were using wire-guided antitank missiles to blow each other up in pickup trucks.

This war was only happening because of technology created far away from here. But happening it was. And if they advanced, especially if they managed to take Aden, a port located on a twenty-mile-long chokepoint for a huge portion of the world's oil shipments, there'd be a global commerce crisis, a spike in oil prices, and disaster for pretty much every country in the world except for poor, decrepit oil producers like Russia and Venezuela. Which meant, even here, what he was doing was related to the security of his home country. In the modern world, everything is related to everything.

After his shift, he went to his apartment just as the sun was rising, and he called home. It was around nine, Bogotá time, and after a discussion of how Valencia was getting along, they reverted to the usual argument.

"Why can't you get a contract here?" She meant a contract working in Colombia. With his old colleagues who'd driven him out, or with Americans, working for interests that were often aligned with, but not the same as, the interests of his country.

"Maybe I should have stayed in," he said. "Dared them to pass me over."

She sighed. "You would have been passed over." Sofia had talked to the wives. She knew. "But if you talk to Colonel Carlosama—"

"I won't live on his charity."

And that was that. He wanted to tell her about his work, about the wedding party, about Jeffie's comment on the strangeness of their work, but of course he couldn't. He asked her about her day, about the women who had remained friends with her, and the women who no longer wanted to see her, and how predictable it all was. How Sofia had, in fact, predicted it. Who were true friends, who were not. As she spoke, he longed to be with her, to be able to touch her, see her in real life, not through a screen. It was a longing deeper than any he'd felt during the many long stretches away from her back in Colombia, and he wondered where it came from. He shook it off. This kind of work would not just set him and Sofia up financially. It would allow them to secure something for their daughter as well. If she really did want to go into human rights, well, that work wouldn't pay. But the money he made here could go into making that lifestyle a possibility for her.

After the call, he remembered Jeffie's invitation and walked to the American's apartment. Jeffie opened the door, and inside it was just him and an open bottle of bourbon. Harsh light came from the windows, which looked out onto drab brown nothingness that stretched in all directions from where they lived, at an air base in the Emirates' deep south, a region of the country known as the Empty Quarter. It was an apt name. Juan Pablo immediately regretted coming.

"Guess what I found out." Jeffie slurred the words as he poured an enormous amount of bourbon into a plastic cup. The room was disorganized. Bed unmade. Papers strewn across a coffee table. An open book with a cracked spine dropped pages-down on the floor.

"I won't stay long," Juan Pablo said. He looked at the book. *An Army at Dawn*. The cover showed a line of soldiers walking across a scrubby hillside.

"You know the Aden screwup?"

The Aden screwup was when a couple of American mercenaries tried to place a shrapnel-laced bomb in the offices of a local political party, Islah, but instead got into a firefight and alerted the whole neighborhood. The thing had been further confirmation to Juan Pablo that using ground forces here for sensitive missions in Yemen was a nonstarter. They just weren't good enough. Even though, supposedly, the American mercenaries were all top quality, a Green Beret, a SEAL, and a CIA Ground Branch guy.

"Turns out the SEAL in the group," Jeffie said, "well, he left the service after shooting a recruit. Training accident. Left the guy crippled. Now he's here, fucking our shit up and making twenty-five thousand dollars a month."

Juan Pablo sipped the bourbon. It was sweet, and burned pleasantly.

"Old Crow, General Grant's favorite." Jeffie pointed at the bottle the whiskey had come from. "Sit down, sit down."

He motioned to a chair positioned toward the window, facing the sun that hung over the empty landscape. Juan Pablo sat, his eyes narrowing against the glare.

"How many guys here got some story like that?" Jeffie said. "Not like, shot a guy, but . . . something must have gone wrong for most of us. From SEAL Team Six to an Emirati kill squad in Yemen—it's probably not how he thought his life would go."

Juan Pablo didn't like where the conversation was going. "Are you about to tell me your past?" he said.

Jeffie shot back the Old Crow and winced as it went down. Then he shivered like a dog shaking off water, and poured more into his cup. "No dark past. I just went bankrupt," he said. He put a hand in the air. "Kid brother had some issues. Of a medical variety. Well, sort of. Complicated." Without asking, he reached over and poured even more whiskey into Juan Pablo's cup. Juan Pablo figured there were at least four shots sitting in there now. He had no intention of staying here long enough to drink it all. But he sipped.

"Right before the end of shift, they intercepted some chatter," Jeffie continued. "Turns out the bomb that went stray killed one of Badr al-Dien's nephews."

Badr al-Dien was a Houthi commander. Not exactly a high-value target, but high enough. "I used to work with an American who'd tell me it is better to be lucky than be good."

"Lucky, yeah." Jeffie stared into his whiskey. "Well, when the funeral comes, I'm guessing the two will put together a package to hit the funeral."

"Logical." It was.

"A wedding and a funeral, we'll have the whole circle of life." He said it dolefully.

"Yes." Some people had the oddest moral lines. In a country where there was starvation, disease, and wide-scale slaughter of innocents, for some reason air attacks on funerals bothered people. When it came to war, even nonreligious men would start drawing magic circles, declaring this and that sacred.

"We killed kids today," Jeffie said, still staring into his whiskey. "Not what I signed up for."

Such fastidiousness. "You're American," Juan Pablo said. "You've killed kids before."

Jeffie let out a little grunt of displeasure. Juan Pablo took a sip of the whiskey, and then took a gulp, letting the burn settle pleasantly. He was getting irritated.

"Have you ever lived in a violent city?" Juan Pablo continued. "I mean, a truly violent city? Not as a soldier. As a citizen?"

No. Jeffie had grown up in Northern California.

"People from places like that only want one thing," Juan Pablo said. "Order."

"Is that why you're here? To provide order? Come on. You couldn't resist the check."

"I'm paid well. There's no shame in that. I provide a valuable service."

Jeffie nodded. Juan Pablo scowled into his whiskey. This fool, this fellow *mercenary*, wanted to believe in clean wars with clear boundaries. Such a thing didn't exist. He thought of his days in Saravena, playing the clown, trying to change the pro-guerrilla culture of the town by seducing the children. Wars are not fought by armies. They are fought by cultures. If the animal you are fighting is communism, then the guerrilla are simply that animal's claws. Drug trafficking is its heart, coca and heroin the blood coursing through its veins, and poor, angry, ignorant people its hide and the flesh underneath. The Houthis were a different animal, sustained by a different type of blood entirely, but the underlying principle was the same. Your job is not to trim the claws. It's to kill the beast.

"This is a good war," he said. "Who is on our side? In our operations center we've got Americans and Israelis and Emiratis and one Colombian. We've got resupply from the United States, arms from half the globe, and if you look closely, see who is supporting this war, directly or indirectly, you will find that what sits behind us is the entire civilized world. And on the other side, we have men and women raised in tents, in a debased culture of rituals and poverty and sacred texts that half of them are too illiterate to read, sending out suicide bombers and laying land mines that will maim and kill for generations, and for what? So they can install the great-great-great-great-grandson of a desert preacher's cousin as king? I am on the side of civilization against primitive nonsense."

He did not add that this was a sometimes lonely side to be on, even in his own family. That his wife and daughter believed in primitive nonsense, in rituals and sacred texts, and it was an embarrassment he hardly liked to consider himself.

Jeffie laughed and shook his head. "Yeah, yeah," he said. "Kids, though. Kids."

Jeffie, who had done support for air missions over Serbia in the '90s, served in Iraq and Afghanistan, suddenly had qualms. Why? Because the quality of the video feed on their drone was good enough to show off a child's corpse. Americans are so very sentimental. Fingers in every conflict in the world, but then they get histrionic about a random dead child and think that makes them a good person.

"Well," Juan Pablo said, "you and I improve the precision of the Emirati targeting? Yes? I suspect there are, in the end, fewer dead children because you are here." Silly. A scrap thrown to Jeffie's conscience. But it seemed to comfort him. Maintaining morale is just as important for mercenaries as for any other kind of soldier.

The conversation stayed with him during his next shift, as he tracked a running battle in a town north of Aden. Friendly armored forces versus rebels who rarely appeared on-screen or gave the opportunity for a successful air strike. Mostly, those in the operations center had just watched on the screens as small boxy shapes spat out little flashes, and then the walls of little buildings crumbled.

It was like he'd said. Civilization versus primitivism. Those armored vehicles could have come from almost anywhere in the civilized world. He'd seen American MaxxPro and Oshkosh M-ATVs here, but also Finnish Patrias, South African RGs, even French Leclerc tanks, though he couldn't make any of those out on the screens before him. If the resolution was good enough to make out individual weapons, he knew he'd see representatives of even more countries. Singaporean 120mm mortars, Serbian Zastava machine guns, Belgian FN minimis, Chinese M80s, and an assortment of small arms and heavy ordnance from Germany, Sweden, Denmark, Norway, the Netherlands, Brazil, and more. The buildings they were destroying were made of local stone, or soil mixed with straw, or burn mud.

Yes, it was an ugly little war. But with the right perspective, there was something majestic at work here. The rebels, whether they were fully aware of it or not, were threatening a main artery of civilization—the Bab el-Mandeb strait, one of the world's most important trade routes. And so civilization, which had never cared much for desert tribesman, had come here and shown its steel.

The day of the funeral, a surveillance team was emplaced in a nearby building to provide eyes on the mourners. They waited. The team radioed about people coming in and out of the building where the funeral was to be held. About "no weapons." About "military-age males," which means any human with a Y chromosome tall enough to piss in a standard urinal. They waited. The early arrivals came. Still no weapons. They waited. Then as the funeral was about to start, a convoy of vehicles arrived. Visual confirmation. Weapons. They were in business.

A photo popped up from the surveillance team. Visual recognition software gave it a 63 percent match on a member of Islah. Not who they were expecting, but a target.

The OpsO called the general. Minutes ticked by. The general called back. They'd send in ground forces. Colombians in cordon, local Yemeni forces making the arrests. They waited some more, watching the movement of the ground forces on the map.

"This is a better mission than I thought," Jeffie said.

Juan Pablo shook his head. Jeffie was pleased they wouldn't be bombing anyone. Instead, the ground forces would round up the funeralgoers and send them to secret prisons where they would be tortured. It was nice to know that all it took to calm Jeffie's nerves was to introduce one minimal step from the actual ugliness of the job.

Minutes passed, the visuals remained the same. Juan Pablo saw Jeffie scratching out longhand division, estimating the remaining fuel on the drone. A convoy pulled up to the funeral. More weapons. The surveillance team radioed that they'd spotted an Iranian ATGM. Jeffie began typing on a keyboard, sending emails back and forth with a JTAC, who promised to reroute some F-15s. And then the Colombians came on the net, and the plan changed.

"Dos urgentes, dos rutinaria, nada muertos," came a calm voice. They'd hit a mine, taken injuries, and identified more mines ahead. Juan Pablo briefed the OpsO and the OpsO called in to brief the general and they waited. The surveillance team called in and identified a building separate from the funeral hall where most of the men carrying weapons had gone.

Juan Pablo called over the OpsO.

"Alternatively," Juan Pablo told him, "we wait for the funeral to end, and then hit the fighters' building once the principals reunite with their security."

The OpsO nodded and called back to the general for guidance. They waited.

Meanwhile, Jeffie circled the fighters' building. It was a multilevel structure with a courtyard. The surveillance team claimed they'd observed only men and boys carrying weapons going in and out so maybe it was clear of civilians. It should be clear of civilians. In theory, the guidelines they operated under would demand better intelligence.

As he waited, Juan Pablo watched the image of the target. It was soothing. At first glance, it was a static image, but then you noticed that it was shifting, ever so slightly, as the drone circled and its sensor camera rotated to keep fixed on the building. He wondered what was going on inside. And what was happening in the nearby building, at the funeral? He didn't know what a Muslim funeral was like. Were they all the same? Or did Yemenis have particular customs? In all his time watching Yemenis die on video screens, he had not once talked to a single Yemeni, or even seen one in person. They were a notional people to him, defined not by experience but by a few articles he'd read, by talk among his fellow mercenaries, and by a few opinion polls he'd sought out to learn about their retrograde beliefs.

Were they as motivated by primitivism as he thought? Was this war of attrition they were fighting grinding down their resistance, or would it spawn pockets of resistance, deep enmities, nonnegotiable hatred? What were they like? He didn't know. It wasn't necessary to know for a campaign like this, which was one half war and one half extermination.

Confirmation came from the general and Juan Pablo let out a breath. Hours of tension building up were soon to be released. Meanwhile, Jeffie was on the radio with the ground team.

"Can you sparkle the building? No, not now . . . but . . . yes . . . good."

If the ground team could sparkle the target, they were set. A perfect mission. Normally, an Emirati pilot in a jet hooked up with a Sniper-Pod would have to shoot a laser onto a target for another jet to fire on. And since the Emiratis tended to fly as high as possible to avoid ground fire, they weren't the most reliable.

"Okay, movement," Jeffie said. There was nothing on the screen for a moment and then figures emerged near the target building. "Yeah, now. Sparkle it now." He switched to a different radio. "You should see it now."

Juan Pablo closed his eyes, took in the hum of the operations center. He wondered if the men who were about to die were capable of appreciating everything that went into their deaths. An American mercenary was aiming a laser at the instruction of an American pilot operating a Chinese drone. They were communicating over an encrypted frequency routed through a Canadian aircraft mounted with Swedish surveillance technology, bounced from repeater hub to repeater hub to the main air-ground tower at their air base in the Empty Quarter. The drone pilot, in turn, was communicating with an Emirati fighter pilot in an American aircraft armed with a laser-guided bomb capable of being launched from nine miles away and forty thousand feet up and still detonating within ten feet of its target.

He heard someone clear the pilots hot. Was it Jeffie? It didn't matter. He knew, as everyone in that operations center knew, that in another country miles and miles away from them men of another religion and another way of life breathed their last. They knew, and the ground team knew, and the pilots knew, but no one else.

Then, tens of thousands of feet above the target building, the pilot did nothing more complicated than push a little button. A series of small charges on a rack mounted underneath his plane ignited, blowing away the hooks holding his bomb in place. It wobbled out into the air. Awkward, ungainly, a baby bird the size of a car, detached from its parent and plummeting through space. Or almost detached. A thin wire trailed behind it, still connected to the jet, unspooling and unspooling until there was no more wire left and it tore itself from its mother. Only then did it open its eyes.

A sensor on the nose locked onto the sparkling building. Four fins at its tail extended outward. It adjusted the angle of its fins. Added lift, stability. No longer plummeting, it flew.

So many things had to happen for these men to arrive at their deaths. Start with the invention of the internal combustion engine. Follow with the development of Europe and the Americas and the rest of the world creating a ravenous appetite for oil, which created oil rigs and refineries and massive wealth for desert princes. Then global supply chains, trade agreements, secure shipping routes, and the law of the sea. Negotiated arms sales, too. Add in the vast edifice of Western science. Computing and radio technology. The space race and the microchip. Silicon Valley and the military-industrial complex. And other, subtler developments. American-pioneered methods of high-value targeting. The post-9/11 explosion of private military contractors. It took all of the massively complex, interconnected modern world to bring these men their deaths. It was a shame they were incapable of appreciating it.

Juan Pablo opened his eyes. On the screen before him lay the same building, now with more figures in the street nearby, exiting the funeral. A flash whited out half of the screen. When it disappeared, the building was altered.

"Hell, yeah," someone said. They called for permission for another strike. Time passed. Permission was granted. Figures emerged out of the back of the building, running. Another flash whited out the screen, and when the flash disappeared some of the figures were motionless.

Juan Pablo didn't know who they had killed, or how the survivors would react to what had happened. He knew he felt satisfied by the day's work. He was a highly paid mercenary, using skills he had learned from the Colombian military, from American Special Forces, and from his own long experience in ugly, dirty war zones, to fight an ugly, dirty war against a primitive enemy. Perhaps this was the future of war, and if so, good. In a war like this, it did not matter how many fanatics swarmed to your side. It did not matter if you stirred the passions of the people by demonizing the government or the capitalists or the Liberals or the Conservatives or the Catholics or the Protestants or the Muslims or the Jews. What mattered was the global, interconnected system that generated the wealth and the technology that ultimately would determine the fate of this war, and the wars to come. That system *was* civilization. It was progress.

Hundreds of miles away, just outside the courtyard of the ruined and blasted building, a boy stared up into the sky. His mind, though full of pain and terror, willed itself to prayer. And he whispered of the day of reckoning, and of the paradise that is the truth, and of the hell that is the truth. And then he was gone.

ACKNOWLEDGMENTS

This book would not exist without the efforts of so many people. First, there are those who read through many drafts of these chapters, providing edits, feedback, and ideas—Christopher Robinson, Lauren Holmes, Matt Gallagher, Elliot Ackerman, Lea Carpenter, and especially my wife, Jessica, who in addition to reading countless drafts helped with research, assisted during interviews in Colombia (occasionally while nursing a newborn), and provided sanity checks during the crazy-making process of writing a novel. Then there is my agent, Eric Simonoff, who stuck by me for six years of writing without ever applying the least pressure on me to hurry up, and whose opinion I greatly valued as the work neared completion. Finally, there is my editor at Penguin Press, Scott Moyers, and his assistant editor, Mia Council, who helped refine the novel into a tighter, better-structured, and far clearer whole. And I should add Jane Cavolina, my incredible copyeditor.

The John Simon Guggenheim Memorial Foundation and Princeton University's Lewis Center of the Arts Hodder Fellowship provided me the time and resources to write and research, and I'm humbled by their generous faith in my work. Also, the brilliant and intellectually omnivorous John Ptacek provided invaluable research assistance through Hunter College's Hertog Fellowship program.

Various scholars and experts gave their time as I was trying to find my footing in tackling this subject. I'm grateful for the advice and expertise of Ethan Kapstein, Jacob Shapiro, Stephen Kalin, Robert Karl, Quil Lawrence, Gavin Kovite, Molly Kovite, Roy Godson, Deni Béchard, Abbey Steele, and Brian Castner. Jacob Siegel, my old friend and podcast cohost at *Manifesto!*, also helped me argue out a lot of the ideas I wanted to engage with in the novel.

While in Colombia, I often stayed with Juan Antonio Restrepo and Ana Isabel Velásquez. Along with Blanca Nora Cardona and Luis Gilberto Velásquez, they looked after me, fed me and my ravenous children, and showered our family with love, while Juan and Isa's daughter Sara Restrepo put in amazing work as a research assistant, particularly in arranging interviews with a wide range of people from judges to academics to ex-military to politicians.

I'd like to thank my parents, Marie-Therese and William Klay, and my four brothers, who in addition to being caring and supportive also helped at various points, connecting me to people who proved pivotal to the book. And I'd like to thank my mother-in-law, Adriana Velásquez, who was a wealth of information on Colombian Spanish and on Medellín, in particular.

I'm also indebted to those who gave their time for interviews, especially Paul Angelo, Hernán Hincapié, Luis Fernando Delgado Llano, Fabio Valencia Cossio, Juan Gomez Martinez, Pablo Hernandez, Pablo Emilio Angarita Cañas, Shawn Walker, Matt Wilson, Andrew Slater, Jason Everman, Joe Reagan, Jhon Jairo Díez, Dr. Samuel Muñoz, Ángel David Marín, Gloria Lia Velásquez, and others. I relied on a variety of books and articles and essays from journalists, fiction writers, poets, and scholars for this novel. Among these individuals and works are:

Elliot Ackerman; Lynsey Addario's *It's What I Do*; the Ahlul Bayt Digital Islamic Library; Matthieu Aikins's "Last Tango in Kabul"; Fatima Abo Alasrar; Shuaib Almosawa; Lieutenant Colonel Charles Armstrong's "Ambushes—Still Viable as a Combat Tactic" (Juan Pablo quotes the opening lines defining an ambush); Deni Béchard; Carlos G. Berrios; Adrian Bonenberger's *Afghan Post*; Virginia Bouvier's *Colombia: Building Peace in a Time of War*; Mark Bowden's *Killing Pablo* and "Jihadists in Paradise"; Deborah Campell's *A Disappearance in Damascus* (there is one direct quote from this book in which, with the author's permission, I repurpose a line from her translator, Ahlam); Brian Castner's *All the Ways We Kill and Die*; Kate Clark; Jesús Abad Colorado; Iona Craig; Jorge Delgado; Jhon Jairo Díez's "Violencia Homicidia y Fuerza Pública: Medellín 1987–1993"; Agusto Bahamón Dussán's *Mi Guerra en Medellín*; Ann Farnsworth-Alvear, Marcos Palacios, and Ana María Gómez López's *The Colombia Reader*; Vanda Felbab-Brown; Jim Grant's "One Tribe at a Time"; Natalia Herrera; Pat Hoy II's "Soldiers and Scholars"; Ethan

Kapstein's *Seeds of Stability* (from which one line is quoted by Juan Pablo, with the permission of the author); Robert A. Karl's *Forgotten Peace*; Juanita León's *País de Plomo*; Kevin Maurer's *Gentlemen Bastards* and *Lions of Kandahar* (coauthored with Rusty Bradley); Emily Mayhew's *A Heavy Reckoning*; Christopher Mitchell and Sara Ramírez's "Local Peace Communities in Colombia"; Luke Mogelson; Alfredo Molano's *Desterrados*; David Morris; Mark Moyar, Hector Pagan, and Wil R. Griego's *Persistent Engagement in Colombia* (as well as Adam Isacson's annotations to that text); P. J. O'Rourke's *Driving Like Crazy*; John Otis's *Law of the Jungle*; Marjorie Pennington's *Bringing Home the War*; María Eugenia Vásquez Perdomo's *My Life as a Colombian Revolutionary*; Mark Phillips's "How to Fell a Tree"; Douglas Porch; Dana Priest's "Covert Action in Colombia"; RAND Corporation's "Building Special Operations Partnerships in Afghanistan and Beyond"; Sune Engel Rasmussen's "Kabul's Drivers Get Their Feelings Across with Windshield Stickers"; John Renehan's "The Devil You Know"; Linda Robinson's *One Hundred Victories*; Edwin Cruz Rodríguez's "La Protesta Campesina en el Catatumbo"; María Teresa Rondersos's *Guerras Recicladas*; Aram Roston's "A Middle East Monarchy Hired American Ex-Soldiers to Kill Its Political Enemies. This Could Be the Future of War"; Noah Rothman; Paul Staniland; Abbey Steele's *Democracy and Displacement in Colombia's Civil War*; Jeffrey Stern's "From Arizona to Yemen: The Journey of an American Bomb"; Winifred Tate's *Drugs, Thugs, and Diplomats*; Michael Taussig's, *Law in a Lawless Land*; Heidi Vogt's "When a Bomb Goes Off in Afghanistan"; Jeremy Waldron's "Named and Targeted"; and Bing West.